RESTLESS SPIRITS

Books by Linda Dunning

Lost Landscapes

Specters in Doorways

"As a writer, Linda Dunning gets the connections she needs with the reader. She does her homework and applies it well. I find her work a true representation of fact and honesty. As an active researcher of life after death for over twenty years, I appreciate this collective information that is both insightful and interesting."

—*Michele Page, ghost investigator, active member of the AAEVP and American Ghost Hunters, having appeared on the Travel, History, Fox, and SyFy Channels, as well as radio programs in Las Vegas, Nevada*

RESTLESS SPIRITS

UTAH'S SMALL TOWN GHOSTS

LINDA DUNNING

CFI

SPRINGVILLE, UTAH

ISBN 13: 978-1-59955-271-2

Published by CFI, an imprint of Cedar Fort, Inc., 2373 W. 700 S., Springville, UT 84663
Distributed by Cedar Fort, Inc., www.cedarfort.com

LIBRARY OF CONGRESS CATALOGING-IN-PUBLICATION DATA
Dunning, Linda, 1949-
   Restless spirits : Utah's small town ghosts / Linda Dunning.
      p. cm.
   Includes bibliographical references.
   ISBN 978-1-59955-271-2 (acid-free paper)
   1. Ghosts--Utah. 2. Haunted places--Utah. I. Title.

   BF1472.U6D86 2009
   133.109792--dc22

                                                            2009042785

Cover design by Tanya Quinlan
Cover design © 2010 by Lyle Mortimer

Printed in the United States of America

10 9 8 7 6 5 4 3 2 1

Printed on acid-free paper

DEDICATION

This book is dedicated to my parents,
who grew up in small towns in Utah and Idaho,
and became curious not only about their
Native American neighbors, but also about
the history of America and the West.

CONTENTS

Book Two
Salt Lake County to Northern Utah County

Book Three
Southern Utah County to Grand County

Book Four
Iron County to Kane County

Cedar City to the Grand Canyon

BOOK ONE

CACHE VALLEY TO
UINTAH COUNTY

STRANGE TALES OF
NORTHERN AND EASTERN UTAH

Logan

I lived in Logan twice, once in my junior high school years when we experienced an earthquake (in 1960) and I lost my junior high school, and again when I taught at the school for the multi-handicapped while my husband was attending Utah State University.

Cache Valley is an enchanting place. We loved the Franklin Basin and all the wonderful hiking trails and canyons. The people in the town are friendly and easy to know. Logan has always held a place in my heart because of my younger years spent there. We had wonderful adventures in our backyard, which bordered on a huge stretch of vacant property that went all the way to North Logan. Now houses have been built there. The never-ending sledding hill, the snow cats in the winter, the parachutists and balloonists, and the endless array of strange events that took place made Logan a wonderful memory for me. I found out about the ghosts much later!

Logan, the largest city in Cache Valley, was founded in 1859. According to the U.S. Census Bureau, as of 2006 the population is approximately 47,660 people. It is a university town and houses Utah State University, which began as a land grant agricultural college.

The first settlers built a fort by the Logan River, and by 1866, when the city incorporated, well over one hundred houses were there. Logan became the center of the valley, because unlike all the other little towns surrounding it, it had an abundant water supply and was located at the mouth of Logan Canyon in the Bear River Range. Mrs. Lydia Hamp Baker settled in the valley in 1877, and in an

3

interview before her death, she talked of the town being mostly willows. She spoke of her trade, which was boot closing (sewing boot and shoe uppers by hand). She said, "The settlers slept in four poster cord beds, with rope stretched on the frame in lieu of springs. They burned willows for fuel, carried water from irrigation ditches for home use, and farmed exclusively with hand tools. Meat was scarce and neighbors gave their peelings and table leavings to help fatten the nearest pig. When the pig was butchered, they received 'pig fry' for their investment—liver, fat, and a little pork. Indians begged from house-to-house, carrying their bundles of biscuits, sugar, and scraps to wigwams in the willows."[1]

The first industries appeared in 1859 when a sawmill was built, an irrigation system was put in, and the town was laid out. Soon this thriving city was focused on agriculture, building a carding mill, sawmill, tannery, several flour mills, and a limekiln.

Construction on the Logan LDS Tabernacle began in 1865 and was completed in 1878, and temple construction began in 1877 and was finished in 1884. The Episcopal Church also formed several parishes there. Brigham Young College was founded in 1878, but it took several years to build it. Ten years later it became the Agricultural College of Utah, and students began attending in 1890. Eventually it was known as Utah State Agricultural College and then Utah State University.

The Capitol Theatre and the old Lyric Theatre both have tales of hauntings, which I cover in my upcoming book *Ghost Lights: Utah's Haunted Theatres, Amusement Parks, and Other Entertaining Haunts.* There were more than 25,000 people who labored on building both the Logan Temple and the Logan Tabernacle. Both buildings are among the few early outstanding beauties of architectural art in the state of Utah, surpassed only by the Manti Temple that sits majestically on a high hill.

Logan is the center of the county government, has two daily newspapers, and technical schools and firms. The city has cold winters and cool summers. In the last few years, the city has really promoted the arts in the valley with such attractions as The Festival of the American West, Jazz Fair, Summer Arts Fair, Lyric Theatre (belonging to the college), drama productions on campus, summer concert series, and, of course, the Utah Festival Opera Company, housed in the beautifully restored Capitol Theatre, now called the Ellen Eccles Theatre.

The "Peepstone" Lady

The oldest ghost story I could find in the area was about the "Peepstone Lady." Stories were told about this woman from the late 1800s to the 1940s.

A man lost two horses, and he went to see the Peepstone Lady in Logan. She looked in her stone—or crystal—and told him where he could find them. It was a cold, harsh winter. He wanted to recover the horses, but he knew it would be too dangerous to try until spring. The next spring when he went to the spot where the woman told him to go, he found the horses starved to death. He felt bad but was surprised to find them exactly where she told him to look.

Another reference to her says that she was Mrs. C. P. of Logan. It says that the woman's parents lost a valuable horse and that she looked in her stone and told them where to find it. They followed her directions and found their horse.

The most interesting claim made about the Peepstone Lady is that she supposedly unearthed a crystal ball to use in her divination when the Logan Temple was being built. The stone could have been crystal, but it is more likely that it was just an ordinary stone from the foundation of the temple and the woman's deep faith made it work. She supposedly used it as a seer stone throughout her life to assist others in finding lost things or to foretell the future. Since the temple was under construction from 1877 to 1884, we can surmise that she was a young adult when she found the stone and more than likely died in the late 1940s. Soon after finding the stone, she became known as the Peepstone Lady and could perform all sorts of miracles using her stone or crystal ball.

A prominent local man disappeared, and they searched everywhere for him. Finally, in desperation, the family went to the Peepstone Lady and asked for her help. After talking with the spirit of the dead man, she was able to use her crystal ball to locate his body and direct the searchers to where he had died. They followed her directions, and sure enough, they found him exactly where she said he would be.

Joseph Smith used seer stones when he translated the Book of Mormon, and from what I understand, in those days it was all right for a Mormon woman to divine as well. In fact, women were given patriarchal blessings that bestowed upon them gifts of prophecy or visions. Some individuals were given the gift of healing abilities, also called "the laying on of hands." Women who had these abilities were encouraged and honored for having and using these gifts, so it makes me wonder if the Peepstone Lady was at first honored and then hid her talents when society's attitudes changed. Or perhaps she achieved such a prominence that she was able to transcend any criticisms or changes in people's thinking.

The Bluebird and Grapevine Restaurants

The town of Logan has two haunted places that I know of. I'm sure more ghosts exist, especially in some of the old buildings in town. My fondest memories of Logan are the homemade ice cream at the dairy store and the big thick slices of homemade bread, with a variety of choices of toppings, that could be purchased on the USU campus.

My all-time favorite activity when I was younger was to eat at the Bluebird Restaurant with my family, or get the best hamburgers in town at the A & W Root Beer stand on Main Street. A much newer place to eat in Logan is the Grapevine Restaurant, which is located in an older home where a real spirit keeps the place hopping. It is said that former employees have several stories to tell, such as dishes suddenly flying off shelves, hurtling across a room, and crashing against the opposite wall. Objects—especially brooms for some reason—are carried up in midair by invisible hands and deposited in a different room. The general pattern is that the activity wanes for a while and then starts up again. It becomes really intense, and then the employees sternly ask that it stop. The activity stops for a while and then slowly starts back up again. My guess is that there is more activity in the wintertime than in the summer, because for some reason, ghosts like the cold. Perhaps the former residents don't like how the restaurant is being run, or maybe they aren't happy about a restaurant being in their home.

When I lived in Logan, students at the junior high school talked about the ghost at the Bluebird Restaurant and how things moved about or shadowy figures were seen in corners. When I later moved back to Logan with my husband, we would hear college students who worked at the restaurant talk about the mysterious happenings. When we ate there a while ago, most of the current employees said there was no activity but admitted that the owners didn't like them to talk about ghosts. I felt something, especially from the upstairs area. We returned for the John Gilbert festival and got a few ghost stories from the employees, or at least a suggestion of ghostly activity. Apparently, while the new owners didn't want that kind of talk at their restaurant, "that kind of talk" had been going on for years, and one or two employees talked to us about their experiences.

The Bluebird was originally located at 12 West Center Street and was started by three partners in 1914. It was more of a confectionery store, where candy and ice cream from the soda fountain were sold. In 1921 the partners wanted to expand, and they built a brand new building at 19 North Main Street, where they could serve lunch and dinner as well. The new location, with beautifully hand-painted walls and ceilings, was opened on Washington's birthday in 1923. An upper mezzanine was constructed for smaller group parties, and the Florentine Room upstairs housed large banquets, as well as serving as a ballroom for dances.

The Depression brought a halt to the thriving business, but in the 1930s, with only two partners remaining, the place was kept open with a lot of hard work and dedication. The Bennett family eventually bought the place and kept it going for years. They served fine food and made the Bluebird a premier restaurant in Logan. Two new private and semiprivate dining rooms were added, along with a brand new kitchen. In 1994 the Xu family bought the restaurant, and they still provide the best of fine dining in the Logan area.

The employees I spoke to said they did not want anyone to know they had talked to me, but they all agreed on one thing—no one liked to go down to the basement alone. When asked why, they said that some of them had been touched by something down there—something not human and certainly not visible.

Logan Cemetery

Another haunting story is about the Logan Cemetery. This story involves a large family and the curse their father put on them from his deathbed. Eight children were in the family, and their father was a stern disciplinarian who must have done some awful things to cause his children to hate him so. He died young, and as he was dying, he cursed his own children by saying that after he died, a child would die every six months thereafter. Six months later, the oldest boy caught a cold, which turned into pneumonia, and he died. The next oldest daughter was killed in an accident six months after her brother died. The six-month cycle continued until all of his children were dead. Six months after the last child died, their mother died as well.

In the Logan Cemetery is a large statue of a woman who appears to be mourning and weeping for her lost children. For decades the locals called her the "Weeping Lady," and she is said to sit over the grave of an unnamed child. Eight graves surround the statue, and all of the occupants died within six months of each other. In order to hear the woman weeping and see and feel the tears on the statue's face, you need to check the date the last child died and go there on that exact date near midnight. Then you will hear the woman weeping and be able to feel the tears on her cheeks. The time between midnight and one in the morning is considered the "ghost hour," when spirits walk the graveyards and the statues weep. What is most interesting about this story is to consider whether the graves or the story came first. Such a story could have easily developed from the strange coincidence of every child in the family dying within six months of each other, and those who discovered this coincidence in the cemetery may have created the story. Still, to see the statue weep would be interesting. When we went there, we could see just how easily this story might have developed. The Logan Cemetery is a huge rectangle, flat and smooth, and located on the hill above town. It is one of the best-kept cemeteries I have ever seen, with a sexton who really cares—not just about how well it is kept, but also about every story related to the cemetery.

According to Richard McOmber, author of *Zion's Lost Souls*, the real story is much more touching and tragic. Olaf and Julia Cronquist, a young Scandinavian couple who converted to Mormonism, immigrated to Utah and settled in northern Utah. Julia was from Denmark and of a fragile disposition. She was ill most of the time. In the winter of 1889, an epidemic of scarlet fever hit the people of Richmond very hard. For weeks she nursed her two young sons, Olif Edward, age six, and Oliver Emeal, age four, but both children died within days of each other. Julia then became ill herself. She never fully recovered from her first bout of scarlet fever, but she did survive the ordeal, and four years later she gave birth to a little girl. Lilean died on the same day of her birth. In 1901 Julia lost her two-year-old twins, Emelia Lauretta and Inez Constance, to another bout with scarlet fever. For the rest of her life, Julia was often confined to a wheelchair. With one of her older children assisting her, she sometimes walked to the graves of her children to weep. When Julia died in 1914, only three of her children had grown to adulthood. McOmber says the following about the Cronquist family in his book *Zion's Lost Souls*.

Olaf had her buried in Richmond with their children, and commissioned a statue from his native Sweden for the gravesite. It depicts a life-sized woman, on one knee, one hand lightly to her forehead, the other holding a wreath. The cost was a reported $2000.00, a formidable sum back then. When Olaf died, the remaining Cronquists buried him in the Logan Cemetery, and moved the rest of the family to join him with matching headstones.[2]

It seems that instead of evil or abuse, it was heartbreak that brought the Weeping Lady to the center of the Logan Cemetery. The statue is the largest and most ornate gravestone there, so it really stands out. It is an incredibly beautiful statue, and the Weeping Lady seems to oversee all that surrounds her.

Several graves of children, all from the same family, surround her, but I could not find eight of them. And the dates, while not exactly six months apart, did follow a pattern as each child died. I came looking for the grave marker of the grandfather of John Gilbert, the great silent film star. When I found it, I could see that the sexton and other caretakers were interested in the story I had to tell them. The sexton showed me other graves with stories attached to them and mentioned an article that appeared in the local paper about the cemetery. I said that next time an article was planned on the residents of the cemetery, he would have to include something about John Gilbert being born in Logan and his grandfather and two wives and an uncle being buried there. I gave them a brief synopsis of Gilbert's stays in Logan as a child and mentioned that his mother was buried in the Mt. Olivet Cemetery in Salt Lake City even though there was obviously room for her in the Logan family plot. Gilbert's boyhood home now has a little plaque in front of it that his daughter dedicated in 2003.

River Heights

River Heights has a small cemetery. A large stake that stuck out of the ground about three or four feet used to be there. Red paint or just red "something" was splashed down the sides of the stake. The kids in town called it "Bloody Stake." River Heights is on a mesa south of the city and was once a separate town, but it is now part of Logan.

The story that surrounds this stake happened a long time ago. A woman we can only call "M" practiced witchcraft. She was accused of witchcraft and beheaded as a blood atonement for her evil ways by those who called themselves "Sons of Retribution," who were probably the Danites.

The Danites were supposedly a secret Mormon organization formed during the Missouri phase of Mormon history. (It is said that the organization was kept a secret in an attempt to protect themselves from their persecutors.) As the story goes, these Danites would retaliate against enemy Gentiles and those of the fold who the Danites felt had broken one of the Ten Commandments. The offenders were often threatened, clubbed on the head, beaten, or even "blood atoned," which meant being stabbed or hit over the head with a blunt instrument and then having their throats cut so that their blood would fall onto the ground and the victim would then be "blood atoned" for entrance into heaven, free of their sins on earth. A few went to their deaths willingly, believing adamantly that blood atonement would release them from their sins.

Other Church members who took the law into their own hands in their communities sometimes imitated these acts of vigilante justice. No one was ever brought to justice for what was done to certain individuals. Fear of retribution kept the perpetrator's identities secret, but the rumors have always been that it was a member of a secret Council of Fifty who formed this Danite group. This practice followed the Mormons to Utah. It was said that before she died, "M" told the vigilantes that she would return to haunt the people of River Heights forever. It was soon discovered that she was true to her word, and her head was seen floating above the end of the bloody stake in the River Heights Cemetery.

The story grew over the years, and the woman was said to laugh and jeer at those who saw her. Apparently she haunts the cemetery but nowhere else in town! I could not find the stake when I visited the cemetery, and no one was around to ask about it. I do know that this is an old story. It's likely that either the stake never existed or it was removed because of the bother the stories were giving the cemetery caretakers. If the story was once based on any kind of truth, then perhaps there was a woman who offended her Mormon kinsmen and paid for it with her life.

St. Ann's Retreat in Logan Canyon

St. Ann's Retreat is in Logan Canyon, and people believe it is haunted. Several ghosts have been spotted on the property, such as a floating nun, a screaming little boy, and children running about the place laughing and talking. Orbs and lights were spotted at night by people in their cars on the highway. Several people believe it was once a school, but it was not. Before the Catholic Church leased the property, these stone buildings were a lodge and cabins built in the 1920s where people paid to stay. If anything happened there before the buildings became a retreat and summer camp, no one seems to know.

The Catholic Church came to Logan in the 1940s. For about twenty years the parish met in St. Jerome's, a small chapel on Fifth North. Monsignor Jerome C. Stoffel was the priest there for thirty years. He built up the Catholic congregation in Logan beginning in the 1960s. He established the Newman Center north of the Utah State University campus and eventually added a chapel to the center. The Center is still a gathering place for non-Mormons and foreign students in the city. At the same time the Catholic Church also operated St. Ann's Retreat in Logan Canyon. At one time they had day camps for children, but the place has not been used for years and is now privately owned.

In Bernice Maher Mooney's book, *Salt of the Earth: The History of the Catholic Church in Utah, 1776 to 1987*, I found the real story of St. Ann's Retreat.

In 1953 St. Ann's Retreat, located in Logan Canyon on land leased from the Forest Service, consisted of two adjoining properties donated to the diocese by the families of L. Boyd Hatch in 1952 and Mrs. Hortense Odium in 1953. The property was administered by the parish of St. Thomas Aquinas and provided a summer vacation retreat for sisters working in the diocese, and later, a recreational camp for youth of all faiths. In succeeding years the camp fell into disuse. Father Donald E. Hope was appointed director in 1978; he closed the camp temporarily while he got the properties repaired. Bishop William K. Winegand established St. Ann's Camp Advisory Board in 1981. During the summers of 1985 to 1987, camp programs were conducted under the direction of Sharon Kaytor, Coordinator of Youth Ministry for the diocesan Office of Religious Education. The camp property was in the process of being sold in 1987, and other sites sought for continuation of camp programs.[3]

Stories about St. Ann's were rather nebulous when I lived in Logan, but I did hear about the place possibly being haunted. Later, when the place was empty, I was told the following story about it. There was a small swimming pool at the summer camp, and a little boy drowned in it. The pool was drained and is empty and deserted now. But when people go there, they can feel a three-foot square freezing cold spot in the dead center of the pool, summer or winter. People have also seen lights there at night. It is either a series of small orbs of ghost lights or one big iridescent glow. People claim to have seen the spirits of children running about the place since more than one child supposedly died there. They don't describe the children, so these sightings are suspect. I guess you could check the town records about deaths at the camp, but my guess is that there aren't any or maybe only one from which all the ghost rumors came. I could only look at it from afar, but from what I saw of it, it is an eerie place. It is well guarded because of some unfortunate ghost hunting incidents in the past. Even the employees at the forest service station at the mouth of the canyon is guarded about giving out any information concerning the former St. Ann's, and with good reason.

The present owners had a lot of trouble with high school and college kids trying to get into the place because of the ghost stories. Because of the trespassing and vandalism, armed guards were hired to watch St. Ann's. In 1997 a whole crowd of teenagers was caught on the property. The guards went a bit overboard and made all of the kids wade into the swimming pool, which was apparently full of water and not empty as everyone had supposed. The kids had to stand in the "empty" pool with their hands on their heads while the guards pointed their weapons at them until the police arrived. There were thirty-eight teens, and three watchmen were holding them at bay with shotguns. The watchmen handcuffed the teens with plastic flexible ties and bound them with ropes. They were told that if they moved, the ropes or ties would tighten and trigger explosives that would blow off their heads. The men also threatened to slit the youths' throats. One shotgun was fired over their heads, and one youth was repeatedly struck with the butt of a gun. While I am sure the kids were being belligerent, the watchmen certainly over-reacted to the situation, which terrified the teens.

Several parents were upset about how their teens were treated. Some of the kids had been downright terrified and were crying in the pool. Even though it was the teens who were trespassing on private property, the parents protested the guards' behavior, and the men were arrested for aggravated assault. Halfway through the jury trial, the three men changed their plea to guilty and got reduced charges in an agreement with the prosecutors. Two separate groups of teens had gone there that night seeking Halloween thrills and instead got a reality experience they will never forget. This event made it onto the show *Inside Edition*, a nationally syndicated program. Since that time, absolutely no one has trespassed on the old St. Ann's property, so while these watchmen went about it in the wrong way, they certainly stopped the trespassing. The kids might have been drinking, and perhaps a little ghostly phenomenon had taken place as well, at least for the kids who were sensitive to that sort of thing.

Since this incident, the old St. Ann's Retreat, which is still private property, tries to keep a low profile. There are wild stories about St. Ann's, and the following story made it onto national websites that describe ghostly places in Utah. The story goes that St. Ann's is a haunted nunnery where nuns once lived and worked. Nuns who needed to be disciplined were sent there to make penance. Some of them were pregnant and awaiting delivery so that the babies could be given up for adoption. One young nun did not want to give up her baby and when the time came and the Reverend Mother tried to take the child, the nun ran away with her baby in her arms. It was the middle of the night, and the Reverend Mother ran after her. Finally, the nun left her baby in a fire pit and covered her with leaves. When the coast seemed clear, the young mother ran back to the fire pit and found that her baby was gone. She returned to the retreat only to discover that her baby had been thrown into the swimming pool and had drowned. Either an evil Mother Superior, other nuns who were humiliated by her sinning, or a hermit in the woods could have done the deed.

In another version of the story, it was the young mother herself, who in a daze threw her own child into the pool and then jumped in and drowned with her. Either way, the story continues, the young mother committed suicide on the spot to join her infant girl. It is this young nun who walks the hills around the retreat looking for her lost baby. Her spirit is haunting the canyons for eternity. This is also why, besides seeing the ghost lights over the swimming pool, that one can hear a baby crying in the woods near the pool. The white glow is supposed to be the young nun running through the woods.

Green Canyon

Near Logan Canyon is a particularly eerie and remote canyon called Green Canyon. It is located to the south of Logan Canyon and almost parallel to it. This mystical and unsettling place gives an ominous feeling to hikers and campers.

In her article, "Deadly Cold," Valerie Vaughn said the following:

> Early settlers knew of the treacherous (Logan) canyon conditions and
> avoided using the resources of wood and building materials the canyon had
> to offer. Instead, they built their homes and some businesses out of adobe
> bricks. When lumber was needed, the settlers would go to Green Canyon,
> north of Logan Canyon, and cut the trees there.[4]

Green Canyon, which is more remote from the settlement, offered easier access,
and the settlers went there often in the early days to cut trees for their homes.
Green Canyon is located in the Waseca National Forest and at the southern end
of it is a place called Wind Cave. At the northern end of the Canyon is the Mount
Naomi Wilderness Area. Perhaps early-day visitors contributed to the legend of
this canyon being haunted.

Within Green Canyon is a certain remote area that I am sure you would have
to hike to, where no bird chirps and no animals live. Even domestic animals will
not go into the area with their masters. Packhorses balk at entering the area. All
sorts of strange things have been reported by people brave enough to go there, and
the overall feeling of the place is one of despair and hopelessness. People say those
who camp there feel depressed until they leave the canyon. There is a strong sense
of evil, as if something bad happened there long ago. Green Canyon is not a large
canyon, and I have no more information about it. I think it would be difficult to
locate the area described, and besides, who wants to go out into the wilderness to
feel evil? On the other hand, tales like this often arise from ancient Indian burial
areas, old battles between the Spanish gold miners and their enslaved Native
Americans, or murders that took place later between miners or trappers. A more
modern event would be recorded, and none exist that I know of. Still, that doesn't
mean that something evil didn't happen there. A wind cave would certainly add to
the mystique, since in the old days people believed that spirits' voices were heard
by traveling on the wind.

Mendon

Years ago, a woman living in Mendon was supposedly caught consorting
with the devil. The townspeople tried and convicted her without formal judicial
proceedings and took her into the mountains to burn her. As they were preparing
her pyre, she shouted a curse on the town. She cursed the spot where she was to
burn and declared that Mendon would not prosper from that day forward. She
said the tree to which they tied her would never die and that her soul would remain
near the tree and haunt it forever. She proclaimed that no animal would come near
it, and no plants would grow around it. Some of the citizens of Mendon believe
that her curse has come to pass, because unlike Wellsville or Logan, Mendon has

not prospered and remains a small town, with most of its population commuting elsewhere.

This event supposedly took place a long time ago, but some citizens believe that the tree still stands by itself in the center of a wide green meadow in the mountains behind Mendon. You are welcome to search for it, but I doubt you'll know where to look, since those who remember this story have probably forgotten the tree's location—if the tree and the woman actually existed. It is hard for me to believe that the citizens of Mendon burned any poor woman to death. Sometimes a story like this gets started because of what an area looks like, and in this case, it may have been the oddly shaped tree sitting alone in a wide meadow. It is more likely that if the story is true, the woman's accusers probably just wanted to scare her by burning a tree as a warning. People in those days did believe in magic and curses and hauntings, so if a woman was practicing medicine or rituals that town citizens thought were unholy and wicked, she could have been driven out of Mendon, especially if a "patient" died due to these practices, or someone believed that a curse had been placed on somebody they knew. This might have been cause to "burn" a witch, but it is highly unlikely that such a thing took place.[5] It's possible that high school kids made up the story. Perhaps a woman who lived in the town was considered a witch. Back then people thought that anyone not following the community norm was "strange." And which came first, the huge twisted tree, or the legend of the woman who was tied to it? Town curses were common then, and over the years Mendon has certainly had its share of troubles. Does this old tree still exist today, and is the woman still haunting it? Only modern-day Mendon residents could prove or disprove this tale.

Mendon City is eight miles southwest of Logan and five miles west of Wellsville. Alexander and Robert Hill, who came from Mill Creek, settled Mendon in 1855. They drove a herd of cattle to where Mendon is today and decided that this little valley would be a great place to settle with their families. In 1856 the Miller family settled just south of Mendon at Gardner's Creek. Settlers began arriving, and by 1859 they had settled in all parts of Cache Valley. A sawmill was built in the area soon after, and in 1860, the first log school house was built and the Mendon Ward was organized. Mendon citizens helped take care of some of the white soldiers from the Bear River Massacre, the largest massacre of Indians in the history of the United States. One would suspect that a citizen or two may have helped some of the Shoshones who were starving and on the run from this massacre, but this would have been done in secret, since at that time the local natives were believed to be hostile and dangerous. At one point, settlers in Mendon began constructing a rock wall around the town for protection, but the rock wall was never finished.

Settlers built a gristmill, several rock homes, and a large rock church. In 1869 the railroad came close enough to Mendon to benefit commerce in the town, and a ZCMI branch was established. The town was incorporated in 1870. Mendon had a twenty-one-member United Order group, which lasted only a year. A

Presbyterian school was started in 1883. Between 1887 and 1900 the polygamous husbands from the area were sent to jail. Wheat farming became central to the town's survival. A new school was built in 1899, and a dance hall was constructed of large rocks in 1896.

Mendon became known for its thoroughbred racehorses, and some racing took place outside of town. By then the railroad had a spur line between Hyrum and Mendon, and people came via train for the horse races. A new LDS meetinghouse was constructed in 1913. High school students went to the South Cache High School on the new electric railroad. Sugar beets became the main farm product and were shipped from Mendon on the trains. By 1947 the railroad ceased operation, and sugar beet production dropped off. Today Mendon is less of a farming community and more of a bedroom community, with people commuting to other jobs in Logan and surrounding towns. In July 2008, the Mendon population was 1,190 people.[6]

Honeyville, Deweyville, Bear River City, Crystal Hot Springs (Madsen Hot Springs), Hensley's Crossing, and Empey Ferry

Crystal Hot Springs were considered haunted by spirits even before white men came to the area, and more stories were told after the Mormon pioneers settled there. People of many cultures and backgrounds have crossed this small territory. The nearby transcontinental railroad workers, especially from China, came to the hot springs at least once a week to bathe.

Thousands of immigrants and pioneers took Hensley's Crossing as a shortcut to California. Besides the lost spirits who wander in this area, there are also interesting homes with some of the most unique pioneer architecture in Utah. With all these layers of history, this little remote area houses some of the most unique apparitions from different decades. As you drive the back road to Logan, the eerie atmosphere of bygone days can be felt and perhaps even seen as white mists rising from the steamy waters in the moonlight.

Honeyville has a population of nine hundred to one thousand people. Deweyville has a population of three hundred to four hundred. They are right next to each other on State Highway 38, on the west side of the mountains that are northwest of Cache Valley. The road up the mountain rises five thousand feet in two miles to reach the summit, and the mountain is the west face of the northern Wasatch. The charms of these two little settlements are the historical markers and grand pioneer houses.

One mile south of Honeyville is Harper's Ward, whose aged rock houses are listed on historical registers and are just about the best pioneers houses still in good repair in all of Utah, except for Spring City. The drive up over the mountains into these two little towns has little traffic and is breathtaking in either direction to or from Cache Valley. When we lived in Logan, we often took a drive on that road just to see the wonderful houses in Honeyville.

Abraham Hunsaker bought land for grazing sheep and cattle and then founded the town of Honeyville in 1860. But it was not until 1866 that the first settlement housed a few families and was called Hunsakerville. Local legend says that Abraham didn't want the place named after him, so it was named after his bee farm instead. Others say the naming was biblical, after the land of milk and honey. In 1865 a stagecoach station and a gristmill were built. A ferry traveled up the Bear River from Salt Lake and took passengers both ways. It was known as Empey Ferry for years. The stage station was moved to Crystal Hot Springs, and the freight and stage line ran west of Salt Creek to Collinston and over the divide to Montana. In May 1872 the Utah Northern Railroad Company built a narrow gauge railroad through Honeyville, and in 1911, Honeyville was officially incorporated. Two railroad stations were there by 1912. One ran electric trains to Ogden and Preston, Idaho, and the other ran between Ogden and Honeyville.

By 1915, the town had a flour mill, blacksmith shop, stores, and eventually four schools and four chapels. An indoor swimming pool was constructed, as well as an ice-skating rink and a hill for sledding and tobogganing that was called "Killer Hill." The school house bell was expensive and unusual and therefore precious to the townspeople. When the school was torn down and a new one built, the railroad company bought the property. They tore out the bell and took it to Sun Valley, Idaho, to go into a building there. The townspeople were upset about losing their bell.

In the beginning, Crystal Hot Springs was named Madsen's Hot Springs, and it still provides the largest hot and cold springs in the United States. The hot and cold springs are right next to each other and are full of saline, which has great healing effects for such things as arthritis and joint pain.

These springs were sacred bathing and healing waters long before the white man discovered them. The Shoshone and their ancestors always camped there. When the white man came, bringing all sorts of diseases with him that the Shoshone and others were more susceptible to, these diseases did not respond to traditional medicine man treatments. Soaking in hot springs was often recommended as a part of the healing, along with herbs and chants. As the people became ill, they would travel to these traditional stopping places to ease the new illnesses. Unfortunately, measles, typhoid fever, chicken pox, scarlet fever, and other diseases were aggravated by the hot springs and caused people to die. In this case, rumors of Indian burial mounds near the springs would seem quite logical and likely, because traveling a long distance away for burial would not make sense since the people had died there at the springs. This is the first layer of hauntings for this area.

Smaller hot springs were all over the area. Not far from Madsen's Hot Springs was another place called Stinking Hot Springs. A pioneer settler named Hiram House, who lived in Corinne, made an agreement with Box Elder County that when he died he would bequeath the springs to them with the stipulation that

15

they would keep it up nicely and never charge the people who wanted to use the springs. With high sulfur content in the water, it was said to have the best healing waters of any of the springs in the area. But the county did not keep its promise, and today the building is disintegrating, the cement pools are cracking, and the place is filthy. People are afraid to go there because of ancient Indian spirits and the superstition that the waters have such a powerful healing ability that the spirits would be angry at how the place was left to deteriorate. As for myself, I think the former owner would be the one to haunt the place. He would be angry with what has happened to his property, especially since it could have great healing effects on people in pain. Perhaps he is prone to drop by and irritate those who are responsible or those who are there to do something about the springs.

Near the hot springs is an old pioneer trail that was never given an official name. Hundreds of pioneers traveling west drove their oxen, cattle, and wagons down through the river. Over twenty-five thousand pioneers used this trail as a shortcut on their way west in 1848. Samuel J. Hensley is credited with being the first pioneer to discover it, and so the place was named Hensley's Crossing after him. This route allowed pioneers to outfit in Salt Lake City and then rejoin their fellow trains at the City of Rocks in Idaho on the California and Oregon Trails. It saved them from having to travel nearly two hundred extra miles. The trail is exactly seven miles long and is 1,084 feet from the cold water and hot water springs, so you can imagine that pioneers probably stopped in this little oasis to rest before continuing on. No one knew exactly where this crossing was until someone in recent years found an old log chain buried right where the crossing was located. The chain was used to hitch teams of oxen together. Further investigation showed that the old Wagon Wheel Trail was also where the chain was found. This is another layer of hauntings for this area.

Tales of Chinese railroad workers are also told about the springs. Because cleanliness was of great importance to them, these men traveled the distance from the transcontinental railroad site to the hot springs area to bathe. They made tubs of cedarwood and let the water flow into them. The hot and cold springs came together within fifty feet of each other, thus mixing the waters to a perfect temperature in the tubs. The Chinese workers could have left a few energy residues at the hot springs. Perhaps this explains the voices heard in other languages around the place from time to time. Between the Shoshone, the Chinese, and the immigrant parties coming from all over the world, Madsen's Hot Springs and Hensley's Crossing were somewhat international places.

The springs became Madsen's Hot Springs soon after the first settlers arrived in Honeyville and Deweyville. In 1901 they became Crystal Hot Springs and were considered a real business enterprise for the town. People used the springs long before anyone had to pay to go there. In 1970 the pools were rebuilt and a waterslide was put in, and now people from miles around enjoy the hot springs. They come from Idaho and Logan or even Ogden to enjoy a dip in the springs. Three hot tubs, a soaker pool, an Olympic-sized swimming pool, a lap pool, and a hydro tube are available to visitors. Crystal Hot Springs is two miles north of Honeyville and has shade trees. Swimming, camping, and picnicking are available in summer, and ice-skating is available in winter.

Besides all of the spirits from so many layers, some things in more modern times happened at the hot springs to cause haunting activity. According to local legend, at least two or more "active" ghosts reside there. It seems that about twenty-five years ago a boy tried to dive from the balcony into the pool but missed his mark and died. Another man was killed when he fell down an outside stairway or deck and broke his neck. The exact years of these deaths are nebulous. The manager has heard several versions of these stories but has been unable to confirm either of them. This doesn't seem to matter since the manager and some of his employees have had their own unexplainable experiences there. You have to understand that the springs are in an isolated area, so if you are locking up the facility at night, no one is around but you. A lot of stories surround the little resort, and some even come from visitors who knew nothing in advance about the ghosts who might be there.

One person who worked there saw a light at the top of the waterslide when he was closing up. He went up the stairs and switched it off, walked all the way back down, and looked up to see the light on again. This same procedure occurred three separate times, but on the third time, the light went off just before he got to it. He ran down the stairs and didn't look back, leaving his coworkers behind and everything unlocked. Apparently, this has happened a few times, with the last one to lock up getting so scared that he simply left without securing anything. An employee was in the attic once and heard footsteps behind him. As he turned to go down the stairs, he felt a cold draft and the hairs on the back of his neck rose. The temperature dropped ten to fifteen degrees in that spot. When he got downstairs, someone had turned off all the video games. The employee was alone. Later, he went back with a friend to investigate what had happened to him by sleeping overnight in the attic. In the middle of the night, both men woke up to a loud thumping noise. When they turned the lights on, they discovered their clothes all mixed up in each other's sleeping bags. They told no one they were sleeping in the attic, so they were really scared by the events that night.

A lot of the employees will not go to the attic alone, especially in the dark. They say they hear music or shuffling feet, or have doors slam behind or in front of them. A staff picture taken several years ago shows a shadowy shape in an upstairs window behind the people in the photograph. They swear the shape is a ghost, and they have nicknamed him "Rob." He has been adopted as part of the staff at the hot springs.

Some of the employees believe there is more than one ghost. One seems to be a younger boy playing tricks on them, while the other seems to be an older man who is not so friendly and nice. The music that is sometimes heard might be explained by the big dance pavilion that is rarely used now but was a big attraction from the 1920s into the 1950s, with local bands coming on the weekend to play for the crowds who came to dance and party.

Many more spirits from the past as well as from the present reside at Crystal Hot Springs. We know the energy there comes in layers, just like it does everywhere else. But because this area has been visited by so many people within the last two hundred years, more layers probably exist there. Among those layers are ancient native peoples, who probably used the waters as they traveled their routes long before the Plains Indians came to be. It's possible they had a burial mound nearby. Others layers might include the Shoshone and other tribes who probably chose to bathe there, perhaps also burying those who did not survive; hundreds of pioneers who chose to rest there before journeying on; the "celestials," as the Chinese were sometimes called in those days, who came a long way to bathe in the spring waters; citizens of this century who might have owned the springs or visited them before they became a commercial enterprise; and, of course, current times and those who pay to swim or dance in the summer and ice skate in the winter. Tourists and locals have used the hot springs for years.

It is no surprise to me that ghost stories are popping up about the place all the time. It is too bad that someone doesn't keep track of them by writing them down. They could be used to intrigue more people to visit.

After tracking down the history of the springs, I am intrigued, especially since I had my own little experience along the Oregon Trail one summer. We stopped at a rest stop, and I walked out by myself to stand where the wagon tracks were visible in a field behind the springs. As I waited for my husband, I had the sense of a little boy approaching me and tapping the back of my legs to get my attention. I somehow knew he was lost and was trying to find his mother and father. He was asking me for help to find them. I tried to explain that they left a long time ago and he needed to go with them. I told him to follow the trail, because it was the only thing I could think of to tell him. I wondered if he had died or was buried there. I later learned that unmarked graves line this trail, especially the graves of children. When I told my husband about it, he said he wasn't stopping at any more places where the Oregon Trail was so visibly marked because I had spooked him!

Bear River City

Not far from Honeyville is a little town called Bear River City that has its own tales to tell about a bridge near the town. The story goes that a woman got really depressed about her life, drove around aimlessly with her two kids in the car, and eventually found herself on the bridge. She may have planned to drive off the bridge, or she might have done it spontaneously. Anyway, she drove off the bridge, killing herself and her two children. Rumors started that she believed the devil told her to do it. It is more likely that she was suffering from depression, or perhaps some sort of mental illness. The high school kids probably added the devil to the story to make it sound creepier.

Local high school kids say that strange things happen there because of the woman's actions. People claim to have seen her wandering on the bridge late at night, or they hear the voices of the children. The high school kids developed a ritual for conjuring up the spirit voices, but few claim to have actually seen the woman's ghostly form. You have to sit on the bridge in your car, with your windows rolled down so you can hear the voices. You honk your horn three times, and then in a few minutes the children can be heard saying, "Don't do it, Mother! Don't do it, Mother!" The high school students believe it is the spirits of the two children calling for someone to save them. Their mother, in her great sorrow, wanders the area calling for them, and the bridge itself "cries" in the dark.

Ogden City, the Oldest Settlement in Utah

Brigham Young chose Ogden as the central railroad hub after the transcontinental railroads were joined, and Ogden City, as it was once called, became the wildest city in Utah. The Shoshone used the hot springs as campgrounds long before the white men arrived. They had their own tales to tell. Trappers and explorers had large rendezvous, both in the Ogden valley and up Ogden Canyon. Ruins of mining ghost towns are all over the canyon. With these mining discoveries came saloons, brothels, and other spirited places. Once the railroad came through, these trains brought in just about anything or anyone imaginable. People came from all over the world to settle in the Ogden valley, leaving imprints of ghosts and spirits behind them. The ghosts and apparitions of this entire city and canyon can be felt wherever one wanders from the old railroad station to the canyon settlements or an old city cemetery. (The Ogden Union Station's entire haunting story is told in a future book on railroading and mining, while the Ben Lomond and Ogden Canyon stories were told in my first book, *Specters in Doorways*.)

Ogden, once the second largest city in Utah, is located where the Ogden and Weber Rivers meet. Ogden's historical reputation as the Gentile city of Utah probably came from being the center of all railroad transportation in the state, if not in the intermountain west.

Ogden City has a colorful and diverse past as a Gentile railroad town. The city has more colorful tales of early mining adventurers than other Utah cities, as well as stories of those who carried out illegal profiteerings during Prohibition. Corinne was the first Utah railroad city. It had an early rivalry with Salt Lake City, but for many reasons, it did not survive as a large metropolis.

Several rich and famous people visited Ogden in the first half of the twentieth century. Some of them stayed to build up entertainment businesses or other enterprises in the city, as well as to build summer homes in Ogden Canyon. One especially colorful mayor named Harman Peery, the "Cowboy Mayor of Ogden," also engendered stories in the 1930s and 1940s of all sorts of promotions, celebrities, and intrigues that took place in the city of Ogden. For example, Mayor Peery created the "Whoopee! Girl." Besides nominating a new girl every year to represent tourism in the city, he had a whole poster and ad campaign that created a famous pin-up girl for World War II soldiers, especially among the cowboy soldiers.

In those days Ogden was a cattlemen's town, complete with huge intermountain west conventions and rodeos.

Miles Goodyear was the first trapper-trader to settle the valley. His home was moved to the Daughters of the Pioneer Museum, which is located right under the shadow of the Ogden Mormon temple. Several of Brigham Young's men bought the fort only three years later, and Goodyear moved on to California. Ogden then became another Mormon settlement early in 1847, the year that the Mormons arrived in the Salt Lake Valley, thus giving Ogden the distinction of the only city or town in the state settled by Gentiles before the Mormons settled there. It was the coming of the railroad that changed the course of Ogden's history. In 1851 what had come to be known as Brown's Fort became Ogden, named after a Hudson Bay trapper, Peter Skene Ogden, who epitomized all the trapping and trading that went on in the area. Hundreds of workers who were building the transcontinental railroad flooded this once rural community. There were workers mainly from China, the British Isles, and Greece. The railroad was completed in 1869, and the famous "Gentile" railroad-built city of Corinne, just north of Ogden near the shores of the Great Salt Lake, was the prospering competitor of the then growing Salt Lake City.

From 1869 to about 1874, the struggle for power between the Gentile city and the biggest Mormon city continued, with strong anti-Mormon politics coming from Corinne and strong retorts coming from the media in Salt Lake City. Brigham Young simply put a stop to it all by having the railroad bypass Corinne, where it was originally headed, and stop in Ogden City to the north of it instead. The transcontinental railroad was originally closer to Corinne than any other city, and Ogden City was the next closest. Brigham tried for years to get a rail line down to Salt Lake City but never could accomplish it. He finally created his own line to Salt Lake to get the railroad there. The coming of the railroad to Ogden City was the death of Corinne, and it is just a small town today. On the other hand, the railroad was the beginning of growth in Ogden. Ogden quickly became a melting pot of immigrants from all over the world, and people from the city of Corinne moved to Ogden. Ogden's black population came largely from those who found employment on the railroad lines, and workers from the transcontinental railroad who stayed to settle there. In 1889 the first Gentile mayor in the state was elected in Ogden, and with the transcontinental railroad completion the same year, the city also became a major railroad town with nine lines going east to west and north to south.

With the growth of the railroad came all of its corruptions as well. Ogden's Twenty-fifth Street, which ran several blocks from the Union Station up to the Ben Lomond Hotel, gained quite a reputation for gambling and opium dens, as well as prostitution and profiteering. The buildings from Twenty-fourth to Twenty-sixth Streets house two layers of hauntings, one from the early days and the other from the two World Wars and the Prohibition eras. Shopkeepers all along these streets will tell you their individual ghost stories, or at least show you the broken roulette wheels in their basements, or secret underground passages from store to store and street to street. They also tell about the strange things they found when they renovated, such as unopened vials of opium or bottles of liquor, or even show you the little smoky glass windows that pepper the floors of their shops to let light into the secret basement rooms.

It is thought that the more well-known ghosts from these early days are some of the famous madams who plied their trades there. The girls would stand on their balconies overlooking the streets and throw down navy beans on the men's heads to attract their attention. The cheaper "crib" girls were located on a side street north of Twenty-fifth Street along "Electric Alley."

At first there were underground opium dens and gambling rooms, and later these became underground bars and tunnels that ran under the city in different directions. One of Ogden's past mayors asked a group of employees to find some of the entrances and exits to the area's underground tunnels so they could be used as a tourist attraction. A few existed before the Prohibition era, but during this time the number of tunnels expanded quite a bit. Some Ogden residents would prefer to ignore their infamous past by minimizing the extent of these now-closed-off tunnels under their city. Others would like to see them located and explored more thoroughly for the tourist trade they would bring to the city's coffers.

Two infamous ghosts from this first era are Fanny Dawson and Patrick or "Paddy" Flynn, who operated in one of the hotels along this street around 1916. They operated a murder company at 352 Twenty-fifth Street, which was a rooming house next to the old Park Hotel. Fanny was president of the company. She was a divorcee who moved there from Idaho with her two small children in tow. Paddy, aka Mickey Flynn, was a con man she enlisted to cruise the bars, hotels, and gambling parlors to scout out men who had either just won a big sum of money or looked wealthy. Paddy enticed the man up to room number four in the boarding house where the three of them had drinks together, only the victim got a few drops of poison in his. It was Paddy who finally confessed to their murder company after being picked up on some other charge. The police interrogated Fanny all night, while her two little children waited by themselves in the boarding house room on "Two-Bit Street." The pair went to prison, but no bodies were ever found, and the number of victims was never determined. Thus arose the ghost stories of murdered men and Fanny's two little children coming back to haunt the area. People claim that arguing voices can still be heard there, as well as the voices of two children laughing.

In the late 1800s, before Fanny and Paddy, "Gentile Kate" became so influential in the city that she purchased one of Brigham Young's carriages after he died and rode in it around the city, flaunting her wealth.[7] However, the truth of this tale is under dispute. Belle London was the queen of the madams and was so successful that a group of wealthy businessmen paid her a handsome sum to move down to Salt Lake City and start something called "The Stockade," which was a whole block area of legalized prostitution. The Stockade was short-lived, of course, because the good citizens of Salt Lake City squashed it soon after.

While in Ogden though, Belle convinced the local businesses to cut an alley from Twenty-fifth Street to Electric Alley so that men could easily duck into the next street unobserved.

Another "ghost" madam came along a little later in the form of Rose Duccinni Davie. She and her husband, Bill, ran four houses of prostitution in the area from 1947 to 1954. People claim to see her with her pet ocelot on a leash walking the streets, or they even claim to see her rose-colored Cadillac cruising the areas where these four hotels were once located, even though Rose died in 1980 of kidney failure.

This area of town prospered with the coming of World War I, even though the prejudices often associated at the time with such a diverse population more than likely existed. An example of this was the never-talked-about social "rule" that black soldiers walked on one side of the street while white soldiers walked on the other. It was extremely dangerous to break this social "rule," and few ever did. Those who did not know about this rule ended up in fights or even dead in some back alley. Hill Air Force base was built nearby in 1938, which brought in more military personnel, as did the Naval Supply Depot in Clearfield and the smaller Utah General Depot.

World War II was a busy time in Ogden City with the arrival and departure of so many soldiers and an average of at least seventy-five troop trains per day. After World War II was over, the people of Ogden City wanted Twenty-fifth Street cleaned up, and there was a big drive to do so. During the Prohibition era, the place was a honeycomb of busy illegal bootlegging and gambling dens so that the ghostly experiences of present-day shop owners are typically the same reports: doors opening and closing on their own, voices and laughter on the streets late at night, the sounds of lovemaking or old time music, and lights going on and off. Up the street a few blocks is the old Ben Lomond Hotel, and down the street is the old Union Station.

For years people from Salt Lake City had to drive to Ogden to catch a train, and even when the depots were built in Salt Lake, it was still more convenient to come in at the Ogden station, which I can remember doing even in the 1970s. Thousands of soldiers departed from and returned to the Ogden Union Station, even during the Korean and Vietnam wars, so the dead could speak volumes from inside this station. After World War II, the railroad passenger business slowly declined, and passenger service to Ogden was reduced to a tri-weekly Amtrak train. The defense industry is still alive in the Ogden area, and freight trains still pass through Ogden, but Ogden did make one big mistake before the recent era of the city's interest in restoration and renovations. In the 1970s and 1980s, the city tore most of its old historic buildings down. A few survived, such as the ornate Egyptian Theatre that is now part of a downtown convention center. The theatre's ghost stories are myriad, and they will be told in more detail in my upcoming book, *Ghost Lights*. Government industries are still the main source of income for the city, and Ogden elected the first black mayor in the history of the state. A new attitude of friendly cooperation between fractions is growing daily within a city that continues to be one of the most diversely populated in Utah.

Ogden City Cemetery

Located at 1875 Monroe Boulevard, this cemetery has been in the news over the years for some strange stories, incidents, and legends. For example, one incident involved the police finding cow tongues slung over headstones all over the cemetery. The police are still baffled as to the reason for this. They speculate that it was either a teenage prank or some sort of cult ritual that they interrupted when called to the cemetery in the middle of the night. Someone might have wanted to be written up in the paper, even if it was anonymously. Since many of the legends revolve around evil doings or cultist activities, it makes sense that there are still groups who want to perform rituals there because of the cemetery's dark past. Ghost hunters who have made several trips to this cemetery say they have gotten their best and clearest "environmental voice phenomenon" recordings (EVPs) there. They pretty much agree that the evil or dark forces that pervade the area get them "spooked" too. Some of the phrases they claim to have recorded include, "I'm not buried here," "I'm okay," "Haven't seen him," "Please Mona," "It's in that room," "All right," "Dragon keeper," "Whispers," and "Remember who you are."[8]

The Ogden City Cemetery is one of the oldest in the city, with over 42,000 headstones on fifty-four acres of ground, and is still an active cemetery in more ways than one! It is built on a sort of hill in a triangular shape, except for the more recent addition of the Tiffany Mack Pet Cemetery, where pets can be buried for a fee of $80 to $100. The military section of the cemetery in the northwest corner apparently is not well cared for, and there have been several complaints about how rundown it is. A yearly historical tour is conducted during which locals, dressed up as famous pioneer characters who are buried in the cemetery, tell the character's life stories. The stories are mostly about Mormon pioneers who were in the Mormon Battalion, or early pioneer women. One famous local person buried there is John Moses Browning, the father of the internationally known Browning Fire Arms Company and inventor of over 150 different firearms. His burial there makes me wonder if spirits killed by his firearms are wandering about. The Browning firearms story can be compared to the more famous Winchester rifle story and Sara Winchester's superstitions about all of her husband's rifle victims seeking revenge. To keep these spirits at bay, Sara, who had lost both her husband and child, continued building onto to her mansion house until the day she died. If the idea of spirit revenge is true, this could have also been true in Browning's case, or even with his progeny. Nothing unusual has ever been reported at the Browning Arms Museum in the Union Station, except for a few visitors claiming to have seen a face floating in the glass, or shadowy figures darting between the glass cases where the arms are on display.

Three famous local politicians—Frank J. Cannon, who was a U.S. Senator from Utah; Morris B. Petersen, who was a U.S. Representative from Utah; and Henry H. Rolapp, who was a Justice of the Utah Territorial Supreme Court—are also buried in this cemetery. While state representatives and senators might be safe from harm, a territorial judge from the Supreme Court of Utah might have a few enemies who followed him in death and are still searching for him!

Ogden City Cemetery has two famous ghost stories. The first one concerns the Broom family plot. Their plot is the only fancy, wrought iron, fenced-in area in the entire graveyard, which naturally focuses people's attention on it. Legend has it that the entire Broom family dabbled in black magic. Ghost societies, which are a bit more prevalent in Northern Utah than in the Salt Lake City area, say they have recorded ominous voices and sounds around this family plot. In one incident, a reporter from the *Ogden Standard-Examiner* accompanied a ghost hunter organization to photograph and record what he could at the Broom family plot. The group was there in the middle of the night, and just as the reporter began to film, an entire cloud of dragonflies gathered together and began hovering over a large granite marker. No other insects hovered near the graves surrounding them, and apparently this dragonfly phenomenon has happened to people before. A second famous legend is also associated with the Broom family plot, and this spirit is called "the blue mist" or the "Blue Lady," who wanders about in search of something. This blue-green ecto-mist has been seen floating about the area for years, but other accounts state that the mist is green rather than blue.

Just at dusk a small blue mist slowly rises out of the ground. Sometimes this is all that happens, yet at other times, people claim that this mist forms into a woman in a long dark blue dress. She is said to wander throughout the cemetery until a few hours before dawn when she slowly dissolves back into the ground near the Broom family plot. No one has ever recorded her on film, but my own intuitive thought suggests a light or sky-blue dress rather than a dark one, and a young woman rather than an older one. She is on an eternal search for something or someone that is lost in time by now. One would guess the search is for a lost first child or a lost lover, and I see her hair as light rather than dark. She is apparently a silent phantom and therefore not among the voices, words, and phrases recorded there. She seems to search grimly and mournfully, but not as something evil. Others claim she is a witch, a member of the Broom family who roams at night.

Members of the Ogden Police Department, who are traditionally big-time skeptics, swear they had their own unexplained experience in the Ogden City graveyard. Once two officers were called to the cemetery to investigate the mist people claimed to see. They both saw it as well. They came back determined to debunk the whole thing by recreating the green or blue mist. They tried several ways to do this, including the dragonfly wing reflection angle. They even studied what atmospheric or chemical interactions might be causing the phenomenon. When they failed, they became fascinated by what they saw and kept being drawn back to the place where they saw it. One night they took their K-9 Corps dog there to exercise, and the dog fixed his attention on something in the dark and refused to step off the road onto the grass toward it. This was a specially trained dog that always followed the commands of its trainer, but on this night, he would not. Other officers, who did not have this experience, say they are tired of being called to the cemetery because of vandals, especially around Halloween. They say the only thing to see there is the ticket you will get for trespassing.

The modern version of the blue mist story surrounds a young girl named Florence (Flo). According to this version, Flo was sitting on a curb waiting for a ride home. A car suddenly appeared out of nowhere, struck her, and killed her instantly. Flo was apparently buried in the Ogden City Cemetery, and her grave can easily be found there. If you go to the cemetery and blink your headlights three or more times, she will supposedly appear as a green light and eventually a young girl, who floats toward your car because she thinks you are her ride home. It is interesting to note how this story evolved from the old into the more modern tale, with a perfect explanation for why parking your car there and blinking your lights would attract this apparition. It has to be a car, of course! Is it any wonder why the local police have to be vigilant in protecting this old graveyard?

Early in the cemetery's history, a heavy rain supposedly washed away part of the hill. As a result, several coffins slid out of their plots and had to be relocated, which resulted in some of the graves being mislabeled. Being misnamed is cause enough for anyone to rise in protest!

Besides the voice recordings and strange sounds, orbs have been photographed all over the cemetery. Green balls of light following people around have been caught on video, especially through the trees behind where the people are walking. For decades locals have reported these strange lights and odd shapes moving among the tombstones. Most of the lights seem to come from the Broom family plot— strange lights that scatter out all over the graveyard.

Because of these legends, Ogden City has closed every cemetery in the city after dark, hoping to discourage vandalism and to stop teens from gathering there. The sexton has also caught people performing animal sacrifices on or near the site of the haunted graves in the Ogden Cemetery.

One other tale exists about the statue of a soldier that stands near the center of the park. It is rumored to represent fallen soldiers from the different wars, and a little research confirmed that it is a veteran's memorial statue. Through the years, people have apparently seen the gun he is holding move slightly into different positions. Some say the head actually appears to be moving its position as well, or at least the eyes look as though they are following you. Others say that the green balls of light come from this statue and not the Broom family plot. They say you can drive by the place at night and see the balls of light scattered about the stones near the statue. Or, if you are in the cemetery, they will come from the trees near this soldier statue and follow you around.

Even though the Ogden City Cemetery is open to few new burials, it is so locally famous that police are still constantly dealing with trespassers who hope to catch a glimpse of something odd or unusual or who are there to perform some sort of strange ritual in hopes of conjuring something unusual. The Blue (or green) Lady continues to walk her path as well, keeping secret whatever interesting tale she might have to tell about her life as a Broom.

Jackson Street Victorian Mansion

The Jackson Street home has been spotlighted on the local news as well as investigated by ghost hunters on more than one occasion. It is presently a photography studio downstairs, with a masseuse and a psychic medium's office on the second floor. The third floor is rented out as an apartment. It is a gorgeously beautiful "painted lady" mansion stuck between commercial buildings and car dealerships on one of the busiest streets in Ogden. Visitors and customers have experienced a variety of things, from breath on the back of their necks when no one else is there, to hair being ruffled by invisible fingers, to being pushed or shoved by an unknown force. The owners claim that at least two children haunt the place and that one of them was caught on the owner's videotape. Several people have sighted these two children playing in and around the outside of the place. Visiting experts have told the brother and sister in residence that there are at least five identified entities in the house. Besides the two children, there are two women, one of whom is named Olivia, according to the EVP recordings. The most prominent spirit is a soldier from the Civil War era, who originally was haunting outside the place but has now moved into the home as well. His name is Curtis, according to the ghost hunter investigations.[9]

When the local news station highlighted this house one year at Halloween, the owners talked briefly about their experiences. Apparently they had a few not-so-positive experiences afterward, especially related to the first ghost busters trying to rid the house of its ghosts. So many different paranormal investigation groups are forming now that they actually compete with each other like businesses do. Because the information is so "out there," with a medium and a clairvoyant on the premises, it makes it difficult for those ghost busters who don't want psychics involved in their investigations, and probably easier for those who do. There are two schools of thought on this issue: one is that solid scientific evidence is hindered by psychics being involved in the investigations, and the other is that psychics can add significant clues to the investigations. The brother and sister who own the home changed the name to The Victorian Place in accordance with the wishes of the ghost, Curtis. The brother lives in the third floor apartment and the sister runs the photography studio on the main floor. It was here, in a family portrait, that they captured one of the ghost children on film. They say the house is over a hundred years old, but little is known about its early history.

Different investigators at different times had their hand rubbed or felt the presence of someone standing behind them. People say they are drawn to the stair area and that one room in the house has a temperature drop of three to four degrees. This room is known as "the cold room." Shadows are seen lurking about, footsteps are heard when no one else is there, and the resident dog will not go into the cold room but stands outside and barks at it. Investigators have had equipment malfunctions, such as a tape recorder that slowed down to its slowest speed and did not return to normal until they left the house. Some of the phrases caught on tape include such things as needing help, saying good-bye, telling people to get out, various names, and asking where they are going.[10]

The Bookshelf, an Ogden Bookstore

The Bookshelf is in an old building located at 2432 Washington Boulevard. Little is known about its past, and no known stories explain the slightly malevolent force that seems to hang around there. The manager says that in all the time he has been there, no one has experienced any sort of strange or unusual phenomena, but one or two employees state that sometimes the books move around.

The Bookshelf is a well-known independent bookstore in northern Utah. *The Salt Lake City Weekly*, a free local paper, voted it one of the best in the state. According to the manager, the large storefront building was built between 1898 and 1904 when the water was first turned on. I can't find anyone who knows what was in the building before two shops shared it for forty years: a Buster Brown Shoe Store in the north side of the building and a Weber Office Supply store in the south side. The present owners have been in their shop for twenty years, which accounts for the building's businesses back to the beginning of the 1950s.

The only odd thing that the present owners could think of was a bank of five lights that insists on turning off and on by itself with absolutely no explanation. Since the owners are not ghost believers but are open enough to have started a large ghost book section in their store, they have enjoyed the attention. They don't feel any presences and figure that eventually they will figure out a rational reason for the bank of lights shorting out.

Besides all of the amazing EVP recordings taken in the store, it is the basement that really entices the ghost hunters. On camera and video they were able to capture orbs passing through walls and a large spiral white light. The owners kept copies of these photos in their store until they were stolen more than once. I suggested to the owners that next time they put them under glass so that wannabee ghost hunters and enthusiasts will have to capture dramatic ghost pictures on their own. My husband and I definitely had our own experiences there, both at my book signing and when we visited the bookstore at a later time.

As for any other occupants of the building before the 1950s, these would all have to be guesses on my part, so perhaps an old timer or local historian could set me straight on what was there before the shoe and office supply stores. My own impressions while visiting the building were that I was uncomfortable in the basement area and did not like being down there. I had few impressions and did not feel anything negative there. Reports of books flying off shelves have been greatly exaggerated, says the store's manager, but the ghost hunters and some customers have reported hearing things being moved around in the basement and people talking down there.

The Bookshelf is still operating and is located across from the Egyptian Theatre and next door to a now defunct shop for New Age enthusiasts called the Capricorn's Lair. The Ben Lomond Hotel is just up the street but under new management. Across from the hotel is the downtown park where street people come and go, and the art deco Ogden Municipal building still stands. There is an amazing atmosphere to this whole Twenty-fourth to Twenty-sixth Street area, so while city planners work on redevelopment, the old converges with the new. The spirits of old Ogden City merge with later generations of spirits along these streets, and each business or building maintains its own haunted quality for those in touch with such things. Perhaps someday soon the city will see the potential of this area, the romance and the drama of all that came before, which the street people have already found. Ghosts are in all of these buildings, and whether owners hear, see, or feel them, some of the spirits have been there for a long time. My husband and I fell in love with the whole area, but especially The Bookshelf, where the old books are still piled high and people of our generation can still enjoy a good "hunt" to find them. The Bookshelf offers books, videos, comics, music, and all sorts of science fiction and comic book figures. The upstairs is loaded with old books of every variety, and the ghosts are there too!

The night of my book signing was the second time I confronted the old man who likes to hang out in the travel section of the book room at the top of the stairs. I think he was the previous owner or manager of a business in the north end of the building. He also loves books and travel and outdoor activities. He doesn't like things out of place and is particular about who comes upstairs to browse. I felt him in this upstairs room and then saw him in my mind's eye on the stairs as I talked to a couple of people in the back of the store. He is tall and thin and definitely an outdoorsman. He probably liked my husband because he is built the same way, loves books, and *appears* to be a mountain man type, even though he really is not.

A second, not-so-pleasant figure was in the comic book section of the store— a young man who probably frequented the place before his death. I don't know if he died by suicide or accidentally. He wore the black outfit that young people wear who are into the occult. He never goes upstairs, and the old man upstairs never goes downstairs, but at times the old man will stand on the stairs to survey the entire shop.

A cistern in the basement makes the area intriguing, and if there are any ghosts down there, they are the oldest residents of the building from the underground tunnel days of Prohibition, or maybe even before then. The old covered well could add to the mystique of the building, but no one has ever seen anything except in the photos taken by ghost hunters.

On our following visit, my husband and I were upstairs in the first book room, and I was walking down one aisle while he walked with his camera down the other. Suddenly there was a loud noise. I looked over just in time to witness some books fall on the floor in front of my husband's feet, strewn out in a half circle before him. He retraced his steps just to see if he could have in any way brushed something that would have knocked this whole row of books off, but circumstances seemed to make this impossible. We discovered that the books were on outdoor camping, hiking, making your own mountain man gear, gunsmithing, and mountain wildlife. It really startled my husband, and he forgot to take any pictures. That evening we came home, and my husband went out to put his newly acquired books in his studio behind our house. When he unlocked the door, he noticed that in the corner of his studio a row of books had fallen off the top shelf. We could find nothing that would have caused this. No other books on either side had fallen, nor had this ever happened before. As he and I turned the books over to put them back on the shelf above him, we found that all of the books were on gunsmithing, mountain man gear, and outdoor travel books. Oddly, I happened to be with my husband to witness this event. Since then, he has been intrigued with our Bookshelf visits and feels that the old man really loves his books and recognizes others who love book-hunting too!

The Pizzeria (Godfather's Pizza) on Harrison Boulevard

This restaurant has the common claim that its building was built over an ancient Indian mound. The phenomena in the place are quite unusual and have been reported as long as the building has been there. The jukebox will turn on and off by itself, even when the circuit breaker is turned off or it is unplugged. Employees have doors shut on them, especially the door to the walk-in cooler. When a staff member tries to get out, some sort of strong force will hold the door shut from the outside. This only happens when no one else is around. Then, just as suddenly, the door will open and let him out. Fluorescent light bulbs that are three feet long have popped out of their casings and crashed to the floor. On one occasion, employees had just replaced several fluorescent light bulbs. One by one the light bulbs levitated into the air and smashed to the floor. Large sections of the floor will bulge up several feet for no reason and with no apparent explanation. A strange whistling sound is often heard with no explanation. Faces and handprints appear in pans of just-baked brownies and other bakery goods.

Employees of the restaurant do not want to go into the basement area alone. Several of them have had the experience of being pushed or shoved by unseen hands. Over the course of time, the current owner has become more interested in letting paranormal investigators check things out. Most of the phenomena have persisted for years, even though the building is relatively new.

In another common sort of occurrence, all of the doors to the place, including the bathroom stall doors, will swing and bang violently all at once and then stop just as suddenly as they began. Ghost hunters who have visited the place report that their tape recorders go haywire. These investigators also think that the main activity is centered in the basement, where they got lots of orb photographs, as well as EVP recordings, which explain the activity.

A theory proposed by those who work there is that the basement is built over an old pioneer graveyard or an ancient Indian mound. The paranormal investigators have also recorded tapping noises that the employees have not heard. The investigators did get one name: "Marcus Finney," spoken with a bit of an Irish accent. His accent is not a good one, making it suspicious.

Several people report seeing fully formed ghosts or apparitions. The most interesting one is a little boy who will run into the kitchen right in front of the employees, stop and smile, run about the kitchen for a while, and eventually leap into a nearby wall and disappear. Other such ghosts will appear in front of visitors, diners, and employees, such as a little boy in a baseball cap, a woman in an Elizabethan costume, and even someone who looks like a pirate. Therefore, I would like to propose one more theory, besides the obvious ones, that perhaps the place once housed a small theater in a building that stood there before this one. This would explain these costumed characters.[11]

When yet another ghost hunting group visited the pizzeria, they captured dramatic footage of orbs and spirals passing through walls, a phenomenon not easily disproven. They also definitely confirmed that not far from this pizza shop is an old pioneer graveyard with mostly children buried in it. In fact, the cemetery is so close to the shop that they proposed that there are other long-forgotten graves outside the cemetery grounds. They feel that the child spirits are visiting the pizza shop and causing a lot of the poltergeist activity there. The ghost hunters thought it possible that there might be a few graves right under the shop and other buildings along the block, but phenomena have only been reported in this shop so far. This is a common ghost lore story of a graveyard near or right under where the hauntings take place. Their dramatic footage would be difficult to disprove, along with the fact that stories of apparitions in the building have been told for decades.[12]

Shupe-Williams Candy Factory

This old factory was located on Twenty-sixth Street in Ogden, and the building was close to a hundred years old. It was being renovated into high-security condominiums that the owners did not want labeled as haunted. It burned down, and since the fire, its fate as a building is unknown. But ghosts know no bounds of this sort, so it will be interesting to see if future tenants of new buildings built on the spot report anything unusual, or if the ghosts will just wander away, unable to find their old familiar haunts.

At one time, the Shupe Candy Factory was a deserted building and was rented out to various organizations, especially from 1988 to 1995 in the month of October for a fund-raiser haunted house spook alley. This sort of function would bring out the ghosts for sure, since it is well known in the paranormal community that the winter months in old buildings are more active, and talk of ghosts will bring the spirits out, especially around Halloween when it seems more acceptable to talk of ghosts and goblins.

According to some who participated in these Halloween fund-raisers, a lot of odd and weird things happened. Attempts were made to get ghost investigators to come, but it never happened. The people who participated in the spook alley reported that there were a lot of poltergeist-like activities that were not of their making. They also reported several cold spots and drafts inside the building that could not be explained. They say it was more than just the usual prankster stuff, even though Halloween actors were performing real pranks right in front of the patrons! Doors slammed and were locked, lights went on and off by themselves, footsteps were heard behind actors and patrons, along with all the other usual indications of a haunting. But what was really unusual were the flying and levitating objects and the things that were put somewhere one day only to be discovered somewhere else the next day. Unfortunately, the fire ruined any chances of renovations or a Halloween venue.

Weber State University Tales

Many Weber State ghost tales are modern and have nothing to do with the founding of the school but rather a recent altercation that took place there. In 1993 a twenty-two-year-old student was angry with his girlfriend and took a gun to class and started shooting at her and the other students. He wounded the girlfriend and others but was shot by a university police officer before anyone was killed. He then bled to death while the paramedics worked frantically to save him. The incident occurred in the social science building on the second floor in the student senate room, and people have reported ever since that they can hear shots and screams at 1:30 PM, the same time this class was going on. Students also report that they feel the spirit of the dead student watching them in this particular area.

Later, ghost investigators tried to film in this room. They had trouble with their equipment but did manage to get faint lights and orbs on their film. Weber State has its own ghost investigation group right on campus, because a couple of professors teach a class on the paranormal each quarter at the school. Several attempts have been made to get photos or EVP recordings in the room where this shooting took place. No one knows the results of these investigations at present.

Newgate Mall Tinseltown Theaters

Once a movie theatre, live performers took over the Tinseltown Theaters and their troupe performed plays in this mall before it once again became a movie theatre. What started the stories about ghosts in the theatre were the rumors that several members of the theatre group committed suicide, but not in the theatre. This is an older mall, and the rumor of these deaths has contributed to the ghost stories about the building. Apparently, people have seen chairs moving inside the theatre all by themselves, heard growling noises when the place was empty, and observed other inexplicable phenomena there. Consistent reports of two black shapes moving through the seats during the showing of films have people a bit scared to go there if they know about the stories. Also, the projectionists are often locked inside the booth and have to yell for someone to let them out.

Dead Haven

Real spirits and Halloween ghouls intermingle in this old warehouse building not far from the old Union Railroad Station at 159 Twenty-third Street in Ogden. Near the main streets of downtown Ogden was an extensive warehouse district. No one seems to know the exact purpose of this particular warehouse in the early days. Later it was a farm implement building and then inexpensive apartments in a rundown neighborhood. In the last few years, this building has housed a spook alley under several different names. Under new ownership, the haunted house, formerly called "The Dark Domain," became "Dead Haven," and the newer commercial haunted house boasts an elaborate display of technological and actor driven "spooks." Since it is seasonal haunted house entertainment, it isn't any surprise that the people who work there began to notice paranormal phenomena that weren't exactly connected to the show. As some employees put it, their show seemed to bring out the real "spooks," which scared them. Talk of ghosts and goblins at Dead Haven brought a lot of poltergeist activity, voices, and even a few sightings of full-fledged apparitions.

In October 2002 the *Deseret News* picked up the story about this unusual partnership between the owners and employees of Dead Haven and the Northern Utah Paranormal Exploration and Research Group (UPER). The story was initiated when the UPER, having heard stories about the place, approached the owners with the idea of interviewing everyone after the Halloween season closed in 2002. In interviewing people who worked there, the reporter discovered that "some strange things have happened that were not readily explained, such as lights going on and off or noises coming from places with no one there. Actors that no one recognized appeared in period costumes."[13]

So on October 31, 2001, several team members spent two hours walking around, taking pictures, and recording. By September of that year, UPER had completed over fifteen investigations of the place. The investigators discovered that the paranormal activity subsided as the Halloween season that began in July waned by the end of November. When the ghost hunters went back the next July, they experienced a woman's voice speaking to them when no one was there and heard banging and other unexplained noises. Various unoccupied rooms had noises coming from them, and dark shadows in human form would glide through walls. Some of them saw a fully formed apparition that followed the owners down some corridors.[14]

In his article, "Who Ya' Gonna Call? Utah's Ghost Hunters," Dennis Romboy wrote about several ghost hunters who took a tour of the old warehouse on an early Sunday morning and identified the spirits of "a wandering man, a moaning woman, and perhaps a young girl" who still remained in the building.[15]

Lately, newly formed ghost hunting groups in Utah have included a psychic on their team. Probably because some are realizing a new paradigm is needed that includes observation and factors not identifiable by current scientific processes. Those in the traditional scientific research field still scoff at this type of research, but some concede that brain research or the environmental voice phenomena recordings may provide something a little more tangible than ghost photography.

This particular ghost hunter group used infrared cameras, tape recorders, thermometers, electromagnetic wave detectors, and eyewitness accounts. At Dead Haven, hoping to catch orbs or streaks of light on their cameras as well as interactive EVP recordings, they recorded a voice saying, "Who's there?" and located on videotape what is believed to be the shoulder and arm of a man who was not there when they filmed the event. They are still identifying the EVP recordings and plan to do more investigations at Dead Haven, if the city doesn't shut the place down. While the investigators did their work, they had the typical mechanical problems that always come up on these types of investigations. They found that brand-new batteries would not work, tape recorders refused to record, and cameras suddenly went dead.

The owner of the building quipped, "How many paranormal investigators does it take to change a light bulb?" He's still a skeptic at heart, but he relates one story of how he learned from the ghost hunters the proper procedure for dealing with trickster ghosts. One night he drove the company van home from Dead Haven. The turn signals and all the dials on the dashboard stopped working, even though they were working fine before. He was still skeptical, but he decided to heed the ghost hunters' advice and politely ask the unseen passenger to leave. As he did this, everything in the van came back on and worked just fine. This made the owner nervous.

What the UPER members soon discovered in January 2003 was that all their investigating caused the activity in the building to stay constant throughout the year, rather than dissipating between November and July as it had previously done. They also discovered that this new burst of activity brought out additional spirits. They proposed a theory that the high-energy levels are caused by fear generated in the high-tech spook alley, which attracts more real spirits. The more the investigators talked about ghosts in the building, the more phenomena appeared. Psychics have known about this kind of phenomena for years, and people theorize that the talk of ghosts simply brings out more untrustworthy tricksters, spirits who rarely tell the truth. The ghost hunters also believe that orbs or lights on videotape show some sort of intelligence by sometimes responding to human voices.

In the process of talking to some of the college students who attended one of these ghost-hunting sessions or worked as actors for the haunted house show, I found that all of them had experienced some sort of phenomena, from capturing orbs on their photos to being really scared by the late-night trip into the building after the show was over. According to the students, one of the college professors who attended the ghost hunt became so frightened that he refused to return to the building and would not talk to anyone about his experience while there. People were present who taught paranormal classes, as well as students who took their classes.

I have learned over the years that nearly all hauntings are harmless, unless of course the live person frightens himself because of not understanding what is happening to him. Sometimes, if the spirit lived a horrible life when alive, his apparition will carry that terrible energy with him, thus causing negative feelings in the building he "haunts." Poltergeist activity can also scare people, especially if a hurtling object hurts someone. Spirits are no different from live people; there are good ones and not so good ones. I have also learned that if someone is taken by surprise by a negative impression, or even a seemingly threatening active spirit, a firm and polite request stops the activity. In a few cases, it takes a strong and powerful command. I am not one to walk into a place where I would be assaulted right and left by layers and layers of historical and negative energy. I am uncomfortable having so much negative energy around me.

In March 2003 UPER updated their website about the latest Dead Haven phenomena. Besides amassing an impressive collection of audio and video recordings, they had now encountered a full apparition in the form of an elderly woman. Photos of her showed nothing but bluish light, but upon investigating the history of the area, UPER learned that in later years the building had become surrounded by a rather rundown neighborhood of old homes and apartments, drug and alcohol users, with quite a few reports of rapes and stabbings in the area. The old building had become a series of apartments, and eventually they discovered that one elderly woman had died tragically and unexpectedly in one of the apartments in the old building. They found photos of her from the early 1970s and placed several elderly women's pictures in front of the eyewitnesses of the ghostly woman's presence. The observers quickly identified this particular woman, but the UPER members realize that they have no real proof of a match from the past.

It will be interesting to follow the story of this nonprofit association as they continue to work together. It will certainly generate some publicity and word-of-mouth that says that Dead Haven is one of the best Halloween activities around. Perhaps the ghosts and goblins of Dead Haven have simply been waiting for an avenue to communicate to the living, or else they are merely impressions and pictures recorded into the building's walls, activated by talking about these energies and echoes from long ago. Once a warehouse and then an apartment building, this old building could host stories and spirits, some of them possibly negative and frightening. Dead Haven eventually closed to make way for a city office building.

Creston Plaza

Creston Plaza is another old building in the area that was built in the late 1800s and still has underground tunnels. The gambling dens, illegal bars, whiskey storage places during Prohibition, and the places where prostitutes plied their trade are closed off now. The Plaza is currently an office complex. The Utah Ghost Hunters Organization has done investigations there. In their investigations they recorded orbs and EVP voices. They also heard children playing in the restroom on the third floor in the middle of the night and noticed that the elevator doors open and close by themselves right in front of the people.

In an article in the *Salt Lake Tribune*, Kristen Moulton states, "For several years, downtown Ogden, with its abandoned buildings and lonely streets, has been a magnet for haunted house entertainment facilities. Now ghost busters at City Hall are putting a stop to the creeping industry." The City Council is clarifying its zoning ordinances in an attempt to ban spook alleys from the central business district. They say spook alleys don't fit downtown Ogden's new image, and they don't want to encourage empty buildings downtown to be used for seasonal activities. Ms. Moulton continues, "Downtown business owners have not complained, but property owners contemplating renovation have expressed concerns about haunted houses going in next door."[16]

Dead Haven has been at this new location for four years. According to Ms. Moulton, "Dead Haven co-owner Jason Bench said Friday that his uncle owns the building, but probably will sell to the federal government, which needs the property for its Internal Revenue Service expansion downtown . . . Bench says that even with all of the development underway in downtown Ogden, he can't fathom why the city wants to get rid of haunted houses. He and partner Warren Braegger have already spent several weeks and $3000 preparing this year's interactive haunt."[17]

No matter what happens to the building, as long as it stands there will be ghosts. It's not the spook alley they need to fear, but the "spooks" inside the old warehouse and other such buildings. My advice would be to warn the internal revenue workers ahead of time, because even if the building changes hands, ghosts don't vacate buildings to which they are attached. It has been my experience over the years that those who banish ghosts from haunts dear to their hearts only succeed temporarily, and the apparitions return when they think it is safe. The activity may decrease for a while—even months or years—but inevitably the spirits return. If the whole building goes down instead of being renovated, some activity will probably remain, and a few intuitive IRS employees may get "spooked" themselves.

Bountiful and Centerville

The miracle of the seagulls happened in 1849 around the settlements of Bountiful and Centerville. Thousands of crickets descended on the fields, and the people of Centerville and Bountiful went out to fight them. They tried to burn them, drown them, and bury them, but they kept coming. Finally, in desperation they knelt to pray. Suddenly, a huge flock of seagulls flew toward them from the west over the Great Salt Lake.

Cynthia Larsen Bennett says the following about the miracle of the gulls:

> At first the pioneers were afraid the gulls would wreak more destruction, but instead, the birds gobbled up the crickets. The gulls disgorged crickets in the lake when they got full and then went back for more. Hundreds of the early pioneers in Davis County witnessed the miraculous event. Because of this incident, the California gull became the state bird. . . . In the early summer of 1854, winged grasshoppers descended on the pioneers' new crops. The pioneers tried prayer again, since all their other efforts had failed to discourage the insects. The next morning the grasshoppers all rose up in the air at sunrise. At that moment a strong wind blew down from the mountains and swept them into the lake, drowning the voracious insects. Thousands of dead grasshoppers later washed up on the shores.[18]

It is too bad that the pioneers did not understand that although crickets and grasshoppers cannot entirely replace crops, they are a great source of protein and can be eaten in addition to them.

Bountiful has one ghost story related to an old abandoned building on Eaglewood Drive that over the years has housed a mortuary, a mink farm, and a small LDS museum. Rumors say that while the museum is now abandoned, LDS artifacts are still stored in it. People driving by this old building have reported seeing dark, shadowy people on the property at night and feeling an eerie presence if they stop to look at the building. Objects and artifacts from old museums can carry all sorts of residual energy and recordings from the past, especially if, for example, the museum houses Indian artifacts or unidentified bones. This is a possibility since many small-town museums either do not know about the repatriation law (which is the process of returning a body back to its place of origin or citizenship, including refugees or soldiers who die in foreign wars), or they don't know they have bones stored somewhere. If this is the case, hauntings are quite likely.

Because of the Ted Bundy connection, the presence of a ghost has been implied at Viewmont High School. The serial killer abducted one of his victims from this high school, and, of course, the high school kids have picked up on it and reported seeing Bundy's ghost, as well as the girl's in the area. They have even claimed to see a ghost car in the form of a yellow VW Beetle like Bundy had at the time. Like most small towns, the kids report apparitions in the town cemetery, and the Bountiful Cemetery is no exception. They report strange smells and sounds, and the fact that one of the tombstones belongs to a man who helped build the Salt Lake Temple. It would be a typically Bountiful story to say that whenever anyone touches this man's tombstone, it is warm, indicating his devotion to his work and faith.

Woods Cross Old Utah Auto Auction

The story of the Woods Cross Old Utah Auto Auction is courtesy of the Ghost Hunters Society website (www.ghostwave.com). I could find no history of the Utah Auto Auction, which might have a different name by now, and I don't have any background information, so you can surmise that if it isn't an ancient Indian mound, the ground has some other history.

As I thought about the place intuitively, three general things came to mind: a tragedy involving some young men who were illegally on the property at night a decade or two ago; a guard who loved the place and did not want to leave, even after he passed away; and something that happened long before the two previous situations. Perhaps a small skirmish occurred between local Indians and the early settlers, or some other altercation that was never recorded. Perhaps there were some sort of fortifications there. As often happens, I have no way to confirm any of this, so perhaps someone out there knows more than I do.

The usual ghostly phenomena have happened for years, but with cars rather than inside a home. Car doors are found open which were supposed to be locked, or dome lights inside cars will go on by themselves. Often these dome lights come on in the middle of the night when the cars are locked. The three guards who worked there would go on their rounds finding unlocked cars. Half an hour later, they would come back and the doors would be unlocked again, or the lights would be on inside a locked car. Dark shadows are seen against fences around the cars. These shadowy outlines are clearly visible but without any source of light that can be identified. One night all three guards saw a filmy female shape float by the window of their guard shack. The apparition then flew toward the cars and disappeared. Neighbors in the area have reported the locally famous ghost lights that people sometimes see floating over an open field late at night. Often there are natural phenomena explanations for lights such as these, and perhaps someday someone will identify just what the auto auction lights are. Maybe they are merely reflections of something nearby.

I found it interesting that an aunt of one of the guards asked him if he had seen any ghosts at the car dealership yet. The question startled the young man, and he asked how she knew about them. She said his uncle worked there as young man and had come home more than once with a story to tell her about them. Perhaps at some point I'll be able go inside and get better impressions. Maybe a local amateur historian can tell me what happened long ago in the area where the Utah Auto Auction now stands—or stood, because it might be under a different name now. This particular story is mere speculation but is interesting to note because of the several generations of employees who claim to have seen the ghost lights, the shadowy apparitions, and the mechanical abnormalities affecting the auto lot.

Farmington

Farmington has a lot of interesting sites, but only one ghost sighting, which was a phantom rider reportedly seen in the late 1800s. This phantom rider supposedly kept reappearing until 1951.

Farmington was settled in 1852 and was originally named North Cottonwood until it became the county seat. By 1855 it housed the first courthouse in Utah, a two-story adobe building. Its nickname was the "City of Roses."

Farmington has always battled flash floods from the mountains behind it, with severe ones in the 1920s, 1930s, and 1980s. In August 1923 its worst-ever flood hit Farmington. A cloudburst in the mountains caused a great rush of water and mud that covered almost the entire town. Boulders weighing in the tons were washed into the town streets, and seven people lost their lives—five boy scouts camping in the mountains, and a couple on their honeymoon in the canyon. The water spread over a wide area, and an elderly woman and a small child were washed downstream into the Lagoon Park. A local doctor rescued them and received the Carnegie Medal for his heroism.

Farmington houses the original 1864 LDS rock meetinghouse and the Franklin D. Richards gristmill, as well as some pioneer rock homes. Pioneers came from Kaysville to settle Farmington and built several mills and a log cabin school house. Besides raising livestock and maintaining dairy herds, the farmers raised sugar beets, alfalfa, and grain. Orchards with cherries, peaches, apricots, and apples were also in abundance.

In the early days, millers, blacksmiths, and other craftsmen also lived and worked in Farmington. The Utah Central Railroad came through in 1870, and in 1896 the huge amusement park, Lagoon, was developed. It is now Farmington's largest source of tax revenue. In 1890 the town replaced the original courthouse with a Victorian-style brick courthouse that was remodeled both in 1932 and 1958. Over 12,081 people lived in Farmington in 2000, and the population has undoubtedly grown since then.[19]

The town's first burial place was in Horse Band, located a little north of the mouth of Farmington Canyon. Locals called this cemetery the Indian Graves Cemetery because it was believed that ancient Indians were buried there first. The second cemetery was located where the old racetrack was in Lagoon. The pioneers interred there are still buried under Pioneer Village, one of the most haunted places in Utah. Besides the ghostly potential of the old pioneer graveyard under the transplanted buildings of Pioneer Village in Lagoon Park, stories about the place being haunted have been around for years. Some of the ghosts came with the Village from its old location, others from the original settlements before the homes and buildings were transported to the Village from small towns down south, and some of the ghosts come from the site itself near Farmington. These stories will be told in my later book on arts, haunted theatres, strange people, and amusement parks.

The first sighting of the phantom of Farmington was reported in 1881. Samuel Morgan told a long story in the *Ogden Standard-Examiner* about seeing a headless figure on a horse galloping down upon him, scaring him half to death, and then just as he thought it was going to run him down, the phantom disappeared. It just vanished into thin air, the witness said. Other reports of the phantom were made in 1905, 1935, and 1951. The story was always the same: the figure would appear along a trail called the Old Canyon Road, which went from one end of Farmington to the other, and then continue north to the area where Pioneer Village is now. One man reported it as "a man who disappears on a horse in a flash." This headless horseman, a dark figure in dark clothes with no head—and not carrying one either—would repeat his performance any time of year, but always along the same route. At that time people believed that the phantom might also be guarding a lost gold mine or that he was an avenging angel or Danite. No modern-day reports remain of this strange phantom.

Clearfield

The town of Clearfield was settled in 1877. Richard and Emily Hamblin, an immigrant couple from England, built a dugout with a thatched roof of sagebrush for their first home. It was originally known as Sand Ridge because of the local prickly pear and sagebrush and the hot dry winds from Weber Canyon. For over two years Hamblin attempted to dig a well but was unsuccessful. When he finally did strike water, it brought more settlers to Clearfield.

The Woods Cross Canning Cooperative was built in 1892 and packed fruits and vegetables grown in the area. During World War II, the plant had larger orders and fewer workers, so they solved this problem by hiring relocated Japanese Americans and German and Italian prisoners of war. A huge fire in the 1970s closed down the cannery for good. The Utah Central Railroad was routed through Clearfield in 1869, and by 1905 the Bamberger Electric train also stopped there on its way to either Ogden or Salt Lake City.

Until 1940 Clearfield was a peaceful farming community. Then the development of Hill Air Force Base on the north side of town brought jobs for civilians, and it became one of Utah's major employers. In 1943 the U.S. Navy bought the land on the south side of Clearfield and installed the Clearfield Naval Supply Depot, essentially making Clearfield a military town.

In her book *Roadside History of Utah*, Cynthia Larsen Bennett says:

> The depot was an important naval installation for the warehousing and distribution of supplies to West Coast supply points. During World War II years, it was difficult to fill employment vacancies, and the supply depot hired almost anyone willing to work. In April 1945, 500 German prisoners of war were assigned to the depot's work crews. After World War II, the depot handled surplus property. During the Korean War, the distribution

workload increased again. After that conflict, the depot began to be phased out. Many civilian workers left to take employment at Hill Air Force Base and . . . the depot was phased out by 1962.[20]

A total of 580 million supplies were shipped from the naval depot during World War II. By 1943 Hill Air Force Base had hired fifteen thousand civilians and had six thousand military personnel on base. In the 1970s townspeople witnessed the arrival and departure of many programs, such as airlift, Strategic Air Command, refueling, communications, test, rescue and recovery, and various fighter squadrons, groups, and attachments. A helicopter-training wing qualified over two thousand pilots and crew members. In the 1980s, Hill Air Force Base continued to operate at its peak. In the 1990s, with dozens of military budget cuts and base closures, the rumor was that Hill Air Force Base was scheduled for closure. Hill Field escaped the "axe" but was definitely downsized.

Today Hill Air Force Base has two interesting places to visit for ghost enthusiasts. One is the Hill Aerospace Museum, and the other is an old white church. The museum has a large display of old military aircraft and continues to add more to its outdoor displays. All the old aircraft probably have their own haunting stories to tell. Tales are told about the old white church being haunted, but the stories cannot be substantiated.

By 1982 private industries moved into the large warehouse buildings of the old naval depot, and it became known as the Freeport Center. The present population of Clearfield is approximately thirty thousand, many of whom are employed by the military and the Freeport Center, which is considered the manufacturing, warehousing, and distribution hub of the west. There are more than 100 industrial buildings and dozens of business firms in enormous structures measuring 200 by 600 feet. The center contains more than six million square feet where the Naval Depot once employed over eight thousand workers with 191 buildings, 41 miles of railroad, and 24 miles of roads.[21]

This old naval depot is purported to be haunted in areas. The Clearfield Job Corps is housed in the old depot, and most of the stories of apparitions are reported from this part of the base, probably because of the Job Corp's young clients. Nowadays, the Freeport Center is nowhere near as active as it was in the 1980s. Old military bases are notorious for being haunted. There are quite a few famous ones across the country. It is fun to add a much newer military base to the list we already have of haunted old forts and camps in Utah.

Hauntings have been reported for just about every building that the Clearfield Job Corps Center uses. The old movie theater on the Center campus was supposedly also used as a military morgue. Back in the days when the old movie projector was used, it would break down under mysterious circumstances. Even new equipment is affected by the building's atmosphere. An older military nurse, whose misty form has been seen by some of the employees and clients, supposedly haunts the tuberculosis (TB Dorm) in the old naval hospital. All of the dorms have a letter name. The TB Dorm, L Dorm, and E Dorm are all supposed to be haunted.

The L Dorm has another apparition that is also thought to be a nurse. In the E Dorm there are three separate apparitions. A girl between the ages of five and six stands by the doorway at the entrance of the dorm. She moves about the dorms and likes to bounce a ball in the hallway. People claim to have actually seen this little girl's ghost. The second spirit is thought to be a former residential adviser who walks up and down the halls making sure that his students are in their dorms. The third spirit is believed to be either a student who died in the dorm a year or so ago, or an unknown spirit coming from a much earlier time. Enough material certainly exists for a ghost hunter group to investigate at night. This huge military base probably has haunting stories from their other facilities as well and not just from the Clearfield Job Corps Center.

One other story about Clearfield relates to the Holt Elementary School, which is near a little pond called Stede's Pond. This more recent story concerns a fifth-grade boy who drowned in the pond in the late 1980s. The boy decided to go swimming by himself in early summer. Later that day visitors to the school spotted his white T-shirt and shorts. Since the 1980s he has been seen floating in the pond in his white T-shirt and shorts, usually in the spring or summer. People have reported hearing crying and calls for help from the pond, and when they rush to the pond, no one is there. Sightings of the boy waving to his observers before he vanishes have also been reported. But most interesting are the reports of the back door to the school mysteriously locking or unlocking, as well as puddles of water or wet footprints appearing on the back steps of the school when no one has been near the pond.

According to local lore, drownings supposedly took place at the pond, although records of early drownings probably don't exist. People going by the pond at night say they can hear cries for help, and sometimes whispering voices. The soft voices and crying can also be heard by the train tracks that run past Stede's Pond. People say they have heard phantom trains going by when no trains were visible. Several deaths have occurred along the tracks as well, especially when the trains ran regularly through the area years ago. Between the haunted train tracks, the haunted pond, and the deaths that supposedly occurred there, the place is, indeed, eerie.

Layton

Layton has an old mall and a place called Hobb's Hollow located in a secluded woodland that are reputed to be haunted. Layton is northwest of the town of Kaysville and was settled by the same group of pioneers who settled Kaysville. Today Layton is Davis County's largest city. A feud erupted between the two towns when Kaysville levied taxes on Layton to build their big, impressive town hall. It took the town of Layton quite some time—until 1902—to make a clean break from Kaysville, but eventually the town achieved this victory with suits and countersuits that went all the way to the United States Supreme Court. The oldest still operating business in Layton is the First National Bank of Layton established in 1905. Another interesting old building in Layton is the Layton Milling and Elevator Company. Layton remained small until World War II when all the military in the area increased the town size from a few hundred to several thousand people. Today Layton has a population of about 65,000 people. Interestingly, one of the huge government housing complexes built for World War II was dismantled and moved to create a community complex that houses, among other things, Layton High School, Layton Public Library and Heritage Museum, a city park, and a wave pool. One wonders what ghosts might inhabit some of these places.

The Layton Hills Mall is reputed to be haunted as well. Perhaps it too was reconstructed from old military housing. The easier explanation is an ancient Indian mound, one of the best ways to explain away any haunting in Utah! Mall employees report ghostly activity in their stores. The night crews and guards report that the most activity involves noises and shadowy figures in the hallways, but the most interesting things reported are that potted plants are often uprooted overnight, or even in broad daylight, with no one around and no explanation for the phenomena. Also overnight, in the locked and secured building, mannequins have been moved into different positions. Phones ring with no one on the line, and security cameras have never caught anyone uprooting plants or moving mannequins about. There have even been claims that the cameras have captured the mannequins actually moving on their own.

Another story from Layton involves an exclusive private neighborhood near the turnoff on Highway 89 leading to Ogden just outside Layton. An old trail leads to what is called Hobbs Hollow, which is located in a secluded forest area near this neighborhood, and there is a small lake. The lake is reported to be haunted in several ways. Voices and screams can be heard when no one else is there but those individuals hearing them. Strange visions can be seen on the lake's surface in the moonlight. People have used rope swings there, flying way out over the lake and letting go. Supposedly several people over the years have disappeared in the lake never to return. Another strange phenomenon reported in the 1970s was a mysterious undertow that got really violent on certain nights even without any wind and sucked some poor swimmer under the water to drown. There are claims that several disappearance cases involving this lake were never solved and no bodies were ever found.

Kay's Cross in Kaysville

In 1847 Hector C. Haight built a cabin where the Lagoon Resort is located today. He was the only settler until a second settler, Samuel Oliver Holmes, moved in northwest of him. Three other families moved there from Brown's Fort in Ogden in 1849. One of these families was the William Kay family for whom the town was named. By 1851 there were 300 settlers in Kaysville. The Presbyterians established a church and school in Kaysville in 1881. While the church continued to operate until 1917, the school closed in 1909 because of the introduction of the public school system in the state. A fort was built in 1854. Some of the early businesses include the white tower of the Deseret Milling Company, which is still in operation. It has become a signpost along the highway when one is approaching Kaysville.

There are two different explanations for Kay's Cross, located in a little wood in Kaysville and built as a memorial by a man whose entire family was either murdered or died in a car accident on the spot. The legends about Kay's Cross were and are fascinating and something the town of Kaysville ought to find intriguing. Here are some variations on the legends of Kay's Cross, whose real mystery is in its secrecy or lack of history. It was a place where evil spirits were summoned and people were warned for years to stay away. There have been reports, even to the present day, of people in black cloaks wandering around, and even of some sort of evil "dog men" who chase people away from the area. A witch cult was said to have burned their victims on the cross. A woman in white flowing robes was said to appear atop the cross and remain floating there, but as one approached the cross, she quickly disappeared. There is also supposed to be a mansion in Kaysville where a man was killed. Whenever anyone passes the mansion at night, steps can be heard in the halls, lights flicker on and off, and one can hear moaning in the building. I would guess that this was the deserted house that may or may not still be standing not 300 yards from where Kay's Cross once stood.

An even older story said that Indians had erected the cross long before the pioneers ever came to the area or that the early pioneers had built the cross over the ground where a massacre had taken place. The spirits of the people who had been killed there had haunted their murderer until he appeased them by building the cross. This story was started because of the eagle figure that at one time sat on top of the cross.

Maggi Holmes, in *Lakeside Review*, writes, "The hollow that shelters the cross from the four winds is supposed to be haunted. It is said that ghosts, goblins and crazed spirits frequent the place on dark, moonlit nights."[22] Over the years the cross was vandalized and the eagle figure disappeared. Still others believed that the founder of Kaysville, Bishop William Kay, had buried his wife there and erected this huge cross in her honor in the 1850s. Another version states that the man who built the cross was a polygamist who murdered his seven wives in this wooded area, entombing one of them upright inside the cross. The wives' spirits lived in these woods and chased away intruders, thus explaining the woman who appeared as an apparition on the top of the cross. The cross also was said to take on an eerie glow that would burn your hands if you touched it.

One can see why the whole area could have at one time been pretty scary, before all the huge suburbs carved up several such hollows full of twisted and forbidding clusters of trees that would have been quite eerie in the wintertime. Especially since the hike to the hollow starts at the gates of the Kaysville cemetery, which one has to walk through first to get down to the first hollow, then go over a high ridge and down again into an even deeper hollow where the cross stood. The cross itself was creepy, having a large "K" in the center of it on either side and a large horizontal "T" on each crossbar, but nothing else was written on the stone and steel-enforced cross. And this was no little cross. It was twenty feet high and about twelve feet wide at the crossbar, and it stood on a large base. As one television reporter put it, "The cross looks kind of spooky even without the stories." Most who visited the place before all the houses were there would also agree that the entire area was spooky and downright frightening, at least in the middle of the night. The story of the old man who guarded the cross and lived in these woods, setting his dogs on trespassers or shooting at them with a shotgun or BB gun, was often used by local mothers to keep their children from hiking out to this spot to investigate.

Explanations for some of the stories are quite amusing too. For example, children who lived near the cross used to love to scare passersby at night by dressing up in a white sheet and climbing to the top of the cross to wave at cars as a ghostly form in the mist. The 1970s and 1980s brought in the witch cult rumors, and the owners would find chickens with their heads pulled off lying around the cross and pentagram graffiti on the cross, written in the chicken's blood. There was an old turkey pen next to the house by the cross. A "haunted" doll lay on top of the pen for years, and rumor had it that if anyone climbed up to see it, its eyes would open and one stare from its eyes could kill you. The abandoned house was about 300 yards from Kay's Cross. Eventually the owners' teenage sons got so tired of trespassers that upon occasion they would hide in the bushes and shoot off a gun in the air to scare the teenage boys away who were there with their girlfriends. The local residents' children played around the cross all the time and never had anything strange or eerie happen to them, except having to deal with all the curious teens who trespassed.

On the other hand, teens who visited the cross fabricated an elaborate series of steps that had to be taken in order to arrive at the cross safely. During the day, the old man who guarded the woods and the spirits who guarded the hollows would be asleep, so one could have a safe passage into the woods beyond the cemetery. But at night there was a group of trees in the cemetery where the first guardian spirit sat on the branches of these trees and waited for trespassers. If the trespasser could sneak through these trees without this guardian spirit seeing him, then all the other spirits in the cemetery would not notice him. Then the trespasser would have to quickly get over the back fence of the cemetery and hide in the oak brush behind it. From there the trespasser had a scary and shadowy walk down into the first hollow where more guardian spirits awaited him. If he made it past these spirits, then he had to climb a high ridge in the dark and descend down into an even darker and more densely wooded hollow where the giant twenty-foot-high and quite eerie cross would rise up before him in the dark, guarded by even more powerful spirits. On occasion, these trespassers would report that their flashlights went out and would not work the whole time they were in the woods, but when they got back to their cars parked near the cemetery, their flashlights would come on again as though they had never gone out.

Locals say that Kay's Cross was actually connected to a polygamy group, the Kingston Clan (not affiliated with the LDS Church in any way), who owned the old home and were suspected of having a hand in fashioning Kay's Cross. A member of the Clan—thus the "K"—bought the property in 1940 as a satellite to the main community in Bountiful. Other people believe that the head of this satellite community might also have had a first name that started with a "K" or that the man intended the "K" to stand not only for "Kingston," but also for "Klan." One of these homes was abandoned for a long time, and that started the haunted house stories, even though there were several owners after Charles and Ethel Kingston, who people believe built the cross. The original leader of the Kingstons had appointed another man to oversee this tiny group in Kaysville, and it was he, Charles Kingston, who had his people build the cross to himself or in honor of some other doctrine associated with the group. According to some sources, this man was eventually ousted from the group and moved away. Since the Kingstons are so secretive, this contributed to the growing number of stories, and Kay's Cross continued to have other rumors created about it.

One of these rumors involved the idea that the KKK had built the cross as a place to have their secret meetings in the 1940s. The children dressed in white sheets at Halloween time, trying to scare off trespassers, might be an explanation for this rumor as well as the "ghost" woman or women stories. Some people said that the Kingston leader was a KKK member, probably because the "K" on the cross looks exactly like one that Nathan Bedford Forest, original founder of the KKK, designed during the Civil War for his flag. The peak activity for the KKK in Utah was in 1925, when they marched through the streets of Salt Lake City and burned a big cross on the hills behind it. They were still active here in the 1940s, although by this time they had few members and had gone underground as well. It is much more likely that this Kingston man had his own religious reasons for designing and building this cross, one theory being that the "Ts" could have stood for the Knights Templar and the "K" for Klan, both Masonic symbols. There is even the idea put forth that the man planned to build his own temple in the woods where his followers could worship. The rumors went on, and on, and on.

On a Tuesday in February 1992, the rumors ceased. Kay's Cross was crumpled to the ground by a large blast of dynamite. Around ten o'clock at night a loud explosion rocked the neighborhood. The blast was so powerful that it was heard all over Kaysville, and one fragment struck and killed a pheasant roosting on a tree forty feet away from the cross. When the police investigated the incident, it was determined that someone had placed some dynamite at the base of the cross and turned the monument into a pile of rubble. They thought that it could be related to a similar incident that had happened a month before when someone had placed an explosive in a dumpster outside a Kaysville convenience store. No one was hurt, but no one was ever apprehended for either crime. It does make one wonder why anyone would do such a thing. They never got any notoriety for it, and as long as the cross stood there, more interesting urban myths and stories would have cropped up with the changing mores of the generations to follow. While the cross is gone forever, the stories still linger. Perhaps owners of the property got tired of trespassers, or maybe a group of teens thought it would be a fun jaunt. An even more interesting speculation would be that members of the Kingston clan, who didn't like the memory of one of their founders dishonored by the continued publicity, destroyed the cross. Most likely, someone who lived nearby got sick of dealing with the trespassers and simply got rid of the whole issue by making the cross disappear. While the cross is gone now, and little is left to visit or vandalize, the dynamiting seems to have accomplished one thing: it stopped the rumors and stories about Kay's Cross. In the thirteen years since, few remember or even know about the cross, nor do they wish to talk about it.

John Ortell Kingston's father was the theologian behind the clan's founding in 1935. His brother Charles Elden Kingston was the founder. But it was John Ortell Kingston who did something not heard of in any other separately founded polygamy groups in Utah. Ortell was a dairy farmer who experimented with his Holsteins to breed superior bloodlines on his dairy farm in Woods Cross. From what I understand, he introduced this theory to his followers, trying to breed superior bloodlines in humans. What has followed is years of inbreeding from incestuous marriages. The idea being that the closer one is to the pure blood line of the prophet of the church, the more like royalty one will become, receiving special dispensations, foods, and money. As a result of this thinking, a number of children have been born into the Kingston clan with birth defects. Of late, the Kingstons have been on the news a lot with several court cases involving child abuse, child brides, runaway members, and "the lost boys" (young men fleeing or even forced out of the group). Although support groups have been established for fleeing polygamy wives, it is interesting to note that few of them actually leave. These details make the real story behind Kay's Cross even more interesting. Something strange and different in a neighborhood, represented by a strange and different cross in a haunted wood, could start a dozen rumors over the years.

When I first came across this tale of Kay's Cross and the haunted house on an old Kingston property in Kaysville, I thought I would simply be writing about another urban myth that I, like other Utahns, had heard several times over the years. I was surprised to learn that this mysterious cross was connected to the Kingston polygamy group. When I researched further, just curious about how and why this huge cross would have been built of huge square blocks of stone, mortar, and steel rods, and then hauled to this obscure farm in the little town of Kaysville, the answer was even more astonishing. As I read about the handicapped children, I recalled my own experiences as a young teacher at a center for preschool multi-handicapped children. We discovered totally by chance that members of the Kingston clan were bringing several of our pupils to the school. The women used different last names, and the children had entirely different handicaps, so it was not until we attended a graveside service in Bountiful that we found out the truth. We had read about it in the paper and so were not expected to be there. We really frightened the women because we were there, and that was when we saw all of the women who had been coming to our school with their handicapped children all together in one place at one time. We speculated that one of the patriarchs must have had bad genes to father so many severely handicapped children.

These memories came flooding back as I spoke to people about Kay's Cross and its real origins and spiritual meaning. As a young teacher with high ideals and intuitive leanings, I had become quite attached to my little charges at the school. One might say that I could read them nonverbally when others could not. I loved them—all of them—but especially those I lost. Several who died were from Kingston families, and my style of teaching made me close to not only the mothers of these children, but also to the students themselves. When Kay's Cross came up in my haunting tales from Utah, I had another haunting to contend with as well. If actually created by Mr. Kingston, the cross, now long gone from its base, represents not just the man who supposedly built it, but what the man did. It represents a few of his progeny who I held in my arms, loved, and cared for as a young teacher, unaware of the undercurrents of this love. I remember these children, their smiling though vacant stares, and their desire to be loved as one would love a puppy or a kitten. But most especially I remember my challenge child, the one who screamed all through every session as I held her and manipulated her through her gestures, her garlic breath (an illegal cure at the time, DMSO was offered as a homeopathic cure for different ailments and caused the patient to have terrible garlic smelling breath), and the day she stopped screaming, smiled for the first time, and relaxed into my body with hers as we worked together.

It was this little girl's grave in that cemetery that I remembered, and her young mother's fear at our presence. Her mother's hidden happiness because we had come said more than any words of comfort might have. In the ensuing years I have come to understand two things: one is that these women, these sister wives, loved their little handicapped children unconditionally. On the other hand, it was the luck of the draw if these women had a handicapped child born to them, since they were taught to believe that if they gave birth to one of these children, they had somehow sinned and were of an impure bloodline on which no blessings would fall. I also came to understand that while all of these women had cared for each other's children, there were really only two of us, a mother and a teacher, who had really known this little girl. We are both possessed by this memory in a strange and invisible connection across time and distance. What is left of Kay's Cross in that pile of rubble in a haunted wood alive with spirits of the dead, and perhaps even a few lost children, has become for me this little girl's epitaph.

Suicide Rock and the Witch of Parley's Canyon

Few people know the old pioneer story told down through the generations about the big old rock sitting in the center of a deep chasm at the mouth of Parley's Canyon and the old hermit who died there. The supposed Indian tale has been lost to time as well. Nor do people today know about an old brewery that was located in the canyon and the beautiful and brilliant brewer's daughter, "Retty" Dudler, who was nicknamed by the local high school kids as the "Witch of Parley's Canyon." Her tragic life and sad demise are part of the canyon's lore that has long since been forgotten. Does she still wander this area searching for her lost child? And do the pranksters who tormented her still remember or even regret their actions?

Highways go up either side of the canyon and across in front of it, so that nowadays the big boulder sits in the middle of a giant triangle with decades of paint jobs on its face. No one really knows just when these rocks became a canvas for boys in love with girls or girls in love with boys. And for decades that was all it was—messages painted on rocks for the lovesick who ventured up its steep sides to paint them. Nowadays the signs have branched out into almost anything, both innocent and foul.

Long before the rocks became a canvas for graffiti artists, the belief was that this giant rock was a lookout post for local Indian tribes. Men kept a lookout for approaching tribes, and women climbed the rock to await the arrival of husbands and sweethearts returning from battle. The legend was that a beautiful chieftain's daughter leaped to her death from the top of this rock after spending days and days waiting for her lover to return. He was a great warrior who had gone off to fight in battle, and when he did not return and she learned of his death in this battle, she flung herself to the rocks below. After this, local tribes shunned the rock, for it was bad luck to go near it or even worse to climb it.[23]

This tall mass of red sandstone now sports, along with lover's messages to each other, fraternity and sorority pledges, sports allegiances, foul language, and even a few occult signs. There is even a marker there now telling the story of the "watch tower" where the maiden leapt from the top of the rock. Skeptics say that the story is unlikely, although they concede that it is an "ancient story" and one that Mark Twain poked fun of when he wrote about his visit to Salt Lake City in his book *Life on the Mississippi*, which was published in 1883. Local rumors say that there has been more than one suicide from this rock over the years, but my research shows that none have officially been reported. Since there are no early records of what did or did not go on at the site of this rock, those rumors will always be just that—rumors. But the story of this rock represents a deeper tale about the mistakes that we make in our youth and their sometimes tragic consequences.[24]

After the first white settlers came to the valley, they decided that a road needed to be built through the canyon. This road was nicknamed the Golden Pass Road because a tollgate was constructed where travelers helped pay for the road. This road shortened the journey that had to be taken by the first pioneers down through Emigration Canyon to the north, because Parley's Canyon had been impossible to traverse at that point. There were various prices for the toll road, all of them under a dollar. One paid so much for a wagon drawn by one animal, a wagon drawn by two animals, extra for an additional animal, and so much per head of stock being driven up or down the canyon. Several mills were built at the mouth of Parley's and on down into the valley, including a sugar mill, wool carding and wool factory, cotton factory, and two ice houses.

There was not enough canal water to irrigate the valley below, and so in 1891 a small reservoir was built completely surrounding Suicide Rock. Later in 1917 the Mountain Dell Dam was built further up the canyon, but this area of the canyon survived several floods. There was a flood in May 1897 and 1922, both of which caused considerable damage. Eventually the railroad went around this little reservoir on either side of it. There was also an old hermit whose name has been forgotten over time, but who lived near this reservoir and the rock in it. He was probably a prospector or an old railroad worker, or even a herder who lived only part of the time in this little cabin by the reservoir. Unfortunately, time and distance have lost his life story, but it is known that he is buried near the rock, and that in times past, stories were told about his ghost wandering the area.

In 1864 a man claimed the land one mile east from the mouth of Parley's Canyon in the bottom of a hollow on the north side of the creek and began building a home there on his three and one-half acres. This hollow was a beautiful miniature valley that everyone who has driven the turnoff to Emigration Canyon where the first pioneers descended into the valley knows about. Going up Emigration Canyon to the end of the houses, travelers break into a little hilly area that winds around until it meets the fork in the road leading to Parley's Canyon. A tiny marker at this location declares that the Donner-Reed Party stopped to rest on their way west. The road continues to the fork and down Parley's Canyon on the north side. The easiest way, of course, is to go up the canyon from Salt Lake City and look for the north creek about a mile up the canyon. It is hard to find exactly where Joseph Dudler built his home and brewery, because the road is so overgrown that it is not really visible from the highway. The only thing left standing today is an old chimney and part of a rock wall on the east end of the Dudler property.

For years some of the ruins of Joseph Dudler's place could still be found or even seen from the highway. Now very little is left to indicate specifically where all of this was. Some of the foundation of his original home and part of the brewery could be seen, and the huge underground cellar he dug for storage was still there. A grove of trees and part of a rock wall stood along the main road, next to the spring where he got his water. But now the main road into his little hollow is so overgrown that there isn't really one to be seen. But when Dudler first built the place, an inn with a large set of double doors in the center of the building faced south. It had three stories and a stone front, with a stairway on the west side that went up to the third floor. The cellar was thirty feet underground, with an arched ceiling that was nine and one-half feet from the floor to the highest part of the cellar. The cellar's walls were two and one-half feet thick and six feet lower than the basement of the inn. It was thirty feet long and about fifteen feet wide.

The inn was seventy feet long and ran north to south. It was thirty-six feet wide in an east-west direction. The foundation was three feet thick and the basement had a ten-foot ceiling. Dudler also built a stone wall that ran along the road as an entrance to the home and the inn. It was nine feet high and about two hundred feet long. A chimney stood about sixty feet north of the house and a barn about fifty feet west of it. In front of the home and the inn were two large troughs for the traveler's horses to drink water from after coming down the canyon or in preparing to go up it. The road up Parley's Canyon was so bad at that time that the railroad had a terrible time building its tracks up through this narrow, brush-covered winding grade. The first Model Ts were driven up the canyon right on the railroad trestles, switching back and forth across the tracks.

Joseph Dudler was a Gentile who came from the east in the 1860s to set up a brewery. He had worked as a carpenter first to earn enough money to do so. By 1870 he had accomplished his goal. The brewery was called the Philadelphia Brewery, and by 1892 he had his own saloon in town where he could sell his brew. The saloon was called, of course, the Philadelphia Brewery Saloon. Later he moved all of his business to Park City and became successful among the miners there. But during this period, he farmed some of his acreage, operated his brewery and the saloon in Salt Lake, and he and his family welcomed weary travelers to his inn. Dudler was a well-liked and respected businessman among both the Mormons and the Gentiles in the valley and never made a single enemy.

The upper two stories of the inn were where his wife, Elizabeth Susan, and his three daughters and four sons lived in the 1890s. Two more generations of family members lived there at times after this, since Joseph Dudler helped his younger relations to get a start in the world. Children were born there, and at least one death is known to have occurred there. People who remember the place think there were more than just one death. Dudler's Inn was also used as a pony express relay station and was also sometimes used as a stage stop. There was a smaller "official" stage stop further up the canyon and a relay station elsewhere. And while the inn was not an official stop, a lot of people made unofficial stops there to refresh themselves with a little home brew. The best quote comes from his obituary where it is stated that Dudler had "made money dispensing liquid refreshments and providing liquid entertainment for the 'happy-go-lucky, devil-may-care' wild and free class of men who then laid the foundation stones for the magnificent civilization that is now reaping the harvest."

Joseph Dudler died in 1897 at the old St. Mark's Hospital, and his wife died in 1904, leaving her beloved home only long enough to die. All of her children had died before she did, except for one daughter, Loretta Elizabeth Dudler or "Retty." This is a story not so much about the inn as it is about the last remaining child of

Joseph and Susan Dudler. Thus, the stage is set for the woman who came to be known as "Crazy Mary," "Bloody Mary," or "Parley's Witch." Being the sole survivor of her family, she inherited the home, the inn, and the brewery all at once.

Retta was a beautiful young woman with striking dark eyes, lovely light brown hair, and all the facial features of a great beauty. She was born on March 19, 1871, and being Catholic, she was proud of the fact that she had been born on the Feast of St. Joseph. As she grew up, it became apparent that she was highly intelligent and multi-talented, with her greatest talents being her musical abilities. Soon it became evident that Retty wasn't just talented. She was what would be termed as a "musical genius." A wide range of people who knew her as a young woman agreed with her family that Retty was amazing. She played the organ and the piano with great accomplishment and had an incredible singing voice. She received local awards for her musical accomplishments but never followed her dreams to become a musician outside her family's home. Instead, she began to run her father's business for him and was known to have a sharp mind in all of their legal and financial affairs. She had basically been running the entire business for her father before he passed away.

It is amazing to hear about someone of such great beauty and accomplishments who did not marry until she was thirty-six years old. On the other hand, perhaps she valued her freedom more, and not marrying at all was one way to keep it in those days. In 1907 she married Harold J. Schaer, and he moved in with her at "the old homestead" as the family always called it. They ran the business together, and Loretta had two sons soon after, Harold G. and Charles J. Schaer. It was the death of her second son, Charles, that apparently broke Retta's spirit. He died at the age of one year, seven months, and fifteen days—every minute counting in Retta's mind. Retta sank into a deep depression from which she never returned. As she grew older, she became more and more strange to the people who had known her when she was young. Once her husband died, she became more of a recluse. She became stilled in time, both in manner and dress, to the time when her child had left her. She got some cats and began to act so strangely that people felt that she had really gone over the edge.

Had she been living in a small town, she would have most likely been politely tolerated as a town "crazy." But with her living out there all alone, the business no longer running and the old homestead chock-full of all kinds of ghosts from the past, Retta found herself being tormented and teased by the young people who did not understand what she had been through. To them she was the old hermit of Parley's Hollow, who acted strange and had few friends to explain her strange ways. Unlike the old hermit who lived in my great-grandmother's boarding house in Kanab, who used to jump out from the bushes around his house and frighten the children away, Rhetta did not fight back. She remained aloof and appeared to be indifferent toward their teasings.

For the teenagers who rode up the canyon to torment her, Retta had become the "Witch of Parley's Hollow," "Crazy Mary," or even "Bloody Mary." Retta was incapable of defending herself against the onslaught of high school kids who drove up there in the 1940s and 1950s and trespassed on her property just to see the "witch." Those who still knew her said that Retta was a special person and a good friend. All of these rumors and wild tales culminated in a terrible tragedy that the people who knew her say broke whatever was left of her spirit.

On October 17, right around the witching season for Halloween devotees, some of the kids set fire to her homestead. It was definitely arson caused, but no one was ever caught or convicted of the crime. The most likely culprits were teens preparing for their Halloween partying in the canyon in the fall of 1952. Luckily, Retta was not home that evening. Any links to her dear husband and her little boy Charles were destroyed in this one cruel act by thoughtless kids who neglected to learn anything about Retta or her life. She was just "Crazy Mary" to them, and the old homestead burned to the ground.

Loretta Elizabeth Dudler died on March 22, 1959, but her close friends said that she died the day that her home died. For after this event, she was never in her right mind again. The portrait of her as a young woman has a mystical quality about it that infers her possession of not only mental and creative talents, but also spiritual and intuitive gifts. In her eyes are the sensitivity and grace and the strength and determination to survive no matter what life sends her way. I myself was heartbroken when I read the story of Retta Schaer. I became aware of such great talent being laid waste by the years of grieving and the one horrible tragedy from which she could never recover. My thoughts went to all such women over the years who lost their way and never blossomed as they should have. Women who worked hard and bore so many children that they had no energy for anything else. Women who because of one great loss in their lives could not leave the tragedy of it behind and somehow move on. Falling into a deep depression, these women could not survive the loss of a child and thus became a shadow of their former selves. As an intuitive, I understand the sensitivity and awareness of the unseen that Retty must have experienced from living a life so isolated in a home where all of her losses had taken place.

So when I think of delicate and yet somehow "crazy" Retta, I think of all the other women whose talents and gifts were denied them, either by force, tradition, or tragedy; the fates playing with their lives; and their will to continue somehow breaking down along the way. When I pass by this area, either coming or going up the fast and sometimes downright scary multiple-lane highway that is now Parley's Canyon, I don't think of ski country or about the wealthy people headed somewhere—anywhere—who traverse this pass at high speeds. I think about when the canyon was quiet, with few travelers and a man who brewed liquor by a small inn there, who had one surviving and beautiful daughter with great talents and promise. Of how she was born on the Feast of St. Joseph, the patron saint of all fathers—and probably carpenters, since he was the foster father of Jesus. How her father had been a carpenter before he became a businessman. Of how she shared her musical talents with others and then could never recover from the loss of a child. And how in one cruel and thoughtless act, a bunch of kids, who would be old men and women today, crushed her with their actions. These old men had to live with their consciences all these years for something they got away with, because in growing older, even some of the most evil men find themselves becoming more contrite and regretful of their foolish and destructive youthful actions.

In my time as a teenager and a young college student at the University of Utah, it was a well-known fact that the "Devil Worshipper's Place" was up Emigration Canyon. Carloads of kids were always going up there looking for this place, which was quite populated with houses even in those days. Up toward the end of the canyon and just before the bend in the road near the Parley's Canyon turnoff was a side road that wound toward the north. At the end of this road was the Devil Worshipper's Place. It was really just an old house with ornate wrought iron fences and gargoyles all around its beautiful gardens.

The people who lived there were constantly being harassed by kids because of the rumors of devil worshipping rituals being performed in the backyard of this house. Carloads of kids went up there in the middle of the night, and at least one brave soul would always jump the fence to look for evidence. The night we went, two guys jumped the fence and almost got caught. I can't say that I was a total innocent in my youth when it came to chasing rumors. I am sure that these poor homeowners got really tired of the constant harassment.

But it did make me wonder—and this may be really stretching it—if perhaps all those rumors from the two decades before about the Dudler Inn might have affected the rumors about Emigration Canyon as well. Perhaps one urban myth affected the other over the years, since the ruins of the old Dudler place was the haunted house to visit, and when it burned down, the talk of ghosts and hauntings increased. Perhaps the whole story came full circle, and once again another generation of kids looking for devils and witches just ended up at the wrong house in the wrong canyon. Retta's ghost was said to wander the old ruins looking for her lost child, and the lost child was said to be wandering the area looking for his mother. Nevertheless, it was Retta's mournful figure that walked among the ruins of her family home, her soft but mournful cries heard across the land there. The stories of her ghost and the haunted brewery faded with the years, and the foliage that hid the ruins of the old homestead covered over what was left of the inn. Retta and her child Charlie, known as "Little Brother," became lost stories that no one remembers today.

Retta's remaining son inherited the property, and he passed it on to his son Harold. This grandson owned the property in the 1950s and was talked into building a sports complex there. It was to consist of a large swimming pool, bathhouses, and a nine-hole golf course. They started digging the pool and built a series of cinder block bathhouses around it. Then Harold's representative took off with all the money that had been raised for the project, and the building had to stop. Neighbors became concerned about the dangers of the open pit, which had been dug for the swimming pool, so a bulldozer was brought in and the hole was filled in. Everyone took the cinder blocks for their own use, and nothing remains of this project today, except for a cement top around where the pool once was. Only old timers now speak of how they were afraid of Crazy Mary and how their friends liked to tease her. Some even remember going up to see the old "haunted house" ruins and spending time hunting for the "Witch of Parley's Canyon's" ghost.

Park City, Heber, Coalville, Cache Cave, Wahsatch, Echo, Neola, North Fork of the Bear River, Kamas, Myton, Tabiona, and Dinosaur National Monument

For me, this whole area has a feel to it unlike any other in Utah. Perhaps it comes from all the lost mine tales, or the prospectors who disappeared, or the pioneers who gave up just as they approached the valley. Or maybe the feeling comes from ancient nomadic Indians, or from the trappers and outlaws who made this area their home. Perhaps it's from a bigfoot or two, or even from the high count of UFO sightings and sci-fi air battles reported in the area. Perhaps it is just that the high mountain air does something to one's brain! All I can say is that spirits do roam the hills in these forests and plains. One can simply look up and find them staring right back down at you from the sky, or from a cave, tunnel, or cellar. Spirits look back at you from a face in a rock, a late-night campfire, an old pioneer graveyard, a spooky miner's hotel, or even a "cursed" or perhaps "blessed" town. Ancient dinosaurs and petroglyphs stand next to a hermit's cabin where outlaws once sought temporary refuge. The Skinwalker ranch is hidden there as well, a UFO tale I have already told in *Lost Landscapes*.[25] These three counties have it all!

Park City Cemetery

Colleen Adair Fleidner, who wrote *Stories in Stone: Miners and Madams, Merchants and Murderers,* thought up one of the most interesting ideas for a book. The book is about a cemetery in Park City, Utah. Fleidner researched many of the interesting people buried there and recorded the most unusual stories. The book contains maps where the people are buried in both Park City cemeteries, and all the stories are fascinating. You may want to check her book out at your local library![26]

Ike Potter's Ghost

A man named Isaac S. Potter has become the subject of Coalville legend due to his untimely demise. Ike stole an ox that belonged to someone living in East Weber. He was caught and arrested but was released on bond. He took off right after his release, returning some time later with a band of desperado Ute Indians and other men who were thieves and cutthroats. Ike was reputed to be the leader of the band. He and his desperados threatened to clean out the community of Coalville for what they had done to him. Catching him alone with only two of his accomplices, Sheriff J.C. Roundy locked them up in the strongest available building, the Coalville Mormon Ward chapel. It would later become the rock school house.

Ike and his two accomplices escaped, and several differing stories exist about how this happened. Some say that vigilantes forcibly removed the men from their temporary prison. Others say that they escaped on their own, and it was totally by chance that they were found so quickly. They never made it out of town. One accomplice was shot as he crossed Chalk Creek, and the other shortly after. Ike Potter was caught in front of the old county courthouse where he was gunned down. No one would claim his body and no one wanted it in the local cemetery, so he was buried on a rocky hillside near the point where the old county road crossed Grass Creek. For sixty years there were reports of old Ike Potter roaming the hillside, his restless spirit seeking revenge on any passersby that were brave enough, innocent enough, or foolish enough to be in the wrong place at the wrong time. Stories were told of seeing a shadowy figure or a strange light. Then Echo Reservoir covered the area where his grave was supposed to be. Forty years later a few human bones washed up on the shore of the reservoir.

Most people in the area believed that these bones were the remains of Ike Potter. Sixty years of reports of his spirit seem to have died when the lake covered everything. But several unanswered questions remain. Were these really the remains of Ike Potter or some unfortunate and unknown accident victim or even an unsolved and undiscovered murder? Perhaps they were ancient bones from a time long past that were never analyzed? Did the bones really wash up on shore or is this only a local legend? Was Ike Potter even buried in the area? Does his ghost still walk the underwater grave without ever surfacing? Perhaps no reports of his ghostly spirit means that no one has spotted him recently walking the shores of the reservoir late in the evening, still seeking to clean out the town of Coalville.

The Spirits of Cache Cave in Echo Canyon

Cache Cave is famous because pioneer wagon trains stopped there on their way into Salt Lake City. For about fifteen years the Mormon trains took the same route through Echo Canyon. Considered a mystical place by the local Native Americans, the whites named Echo Canyon the "Valley of the Red Forks." The pioneers traversed down the south side of the canyon, and by 1860 thousands had passed through this area, crossing Yellow Creek and going on down to Cache Cave on their way into the Salt Lake Valley. Immigrants and locals identified certain rocks and formations, not only to provide direction signs, but also to encourage those who journeyed to the Mormon's promised land. Castle Rock was famous, but Cache Cave was even more famous. Orson Pratt's journal description of the cave said that the opening was like the door frame of an outside cellar, and that originally it was called Redden's Cave after the man who had first visited it. There are 135 pioneer names carved into the cave's walls, and a lot of people left behind supplies and other things, intending to return for them later. In 1855–56 the Mormon handcart pioneers were greeted there by a storehouse of badly needed supplies.

When Johnston's Army approached ten years later, over twelve hundred Mormon men were assigned to dig breastworks and fortifications in Echo Canyon in preparation for a war thought to be inevitable between the U.S. government and the Mormons. The area was manned until the winter of 1857 when the men were sent back to Salt Lake City. While no shots were ever fired, the Mormon men did delay the advancement of Johnston's Army so that they did not march into Salt Lake City until the following summer, which probably prevented an immediate war between the two factions. Some of the fortifications and breastworks can still be seen in the canyon today. From April 1862 to October 1861, Echo Canyon was part of the Pony Express route, which stopped at way stations inside Echo Canyon along with overland stagecoaches. Mark Twain even mentions it in his book *Roughing It*, which tells of his stagecoach journey through Echo Canyon via this route. The telegraph was put through Echo Canyon, with Brigham Young's first message reading, "Utah has not seceded but it is firm for the Constitution and laws of our once happy country." In 1868 the Union Pacific Railroad built tracks through Echo Canyon.

After the huge influx of pioneers was over, the cave became a place for fur traders, thieves, and robbers. These outlaws not only hid out in Cache Cave but also stored their loot inside. Charles Wilson and Ike Potter frequently used the place as a hiding place before they were shot in Coalville. They kept their stolen grain there, along with other supplies and stolen items. Cache Cave is thought to be haunted by the different groups of people who stopped there over the years, but especially by the spirits of the two ruffians, Wilson and Potter. Stories are told, and it is indeed an eerie place to visit. How many people left their caches in this cave and then never retrieved them? Who might have spent time there? The wind does blow and voices can be heard as you approach the area. It is what I call a "talking cave," where so many voices can be heard that I could not understand any of them.[27]

Skeletons in Echo's Saloon Cellars

The town of Echo is at the mouth of Echo Canyon. It was named for the echoes that reverberate off the walls of the canyon. James Bromley was the first resident of Echo and operated a Funk and Walker Stage Station at the mouth of the canyon beginning in 1854. Echo was quite a boomtown during the time the railroad was being constructed. The first locomotive came down the tracks in January 1869. By the 1880s, Echo was a busy railroad town. Trains used about two thirds of their fuel supply between Ogden and Echo and then needed to refuel to get to Evansville, Wyoming. In 1960 the last locomotive went through Echo, leaving a few haunted places behind it.

When temporary saloons followed the railroad as it was being constructed, the saloon owners left garbage pits in their cellars. It does seem unusual that a garbage pit would be dug in the basement of these temporary saloons rather than digging it some distance from the town to avoid the smell. This practice brought about rumors of foul play only after some of the cellars were discovered and excavated years later. An explanation for why they were being excavated was never given, but one could guess that the town was either building something and digging a basement for the foundation, or someone was digging around for that one great find—an old bottle or some other artifact.

As they were excavating some of these cellars, they found seven skeletons in one of them. Nobody knew how they got there or who they were, and obviously from the way in which they were haphazardly buried, they weren't meant to be found. These men would certainly have a reason to haunt the town of Echo, having probably died by foul means and being unable able to tell their true stories. This find also suggests that this might have been a practice for saloon owners wanting to cover up murders, gunfights, or any other type of foul play during the years that these saloons operated in these rough railroad towns all over the west. Perhaps Echo had more than one such saloon death pit that was never found.

Johnny Cash and the Kozy Café

The Kozy Café in Echo is just above Coalville as you are heading east toward the Wyoming border. It is a favorite stop for the motorcycle groups who like to travel the byways of America. They have great food, and it is a fun place to gather with your friends while you are out on the open road. It's one of those places that the Travel Channel might want to highlight on one of its old highway programs. The ghost there is supposed to be the owner of the café. "Fat," as he was known, passed away a few years ago. Since his death, waitresses have heard voices near the bar and have often heard someone order a refill on coffee when no one is around and the café is closing. Both employees and patrons report hearing bar stools squeak and turn when no one is on them. People have also reported hearing old cowboy boots scruff across the floor to the jukebox. This especially happens shortly after a certain Johnny Cash song begins to play on the jukebox. Apparently, this old song was Fat's favorite. Whenever the song starts to play on the jukebox, the volume suddenly goes up when no one is near, and sometimes the song plays when no one has selected it. Apparently, Fat had such a strong presence in his little café that some of his personality remains to haunt the place, even if the café has changed owners.

Railroad Spirits of the Wahsatch Tunnels

As you leave Echo, Utah, and turn northeast on I-80, passing the town of Castle Rock, a few remains of an old construction camp come into view just before you reach the Wyoming border. This town was called Wahsatch, and whatever is left of the town site is on private railroad property today. As the Union Pacific Railroad surveyed the area, this was the last location on the flatlands before the railroad dropped down through Echo Canyon. From 1860 to 1868, hundreds of workers lived there, and the town was not only a major construction camp, but also a major supply area for the railroad. While Echo Tunnel was being drilled, a roundhouse, locomotive shops, boarding houses, and warehouses were built in Wahsatch. Once the tunnel was built and construction crews moved on to other sites, Wahsatch continued to be a place for engine changes, serving facilities, and a crew rest stop. In May 1869 passengers who waited for local train changes were able to have a good meal there. During this time, the use of helper engines carried heavy freight trains up the canyon to where they were serviced. The freight trains were then turned around and sent back down the canyon.

Evanston, Wyoming, was also originally a construction camp, eleven miles to the northeast, but unlike the town of Wahsatch, it grew into a small city. It was Evanston that proved to be the demise of the little town of Wahsatch. In the 1870s, most of the buildings were razed except for the depot, loading docks, and maintenance buildings. For years after that, sheep and cattle loadings took place from the Castle Rock area, and the track crews lived in Evanston. Later, Echo was the headquarters for the construction of the new tunnel that was drilled in 1916 not far from the first one. A second track was laid to decrease the grade coming up Echo Canyon.

> The old abandoned 1916 tunnel is the only thing of interest in the area now. The east portal of this tunnel is a few hundred yards west and downhill from the town site and can be viewed from the edge of the ravine. By diligent searching, remnants of the way in which the locomotives were turned can be seen in the immediate area of the vacant section houses which date only back to the 1930s. The depot built in the 1930s and unused for many years was torn down in 1969.[28]

People believe that when this camp was in operation and many of the workers were "celestials" from China, opium dens and the like were dug underground. More pertinent are the rumors that when some of these men died, the crew foremen buried the bodies in the solid rock walls of the underground tunnels, as well as within and under the old abandoned tunnels that were originally built for trains to pass through on their way down the canyon. While men of other nationalities may have occasionally had this happen to them, it was more likely that single

Chinese men who had no family in America to search for them met their fate in this manner. These "lost" men supposedly haunt the old tunnels and railroad grades even now, because neither their spirit ancestors nor their descendents have been able to find them.

The old tunnel has long disappeared, but its unquiet spirits might still haunt the area nearby the newer 1916 railroad tunnel. The newer tunnel always remains freezing cold inside and has a layer of ice in the middle of the tunnel even during the summer months. This tunnel is thought to be very haunted. Locals that have hiked out to the area say that not only can you hear the crying of the unblessed (buried without ceremony), but you can also hear their voices whispering in the middle of the night. The tunnel itself is one giant "cold spot." Ghost trains have been seen coming down the long-deserted tracks with sparks flying high in the dead of night. Most interesting, though, are the rumors that since the walls of the tunnel are decaying, you can now see some of the bones of these men. Many Chinese believed or still believe that if spirits are buried right where they die, they are less likely to haunt the area and will find their way home. But if the men are not given a proper burial at the time of their death, with their families and priests present, they will stay there until they are found by their descendents and properly blessed. In addition to this, these men may also have been the victims of foul play or simply not respected enough to be given a proper burial. Whatever the reasons, these men deserve to be honored by their descendents, and if they were not at the time, they will continue to haunt the tunnel and the land surrounding it until such ceremonies take place.

Considering the fact that some skeletons were found in the garbage pits that the old saloon keepers dug in their cellars and so casually left behind them, it is not hard to believe that more bodies were buried in this fashion—under the temporary saloons and under the railroad grades and tunnel walls. It is staggering to imagine just how many men may have lost their lives this way. History has confirmed that some of these workers never did come home. Some had no one to miss them or no means by which to locate them. Descendents now are looking for information on some of these men—Chinese, Irish, or of any other descent. Some were probably buried with the usual ceremonies after dying of illness or an accident along the grade, but others may have met with foul play and had no chance to right the wrongs done to them. Unless they were buried on the spot where they died and the ground was consecrated, spirits of this type lay in wait for anyone to come along that they can tell their story and scare those who stand over or near their unmarked graves. Really, this is not what they want. What they want is for those of the living to hear them, listen to their story, and help their descendents find them. They simply want to be found.

"Hyrum Smith," the Old Miner Campfire Stories

I first heard the "Hyrum Smith" stories associated with Heber City, but the area doesn't matter. Hyrum, not to be confused with the brother of Joseph Smith, nearly always ends up in a scout camp story on a dark night around a brightly lit campfire. Hyrum is supposedly roaming the hills in spirit form, and he jumps out and grabs someone, which comes at the end of a long and involved tale about his life. A stand-in scout or counselor then imitates his apparition. Hyrum is most often associated with the area from Heber and Coalville to the north fork of the Bear River on the Wyoming–Utah border in the Ashley National Forest. Old Hyrum tales can be heard even as far away as Duchesne. The common ones are basically well-known urban myths, such as the famous one about the hitchhiker who is picked up in a heavy rainstorm, turns his head, and the other side of his face is all mangled. The driver, scared to death, drops the hitchhiker off where he wants to go and then guns the accelerator and drives fifty miles down the road before stopping. When the driver gets out of the car and walks around to the other side, he finds the man's hand, or sometimes even more menacing, a hook, hanging on the door handle. This is only one of several dozen such stories.

Hyrum's beginnings are clouded. In one version he was working on the Duchesne tunnel, which allows water from the Provo River to reach Duchesne. He was killed in an unusual explosion there, and no trace of him has ever been found, so his ghost has been seen hiking along the roads from Duchesne to Heber City. In another version, Hyrum is a miner, a young man sent in to set a dynamite charge in the mine. At the last minute, he foolishly goes back in to get something. The blast erupts and blows half his face away. Hyrum survives but dies shortly after. He roams the hills above Heber to Coalville searching for the other pieces of his body. The worst thing you can do is to get in his way when he is looking. What interests me is how much territory he has to cover to support all of these tales. He has to travel all over Summit and Duchesne Counties, so it is probably good that he is a ghost.

The "Sweddish Logger" Story and the Boy Scout Camp

The "Swedish Logger" story is related to the specific area of the east fork of Bear Canyon thirty miles south of Evanston, Wyoming, but inside the Utah border. It is a place called Scow Creek, where a Boy Scout reservation exists today. The story is repeated to new sets of scouts each year. Even the locals in the area have told this one for decades. It seems that at the turn of the century, a Swedish logger was working at a logging camp in the area. He was writing to a girl in Denver. One weekend he went to Denver and asked her to marry him, and she accepted. He brought her back to camp with him. They needed a home, so he set to work building a cabin. When it was completed, they moved in. He had warned her several times about a rogue cougar that was roaming the area around their cabin. He told her to keep the door locked and bolted and to never open the door, especially at night.

One evening before the logger returned home, his young bride thought she heard a baby crying outside. She opened the door and was instantly the prey of this giant cougar. When the logger came home, he saw his young bride mangled and dead before the front door of his cabin. Distraught and beside himself with grief, he dug her grave next to the cabin and left the cabin just as it was, never to return. The remnants of the cabin are still in existence today, and inside the walls are newspaper clippings from all over the United States, because the logger had been quite a wanderer before he had settled down—however briefly—with his new bride. Upon wandering into this area, it is said, you can hear a baby crying in the distance. If you walk through the woods anywhere in this area, you might also hear a woman screaming.

Edwin, the Neola High School Ghost

On the other side of the Ashley National Forest and to the south is a little town called Neola. Union High School in Neola is due north of Roosevelt and not far from the Uintah River. As many schools claim to be, it is supposedly built over an ancient Indian burial mound. In the auditorium of this old school is a ghost that has been nicknamed Edwin. Edwin has apparently been there for years, through various school productions and dramas. He likes to play tricks on people, especially when there is a person alone in the auditorium. His favorite is to turn all the lights off in the auditorium when only one person is there to scare the wits out of them. Edwin's other favorite ploy is to hang costumes on the curtain tracks or place things in unusual places. One of his most famous tricks occurred when the drama class at the school put on a production of *Dracula*. The actor playing the corpse inside the coffin was pushed off the stage by unseen hands, coffin and all.

My guess is that Edwin is being helped by some prankster high school kids, especially around Halloween. There probably is some phenomenon in the school that I hope to check out soon for myself. Perhaps Edwin is really a former high school student who died tragically, or perhaps a disgruntled actor who never made it in Hollywood and found it easier to do away with himself, returning to where he once was a star. Perhaps he is an old Indian, but I don't think so. My gut reaction is that there is a lot of hanky panky on the part of the students to perpetuate the myth, which only covers over the real spirit's presence in that auditorium. A good way to identify a ghostly presence is to stand up and acknowledge the ghost and then wait to see if a door slams or something heavy drops or something bursts like a light bulb. Apparitions just love letting you know that they are there, especially angry ones.

The Lost Pioneer Graves of Kamas

Kamas, a small mountain town high in the Wasatch-Cache National forest, not far from Mirror Lake, has one ghost story. We used to go camping there all the time when I was growing up and were told stories about how Indian spirits haunted the lake. The South Summit Middle School in Kamas is supposed to be haunted by what the students call the "pool ghost." Apparently, a girl drowned in the pool, and the story goes that she can grab you by the ankles and drag you down into the pool. Supposedly two other students have died in the pool because of the "pool ghost." The pool was probably covered over and was where the basketball court is now, since she is still haunting the area. A call to the South Summit Middle School produced the following quote: "No ghosts here!" But there is more to the story than this, because recent articles in the paper have confirmed a pretty big reason for why there would be more than one ghost haunting this brand-new middle school.

Five pine coffins discovered on the future site of North Summit Middle School had some students concerned ghosts would haunt their hallways, while others wondered what would happen to the old bones. The coffins, containing the remains of one man and four children, were found while construction crews finished footings on the new building. The workers found the first grave on Dec. 10 and the last—the coffin of a 1- to 2-year-old child—was exhumed. "We knew there used to be an old cemetery here," said North Summit Middle School Principal Lloyd Marchant. "But this was unexpected." Rumors circulated the bodies were those of American Indians, but a forensic archaeologist told the school and the sheriff's office that the bones are of Norwegian descent, possibly those of Mormon pioneers.

The old graves in that area were relocated to the present cemetery in 1868, . . . but some were obviously left behind. Other such graves were located when North Summit High School was constructed across the street and when a swimming pool was added. A Summit county sheriff spoke to the high school students at that time to assure students that no ghosts would appear. He again spoke to the middle school students when more graves were found, assuring them by stating the ages of the bodies: two 1- to 2-year-olds, one 2- to 3-year-old, one 12- to 13-year-old, and an old gray-haired man. He also told them that there was little possibility of finding out the deceased's identities. The school participated in the reburial ceremony at the Coalville cemetery. The bodies were placed in new caskets, and sheriff Alan Siddoway used his personal horse-drawn hearse to cart the remains from the school to the burial site after the archaeologist finished working on the site. One teacher planned to have her eighth grade class write an historical fiction on the life of one of the bodies found at the new school.[29]

Myton's Curse

This is a tale of how "the curse" was reversed. Bridge City was renamed for Major H. P. Myton, who was the first postmaster appointed by the United States government. The town had only become Bridge City because all the mail for the Uintah Basin at the time was sent to the bridge. Several of the Gentile families who went to the town for government assignments decided to stay in Myton. Still others went to work on the canal system built for the Indian allotments. Bridge City became a huge crossroads for the whole basin, and all this travel across the river brought in wild times.

By 1908, Myton was 90 percent Gentiles, and they were much united in their desire to keep the Mormons out of town. People believe that this is the real reason for the "Mormon Curse" or "Myton Curse," as it was called then. A calculated and well-organized Mormon plan began. The Mormons were determined to gain control, not only of Myton, but also of the whole Uintah Basin. The Mormons got control of the newspapers, water, and school locations and superintendents. Then they dealt their final blows by closing the Myton State Bank, and finally by taking the bid for the county seat away from the town. These moves essentially killed Myton as the number one city in the basin.[30]

When Myton lost its bid for the county seat, the curse was in place for good. There are several versions of the literal Myton curse, and to do it justice I will relate all three. In the most well-known version told to me by two former residents who grew up in Myton, a meeting was held in Myton about a proposal to build a new stake center for several Mormon wards. The Gentiles, who outnumbered the Mormons at the time, shouted the speaker down and threatened to tar and feather him and run him out on a rail. The LDS stake president then told the crowd that the building would go up in Roosevelt and that Myton would from that day forward go downhill until weeds grew in the sidewalks, rabbits played in the streets, and every street in Myton turned into a swamp.

In the second version, the stake president in Roosevelt, dismayed at the behavior of his members in Myton, who seemed to tolerate the local saloons, with some even frequenting them, warned the members that if they did not change their ways, Myton would fall into wrack and ruin and weeds would grow in the cracks of the sidewalks.

The third version relates that an LDS committee from Roosevelt came to meet with the non-LDS town council of Myton, wanting to buy into businesses in town. This request was vehemently denied. The head of the LDS committee, a stake president, then uttered his curse: "If you do not allow us to buy into your town, you will see the day when only jackrabbits and tumbleweeds inhabit your main street."

And Myton did go downhill, just as "the curse" had predicted. When the road was switched in the 1920s from Indian Canyon Road (U.S. 191) to the road that went to Heber (US 40) traffic through Myton was greatly reduced. By this time the Masons had built a lodge there and began to feud with the Mormons financially. A fire razed the business district in 1915. More fires followed in 1925 and 1930, and then the Depression dealt a final blow when there were no funds for rebuilding. A financial scheme to revitalize the area by bringing the railroad through town failed, and this, coupled with poor crops and another big failure to bring a huge irrigation project into the area, caused Myton to dry up in every way possible. Some river flooding made temporary swamps in the area, but not where they really needed the water to be.

Until recently, Myton citizens were proclaiming even on their website that the Myton curse had been lifted at last. After my last visit, I have come to believe this. Improvements have been made to this once-cursed little town. A former town mayor, Ludy Cooper, who has since passed away, put it best when she said, "For all these challenges, there are paybacks. Even though the wind does blow hard, we don't have tornadoes. We don't have floods, we only need air conditioning a few weeks out of the year, and we can depend on the weather to cool off at night so we can sleep. When we wake up in the morning, we can breathe in the cool, clean air. We may have a bit of fog in the winter to turn the trees into glistening white monuments, but we don't have any smog to smother us. We do have the most spectacular sunsets in the whole world. We do have quiet—so real you can hear it."[31]

The irony is that in the end, the curse on Myton not to progress became a blessing in disguise.

Stone Face, Tabiona

> He looms as a stony sentinel over the North Fork of the Duchesne, with only one good eye guarding the valley and hundreds of years of secrets.[32]

To find "Stone Face," take U.S. 40 to Duchesne, located in the Uintah Basin, and turn north on Route 35. Keep going until you are about twenty miles beyond Tabiona. You will pass through the Uintah and Ouray Indian Reservation and then the town of Hanna before getting to the turnoff for Stone Face, which is about three and one-half miles further on. Mostly only locals and a few gold miners and treasure hunters know the story of Stone Face. The twenty-five-foot-tall rock outcropping looks like a one-eyed man with high cheekbones and jutting jaw. His secret is that he points the way to a lost Spanish gold mine. Stone Face supposedly has directions marked on his face for the old trails that lead to the lost mine.

These trails take you to the Granddaddy Lakes, where an old cabin stands as the last marker before reaching the lost mine. It is one of several legendary locations in Utah for the "Lost Rhoades Mine."

> The legend is that the Spanish Conquistador Hernando Cortez dispatched exploration parties as far north as Utah in search of the Seven Cities of Cibola. In the Uintah Mountains, they supposedly struck gold. But after the conquest, the mine lay dormant for centuries until Brigham Young sent Thomas Rhoades to find it. With the help of a Ute Indian chief, who knew the secret location, Rhoades brought forth enough gold to help establish the Mormon empire—or so the story goes.[33]

Local lore about Stone Face is that the outcropping is not entirely a work of nature. Locals believe that years ago a man used to go up there to work on it late at night to make the outcropping look even more like a face. Others will tell you that it was put there by a higher power in order to watch over the valley. And still others have a different name than Stone Face for the outcropping. A man who owned a dude ranch had been in an accident resulting in his having one permanently shut eye. His name was Lou, so locals began calling the outcropping One-Eye-Lou. Ranchers who have lived in the area all their lives say that the face has been there for as long as they can remember, and they really don't care whether Stone Face gets more attention or not. Perhaps someday the treasure hunters will find the old cabin and the old mine. In the meantime, Stone Face watches over the area in a silent vigil that has lasted for decades.

Dinosaurs, Petroglyphs, and Hermit Outlaws

Around Vernal and Roosevelt, the land has enough visible layers of fossils and dinosaur bones to entice anyone to visit Dinosaur National Monument. But not everyone will know what lies on the government land behind it. There is a long road to a boxed canyon where the famous hermit, Josie Bassett, lived for years by herself. But she didn't get to die there and had to be forcibly removed so that her relations could help her in her last years. The cabin, the old corrals, and even the bridge over a small river have become part of the national monument.

Along this road are several mural-sized petroglyphs that people claim have not only definite UFO spaceships on them, but also the well-known space alien grays, with large black eyes and no mouths. From the time you leave the monument to the west and then curve back east along this road, you can feel the eeriness of the area. Ancient Indian spirits abound, and Josie's apparition quite clearly inhabits her little cabin. The locally named "Hide-Out" box canyon where Josie's corrals are located is so full of energy that most who happen to hike up there find it downright scary. On the cliff is a cave where the only way in and out is by climbing a rope. Old outlaws used to hide there. They would lower a rope and bucket, and Josie would fill the bucket with food or water. The outlaws then raised the bucket to the large cave they were hiding in.

It is rumored that besides members of the Wild Bunch and other Utah outlaws, members of the Dalton Gang hid out there from the law. In 1954 a small plane crashed a few miles east of this canyon, and the two men walked out through this area. They both survived the crash, but one of the men died later from internal injuries. Josie's entire story will be told in my old west tales. Suffice to say I have been there twice and felt myself walking back in time to a different era, getting lost there and having a terrific time finding my way back. I intuited a lot there, and the story about Josie and my conversations with her and whatever spirits roam there came in layers of history, from ancient dinosaurs and Indians, to outlaws and lawmen. Even Josie Bassett haunts Split Mountain.

The beautiful Ann Bassett was both cattle rustler and rancher, and her little sister, Josie, got to know all of the Butch Cassidy gang, as well as other outlaws they offered shelter to. Ann Bassett is one of the claimants to the Etta Place title as girlfriend to either Butch or Sundance. In the 1950s, Josie even had a

Hollywood musical completed in her honor, with Doris Day as the leading lady. In her nineties, she was the local rodeo queen and grand master of the Pioneer Day Parade. She was also famous for having poisoned one of her husbands and getting away with it.

Both sisters' stories are amazing, but it is Josie's little cabin, where she lived several years alone, that still houses all her energies and memories for those who intuit such things.

All in all, a trip to the dinosaur quarry is worth it on its own, but don't forget to go down Dinosaur Quarry Road and stop and walk out to the petroglyphs. Be sure you sit in Josie's cabin in the Split Mountain area for a few minutes, and then hike up the box canyon to the corral ruins behind the quarry. If you don't meet some spirits you will certainly feel them there. This is one mystical canyon!

Notes:

1. Ward J. Roylance, *Utah, a Guide to the State* (Salt Lake City: Utah Arts Council, 1982), 400.
2. Richard McOmber, "The Weeping Lady," *Zion's Lost Souls: Utah's Notorious Ghost Legends* (Bloomington, Indiana: iUniverse, 2004), 39–41.
3. Bernice Maher Mooney and J. Terrence Fitzgerald, *Salt of the Earth: The History of the Catholic Church in Utah, 1776 to 1987*, 1st ed. (Salt Lake City: University of Utah Press), 224–25.
4. Valerie Vaughn, "Deadly Cold: Jim Bridger, Brigham Young, and FDR Shape the Human Imprint on Logan Canyon," *Hard News Café* (Utah State University Communications Department, Nov. 11, 1999).
5. *Popular Beliefs and Superstitions from Utah*, collected by Anthon S. Cannon (Salt Lake City: University of Utah Press, 1984), no. 10058, 316.
6. City-Data.com, http://www.city-data.com/city/Mendon-Utah.html, accessed Jan. 14, 2010.
7. Lyle J. Barnes, "Did 'Gentile Kate' Really Buy This Carriage?" *Notorious Two-Bit Street* (West Conshohocken, Pennsylvania: Infinity Publishing Company, 2009), 69–74.
8. GhostWave, http://www.ghostwave.com/ogdencity.html, accessed Mar. 2008.
9. Ibid.
10. Salt Lake Ghosts and Hauntings Research Society (http://www.slcgh.org) and the Utah Ghost Hunters Society (http://www.ghostwave.com).
11. Mark Sail, "Life at the Top: Pizza Place Incurring Wrath of Wraiths," *Ogden Standard-Examiner*, Oct. 20, 2001.
12. Alan Meyer, *Ghost Hunting in the Unknown Zone*, documentary (Rogue Entertainment, 2002–3). For more information visit www.alanmeyer.com.
13. UPER Investigations, http://uper1.tripod.com, accessed Mar. 2008.
14. Ibid.
15. Dennis Romboy "Who Ya' Gonna Call? Utah's Ghost Hunters," *The Deseret News*, Oct. 30, 2002.

16. Kristen Moulton, "Ogden Is Spooked by Haunted Houses," *The Salt Lake Tribune*, June 28, 2003, B.

17. Ibid.

18. Cynthia Larsen Bennett, *Roadside History of Utah* (Missoula, Montana: Mountain Press Publishing Co., 1999), 114.

19. Ibid., 183–84.

20. Ibid., 100.

21. Roylance, *Utah, a Guide to the State*, 431–32.

22. Maggi Holmes, "Mysterious Cross Casts Eerie Shadow On Kaysville History," *Lakeside Review*, Oct. 28, 1981.

23. Florence C. Youngberg, *Parley's Hollow: Gateway to the Great Salt Lake Valley* (Scottsdale, Arizona: Agreka Books, 1998), 88.

24. Brett Hullinger, "Utah's Myths and Legends," *Salt Lake Magazine of the Mountain West*, Feb., 2005, 77–84.

25. Colm A. Kellehar and George Knapp, *Hunt for the Skinwalker* (Paraview, New York: Paraview Pocket Books, 2005).

26. Colleen Adair Fleidner, *Stories in Stone: Miners and Madams, Merchants and Murderers* (Mabank, Texas: Flair Publishing, 1995).

27. Dan Hampshire, Martha Sonntag Bradley, and Allen Roberts, *A History of Summit County* (Salt Lake City: Utah State Historical Society; Coalville: Summit County Commission, 1998), 124–25.

28. Stephen L. Carr, *The Historical Guide to Utah Ghost Towns* (Salt Lake City: Western Epics, 1972), 58.

29. Matt Canham, "Old Graves Found at School Site Were Possibly Pioneers," *The Salt Lake Tribune*, Dec. 18, 2004, B.

30. Alexia "Ludy" Cooper, "The History of Myton," http://users.ubtanet.com/myton/g_godly.html, accessed Mar. 2008. Ludy moved to Myton in 1946 when she married her husband and lived there for the rest of her life. She was the mayor.

31. Ibid.

32. Christopher Smart, "Face in the Rock Keeps Its Secrets," *The Salt Lake Tribune*, May 16, 2003, B1 and B4.

33. Ibid., B4.

BOOK TWO

SALT LAKE COUNTY TO
NORTHERN UTAH COUNTY

Strange Tales of Central Utah

Sandy City

Sandy City Cemetery

The Sandy City Cemetery has some great stories too, the best one being about the man buried outside the gates of the cemetery on Seventh East. One national book, *Ghost Stories of the Rocky Mountains*, by Barbara Smith, has a short story in it called "Too Close for Comfort," with reference to an old house in Sandy City. Old-timers who live in Sandy could not confirm this story, but residents do remember a home by the cemetery that was empty for years and was considered the town's haunted house. Either when Ninetieth South was expanded or even long before that, the old house located to the west of the cemetery vanished. According to this story, before this Sandy home was torn down, residents experienced doors slamming and cupboards opening by themselves. When anyone tried to watch a show, the television turned off and on by itself. Even though the owners kept quiet about their experiences, according to the accounts I heard, the house's reputation was well known around the town. City workers refused to enter it, and neighborhood children constantly passed by in hopes of seeing a ghost.

Apparently, after this home was demolished, when the road on Ninetieth South was being widened, crews excavating the area found a grave and its marker buried under the house's location next to the cemetery. When I asked other old-timers at the museum, I got a different version—a much older story—concerning this event. In this tale, everyone knew that the man had murdered his wife and gotten away with it. The man eventually died of old age and was buried in the Sandy Cemetery. The townspeople were so irate at this man getting away with his crime that some of its citizens went into the cemetery in the dead of night, dug up his coffin, and transported it outside the cemetery gates and reburied it there, thinking that he would no longer be buried in hallowed ground and therefore couldn't get to heaven. No one seemed to know what decade or era this was, but several people knew the story. Another version, which turned out to be entirely false, was that when Seventh East was widened some time ago, they covered part of the cemetery. The city offered the families a chance to move their relatives' remains, but not every body was claimed. Actually, the newly widened street didn't even touch the cemetery's boundaries, but it is true that at least one man is buried under Seventh East.

Maybe this is the man the citizens of Sandy buried outside the gates for his sins, or even some other man whose story may never be told. The man, whoever he is, will probably never be found. His spirit is probably still trying to get in the gates of the cemetery, or perhaps now his apparition is free to roam wherever he wishes. So who is this second man buried under the old house to the west of the cemetery? With this old house gone now, is there still a grave there, or was their ever one in the first place? Could more than one grave be outside the bounds of this graveyard, even though the Indian burial site was to the west of the cemetery? Or is this never-found burial place an ancient Indian grave instead?

Settlers started the Sandy Cemetery in 1873 when a man named Allsop donated two acres for this purpose. The north part of the land had originally been a burial place for local desert Utes who lived along the Jordan River. The Utes had made caves in the sand banks for homes, and some Paiutes also lived among them. The white settlers called them the "Yo-No's," and they were very poor. They told fortunes for money, wore colorful beads, begged for supplies from the people of Sandy, and lived off rabbits, squirrels, birds, fish from the river, and crickets and grasshoppers. A wealthier band of Utes also used the land as a burial ground and lived nearby on Flat Iron Mesa. Their chief, nicknamed "Big John" by the whites, lost his first wife, and she was the first person to be buried at the foot of Flat Iron Hill near the present-day Sandy Cemetery. This tribe lived in wickiups and hunted and fished for food. Much later, one aged citizen of Sandy remembered going with his father and some other men in 1927 to meet with the present chiefs of these tribes to negotiate with them to obtain the land on the south side of the cemetery for the citizens of Sandy.

Up until this time, the LDS Church had owned the property, but in 1927, the city of Sandy took over the operation of the cemetery. Burial plots when the LDS Church owned the property were only ten dollars apiece. All sorts of improvements were made in the late 1920s. Grass was planted for the first time, and the huge trees that line the cemetery now were planted. One of the planters, who was a child at the time, is now a Sandy octogenarian. A full-time sexton was employed in 1929, and an office and tool house were located at the west end of the cemetery. A long line of sextons oversaw the business of "perpetual care" for years, and while the office and tool house are long gone now, the cemetery continues to have a few burials in full view of the two busy streets that surround it. There is no longer a sexton for the cemetery, and Sandy City employees take care of the cemetery's lawns.

Ghost hunters who have visited the Sandy Cemetery consider it quite an "active" one, as well as the most ominous cemetery in the city. They have recorded several words and phrases, many the comments being quite hostile toward visitors. The ghost busters who have gone to the Sandy Cemetery all agree that there is a malevolent force pervading its ground. I have a friend whose parents are buried there, and I was joking with her about this. She said that this made her worry that her long-gone parents, along with the other good folk buried there, might need protection. This malevolence may have something to do with the colorful history of the cemetery, with quite a dark period of mining camp followers who are buried there. It seems that at least a dozen or so persons buried there were probably pretty unsavory characters. The negative energy in the place has provided some of the clearest EVP recordings ever, and the ghost hunters warn others to watch what is said in such a place, because quite often you will get responses, wanted or not. Ghost hunters believe strongly that spirits do interact with the living and are not just pictures or energies from the past. When you enter such a place, be careful and respectful. The ghost hunters have gone to other cemeteries where the feeling was one of "Come back!" or "Visit again!" But at the Sandy one, they have recorded warning messages and quite blunt requests to leave, with one ghost hunter actually being pushed out of the cemetery gates by an unseen force.

The Sandy Cemetery is still an active cemetery and is not hidden at all but very exposed, as anyone driving on Seventh East or Ninetieth South can attest. It is easy to get to but seems to be well taken care of and guarded. It might also be important to mention that there have been reports of haunted houses near this cemetery, the older ones being built when Sandy was a mining and smelting town. There are stories of hauntings in the old houses around this cemetery, both those torn down and those still present, that one wonders if the hauntings are merely residue images of the original town, or active, ghostly residents of the cemetery out on a lark in the area. Local teens may just be pulling pranks, but there is no evidence of vandalism anywhere in the vicinity. Last, there are the old Ute and Paiute spirits wandering around the area, probably a much wider area than the cemetery itself.

When one ghost hunter group asked if anyone was there, the response was "Watch what you say." When one of the ghost hunters made a comment about a man's polygamous wives buried around him, there was no response, yet when they played back the tape later, it said right after the hunter's comment: "You –itch!" I have listened to hundreds of EVP recordings and feel that at least 50 percent of them are so unclear that absolutely no one would agree that anyone was saying anything. Another 25 percent seem clear enough to be a voice, but what is interpreted as the word or phrases spoken is quite questionable. The remaining 25 percent are very clear and say exactly what the interpreters say they do. These recordings are the ones that make you wonder, especially since the whole tape can be heard, and you can hear the living person talking while a voice appears to be answering every comment they make with one of its own. I would guess that many of EVP tapings are faked, but a small percent are real. The question then is, from where are the voices coming? Are they coming from the people buried in the graveyard or from the minds of those visiting there? Someday we will know the answers to all these questions and will chuckle at how oblivious people were then.[1]

One story I ran across might help explain this ominous feeling in the graveyard. Apparently, there was a period of time when the Ku Klux Klan was quite active in Sandy, reaching its peak across the country in about 1925. In 1915 the Klan experienced a short decade or two of insurgence or revivalism. This new Klan was organizing all over the country but especially with unions such as the carpentry and miner's unions out west. My father's favorite story about the Klan happened in the 1920s when his family moved from Magna, Utah, where my grandfather was a carpenter at the Magna Smelter, to Pocatello, Idaho. One day his father came home and told everyone to get dressed up since they were going to a picnic. Grandpa drove them out to a grassy valley. My father's dad left them all in the car and went down to check things out. A little while later, my grandfather came back quite red in the face. He slammed the car door and they drove off, without going to the picnic. This was my father's one family experience with the Klan. My grandfather never again mentioned how he had been taken in by a racist organization.

In 1921 a group of anti-Mormons, Masons, and non-Mormon businessmen started the Salt Lake City Klavern No. 1, but local newspapers and Mormon Church leaders soon squashed it. Another chapter soon followed in Ogden in 1923, formed by anti-Catholic Baptists. A nationwide membership campaign in 1924 and 1925 brought about members in at least ten Utah counties. The Klan became most active in Ogden, Logan, Provo, and in two predominately mining towns, Helper and Price. While the Klan mainly advocated white supremacy, Protestantism, and being 100 percent "American," some members also advocated violence and hatred. Cross burning, outdoor initiations (picnics), parades, and other covert acts of intimidation have always been their trademarks. The Salt Lake City chapter had a women's auxiliary and hosted regional meetings. Only two documented violent incidents took place in Utah during this brief resurgence. One individual was an Italian man in Carbon County who had a heart attack while being chased, and another was a black man who was lynched by a mob. The original dramatic entrance into Utah during this membership campaign involved lots of organizing in the Bingham, Magna, and Midvale areas, where the main mining and smelting mills were located. Sandy men worked in the Midvale smelters and mines all around the valley.

The Klan's 1925 parade into Salt Lake Valley also included a series of events involving Ensign Peak. The Klansmen raised a fiery cross on the hillside above them and then opened their state convention. They set up fiery crosses all around the valley during the April LDS general conference and gathered around altars while sentries guarded their automobiles. The firelight cast an eerie glow all over the city. Thousands of people watched the spectacle, and the Klan pronounced it a great success. A group of Greek children in Magna unmasked several important townspeople as they paraded through their streets. City commissions passed ordinances banning the wearing of masks in public in hopes of curbing the KKK. That Christmas all the Santa Clauses and their male helpers were hit by the ban as well, and little children had to visit Santa minus his beard. The LDS Church issued strong anti-Klan statements and told members not to join the racist group. The immigrant populations in the mining towns were too large and powerful to allow this kind of community discord. By the late 1920s, only a handful of members remained.[2]

The first public presence of the Ku Klux Klan in Utah happened on April 19, 1922, in the Sandy City Cemetery. The Klan was trying to improve its image, so members attended a murdered policeman's funeral and began donating to charitable causes. In their book, *Riverton: The Story of a Utah County Town*, Melvin L. Bashore and Scott Crump say the following about the Klan:

> It was at the funeral of a young Salt Lake County deputy, Gordon Stuart, who had died in the line of duty. Nearly five hundred mourners were shocked to see eight or nine Klansmen in full regalia appear during graveside services. They formed a human cross and approached the casket. They placed on it a "cross of lilies," bedecked with a banner inscribed "Knights of the Klu Klux Klan, Salt Lake Chapter No.1" and then turned to the west, raised their left hands toward the sun, and hurried silently toward idling automobiles chauffeured by their fellow Klansmen.[3]

While the young officer had or did not have a connection to the Klan, it does make one wonder if some of the policemen in these then small towns didn't have a connection of some kind!

A Mayor's Story—The Young Man on a Board

On a lighter note, this wonderful story about Sandy concerns the life of a first-celebrated town citizen. I consider this Sandy's best ghost story from the early settlement days.

With tears in his eyes, the former mayor Noal Bateman told this miraculous story to me, even though a century had passed since the events occurred. A story like this could be at the real heart of any small town's history, but as long as it is not recorded, it exists only in the minds and hearts of those remembering it. Many father-son and father-daughter stories are in books and on film. They tell of redemption or loss, or even awakenings, and they share one common theme—that of redemption, reawakening, and finding one's "field of dreams" in life.

As I stood in the little Sandy Museum that day, listening to the mayor's story about his father, I found this true story even more moving, though it is certainly less dramatic than in the movies. It was a story of a boy's journey to manhood and the father who taught him faith, hope, generosity, and strength. *It is indeed a ghost story*, I thought as I gazed at the 1917 photograph of this man's father in his wheelchair in front of his hay and feed store and coal yard.

I was the one who started the conversation when I asked the ninety-three-year-old man if his father had been an invalid and how he had gotten that way. It was a ghost story that I was meant to write, or I never would have heard it. It is George Bateman's story, told by his son Noal as the two of us sat before a poster-sized photograph of a young man in a wheelchair. As Noal told his story, the young man stared back at us as though he were there with us. Interviews and conversations about this "boy" and his father followed our first meeting. It was something that was meant to be.

In the late 1800s and early 1900s, many people believed in magic, healers, fortunes, and herbal cures. During this era in Utah, the current prophet of the LDS Church, Brigham Young, set the tone by not trusting doctors. He encouraged herbalists, healers, and midwives as an alternative to seeking help from the medical profession. There were few doctors this far west at the time anyway. Later on, several sons and daughters of Brigham Young became physicians, and Brigham Young himself was attended by at least three doctors in his last years. But during this transitional time, there were also members of the LDS Church who traveled about performing healings. They supposedly used wood from Joseph Smith's coffin and pieces of a cape, canes, and handkerchiefs that had belonged to Brigham Young.[4, 5]

The LDS Church at first sanctioned those members who seemed to have healing gifts, but after the turn-of-the-century, healings and washings and anointings were less prevalent among the lay members. Healings became the duties of those in leadership, and by the 1920s, while lay members continued this practice, they were neither sanctioned by their church nor discouraged from practicing. Priesthood holders of the Church did perform blessings and what they called the laying on of hands to help heal their members. As late as the 1930s and 1940s, members of the Church who had special healing gifts continued to move from community to community performing healings.

Other people in the late 1800s and early 1900s traveled as healers. They may or may not have helped people with cures or remedies to ease their aches and pains. Sandy had two such visitors who came regularly to the community. The first visitor was a white "medicine man" named Dick Lorenzo. He visited the town at least four times a year, bringing with him remedies for colds, rheumatism, scarlet fever, and anything else people had. He would stand at the back of his wagon and entertain the children by balancing a wagon wheel on his chin or a feather on his nose. He had an old organ, and his wife played while he sang popular songs. He had a good singing voice and was known as Sandy's "Kickapoo Man." The controversy continued about whether belief in his cures restored good health to those who used them, or if the cures themselves worked miracles. There were folk medicines that did work and have been transformed into modern medical cures under different combinations and names. Instead of poultices and concoctions, we now have plant-based and synthetic pills that the powerful pharmaceutical companies peddle through the mass media instead of from the back of a wagon.

The other man was nicknamed "Five Drop" Petersen. He was a local man who concocted his own brew to cure all manner of things. You only needed five drops of the magic liquid to cure anything, thus the name "Five Drop." People swore by his cure, even though it is well known that such cures often had a bit of liquor added to them. His tonics eased aches and pains but did not cure anything. There were herbal remedies which did work, and after all, much of our modern medicine comes from plants in the rain forests of the world, not much different from the plants that the Native American medicine men have used for decades. The differences are only in the presentation and packaging of these remedies, but medical people would argue that their remedies have been tested more thoroughly. But back in those days, these remedies were done simply by trial and error and then if they worked they were advertised by word-of-mouth. "Five Drop" Petersen apparently helped cure quite a few people with his special brew.

In addition to these two healers, Indian fortune-tellers came around to get payment or to barter for their fortune-telling, especially at Christmastime when people were feeling generous. In the summertime, the gypsies would pass through town and either bless your money or tell your fortune, along with offering another kind of solace to the tough times people were having even before the Great Depression.

Last were the traveling healers, who brought with them both hope and spiritual advisement, along with their healing gifts. Without doctors in the early days, midwives went out into the rural communities and helped bring hundreds of babies into the world while performing minor surgeries and sometimes even major ones, along with offering dental services. Later, when doctors made rural visits, the healers were still called upon when no hope could be given by the medical profession. Even today, having been a teacher of severely handicapped children, I do have a special understanding of the desperation that parents and loved ones feel when the medical profession can no longer offer any hope for a cure, or anything that will ease someone's suffering. My memories of those experiences taught me a lot about not only the process of dying but also how powerful belief in healing and acceptance of one's fate can be.

When he pointed out his father in front of his store, I asked Noal if he had been an invalid. I apparently hit on a chord of memories which came rushing back to him, and the story spilled forth. His grandparents had come from Brigham City with his grandfather's two brothers to settle land on the west side of the Jordan River. They eventually built a large house there for themselves and their thirteen children. His grandfather and his boys hauled ore from Bingham to Welby, and his grandmother, after completing her morning chores every day, made fifty pounds of butter to go with the eggs, fruits, and vegetables that they would sell in Salt Lake City once a week. His grandmother developed gallstones from the hard drinking water, so the family moved to the east side of the valley to Sandy, Utah, to get fresh mountain water. They bought a farm there and turned over their other land by the old Gardner Mill to their sons to work. They continued to have a large fruit orchard, a herd of sheep, cattle, and horses while their sons worked the land in West Jordan.

Noal Bateman's grandmother was well known in the area for feeding a free meal to transient miners in Sandy. His grandfather ran a hay, grain, and feed store in Sandy and also kept a coal yard. His boys operated a steam threshing machine to work on the western range. One of his sons, the former mayor's father, hauled coal to the thresher from the coal yard. The year was 1912, and his twenty-five-year-old father with a wife and family of three already had a lot of responsibility. According to Roxie Rich, George Bateman was seriously injured when he was crushed by a load of coal. Rich says the following in his book, *A History of Sandy City*:

> George was hauling coal to the thresher from a coal yard across the road from the West Jordan Flour Mill. The pile of coal was at a lower elevation than the road. He got his load on a flatbed rack wagon. Then he had to make a circular turn to get up on the road. The turn was a little too short, and the right hind wheel sank down. There were some ties in a pile. He took one, thinking he could brace the load. Just as he approached the load, the whole thing came down and crushed him under the coal. He was never able to walk after that. After a few months, when George was able to handle his wheelchair, his father turned the business store and coal yard over to him. He not only managed the business, but he was also in charge of the tree spraying in the south half of the county. He also held city jobs for Sandy City.[6]

The whole extended family was close, and George was a positive person. People who visited him to offer sympathy would go away feeling less sorry for themselves. His wife and three children were strong. They loved each other dearly. Always in terrific pain, George still remained cheerful, as did his wife and children. The extended family took trips together, such as an annual visit to Yellowstone National Park.

Also from Rich's *History of Sandy City*: "To keep the bears out, George always insisted on sleeping next to the opening of the tent. We carried him down the 368 steps to the bottom of the canyon below the falls."[7] One of his sons took over as city treasurer with his father who could no longer handle the job. His son, Noal, later became a city councilman and eventually the mayor in 1954.

But this is the official story and not the true one told to me that day by an old man remembering his father. George had transformed into the cheerful and generous man in Roxie Rich's account of the accident for a reason not told about in her book. For almost a whole year after the accident, George laid flat on a board in excruciating pain. He was unable to sit up or even move, and family members, who knew nothing could be done, prayed for George to be delivered from this life to a better one in the hereafter.

One day George's wife piled her children into a wagon and headed to Springville. (The mayor was four years old at the time, too young to remember. His mother later told him the story.) She had heard of a traveling LDS healer named Brother Hall, who was visiting in the Springville area, and she was eager to try anything that might help to lessen some of her young husband's constant pain and suffering.

Brother Hall stood six-foot-six-inches tall and was a powerfully built man who had come to Springville to heal a little girl of her clubfeet. George's wife watched as a little girl's feet and legs were straightened out and little girl could stand up and walk properly. Afterward, George's wife invited the healer to come to their home to see what he could do for George. By this time George weighed only about 125 pounds, and his emaciated and pain-racked body had certainly not allowed him to be cheerful or even desirous of being in this world. Brother Hall assessed the situation and then sat down with the family to talk with them. He instructed George's wife in some methods to ease the pain, and then in the administration of some herbal remedies. He told the children to heed his advice.

"I want you to take turns rubbing your father's legs. This is something you must do for as long as your father lives."

Noal, with tears welling in his eyes, turned to me and said, "You know, from then on our father's legs were as pink and healthy as a baby's."

Then this giant of a man stood up on something high, lifted Noal's father up in the air, and suddenly dropped him, jumping down just as quickly to break his fall. Whatever Brother Hall did popped George's spine back into place, and the next morning, Noal's father was in a lot less pain and could sit up for the first time in months. Soon he was able to manage a wheelchair, but most important, his whole attitude changed, as did that of his family, having at long last been given hope.

Noal Bateman's father lived to be fifty-two years old and had a full and active life. I asked the mayor if his father was still in pain after Brother Hall helped him, and Noal said that he was, but the pain was cut in half. They were also able to find remedies and physical exercises to help to reduce the rest of the pain.

George Bateman went on to hold city positions, including being on the town council, and his store became the gathering place for the town. George seemed to know what to do and where to find things and what was needed to get the job done. He eventually became an unofficial leader of the town.

Noal can remember driving his father all the way to Elko, Nevada, when Noal was only twelve years old, to pick up the six-foot pine trees that were to be planted in the Sandy Cemetery. Along Seventh East today, this break of pines towers dozens of feet over the streets around it, and a little memorial dedicated to Noal's father stands in front of the cemetery.

Throughout his years on earth, George Bateman continued to deal with a lot of pain. Several years later, the full force of the pain returned, and he was bedridden again. This time the family went to a young doctor in town and asked him for help. Being young and confident, the doctor said that he thought he could help. He operated on George's legs in the back of George's feed store and severed several of his tendons. This reduced the pain, and George was able to live several more years with tolerable amounts of pain.

Later, in the last years of his life, when the pain returned full force again, the family sought out the same doctor who was now a famous surgeon in Salt Lake City. The doctor apologized to the family and to George, saying that he had been young and foolish and could easily have killed George by performing the operation. He said that he could not help George now, and there was nothing to be done. No amount of healing, prayers, or medical expertise at that time could help his condition, and George Bateman died at home with his family and brother by his side. He lived twenty-seven years longer than anyone might have expected. He left behind several children and grandchildren and a wonderful legacy to the town of Sandy. His son Noal went on to serve in city positions, including several terms as mayor. Both George and Noal lived in Sandy all their lives. At ninety-three, Noal Bateman saw the value of having his father's "ghost" story told, however briefly, in this book.

As a ghost researcher and story collector, I find that the apparitions and ghosts are nearly always interwoven into the landscape from which they come. As an intuitive person, I also know that hauntings are not as rare as people think, and few are negative. Even as I interviewed Mr. Bateman in his home, there were signs of his recently departed wife all around me in the flickering lights and in the very atmosphere of the home. Perhaps his father was there too as his story unfolded around me. I wondered at the time that if I visited the Sandy Museum after this book came out, would George Bateman also give me a sign of his approval or sanctioning for the little I told of his story? Would he acknowledge my efforts in some way, such as the flicker of a light or a light breeze? I hope he will be pleased. I read in the paper about Noal Bateman's death and was saddened to think that he would not get a chance to read it in print. I'm sure there was a reason for this as well.

After two interview sessions, lots and lots of phone calls from Noal, and a lot of hard work on my part to get the story just right and to make sure he understood what kind of book it was going to be, Noal called me one day and told me that I could not use the story. I was quite surprised but knew that I had to honor his wishes. I dropped off all the tapes and the story to him. I pulled the mayor's story out of my Sandy piece. A year went by, and then one day on my answering machine I received what sounded like a desperate message. Mr. Bateman was in tears. I called him, and he apologized to me for having been so rude. When he asked me to pull it, he had just had a stroke and wasn't in his right mind. He was confused and thought the story was about him instead of his father. He said at the time that too many stories had been written about him already, and he didn't want any more done on him. He had never read my story. He found the copy while going through his papers and read it. It was wonderful, he said. He also said that his children had been angry with him for not allowing the story to go in the book. He was desperate and wanted to know if there was still time to put it in. My book didn't have a publisher at the time. I assured him that no matter what, his father's story would never be cut from my book.

I always think about Noal and his father's story when I drive past the Sandy Cemetery on Seventh East. I look at the huge pine trees that they planted together. I think about the silent grave I am driving over on that street and realize that George and his son Noal are now buried together inside the cemetery. I am haunted by their stories and dozens of others, such as all the lost stories from people in the past, those who were never fortunate enough to have their lives written down.

I remember being in a shop one summer in Cripple Creek, Colorado, before the town became a tourist center. I remember looking down at baskets and baskets of old 1800 photographs. When I asked the shop owner where they had come from, she said that she had purchased them in bulk and had no idea who any of them were. It haunts me still today as I remember the photographs of all those people whose stories are lost. I think, *Who were they and what happened to them?* They must have had family, people who cared about them. How could all those stories be lost forever? I profoundly feel a deep desire to preserve as many people's experiences as I can. They were all "ghost" stories as far as I was concerned.

Millcreek, Murray, Kearns, and Magna Haunts

The Cranky Cowboy of Cassady's Bar

No one seems to know just when the building on Thirty-third South was built, and several other bars occupied it before Cassady's Bar. In the late 1960s it was the Celebrities Club, and then in the 1970s it was a disco place. After that, the bar changed hands several times, going from Fire and Ice to the California Club and then the Million Dollar Saloon, which was a strip club. After this, the building housed Life of Riley and then City Limits. It finally became Cassady's. At some point in the history of the building, the bartender says there was a shooting in the parking lot where a guy died. One thing is for certain, the current owners say their ghost has been in the building for a long time.

Two previous owners had experiences with the resident ghost, and the former owners told those who wanted to buy the bar that it housed a ghost. The Celebrities Club was the first bar in the brand-new building on land that no one thinks ever had anything on it before. Several people are certain that the ghost established himself there sometime after the first club was opened. Some think he could be associated with the parking lot shooting, although this was a much later event. Most people think he was probably a customer who hung out at the bar from its beginnings, and after he died, he decided never to leave the place. Old-timers remember his presence there being discussed from as far back as they can remember.

One area near the bar seems to remain conspicuously different in feeling and temperature. People who happen to be in this area get the chills even when there is no air conditioner running in the heat of the summer. The ghost is most active between eleven o'clock in the morning and one o'clock in the afternoon. Closing time is another active period. Former owners always warn the new owners about "Jack," as they've come to call him. Apparently the apparition comes with the property. Former owners have seen Jack in the bar a lot. He is dressed like a cowboy, and his outfit seems to resemble someone from the late 1950s or early 1960s.

While patrons, employees, and even ghost hunters have pictures of orbs or light streaks on their film, Jack is not a "static" ghost, only an interactive one. The last owners saw a tall, thin man in cowboy clothes and a black cowboy hat, and they describe him as having a weathered face. One former employee claimed to have seen Jack sitting in a booth on more than one occasion. Several people have reported hearing someone playing pinball in the early morning when the machines were turned off and no one was in the bar.

The present owners had so much poltergeist activity directed negatively at their adult son that they called in a psychic to help them. This generated enough publicity that the bar ended up being on a television news spot around Halloween. Before they called in the psychic, the owners had experienced several things going on in the bar. The activity started with people claiming to feel two strong hands shoving them off their bar stools, and then their five-year-old grandson began reporting that he had seen "the cowboy," as he calls him. Patrons also reported having their hair yanked on the back of their neck when there wasn't any one standing behind them. These were not gentle yanks, but a good, hard pull that hurt. It ceased to be funny when their dog barked at the air and ran away to hide, and when a customer thought he had been kicked. Another patron was pushed so hard that he nearly fell off the bar stool. Finally two strong—but invisible—hands pushed their son so violently to the floor that it nearly knocked him out.

The phenomena began increasing when the ghost began aiming all of his attentions at the owner's son. Glasses started flying off the glass rack, sometimes hurtling forward and smashing on the floor at their son's feet—or literally almost hitting him. Finally, one of these glasses narrowly missed him, but there were more deadly attentions soon to come. One night he was shutting off all the machines, and two strong hands shoved him onto the ground from behind and held him down for what seemed like several minutes. The owner's son is a big guy and not easily shoved. Finally, a fifty-pound "smoker" flew forward and hit him so hard that he had to have stitches.

The owner and her son decided to call a psychic for help. The psychic came late in the evening and confirmed some things, such as them calling the apparition "Jack" and what others had said he looked like. She was not given a description of the ghost before she told them what he looked like. This confirmed the descriptions of the apparition that others had given them. The psychic then asked the apparition to stop his cantankerous activity, and for a while after this, there was no more activity at the bar from cowboy Jack. Of late, things have started up again and around Halloween caught the attention of local television reporters and a few ghost hunters. Something interesting that the psychic mentioned was that the ghost said the owner's son reminded him of his own little brother. The apparition must have either really disliked this brother or simply liked to tease him unmercilessly.

Of late, Jack continues his interactive activities, just as he has done for several decades. No one seems to know where he came from or why he so stubbornly stays in the building that has always been a bar of one kind or another. Perhaps one of these bars was a cowboy bar, and Jack was a regular customer then. Or perhaps he was a nearby rancher or farmer before the building was there. More likely, he had some great attachment to one of these bars, or perhaps to the bartender or landlord of one of them. He may have simply been a patron who, when he died, had no other place to go.

One former owner reported to have actually seen Jack moving around in the bar, and he gave a description of Jack similar to that given by others. The mystery to the present owners is why Jack is directing most of his negative attentions toward their son. Perhaps Jack is one of those confrontational spirits with a little bit of testosterone, who likes to pick fights at bars with the most burly guys in the place. One way to find out if this is the case is to find long-time patrons or employees who could confirm the same kind of activity directed toward another burly guy in the past.

Cassady's became a bit famous after a Halloween ghost spot on television, which helped the little bar out considerably. Quite a few people then wanted to visit the place to meet the resident ghost. Cassady's still retains its low profile and regular clientele. The bar's notoriety grew to the point where more than once a local rock radio station broadcast their morning show from the bar, and a local television station broadcast their story on Halloween. Perhaps this will become a tradition!

Murray's Haunted Mansions, Homes, and Schools

Murray, Midvale, and Sandy were all separate small mining and smelting towns during the industrial era. Now all three are suburbs of Salt Lake City. Each of the three towns has its own set of ghost stories to tell from their mining and smelting days. All three are considered haunted areas in the Salt Lake valley. Midvale's stories never seem to make the national ghost books, but Sandy's and Murray's ghost stories can be found in several books and on a lot of websites. The authors often neglect to give the background information on the mines and smelters that once existed in these areas. As the industrial era waned, this melting pot of people, with various immigrant nationalities spread out to different parts of the valley, became Mormon-dominated, but Spanish-speaking people now dominate Midvale. Murray still has a melting pot of people with various ethnic and religious backgrounds, and Midvale also has its ethnic nationalities. Sandy, on the other hand, has become a homogeneous middle class suburban sprawl.

Among the intriguing stories of hauntings from Murray—besides those about schools, the park, the cemetery, and the area around the smokestacks, which is now a huge shopping complex and hospital—are also stories of individual homes. More than one ghost hunter group has been to the Murray Cemetery and also to the old smelter buildings before they were torn down, as well as answering calls from private citizens who are having a lot of unexplained activity in their older homes. The location of the old Franklyn Smelter seems to have a lot of activity, as does one older mansion located in the Murray area. Hauntings have been reported at newer buildings, such as Union Middle School and Grant Elementary School. A private mansion that was reported to be haunted was once an old nursing home, and current residents are claiming that there is a ghost in their house.

There's also another older home in Murray that was built at the turn of the century and was later used as a place for pregnant, unwed teenagers. Stories have been told for years of illegal abortions performed in the house, as well as of babies buried in the backyard or under the house. Odd phenomena occurred in the house while the previous owners lived there, and they always felt it was connected to these young women's traumas, as well as to the deaths in the house of little unborn souls. The abortions might have been mere rumors, but the mansion did serve as an unwed mothers' home from the 1920s to the early 1940s. When the home became a private residence again, unusual phenomena were reported, such as young girls crying, babies crying, footsteps, shadows, voices, or even whole ghostly conversations. For obvious reasons, these private homes must remain anonymous.

The sixty-year-old mansion that was once an old nursing home has a smaller home built in front of it where the current owners claim to be experiencing ghostly activity. Phenomenon reported in the larger mansion include a little girl ghost who walks up and down the halls, moves things in the rooms, makes a rocking chair rock, and also plays with the owner's pets making them agitated. The activity in the larger home seems to have gradually moved into the smaller home too. The owners of both homes have reported footsteps and shadows coming down the stairs. An apparition of a little girl's shoulders and head has been seen floating in the air. There is a large bow on the top of her head, which makes the residents think that she comes from the time that the house was first built. The owners have also heard sounds of a cash register or Nintendo. Sometimes the TV, VCR, or Nintendo games have been left on all night or turned on early in the morning when nobody was there to do it.

Students report dark shadows running across hallways at Union Middle School, as well as the usual haunting phenomena, such as footsteps, lights going on and off, strange unidentifiable sounds, and doors opening and closing by themselves.

A more modern ghost has been reported at Grant Elementary School. It seems a particular band teacher at the school died in a car accident on the way to his job one morning. He is heard playing the piano in the cafeteria-auditorium. People have heard this piano playing not only in the evening, but also in broad daylight when no one was in the room.

As for Murray Park, nothing specific as ever been reported, but many people who go there feel a dark energy that bothers them while they are in the rather large park.

The most interesting story from Murray is about a small late-1890s house built by a man named Tobias Gibbs. In 1968 the story received some local publicity when a famous ghost investigator and local radio talk show host attended a séance in the house's attic. The house was built on solid rock and had no basement. A nine- by fifteen-foot room comprised the attic space. Since there is no room for a staircase, you must get to the attic room by going through a three-by-five-foot hole in the bathroom ceiling. A rope is pulled down through the hole with a noose or stirrup tied on the end of it. You place one foot in this noose and then swing up through the hole into the attic room, a tremendously inconvenient way to get anywhere—and rather dangerous too. From the HauntedHouses.com website:

> Next to this hot, little attic room was the furnace and storage room, which had a rather odd entrance, located 39 inches up the wall in the attic room. One has to step on a chair, and/or hang onto a rope, which hangs down from the rafters, to reach the crawl-through hole, 30 inches square, to reach the entrance to this furnace/storage room.[8]

Eventually, the new owners learned that the original owner of the house had not committed suicide, in spite of appearances and the neighborhood story that the man's body had been found hanging from the attic rope, with his body dangling down through the hole in the ceiling of the bathroom. Tobias was a young man who had recently gotten married, and he and his wife had purchased this little piece of land on which to build a house. After the house was built, Tobias tried to dig a basement. Discovering the solid rock foundation, he realized he would have to build an attic for storage space in the house. Instead of building a ladder to the attic, which was obviously added much later, he tied a rope to the rafters with a noose on the end so that he could use it to get into the furnace room in the attic.

The new owners knew there had been a death in the house, because Tobias's grandson James Gibbs, who sold it to them, had told them the story of Tobias's suicide. It was the new owners who solved the mystery about his death that had puzzled people for years. Why would such a young man, just recently married and seemingly content in every way, suddenly commit suicide? Years after the event, the new owners proposed a new theory about Tobias's death. They said that Tobias, instead of purposely hanging himself as everyone had supposed, had come out of the furnace room, stepped down on some object that had collapsed under him and then fallen. When he fell his head slipped into the noose at the end of the rope, and he then fell through the attic hole, hanging himself accidentally. The owners of the home would have continued to believe the family suicide story, but for a series of events that the spirit in the house perpetrated in order to get their attention.

When the new owners moved in, they knew almost immediately that there was a ghost in the attic. Sounds, footsteps, and other odd things were disturbing their children. The mother was hearing strange noises in the attic constantly and found herself being touched by unseen hands when she was working in the kitchen or other rooms in the house. Then one night she woke up feeling something touch her leg, and when she looked up, she was sure she'd seen two eyes looking at her in the dark of her bedroom. She began trying to communicate with the ghost, and whenever she was alone in the house, she would call out to him to give her his name. Each time she did so, sounds would come from the attic. They were always the same—two sounds, one like an oboe and the other like a tuba. When put together, they sounded like "To-by" to her. The mother also investigated the history of the house, trying to find out as much she could about the previous owners.

James Gibbs, who sold them the house, told the family that his grandfather had built it. When they learned that James's grandfather's name was Tobias and it was he who had committed suicide in the house, they felt they had identified their ghost.

The owners eventually decided to go public with the activity in their home and in 1967 agreed to hold a séance, hoping to discover why Tobias was bothering them. Talk show host Tom Carlin and ghost investigator Douglas MacGregor brought some college students with them to do the investigation and séance. There were no electronic equipment malfunctions or temperature changes, but the talk show host was startled by one particular event.

> Douglas had given everyone . . . a sealed, foil package of 4 x 5 press camera Polaroid film, which Tom decided to sit on top of, to make sure no one tried any funny business with his film. During the séance, in the blazing hot attic room, Carlin felt cold chills around his neck and ears, which traveled down his back. After the séance, which had no true manifestations, McGregor checked all the film packages. All the film was blank, except Tom Carlin's, which gave the ominous warning, 'DANGER!' Then Carlin thought it was a poison pen letter, totally making him a believer, vowing never to go up in this attic again! He felt the ghost could stay up in the attic, and he would stay out.[9]

In May 1968 the mother's religious leaders completed an exorcism in the house. At the same time, she had a vision in which she saw the figure of a twenty-year-old man she now called Toby, with two white figures on either side of him. She assumed that the spirits or angels had come and taken Toby away for good, probably to heaven, and that her Mormon elders had eradicated the problem. But in October 1968, the mother awoke again in the middle of the night to see a young man sitting beside her on her bed. He spoke to her for the first time and said that his work was not done yet and promptly disappeared.

In December of that year, the mother was using a folding chair to check for Christmas decorations in the furnace and storage room. When she stepped back down onto the chair from the last ladder rung, the chair started to fold up on her feet. A strong, sharp voice told her in that instant, "Go with the chair!" So instead of jumping off the chair, what anyone would instinctively do, she followed the voice's advice and just let her body fall.

"After recovering from her fall, she realized that if she had jumped, she would've fallen through the entrance hole to the attic and would've been found dead on the bathroom floor. It was in the same instant that she realized this that she heard the young man's voice again, saying: 'That's how I died.' "

She understood two things then. Tobias had not committed suicide but had died from an accidental fall and consequent hanging. She also understood that the "DANGER!" scratched on the back of Tom Carlin's negatives had not been something to scare him out of the house but rather to warn him away from impending danger in the attic. It seems that Tobias had realized in the most ultimate way that he had inadvertently built a dangerous addition to his house and was trying to prevent anyone else from dying in the same manner he had. The owners of the home found a way to make this area of the house much safer, and when the renovations were completed, Tobias Gibbs seems to have retreated from haunting his own house. No more reports were ever published about the house. Perhaps Tobias had found peace.

The Malevolent Murray Cemetery

At the Murray Cemetery, ghost hunter groups have gotten intriguing EVP recordings. Ghost hunter groups have recorded such phrases as: "We could help," or, when asked if he could be seen, the ghost replied, "Yeah, I could." Other phrases recorded from the cemetery included such things as, "Help me," "Get it over," "Leave us alone," "Make it quick," and "Get out!" Ghost researchers say that the cemetery is very active and has a strong phenomenon all its own. It seems that the cemetery must be entered from the east in order to get clear recordings. Entering from the north, south, or west yields no recorded phrases at all on the tapes. But the northeast corner produces all kinds of recorded phrases every time the ghost enthusiasts go there. The ghost hunters say the force is negative, while those who buried their relatives there say this cemetery is just like any other cemetery in the valley.

Spirited Hijinks in Kearns

I found only one story about Kearns, which relates to the Kearns Junior High School. The students there report that over the past few years students have seen a family standing at the top of the main stairs in the building. Everyone agrees that there is a father, a mother, two girls, and one little boy staring down at the students as they pass by. No one describes what their clothing looks like, so no time period can be established. This is probably a story started by the students based on the scene in *The Sixth Sense* when the little boy goes to his school, glances up at the top of the stairs, and sees where the old gallows were located before the school was built there. One would have to research the area to see if anything was located on the property before the junior high was built, and this might help find out what really happened. Otherwise, the story is probably due to the active imaginations of the students.

Haunted Schools in Magna

Magna has some great stories because of its history with mining and smelting. There are old train and smelter stories, which I will tell in an upcoming book on the older history of Utah, as well as an old movie theatre whose story warrants a whole section in my future haunted arts book. I just want to mention a few stories about places in the town that people feel are haunted besides the old theatres and other places. There is a beautiful old stone Catholic church that is worth driving out to see, too.

The most famous haunt in Magna was the old Webster Elementary School. Ghost hunter groups had been out there several times. The old school managed to be still standing because it was fenced in on Kennecott Copper property. It sat in a sort of limbo state, deteriorating and yet not torn down. Over the years there had been discussions about what to do with it, including turning it into a town museum, but the company and the town did nothing with it. The stories revolved around spirit children who were supposedly heard screaming, laughing, and crying, even during the daylight hours. The way the building sat at the end of town behind a high fence with the open fields to the west did make it rather spooky. The ghost hunter groups got permission to explore the school, and in spite of the usual camera equipment failures, they were able to get not only dozens of EVP recordings, but also orbs and light streaks on their camcorders. They found the place fascinating, probably because it had been standing empty for fifty years or more, much longer than other haunted locations. Nothing was negative about the building, but sounds and sights remained within its walls for the ghost hunters to capture on film.

Jack Goodman, a columnist for the *Salt Lake Tribune,* wrote about the old Webster School when he was still alive. He hoped that something would be done with it. He said that the school was built in 1912 and was originally called the Magna Elementary School. It cost $13,512 to build and only had six classrooms at first. It was later called the Hayes Elementary School, and in 1922 it became the Webster School. Six more rooms were added at the time. By 1927, another six rooms were added, making a total of eighteen classrooms. In the 1950s it housed 20 teachers and 675 students. The new school was constructed by 1955, and the

Webster School was shut down, even though a brand-new gym and auditorium had just been added in 1953. A mining museum and then a county office space were discussed, and yet nothing ever came of the ideas. So the school sat idle for fifty years, not being torn down or restored.

If the school district had still owned it, the school would have been long gone and the property sold to put money into the coffers of the starving district. But since Kennecott Copper owned the land and the building, I wonder whether it had just been forgotten or someone was keeping it for sentimental reasons because they had attended school there. Its location would not have been prime commercial property for anyone, and its reputation for being haunted might continue even after its demise. Nearly all the windows were broken, and it stood three stories high, so it was a prime place for ghost hunters who wanted to explore an old abandoned school. Signs were posted all over the place, and it seemed to be well guarded by the neighborhood.

We visited this old school and it was intriguing. We took some photographs, intending to return because it was such an interesting building. Just days later, the Webster School was no more. I remember thinking as I watched the news that both the town of Magna and the Kennecott Copper Corporation should be ashamed of themselves for not doing something sooner with the building. On June 22, 2004, sometime after 5 AM, the Webster School was reported on fire. By the time the fire department got there, flames were shooting out of every window, and the roof and the interiors were gutted. Deemed a fire hazard with only the walls left standing, the following day the entire structure was demolished. Speculation was that it was either arson on the part of local teens, a transient trying to build a fire inside to cook, or even ecoterrorism. Another building had recently burned down, and this ecoterrorist group named Kennecott Copper Corporation as one of their three main targets. A smaller fire was started by a transient several months before the final fire, but that fire was contained. Three young men, twenty-six, eighteen, and seventeen, were arrested as the arsonists who destroyed the building. Investigators discovered that there were at least two points of origin for the fire in the building. The young men maintained that they were just playing around, but the fire investigators said that the fires were deliberately set in more than one area of the structure.

Any ghosts probably went down with the burned building, or did for sure with the wrecking ball. Once again I have to pay homage to Jack Goodman, who loved the old building along with other historical sites in the state, and I hope his paper will publish more of his articles now that he is gone. It would be a real tragedy to lose all of his research, stories, and drawings. As for the ghosts, perhaps they won't leave an empty field or the ruins of the old school. If something else is built there, which I doubt because of the area, maybe the new employees will hear the children laughing. And even Goodman might visit his favorite old buildings around the state, including the Webster School.

Opinions on the loss of the school varied from tears and whole families who had attended the school voicing their sorrow, to one woman who said it was about time the old building went since nothing was being done with it anyway and it was just an old eyesore. Kennecott Copper Corporation claimed that in only three more days they had intended to transfer the property to the housing authority so they could build low-cost housing. The town of Magna did not voice any real community opinions at all, except to say that it had been difficult to protect. When the building burned down, the townspeople came out to watch, and many of them were crying because they had gone to school there or knew someone else who had. The best comment and the one I agree with the most came from Ernie Colosimo, who owns Colosimo's Standard Market just down the street on Magna's Main Street. (His parents founded the market in the 1920s.) "A renovated building wouldn't have been the subject of kids playing around."[10]

Cyprus High School is the other haunted locale in Magna. It is still operating as a school and was constructed in 1910. At least two fires have erupted in the building over the years, and quite a bit of remodeling has been done. Everyone is certain that the auditorium is haunted, and ghosts have been spotted in other parts of the old building. The premier ghost is a man dressed in 1930s clothing, perhaps a teacher from an earlier time who did not want to leave. And the auditorium has all sorts of troubles with its electrical equipment. Stage lights go on and off all the time, and strangest of all are the bats whose nests have not been located and who fly through the auditorium during assemblies. I imagine that several student stories about this building exist, and having driven past the school, I can see why there would be stories. The school is definitely affected by the layer of history that came before it in this old mining and smelting town.

Ghost Builders of Riverton and Herriman

Many of the first settlers in Riverton, Utah, came from Denmark and other Scandinavian countries. They lived in dugouts and log cabins on the bottomlands of the Jordan River and watched the fog and mist rise up from the river where Native Americans had stopped to camp and bath in the healing waters of the nearby hot springs. Archibald Gardner, the man who built several mills in Canada and the Salt Lake Valley, was one of the first settlers and dubbed the town Gardnersville. Archibald later moved to West Jordan where he built several more mills, married many wives, and left a series of ghosts behind him.

The settlement of Gardnersville stayed small until around 1876 when South Jordan Canal was opened, bringing more water to the area for farming. Another canal called the Utah and Salt Lake Canal was completed in 1881. Earlier, in 1867, Gardnersville became a part of the South Jordan Precinct. In 1879, with a judicial precinct and more than one hundred people in the settlement, the town changed its name to Riverton.

Early Mormons in Riverton met in each other's homes for educational, cultural, and religious meetings and formed an LDS branch in 1870. In 1886

Riverton formed its first LDS ward and built a meetinghouse for school and church functions. (A ward is like a parish, and several wards make up a stake.) The church building was completed in 1879. By 1900, there were about five hundred people living in Riverton, and by 1908, construction began on the domed meetinghouse designed by a locally famous and creative architect named Richard Kletting.

The commercial building on the corner of Riverton's main intersection had two floors and a round turret on the corner of the upper floor. A barbershop, a beauty parlor, a post office, and several notions stores were housed inside the building. The commercial building was never used as a church, but the downstairs rooms were used as a primary grade school for a few years. On the second floor of the building was a large auditorium and stage where plays and other programs were presented. The second floor was also used as a roller skating rink. Sadly, the domed meetinghouse was demolished in 1940. A story about the haunted stage area still exists that was told in the community over the years by old-timers.

Riverton Elementary School

Modern and historical ghost stories about the old Riverton elementary school seem to have merged into each other over time. There are also stories about the Crane Museum, both when it was located on Redwood Road and then when it was moved to its new location close to the town's original cemetery. As a descendant of the tall, red-headed Cranes, who were founders of the area, I find these stories fascinating, because ghost hunters never think of meeting their own ancestors at the cemetery where they were buried or in a house where they lived. But Riverton has a fascinating history even without any ghost stories. Robbers, lost treasures, haunted houses, the KKK, and the apparition of a matriarch of the town all add to the mystique of Riverton.

For decades children were afraid of the ghost that lived on the stage of the old playhouse. Chairs would tip as though pushed by invisible hands. Lights would go on and off when no one touched the switch. The scariest occurrences were when the curtains surrounding the old stage blew way out when no one was behind them and no wind or air current could have powered them. Once a human hand and arm formed behind the curtains, and when people quickly investigated the other side of the curtains, no one was there. Whoever the ghost was, the apparition went down with the building, and the people at the café that replaced it haven't reported any strange incidents since the new building was built.

In 1879 a one-room school house was constructed, and in 1892, a more permanent two-story brick school house, the Riverton Elementary School, was built on Redwood Road. In the 1920s, new elementary and junior high school buildings were constructed. After many years as a school building, the old Riverton Elementary underwent extensive renovation to ready it for use as a community center and city offices. In the past, the school also housed a Montessori school and dance and exercise classes. The town has grown fond of this old elementary school, especially since it is one of the last remaining historical sites in Riverton, but there are still those who want to see the old building come down. Recently there was a fight going on to keep the school as a community center, and a town bond passed with an overwhelming vote to keep and renovate Riverton Elementary School.

Ghost stories have been told about this school for years. The stories stopped when Riverton Elementary replaced its old boiler room downstairs with new gas furnaces. That doesn't mean that some of the people working in the building today don't hear things from time to time. People could often hear moaning and groaning sounds coming from the boiler room. Disturbing to many people was that these sounds seemed to be of human origin rather than the typical sounds you hear from an old boiler when it is in operation. Most disturbing was the fact that the sounds were often heard in the middle of the night or on days when the boiler wasn't operating. Most of the students believed that a ghost lived down there, and this came from an old tale passed down through the generations.

The story goes that in the early days of the school a particular custodian was working in the boiler room when an accident occurred and the man was badly burned. He died a short time later. People claimed that this man's apparition haunted the old school's boiler room, but even with all of the people employed in this building at present, no one seems to have any recent stories about this ghost, although the younger generation seems to be adding to the building's haunted history on the Internet. Stories have begun to surface on ghost hunter and ghost story websites concerning the Riverton Elementary School. Most of them mention the fact that late at night you can hear children's voices as though school were still in session. And there are people who claim that they hear footsteps behind them in the hall. Details have been added to the original stories, such as a little girl crying because she accidentally fell down a chute to the boiler room. No one knows if it is true, but if it is, why would the little girl's spirit still be there? Are people implying that she died there or that her spirit was trapped there? It is more likely that the story is not true, but it is a good one and adds to the mystique of the building.

Page-Hanson, or "Rollies" Store

Riverton's agricultural growth was steady from the 1890s to the 1930s. Like other places around the state, the Great Depression hit the town's farmers hard. Farmers grew alfalfa, sugar beets, wheat, and tomatoes. The town also had an alfalfa feed mill, a canning factory, an egg-processing plant, and a dairy cooperative. Many of the townspeople were farmers, sheepherders, or builders. The original business district is almost gone now, having been demolished by widening the street along Redwood Road. But in its heyday, two particular buildings were of interest because of stories about ghosts. One was the two-story commercial building built in 1893, and the second was the Page-Pixton Store, later called the Page-Hansen Store. Locals called it "Rollies" or "Rol-Save," and for years it was the main variety store in town where people could buy just about anything without having to travel to Salt Lake City.

When Thomas Page grew older, he turned over the management of his store to his son Roland. Another son, Meredith, eventually bought a controlling interest in the company stock and took over the management of the store. A granddaughter worked in the store from 1926 to 1930 when this transition was taking place and remembers her grandfather Thomas P. Page growing old and developing a lot of funny ways.

> He never made a mistake. You couldn't ever tell him that he'd made a mistake. I was supposed to check all of the mistakes, but if you told him he made one . . . he didn't appreciate that. . . . They had shoes and groceries and corsets and hats and dresses. You name it, they had it. He called it a department store, and that's what it was. Everything was sectioned off. If you had a customer, you followed the customer to all the different departments where they wanted things and wrote it all down in a book and added it up. All those sales slips had to be checked by the bookkeeper the next morning to make sure that nobody made a mistake . . . the groceries were on the highest shelves, and you had to climb one of those ladders that roll on a track to get to them. You'd have to roll the ladder to where the peas were and climb up and get them off the shelf. A box of the corsets or something in the corset room—they had a ladder in there. . . . Everything was segregated into departments.[11]

A few locals suggested that Thomas P. Page might have haunted his store for some years after he passed away because his presence was so strong there when he was alive. I found no specific stories to substantiate this.

This historic store was leveled on Father's Day of 2008, a somewhat ironic move according to those who tried to save the last remaining town father's building while celebrating Father's Day. Thomas P. Page died at the age of eighty-two in 1933, and in 1934, the Page-Hansen Company opened up another branch in Midvale. By 1937 the company stockholders decided to dissolve the corporation because of the effects of the Great Depression. Some felt that Rollie Page might also be haunting the place along with his father. Perhaps the new Walgreens built on the land will report an odd occurrence or two now that it is open for business. Since old Mr. Page loved his store so fiercely, perhaps he will stubbornly hang on to his haunting habits. According to residents who remembered him, everyone knew and loved Rollie, who ran the store while his father Thomas grew a bit strange with old age.

After Mr. Page passed away in 1933, people would both literally and figuratively feel his presence in the store. Mr. Page's ghost didn't just oversee things quietly. He liked to shove people around, poke them, and make the hair on the back of their necks stand on end. Customers and employees got used to this activity and often expected it, especially when they were stocking the shelves. Old

Mr. Page's apparition seemed to like to oversee everything going on in the store, and employees got manhandled once in a while by invisible hands. Sometimes they would feel someone shove them aside when no one was around, or try to slide them off the rolling ladders.

The bank in which Rol-Save was situated was robbed twice. The first time was in 1924 when the thief shot into one of the store's doors. When the old building was demolished, the hole produced by the gun blast was still in the store's door for all to see.

The big robbery, though, was in 1929. The robbers broke a window to get in. They entered the bank at 10:00 AM, and one of them stood in the doorway, leveling his gun at the people inside, while the other robber scooped up the money into a canvas bag. They cut the telephone lines in the bank, locked everyone in a closet, and made their getaway. With several heavy bags of silver dollars in their possession, the robbers took off on what is called "the flats" near the Jordan River. The bank teller broke out of the closet and in his car he chased the two bandits. The two robbers got in their car with the bank teller right on their tail.

Two miles south of Sandy, the two robbers exited their car and began running toward Draper. The teller got out of his car and began running across the field after them. When the robbers realized the bank teller wasn't going to give up, they proceeded to throw silver dollars out of the bags to distract the teller and to lighten their load. The teller, who was a former running back football star at the University of Utah, gave chase, and with the help of another cashier, tackled both young men. People in town figured that it was a two-mile run to the other side of the river bottoms down by the railroad tracks where the teller finally tackled one of the guys, punched him out, and held him down until the authorities arrived. The thief's gun jammed, and according to the authorities, that was why no one was wounded or killed.[12]

Over the years townspeople have combed the river bottoms looking for some of the silver dollars, which might be worth a fortune today. Supposedly no one ever found any silver dollars, and people have quit looking for them. If anyone ever found any of them, they are not telling, but older citizens who know about this story might tell you otherwise.

Riverton incorporated in 1946, and by the 1970 census was taken, the town had almost three thousand people. By 1990, over eleven thousand people lived in Riverton. The small farming community had become a residential community—almost a suburb of Salt Lake City—although the proud "Rivertonites" would disagree with this evaluation.

People in Riverton are proud of their heritage and ancestry, even though the transplants defend their independence as a community. Now termed as a "popular country-style suburb," Riverton has formed the Riverton Historical Society and has been fighting to save its last historical buildings. Riverton has lost a lot of interesting hauntings and stories, including one of the Crane houses that was moved from Redwood Road to its present location. This mansion home was haunted long before its move, along with the two others that once stood by it on Redwood Road. Karen Bashore, president of the Riverton Historical Society, and Mel Bashore, a historian for the LDS Church, were coauthors of *Riverton*, which won a national award. Mel still does research and writing about the area. When Karen was the director for the Riverton Arts Museum and Historical Society, she completely renovated and restored the Crane House for their headquarters.

The Heb and Mary Crane House, Now Riverton Museum

The story of the Crane House is typical of many such stories—small towns trying to save their last historical buildings before they are removed due to progress. Besides its evolution to an art and historical center, the house has three added bonuses for me in that my great-grandfather and his brother built the mansion. A miniature furniture collection built by one of my relatives is displayed there, and a resident female ghost haunts the place.

Annie Crane, my great-grandmother, was born in Herriman, Utah, ten miles west of Riverton. Her father, James Crane, was a polygamist with three wives and at one point was both bishop and mayor of Herriman. Annie and her two brothers, Heb and Will Crane, eventually moved to Riverton. Annie married Carl Madsen, a man with carpentry in his blood, and they lived in Herriman for a while until Carl got a good job doing carpentry work in Draper, about ten miles east of Riverton. Annie refused to leave her family and friends in Herriman, so Carl simply told Annie that he would take a second wife, a pretty girl he had his eye on, and live in Draper during the week. He said he would come visit Annie in Herriman on the weekends. Annie immediately moved to Riverton so that Carl only had to ride his horse ten miles to Draper, and no second wife was ever taken.

When circumstances allowed, Annie Crane would spend more time in Herriman than she did in Riverton. Her husband went on three missions to Denmark for his church, and Annie was afraid to be alone with her twelve children even for one night. One time he was going to be gone just overnight, and she piled up furniture against the front door, tied the dog nearby, and had each child—with a poker in his hands—take a shift staying up to guard the house. One time, in the middle of the night, the child on guard fell asleep. The dog broke his rope, jumped on the furniture, and knocked it all over. This commotion nearly frightened Annie to death!

Carl Madsen Bradt was a hard worker, but he never did make much money at his trade, so Annie also had to work. When they argued about him going on his first mission, he finally slammed his fist on a table and declared that he would leave her and his family to go on a mission. Annie finally agreed. While he was gone, she sold eggs, did washing, cooking, and anything else she could so that when he got off the train and said, "Well, how much money do we owe?" she could

95

answer him by handing him the deed to their house—paid in full. It was a matter of principle for Annie.

Annie was only seventeen years old when she married Carl, who was a widower with two children to raise. There is an explanation for Carl's stubborn bitterness and disappointment in life. For six years he was an apprentice to a man who beat him. He is quoted as saying that he stayed the whole six years because that was what he had to do to learn the trade. He then married his childhood sweetheart and they were happily married until right after the birth of his second child when his young wife and the love of his life died in his arms. He married young Annie less than a year later, and Annie made the best of it. After all, she was a Crane, and the Cranes, besides their red hair and fiery tempers, also had a great sense of humor, which her children enjoyed. Her oldest son, Jim, who was a favorite of hers, died in the influenza epidemic in 1918, and one of her youngest died as an infant.

Without telling her husband, Annie would hide money in his old overcoat in case they needed it for a rainy day. She knew that if he found it, he would spend it. He never wore his old overcoat, but one day, he got up, dressed, and came out of the bedroom wearing his hat and the old overcoat to go to town. Annie was devastated. All day long she wrung her hands and anxiously waited for him to come home. The children were worried too. That night she eagerly met him at the door, immediately took his hat and coat, and took them into the bedroom. A few minutes later, she came out smiling, and all the children knew that everything was all right.

Another time, Annie was working for a man and his wife. The man was super religious and prayed all the time. Annie and his wife would kneel on the floor and pray with him, and then, when he was deep in concentration, his wife would get up make biscuits, roll them for cooking, put them in the oven, kneel down and pray again, take the biscuits out when they were ready, and continue praying with her husband. Annie got away with more because she wasn't married to him. She would get up, strain the milk that his boy brought in each morning, wash the bucket, give it back to the boy, sweep the floors as much as she could, and complete several other chores in-between the prayers. But when they ended, Annie would always be on the floor again, her head bent in prayer.

Tramps would come to Annie's back door to earn a meal by chopping wood or some other chore. She would always oblige them. They would do a little job for her, and she would feed them and send them on their way. Annie felt sorry for one of them because he looked terrible. She invited him in for lunch first, and he ate all that he was able to. After lunch, he turned to Annie, said thanks, and then told her he would chop wood the next time he came through. He left without chopping the wood. This only happened once, since Annie had learned her lesson. From then on, the tramps had to work hard for their meal—before they ate!

This story is my favorite. One morning at breakfast, Annie playfully flipped a teaspoon of water into her husband's face.

He told her to stop, but she went right on doing it. Finally, he said, "Annie, if you don't stop you will be sorry." She threw one more teaspoon. He jumped up, and she ran into the bedroom and locked the door. He was right after her with a bucket of swill that was there to feed the pigs. He broke the lock on the door and threw the swill. Mother dodged it, and the swill hit the side wall. What a mess! That was another time she called him all the Danish names she could think of.[13]

Annie and Carl Madsen built their home on Redwood Road, the same road and not far from where Hebert and Mary Crane built their somewhat larger home. Heb and Will became sheep owners and carpenters and were quite successful at both. Perhaps one reason Heb and Mary Crane's house was larger— besides their financial success—was that they had ten children and the money to accommodate them all. Will Crane's home has apparently already succumbed to progress, and the Carl Madsen home, which is privately owned, is still standing along Redwood Road. My father spent two summers there in the 1920s, living with and working for his grandparents in Riverton. He says he remembers what a hard taskmaster his grandfather was, but it was his grandmother who was the harder worker. She got them everything they acquired in life in terms of property and finances.

The Heber and Mary Crane mansion was saved, but not without a fight. The mansion was moved from its foundation and original location on Redwood Road to its present site. A grass roots Riverton group was able to have the house moved to its present quieter location only a few doors west of the town cemetery. The man, who donated the land to them, let them move the house to its new location on his property and then declared that he wasn't going to give them the deed for the property. The former mayor of Riverton stepped in, apparently a distant cousin of mine, and did some political maneuvering, presenting the deed to the Riverton Town Council.

Some people believe that Mary Crane kept a stash of money in the house. Those working on the house, including descendents of the Cranes, searched the foundation thoroughly and even some of the walls, but no money was ever found. The irony is that since the house was moved, Mary is now buried only a few doors down from the house she designed and that Carl Madsen helped to build.

One interesting feature of my Crane ancestors and relatives is that the women are tall, big boned, and often have bright red hair. My father remembers going to a family reunion years ago where he had never seen so many red haired people in one room together. He called them the "Great Danes."

The ghost in the home is, of course, Mary Crane. Mary was a small, slight woman of great moral fiber and was quite fastidious in her habits. She kept her home spotless and expected everyone else to do the same. She designed and decorated the home, lived in it all her married life, raised ten children in it, and died there alone since Heber passed away ten years before her.

An interesting feature of the mansion is a large upstairs dressing room with window seats and built-in dresser closets at each end of the room. Karen explained to me that this room was divided in half by a partition because it was where the girls and boys got dressed each morning on their side of the partition. There is a kitchen, a dining room, a large parlor, and two bedrooms and a bath downstairs. The Arts Museum and Historical Society created a full basement with meeting rooms and classrooms, and upstairs, where the back stairs are located, is an open meeting area, several bedrooms, and the large dressing room. The main oak wood staircase, which is located directly in front of the front door, was added later when the home was an elegant restaurant on Redwood Road. A small alcove with beautiful leaded glass is just inside the front door, and a portrait of Heber and Mary Crane and their family hangs there. To the right is the large parlor with two adjoining rooms and large sliding doors on either end, as well as intricately carved fireplaces. The Art Museum uses the upstairs rooms as an art gallery, and local Utah artists display their work there.

Mary Crane was known in her later years to be quite grumpy and rather mean and cantankerous. When groceries were delivered to her back door, the grocery boy had to stay outside and pass the groceries through to her in the kitchen since she didn't want him to get her floor dirty. Perhaps her own children had to take their shoes off at the back door! On the other hand, if she liked you, she was a loyal and good friend and could make you feel welcome and comfortable in her home.

One old-timer tells the story of living in her neighborhood and walking past her home every morning on his way to school. He would click a stick along her picket fence, but he stopped doing it when she finally came out and gave him a scolding for bothering her fence.

Mary died in her home at age eighty-seven. She left specific orders that her funeral was to be held in her parlor and not at a church. This was an unusual request at the time, since nearly everyone was Mormon and funerals were always held in the ward house. Karen Bashore thinks it a bit ironic now that Mary Crane is buried only a few doors up from where her own funeral was held in the home she so loved.

Most of Mary's children married into rich families, and most of them moved back east, never to return to Riverton. All of the boys were quite handsome and all of her girls were considered a bit wild and beautiful. One of her daughters married into the Pierpont family, and only one son—the oldest, Heber—stayed in Riverton. Nearly all of them went to college, and most of the boys knew how to build. One of her other sons, Milton Crane, eventually went to Los Angeles and built some homes for Hollywood's elite. It was Milton who constructed Rudolph Valentino's Falcon Crest, the home Valentino built hoping to save his marriage to Natacha Rambova, formerly Winifred Shaunessey of Salt Lake City. It was exciting for me to find a family connection to Hollywood's silent movie days. A display of miniature wooden furniture, originally designed by Milton, is in a glass case in the home. It is said that Milton's wife always claimed that she fell in love with his miniatures first and didn't fall in love with Milton until later. Mary Crane, whose husband was often absent due to his church callings, building, and sheep-herding duties, raised an extraordinary family.

Mary was a great beauty herself and passed away in the 1950s. The mansion then became a fancy town restaurant called "The Evergreen." As long as the restaurant was open and run by Mormon people who had the same viewpoints as Mary, not much was reported in the way of ghostly activity, or at least the stories were kept within the family's restaurant business. There is one amusing story, however, especially if Mary was the perpetrator. It seems that the restaurant managers needed a new coffeepot, so they bought a big two-gallon coffee maker. The next morning they set up the coffeepot, filled it with water, and put in the filters and the coffee for their first restaurant customers of the day. It was early in the morning before the restaurant was open. The coffeepot was percolating away when all of a sudden it rose several feet into the air and propelled itself across the room, hitting the opposite wall and splattering its hot contents all over the kitchen. Obviously, since Mormons are not supposed to drink coffee and the smell of it can permeate the whole building rather quickly, Mary and whatever other ghosts might be there didn't like the smell of it.

When some Chinese people—and possibly "Gentiles"—took over the place and opened a Chinese restaurant, they reported a lot of ghostly activity in the house. They told everyone that the spirits in the house didn't like them, and they had a few good stories to tell as to why they felt this way.

On more than one occasion the cook went down to the basement alone. He would reach up, pull the chain cord to turn on the hanging light bulb, and begin to look for his supplies. The light bulb would often grow dim or go completely off, but this time, as he turned his back to the cord, he distinctly heard it being pulled down and shut off with a click, which left him in pitch-black darkness. The light did not come on again by itself, and he had to feel his way out of the basement. He sensed that he was being followed and was positive that something (or someone) tapped him. The cook refused to go down to the basement again, and everyone else felt uneasy about being there alone. The Chinese owners said that the ghost never liked them and that a few other things happened when they ran the restaurant. It was shortly after this that the Crane House was saved and moved to its new location where it underwent several years of renovations. A Taco Bell now sits where the Crane house once stood.

As Karen Bashore began her work on the house, she began to realize that Mary was still there. Several incidents convinced her that there was at least one ghost in the house, and it made sense that it was Mary Crane. Soon most people who came to the house just accepted that it was her. Some of these incidents occurred while the house was being renovated. One time two workers were in Mary's bedroom upstairs either painting or repairing things, when they suddenly came downstairs and said that they did not want to go back to that room. There are two built-in corner cabinets with mirrors and latches in two corners of this bedroom. The cabinet to the west is extremely difficult to open and must be yanked full force to get it open. The men went over to snoop, worked the door open, checked out the contents on all the shelves, and then, with some difficulty, shut it again. As they turned to go back to work, the cabinet door opened by itself and swung halfway open as though it were trying to get their attention. When they looked, the door slowly swung the rest of the way out with a long, deep creaking sound. The two men stood frozen to the spot and watched as the cabinet door then slowly swung shut and firmly latched itself. Karen thinks that Mary was upset with these two men for snooping in her house.

While Karen was working on the roof over the front porch of the house, in a place where the Crane girls used to sun bathe, she slipped and fell twelve feet. She was alone at the time, and all she remembers is that she woke up, crawled to the house across the street, and with her fist pounded on the bottom of the door. The neighbor woman came to the front door. Karen asked her to call her husband and let him know what happened. She told the neighbor that she was going to get her car and drive herself to the hospital. The next thing she knew she was in an ambulance headed for the hospital. The only thing she broke was her elbow. One other thing she could remember was that she felt as if two giant invisible hands came underneath her body and cushioned her gently to the ground. People tell this kind of story all the time about falling from a great height and having the hands of God or an angel lower them gently to the ground. It was amazing that Karen only broke her elbow and had no other injuries. She believes that Mary had a hand in this—literally.

One day Karen was hanging a painting over the stairwell and leaned across the railing to do so. Two visitors to the gallery were standing in the central meeting room upstairs watching her. One of them said suddenly, "Who is Mary?" This startled Karen so much that she almost fell into the stairwell. By this time there had been so many unusual incidents that Karen had begun to call the ghost "Mary," yet these visitors were total strangers to the house. Karen asked the woman how she had thought of the name "Mary." The lady signaled for Karen to come around where she was standing. Karen painted all the walls upstairs herself and knew they had been dry for some time. There in the paint over the stairwell was the name Mary written in cursive. It is possible, Karen says, that someone could have sneaked into the house and written the name just to label the house as Mary Crane's possession. But she is sure that when she painted she was alone and that the paint dried before anyone else was in the house. How it got there is a mystery to everyone. One solution to the mystery is that someone could have done it as a practical joke when Karen wasn't looking. This seems unlikely to Karen.

Later, as the Riverton Art Museum began to hold classes and tours and other events, more unexplained phenomena occurred, making Mary a rumored fixture in the house. One of the most interesting incidents involves a bunch of teenagers messing around in the kitchen on Halloween. They started making up Mary stories, and eventually one of the boys thought it would be funny to go to the back porch door, the one that faces down toward the cemetery, and yell out over and over again, "Mary! Come home! Mary! Come home!" The teenagers turned off all the lights for effect, and when they all came back into the kitchen, the boy who started the whole thing reached around to turn the lights back on in the kitchen. As he touched the switch, a huge ball of blue light came out of the switch and he was almost electrocuted. There was never any trouble with the wiring before or after this event. Since then no one has called to Mary Crane in the place where she was laid to rest. Apparently she had another quality besides liking orderliness, cleanliness, and quiet, and this was demanding respect for one's elders.

Riverton's only other infamous claim to fame happened back in the 1970s when the Klu Klux Klan began to get a following in the area. A graduate of Bingham High School organized a Klan branch in Riverton, Herriman, and Bluffdale. Riverton was experiencing an economic depression at the time, so it was easy to start the Klan there. The organizers set up an initiation ceremony at the Point of the Mountain in August 1975. A few public Klan-related incidents were reported in the late 1970s. Hate flyers were distributed and tacked onto public buildings and telephone poles in the area. The Klan also held several mock executions in the Riverton Cemetery. They hung the effigy of a black man, shot it in the stomach with a shotgun, and left dead ducks below it on both sides of the cemetery gate. These mock executions continued in the cemetery during the months of October and November of that year, with the letters KKK painted on the street below the dummies, and several of the surrounding streetlights were shot out. The Klan began to recruit people in the area and did succeed to some extent. By the early 1980s the Klan had reached a membership of over one hundred people. They began barging into stores in Riverton, ordering black clerks to get out of town. Raising money with cockfights and dogfights, Klan members bought arms and ammunition and stockpiled these weapons near Camp Williams, south of Bluffdale, and held guerrilla-training exercises there. Soon after this, the whole movement died out, leaving the town of Riverton with an unwanted notoriety that lives on to this day. Some feel that the whole movement did not die out but simply went underground, because occasional dead cats and rabbits are found hanging on farmers' fences as a reminder.

It is interesting to note that the Crane House is located close to the cemetery where some of these incidents took place. Mary Crane was probably upset about what these men were doing to her place of rest. Karen Bashore felt that Mary Crane liked how Karen fixed up her home. She also felt that Mary spent most of her time upstairs in the Crane House. After the renovations and restorations were completed, the ghostly activity in the house died down. I enjoyed visiting a house purported to be haunted and a place where some of my own ancestors lived and died. The irony is that both the best and the worst of Riverton's history ended up being represented on this one street. The wonderful work that the town citizens are now doing to preserve their history, and the old copies available of the newsletter, *Riverton Yesterdays*, that Mel put out when he volunteered there, make Riverton a charming place to learn about and visit.

Today, the Bashores have retired from their duties at the Riverton Museum, and younger town citizens are running the Crane House. While the people there now have never heard the ghost stories, they did express an interest in learning about them for their museum's "mystique" and archives. I have already shared my ancestral stories with the new committee by giving them a copy for their archives. They will get a copy of this book when it comes out, and perhaps they will add more ghost stories once they get Mary's background information.

The Herriman Cemetery

Herriman Cemetery is a small cemetery in what was once a small town. Nowadays, Herriman is fast becoming a huge suburban sprawl of large expensive homes and new schools, with the Jordan School District being one of the fastest-growing districts in the state of Utah.

The Herriman Cemetery has many of my ancestors buried in it. Therefore it is interesting to me that ghosts in the form of dark, shadowy apparitions and misty white shapes have been seen there in the middle of the night. My great-great-grandfather James Crane was the founder and Mayor of Herriman. He and his three wives are buried in the Herriman Cemetery. It's a bit scary to think that someone could get an EVP recording of my own great-great-grandfather, or even the voice of one of his wives. I for one am not about to confront the spirits of my own ancestors. I enjoyed reading all the interesting stories about the history of James Crane's poverty-stricken life in England and the stories of his three wives and their children.

Herriman is about ten miles due west of Riverton and is out on the desert plains. I think the Salt Lake City suburbs will reach it soon and engulf it like the rest of South Jordan, Draper, and Riverton. Perhaps my great-great-grandfather enjoys his privacy and doesn't like what is happening out there! The idea of talking to my own distant ancestors via EVP recordings is a bit creepy to me. James Crane's large black tombstone towers over the three smaller ones spaced evenly in front of his, right in the middle of the little rectangular cemetery. I put flowers on their graves occasionally just out of respect. Unfortunately, I can only honor from a distance my roots and the religion that brought them here. And yet, the stories of some of my ancestors who settled this valley are talking to me from the quiet of a little cemetery where ghost hunters say they are speaking back.

Ghosts of Grantsville

In 1846, in a little town called Willow Springs, a group of pioneers, later called the Donner-Reed party, camped on their way to infamy. They stopped at Twenty Miles, a hot springs where they bathed and rested, and then they were on their way. Unfortunately, they were already a month too late to be crossing the Sierra Nevadas.[14]

As well as leaving artifacts behind, the party also left a mystery as to where the gold coins they carried with them are buried. Most people believe that the coins were buried much further out into the desert, somewhere just before they went into the mountains. Years later, when Willow Springs became the town of Grantsville, residents gathered the things together that were left by the Donner-Reed party. When a man from California offered to buy the artifacts for exorbitant amounts, the townspeople refused to sell them. A few townsfolk, hoping to make a lot of money, stole many of the artifacts, but it's not known if anyone ever did make any money from them. What little remains today has been put on display in the tiny town museum, an old one-room school house which once sat inside the original town fort.

Hilda A. Erickson, once the oldest living pioneer in the state, was a citizen of Grantsville. She lived a long and fruitful life in the service of others. Born in the village of Ledsjo in Sweden, her parents joined the Mormon Church in 1856. Unable, after ten years, to earn passage to Utah for everyone, the family separated. Hilda, her mother, and her younger siblings came without their father and two older brothers. Hilda and her family were finally reunited after they survived a cholera epidemic onboard ship. They made an oxcart journey across the plains. Hilda in later years was lauded as the last living pioneer in the state, having traveled with the last wagon train to come to the Salt Lake Valley.

After the family was reunited, they settled in Grantsville. Hilda's first profession was as a skilled dressmaker and tailor, for which she took courses in Salt Lake City. Hilda was described as straightforward, honest, hardworking, and clever. She kept a journal and was an interesting writer as well, giving away important details about her life, probably without realizing it. She was pretty and was pursued by many suitors, until finally one suitor pursued her incessantly. An impression from her wedding day, in a description from her journal concerning the man who won her, it becomes clear that at the time her desire to attend another dance was much stronger than her love for any of her suitors, but over the years her love grew stronger for her husband. For fifteen of these years, she and her husband ran a mission to the Goshute Indians in Ibapah where they had a small ranch in the Deep Creek Valley. Becoming self-sufficient in every way, Hilda took care of her children, did mission work, continued to sew for extra income, and gained a reputation for being an excellent cook.

In the fall of 1885, Hilda went to Salt Lake City again to take coursework in obstetrics at the Women's Deseret Hospital. She gained her midwife license and returned to Ibapah. Over the next year, dressed in long dark dresses and a bowler-riding hat, she rode sidesaddle through the valley to deliver babies both for Indians and whites. She wore a gray buckskin mask to protect her face from the frequent winds, which even today create fogs of dust, sometimes making visibility suddenly near zero on the highway. Traveling day or night, Hilda or "Angapony" (Redhead) as the Goshutes called her, brought many children into the world and provided other medical and dental services to all who lived in the valley. She once threw one drunken and belligerent patient out of the house by grabbing him by the collar and using a stove poker to subdue him. Both her dental tools and her rattlesnake collection are housed at the Daughters of the Utah Pioneer Museum in Salt Lake City.

In the next phase of Hilda's life, the Ericksons acquired The Last Chance Ranch. While continuing her midwifery and medical practice, she crocheted gorgeous laces for her home and began cooking for pay. Like most good cooks, she used a handful of this and a pinch of that and created her own recipes. She used whatever was available when she didn't have all the ingredients required. While her husband went on an LDS mission to Sweden, Hilda ran the ranch and maintained a second home in Grantsville so that her children could go to school. Taking up to six trips a week, Hilda rode alone through bad weather, bad roads, and the possibility of Indian trouble or even "bad men." For the next twenty-four years at Hilda's and John's Last Chance Ranch, John farmed and raised cattle while Hilda made home-cooked meals for others and raised and sold her own herd of sheep for extra cash. Instead of staying up late in the night to sew, Hilda was now staying up late to cook meals for the people who passed the ranch. She charged twenty-five cents a meal and fifty cents to feed and board the travelers' horses.

In 1924 Hilda and John moved to Grantsville and decided to build a store and maintained a Texaco gas station and a small lumberyard. Hilda was the manager, buyer, and clerk for the next twenty-one years until the store closed in 1945. For years she kept ledgers of all her medical cases and business dealings and was good at math and figures. When she had to close the store, those who assisted her found thousands of dollars of unpaid bills from those she had helped out over the years. One man came to visit Hilda when she was one hundred years old and gave her a hundred dollar bill, saying he couldn't in good conscience go on a trip to Hawaii without first paying back his debt for the year that Hilda kept him and his family from starving.

"I have traveled by ship, ox team, mule team, horseback, horse and buggy, wagon, bicycle, car, and plane. My biggest thrill was by airplane. I've yet to ride in a jet. I kept my driver's license good until 1954."[15] Hilda continued driving until she was ninety-four years old, later taking buses to visit friends and relatives. Hilda received recognition from both the Governor of Utah and the President of the United States when she turned one hundred. She continued to read her romance novels as long as she could. When she was much younger, she rode her horse back and forth to the closest town to retrieve the latest chapter of a romance novel being published in the local newspaper. She had her one brush with politics in 1922 when her name was put on the ballot for the State Legislature, but she lost to a Republican candidate.

Living to be 108 years old, Hilda Anderson Erickson said her longevity was due to right living, exercise, work, good nutrition, early to bed and early to rise, and a positive attitude. She was quoted as saying, "More people rust out than wear out."

She rode on a float in the Days of '47 parade in Salt Lake City when she was 101. She passed away on January 1, 1968, and is remembered as quite a character by those who knew her. A life-size bronze statue of her, riding her horse and dressed in her long skirts and bowler-hat, was placed in front of the Grantsville City Hall in 1997. Some say that the younger Hilda can be seen on horseback still, riding in silence to her ranch or riding hard and fast on her way to deliver a "ghost" baby.

Meanwhile, along the Donner-Reed Trail and in the Great Salt Lake Desert, the abandoned wagons and supplies and the story of this now-famous tragedy often supersede another interesting story about Grantsville. It is the story of an adobe Italianate box house, something pretty much unheard of out in the desert. Only eleven such houses exist in the state of Utah, nine of them in Salt Lake City. The Rich-Sutton house is the only one built of adobe. The other homes of this type are listed in the National Register of Historic Homes. Most of the characteristics of the three main styles of the Italianate box homes were incorporated into this one home, along with large bay windows.

The Rich-Sutton mansion has miraculously survived and is now on its painstaking way to total restoration. This house took my breath away when I first saw it, and I can see why the town mayor fell in love with it. This is the story of a house becoming a man's passion in life.

John T. Rich arrived in the Salt Lake Valley from Galena, Illinois, in 1847. He was born in Mineral Point, Illinois, in 1840. In 1872 John married Agnes Elizabeth Eola Young, who was a beautiful socialite from the east. She was originally from Kilbirnie, Ayrshire, Scotland. John and Agnes and their two small daughters moved to St. Iohusa, an old town that once existed in Tooele County, but they soon moved to Grantsville, which was a larger town.

John was a well-to-do sheep rancher who hoped he could keep his wife happy by moving her from the dry dusty desert into a slightly larger town. In an attempt to keep her content, he built five successive houses, each one larger than the last. The Rich-Sutton house was the last and grandest of them all. The home was built after the Riches took a trip to San Francisco and Agnes saw the Victorian "painted ladies."

An architect was hired, which was unheard of at the time. Most homes were planned and built by local builders. The house was built of adobe brick and decorated with Romanesque window casements, porches, and other enhancements that an Italianate style home would have. When the house was finished, John returned to his church duties and attending to his flocks of sheep in the Skull Valley. He was not home much, and Agnes was left alone most of the time. Agnes won out, and in 1887, eight years after moving to Grantsville, the family moved to the bigger town of Brigham City. Rich settled there with his family and became a wealthy banker. Legend has it that he sold his beautiful mansion for eighteen sheep and some cash items, but this is not what really happened.

Eventually Agnes ended up in California and died in Alameda in 1894. It is interesting that this is where Agnes died, because Alameda Island was once a summer home playground for the rich beachgoers. It is filled with some of the more ornate "painted lady" Victorian homes in California. She was buried in the Salt Lake City Cemetery.

The current owner is part-time mayor of Grantsville. He has done some research on the houses's first owners. In truth, Hyrum Sutton bought the home in March 1890 with a loan from Rich, and he also leased 2,000 sheep from him in 1893. He continued to be a sheep raiser until 1913 when he retired. He also did some cattle raising and dairy farming. He prospered nicely and was never interested in political offices in town.

Sutton had four successive wives. He was not a polygamist but lost three wives to childbirth, or "blood poisoning," as they called it in those days. This would account for some of the spirits living in the house, since in those days women usually bore their children in their own homes. The wife who is said to haunt the house is his last one, Clara Sutton, who survived to old age.

The Suttons owned the property into the 1950s before selling it. It had several owners and at one point was turned into apartments. Byron Anderson, who is the present owner of the house and part-time mayor of Grantsville, remembers walking by the place on his way to school every day. It was old and run down, and he and the other children would throw rocks at the windows. Abandoned, it was rather spooky with its rotting roof and crumbling adobe. The 124-year-old mansion was headed for destruction.

Finally, Shauna Elkington, an artist, bought it and worked on it herself. She added ceiling wall trim and painted and restored some of the wood. She encountered Clara Sutton's ghost several times while living in the house. But it was Corrie Anderson, Byron's wife, who saw the full-fledged, three-dimensional apparition when she entered the home alone for the first time while awaiting her husband's arrival. She saw a misty shape form into what she says was a "floating white and bright personage." Corrie ran one way. The ghost went the other. Corrie went outside and sat on the porch and waited until Byron got there before she would go back inside.

Shauna and Corrie had similar experiences in the home, but Corrie Anderson had only this one-time encounter. Both women believe the ghost was Clara Sutton, the fourth and final wife of Hyrum Sutton, since the apparition looked like a photograph of her and her family on the porch of their home. Clara is small and round, with dark hair pulled back in a bun.[16]

Byron Anderson and his wife, Corrie, took on the task of carefully restoring the house back to its original beauty. To match woodwork, plaster, paint, and wallpaper colors, they used old photographs and scraps that they found as they worked. They worked on the house for two years before moving into it themselves. Byron worked room-by-room on the interior and window-by-window on the exterior. During the course of his work, he got a little publicity, and the Sutton descendants heard about him restoring the house. A few of them sold him furniture pieces, which he was able to place back into the home, including a settee, a hall tree, a love seat, two side chairs, two rockers, and a mantelpiece that did not have to be refinished even though it was stored in a chicken coop for a time. Florence Bell of the Sutton family had the mantelpiece in her home in West Valley City and sold it to the Andersons when they were looking for original pieces from the house. The other mantelpiece in the house came from Brigham Young's Beehive House and has a carved beehive on top.

The house was restored to structural soundness, and new wiring and plumbing were installed. The Utah Heritage Foundation helped Anderson get in touch with Jan Gorter, one of few remaining experts in wood graining, who spent more than two months at the Andersons' home. The house had original faux graining on fir. Jan regrained the wood with an oak grain and a mahogany color. Piece by piece, Anderson removed all the molding and restored each one. Some missing pieces were reproduced exactly, and some of them are silicone with a polyurethane cast. Jan used a process similar to what was used to preserve objects in King Tut's tomb.

The most interesting adornments in the house—besides the amazing carved wood staircase—are the ceiling medallions around the hanging chandeliers. They were found in small pieces and were glued back together and repainted. The home is painted in a five-color combination typical of other painted ladies: off-white, mustard yellow, dusty taupe, rose, and burgundy. All of the decorative trim on the outside of the house is being restored. The house is on two acres, with fifteen fruit trees and a huge lilac bush in the backyard. There is also a covered well house and a workshop garage added on by the Andersons. The house is 3,200 square feet. The main floor has a living room, dining room, parlor, entryway, half bath, kitchen, mudroom, and an attached summer kitchen in the back. The second floor has three bedrooms and a large bathroom with a tiny spiral staircase that was added later so that the attic could be accessed and turned into an additional bedroom. The home has been placed on the National Historic Register.

When the Andersons first owned the Rich-Sutton home, Corrie had some other experiences with Clara Sutton. Things would disappear and reappear later on. For example, Corrie bought a Barbie doll horse as a Christmas gift, and when she brought it home, it immediately disappeared. It reappeared under the tree on Christmas morning. Other things mysteriously disappeared and then reappeared in odd places, and everyone claimed to not know anything about it. Most of the activity took place around the sewing room upstairs, and Corrie says that when they turned it into another bedroom, most of this activity stopped. My impressions were that there are at least eleven spirits who visit the house on occasion. The three main spirits are a teenage girl, a little boy, and a woman who looks like Clara Sutton. When I walked into the front hall for the first time, I saw in my mind's eye a small, round, dark-headed woman clothed in a long dark dress at the top of the winding staircase. She was checking me out. I felt that she spent most of her time upstairs between the sewing room and the back north bedroom.

The teenage girl and little boy hung around the dining room and the parlor. I later had some theories as to why I saw these two spirits in that particular area.

The front parlor is the last room that Anderson intended to work on, saving renovation of the best for last. The room was full of all kinds of things that would be interesting to children, especially the Andersons' own grandchildren. It was full of toys, dolls, and books. It was the room less likely to have visitors, as the sewing room probably was when it was a bedroom. Later, I learned that one of the Sutton children died in a diphtheria epidemic when she was fourteen years old and was laid in state in the front parlor. Neighbors and friends had to attend her viewing by looking in through the parlor windows. This partially confirmed what I saw and sensed earlier. Whether I was viewing an impression of these events or if it was just the girl's spirit who chose to visit the place of her demise from time to time, it fit my and my companion's impressions. We also felt that the young boy was probably another child who was lost to illness or accident while living in the home. All of the spirits were from the earlier eras of the house and not from a more modern time. Three women and the children they were giving birth to died in the home or returned after their demise. The three other spirits that my companion and I sensed had also died there or returned upon occasion to a familiar place. When we later compared notes, my friend concurred with me on the locations of the apparitions we felt there.

When asked why he chose to take on this task of restoring the home in every detail, Byron Anderson was hard pressed for an answer. He has time as a retiree, but he still has all the duties of part-time town mayor. Mr. Anderson clearly loves the home, the preservation of other historical buildings in his town, and his hometown in general. Whether his fascination with the mansion grew out of those haunted-house-days of his childhood or a later interest in architecture and preservation, it is obvious to anyone that a project of such magnitude and such care for detail, goes beyond what most people would do. At any rate, the Andersons have created a thing of great beauty in this small desert town.

When I was looking for this house, I wandered around until I came upon it. I was literally blown away by the western-style Victorian mansion hidden in the little community of Grantsville. The owner, Byron Anderson, was painting the porch and chatted with us. We caught one glimpse of the interior when Corrie came out onto the porch, and the soul of the house reached out to me. I knew then that I must come back to visit.

The ghosts of the house aren't gone, but I'm sure those living in the home would like them to be. I think the spirits are content with what is being done, and they don't want to disturb the work. Quite satisfied with the painstaking and detailed task of saving their dwelling, they seem to be more like observers of the passing scene, or snatches of old silent films being played over and over again. At least one interactive apparition still seems to be wandering around.

The Andersons called me with an additional ghost story that they remembered about their house. It seems that when their son, Byron Lee, was still living at home, he was sleeping in the loft room. This is an interesting room because of the spiral staircase that Shauna Elkington added to it. The narrow spiral staircase in the center of the room was built for children to climb, and it goes to a private attic room that was remodeled into an additional bedroom. The staircase is the only entrance and exit to the hidden room. One night Byron Lee went up to bed in the dark and was confronted by three grown men playing cards on his bed. He turned the light on and the men disappeared. Just to make sure he really saw what he thought he had seen, he turned the light off again and the three men reappeared. He tried this several times and the same thing happened. It didn't scare him, so he finally went to bed in the bed next to his own. The men eventually left, and Byron Lee was able to go to sleep.

The next morning he told everyone about the three apparitions he had seen, and they asked him to describe them in detail. He had never seen a picture of Hyrum Sutton and his two brothers, but his father, Byron, had. The descriptions sounded so familiar that Mr. Anderson went and searched for the picture and brought it to his son to look at it. He asked his son if these were the three men he had seen, and Byron Lee said, "Yup, that's them." It makes sense that the three men would be playing poker in an attic room where their wives would never discover them, but these three apparitions never reappeared to any other family member staying in the attic room.

Not long after I finished this story, the pictures I had taken of the mansion came back from the developer. There was nothing unusual at all in the photos from the Rich-Sutton mansion, but I was startled to discover that I had captured some sort of activity in the little Donner-Reed Pioneer Museum. I went to the museum out of curiosity and at the insistence of the mayor, not really expecting to find anything. I wandered around the museum, went outside and read the plaques, and went over to the little one-room log cabin that had been moved log-by-log to its new location in the museum's small park. The caretaker and his grandson went to check on the log cabin and the outdoor machinery on the premises, leaving my companion and me alone in the one-room school house that was now a town museum. We found interesting items besides the little exhibit of the Donner-Reed party artifacts.

My friend ran out of film before she could take a picture of an interesting handwritten wedding certificate and poem that were hanging on the wall. She also wanted a picture of the leather sidesaddle that Hilda Erickson used in her travels around the valley as a midwife, doctor, and dentist. When we got back to the car, she told me that she wanted these pictures, and so I grabbed my camera from the car and ran back up the little hill. I hurried inside the museum, probably surprising any spirits around who thought we were gone. I quickly took a picture of the saddle and then ran around to the other side of the museum and took two pictures of the wedding certificate and poem.

There are probably explanations for the images and light changes in the pictures, yet the circumstances in which they were taken makes me wonder. It could have been the angle from which I took the photos, or the way the light from the front door was hitting the objects. In the case of the wedding certificate and poem, I could have shifted the camera slightly, which allowed light from the top of the door to affect the photo. Still, the pictures are dramatic. An old rocking chair to the left of the saddle appears to have the soft, misty shape of a figure standing behind it. No mist is on the seat or legs, and yet from the bottom of the back of the chair to a couple of feet above it, you can see someone standing there. As we examined the photograph, we discovered that there was a second misty figure to the right of the saddle, behind the old funeral carriage harnesses. The most dramatic pictures were the two sequential wedding certificate photos. I don't remember the order in which the pictures were taken, but in one of the photos, the certificate, protected by a plastic cover, is easy to see. The writing on the poem is clear, as are the photos of the bride and groom and the pen and ink drawings of flowers. In the other photo, a misty white figure with a round head appears to be standing in front of the certificate, and his shoulder extends midway across it.

Other explanations may exist for the figures in these photos, but when I think about it with spirits in mind, the following could also be a likely scenario. As I rushed back in, I could have surprised the spirit or spirits who thought we had departed for good. I ran to the saddle where one or two ghosts could have stood watching me take the picture. Another spirit could have been leaning against the wall when I took the first photo of the wedding certificate and poem. He may not have had enough time to get out of the way. When I took the second picture, the light may have shifted or the spirit moved. Or perhaps the spirit *wanted* to be in the first photo and moved in front of the camera when I snapped it. Either way, I think I surprised at least one or more spirits when I came back into the museum. What was eerie to me was the fact that, if they were spirits, one of them had been standing right in front of me not a foot away, staring directly at me as I took the photos. Since I am almost six feet tall, that would make the figure about five foot eight inches.

There may be ordinary reasons for the misty figures being caught on camera that day, but it does make me wonder why the spirits hang around where they do. Do they visit for old-time's sake, or are they unable to leave, condemned to stay where they are for all eternity? I prefer to believe that they make visits to places that are familiar to them, and with the museum having once been a one-room school house, it would be familiar to quite a few spirits. Another theory is that they are hanging around a particular building or object because they want something done with it. Maybe the ghosts are simply waiting for someone to complete a task. Because many of the objects in the museum come from the Donner-Reed party, I wonder if a few of the spirits are angry and want retribution for what happened to them. Or perhaps it was something simpler, such as hoping that their possessions might be given to their descendents.

Or, as most people probably believe, my photographs were only capturing light shifts and changes when I moved slightly as I took the photos. Whatever the reasons, these photos were dramatic enough to go into my file of the top ten places I visited in Utah where so-called ghost images appeared on my film.

110

Orem, Pleasant Grove, and Provo

Orem Tales

There is one tale of a haunting in Orem that has often been mistaken for two separate stories. It involves an old bomb shelter that is underneath the Scera Shell Theater. The story goes that either by standing near the old bomb shelter or actually getting inside of it, you can hear a girl crying out for help and a man's muffled voice. The shelter has apparently been abandoned for years, and the rumor is that a girl was dragged down there and raped. Those who have gone inside it say that it is dark, wet, and cold. Volunteers at the theater call their ghost "Eleanor." The regular employees claim that the whole story was made up to keep the volunteers from exploring the basement. Eleanor supposedly walks around in the basement and occasionally shows up in the old original part of the building. She appears to be a young woman, and there is a green or blue glow around her body as she walks. She is not harmful in any way and adds to the interesting charm of the building. The volunteers have seen her, but none of the regular employees have.

For some strange reason she likes to appear on Wednesdays. Some people have surmised that she once worked there every Wednesday, perhaps as a volunteer or an employee. Others have speculated that she died before work on a Wednesday and, not realizing she's dead, still goes to work every Wednesday like clockwork. The explanation could be much simpler than this, for instance that she once had a special task to be completed on Wednesdays and continues to do it over and over again. Volunteers, mostly junior high, high school, or college kids, believe they have seen her in the building, along with the usual shadows in a darkened theater. Since first researching the Scera Shell Theater, I have heard that some of the volunteers are doing court-ordered community service, which, if true, would explain my own experiences there and why this ghost is probably made up. There is one interesting story, though, of a projectionist in the old days who saw the girl's face reflected in the glass plate as he worked on the projection machine in the booth. I did feel that there were a few residual apparitions or impressions, but not an interactive spirit like Eleanor is supposed to be.

In the Scera Shell Theater, we were able to see one of the first Indian Company motorcycles that was ridden by the "Mormon Daredevil" who won national and international races in the early 1900s. What people often don't understand is that ghosts and residual energy can attach themselves to certain objects or people. Objects or people who meant a great deal to the spirits when they were alive can hold on to their memorabilia for quite a while. To me the most interesting thing in the entire theater was the bright red motorbike. I feel that the man who rode it does come occasionally to revisit what was probably an exciting life for him, alive or dead. The real ghosts at this theater, such as the Mormon Daredevil Indian motorcycle racer from the 1900s, probably visit regularly because of the Orem Heritage Museum housed next to the Scera Shell Theater, which contains prized objects. The recent movie *The World's Fastest Indian* is an echo of the real story of an international champion racer and the New Zealander who wanted to imitate this man on the Bonneville Salt Flats. As a much older man, Anthony Hopkins plays Burt Munro who came here in 1963 to race his 1920s Indian motorcycle to a world speed record. I believe that real events echo through time, and the objects used in these events, if they still exist, carry ghosts with them.

People who lived in the area have set me straight on a few things since I visited the theater. There were apparently two swimming pools, one to the north of the theater and one behind it. The larger rear pool was filled in, and a parking lot was constructed over it. A few drownings have also contributed to the history and hauntings of the place. Most of the people who eventually used the community center worked at Geneva Steel, and, in fact, the whole town of Orem grew up around the steel plant. Dover and Alice Hunt, apparently the couple whose presence I felt while in the theater rooms, ran the Scera Shell Theater and community center as the original owners.

In the 1930s, the Scera Shell Theater sponsored for one night the beautiful and petite internationally known contortionist, Miss Ruby Ring. Her real name was Ruby Norr, and she was originally from Salt Lake City. It is interesting to see the difference in advertising from her New York appearances and her Utah performances. At the Scera Shell Theater she was shown in a long ball gown and advertised as a wholesome hometown acrobat. At Loew's in New York City, in a skimpy midriff and tiny skirt, she got this review: "Ruby Ring is the only really solid act in the whole show. Fem twister works with remarkable ease and purveys a top line of sensational contortions. Mob sent her out with a hefty palm." While the "Eleanor" ghost is probably pure fantasy on the part of the teens who work there, the real ghosts and residual energies at the Scera Shell Theater are much more interesting than anyone there now would suppose.

The Planted Earth

One other well-known ghost resides in the Orem area, and she is in an old mansion along State Street, the main drag in town. While presently an antique store called the Planted Earth, this home was one of the first mansions in the Provo valley. The old mansion also sports one of the few historical signs in the entire state where the ghostly presence of the original owner's wife, Edna, is mentioned. It was built in 1898 by William Cordner, who was the first to settle with his family along the Provo bench in the winter of 1877. They soon had huge orchards, became quite prosperous, and built their mansion house some years later. The Cordners are also highlighted at the Orem Heritage Museum, being one of the first founders of the city of Orem. The family lived in this home until 1942, or at least Edna did. She passed away in the home that year, and for the next six years it stood empty. After that it was host to a series of businesses, until the Planted Earth arrived and filled the place with all kinds of antiques. The historical plaque is unique. Almost hidden from view, it is free standing, silver, and has writing on it. Its very appearance is mystical.

The owner of the shop says that Edna stays upstairs and rarely comes down to the main floor. Customers and employees have seen her as a black gliding shadow passing by them or across the door frame of the narrow stairwell that leads to the second floor. While the owner has never seen her, she says that others claim to have seen her, or at least they have felt her presence at times. It is a warm and loving feeling, she says, and she believes that Edna is content with what they have done with her house. Antique stores offer a variety of "haunted" objects anyway, but apparently Edna has been sensed, felt, and seen. As a vague shadowy outline or just a sudden feeling of warmth and tingling, she arrives with the smells of baking or other scents that are recognizable only to her. Edna has remained in her home as a visitor, and perhaps in the future, when at long last her home is in jeopardy of coming down, she will appear as a full-fledged apparition. This is often the case in such situations, and when that happens, Orem will have one of the best ghost stories of all to tell.

Pleasant Grove

Pleasant Grove is in the heart of Mormon country, where a certain way of life is rarely disturbed by outside influences and dangers. But the publication of a little book called *Jay's Journal* changed all that. Rumors of ghosts, demons, satanism, and witchcraft, kept quiet for years, grew into what most believe was an entirely unfounded story that ruined the reputation of a grieving family. Most of this information is taken from an excellent investigative report published in the free local paper, *Salt Lake City Weekly*. This paper does an excellent job of reporting the story behind the story, and the real stories behind the mythical ones are usually more interesting than the hauntings themselves.[17]

Pleasant Grove was settled in 1850 and was incorporated in 1855. A conflict between Indians and settlers gave the town its first name, Battlecreek. The Indians called it "Mepha," meaning "little waters."

Pleasant Grove is at the foot of Mt. Timpanogos. Groves and orchards were its main source of income, along with sugar beets and potatoes. From 1920 to the 1950s, it was known as Utah's Strawberry City, with an annual three-day Strawberry Days celebration. In later years most of the townspeople sought employment outside the city, and recently, because of its beautiful surroundings, it is fast becoming a bedroom community with large and beautiful homes, churches, and schools.

The idyllic nature of this town is the irony in the legend of *Jay's Journal*. Maybe bored teens put this tale together for a writer who was eager to find such fables. Or maybe, just maybe, it has some truth to it, in which case something not so pleasant took place in the quiet town of Pleasant Grove in the form of a real witch hunt when a writer invaded the privacy of a grieving family.

According to legend, Jay ran a coven of witches or devil worshippers of the darkest variety. Devil worshippers supposedly gather in the cemetery on the anniversary of Jay's death and also on Halloween and All Saints Day to chant and call to him to release his journal that contained hidden secrets of great powers. No one to date has found the journal. Per legend, the journal was buried with Jay on one of these ceremonial dates, and in the future, Jay will miraculously cause the journal to rise from his coffin. Then supposedly, all his dark knowledge and secret powers will be released.

Local teenagers are probably still scaring people with this story. They are probably still visiting the cemetery late at night, only to be arrested for trespassing. In the version told me by those who grew up in Pleasant Grove, the story of *Jay's Journal* comes from a real event. Apparently in the late 1960s, six teenagers, of whom Jay was one, were gathering by a certain crypt in the cemetery to practice witchcraft, use a Ouija board, and chant incantations. Three of these teenagers died within months of each other under mysterious circumstances. Two of the teenagers were killed in unrelated car accidents, a third in a motorcycle accident, and Jay took his own life. Some time later, a fifth person from this group also killed herself. The legend is that Jay kept a journal of their activities and buried it near their gathering crypt in the Pleasant Grove Cemetery. Such activities, if true, could not be mentioned again for fear of reconjuring whatever the six teenagers conjured up in the first place.

The teens supposedly conjured up a large spirit who, with gnashing teeth, came toward them, threatened them, and then disappeared. Legend is that this spirit managed to kill the four male teenagers within the next year, all of them dying from a blow to the right temple. So finding *Jay's Journal* might be quite dangerous, to say the least! Over the years, the teens who have gone there in search of Jay and his journal say that an eerie green glowing light appears around the grave at night and it follows those brave enough to enter the cemetery.

If the book about this legend, *Jay's Journal*, was meant to deter teens from pursuing witchcraft and satanism, it did not succeed. Local police say there was little evidence of these practices in the cemetery, but after the book came out, more evidence of individuals having been there was found. The police found such things as white and black candle wax (something used in the book) and blood stains. Vandals smashed a clay portrait of the dead teen that once adorned the headstone.

Local people have known individual teens who have visited Jay's grave or have at least become immersed in the study of witchcraft. One boy supposedly built an altar to Jay in his bedroom and prayed to the shrine, complete with satanic symbols and blood.

It does not surprise me that teens would perpetuate this story. Suppression or oppression of expected behavior, as opposed to allowing for the unexpected, keep such things alive. Truth has become rumor, and rumor has become truth, depending on individual perception. Good intentions, sincerely felt, ended up hurting a lot of people long after the real Jay passed on.

Like all stories, there is a real story behind the myth, much more poignant and scary because of the real people and events involved. The real Jay was a boy named Alden Barrett, who shot himself in 1971. The real journal had nothing about witchcraft or satanic worship in it—anywhere. Instead, Alden wrote about his concerns at the time, such as rejection by a girlfriend, his anti-war and anti-government sentiments concerning Vietnam, his interest in Eastern religions, and his lack of belief in the LDS faith. His journal revealed a brilliant mind and a tender heart, tortured by his own personal questions about who he was and what he wanted to become. Most people who knew him believe that he killed himself over the loss of his girlfriend, but intuitively I believe there was more to it than that.

Trying to cope with so much grief and tragedy, Mrs. Barrett, Alden's mother, sought solace and possibly a little redemption when she read a newspaper article in 1973 by Dr. Beatrice Sparks, who was a Utah adolescent psychologist. Dr. Sparks was writing books about overcoming teenage adversities, with such timely topics as teen pregnancy, AIDS, drugs, and alcohol. Mrs. Barrett contacted Dr. Sparks and agreed to have her son's story told in one of Sparks's books. Dr. Sparks, when interviewed, said two revealing things: one, that she wished she had never written *Jay's Journal*, and two, that the family was in denial about their son and she stood by what she had written, having obtained most of the information from Alden's friends and acquaintances. As a result of the publication of this book, Alden's mother, having survived the untimely death of her first husband and her second husband leaving her for another woman, lost both her sons—one to suicide and the other, at the time, to estrangement.

Mrs. Barrett had hoped "that Sparks would produce an account of her son's life as a cautionary tale to other teenagers wandering perhaps too far from mainstream society and family tradition." She went on to fill two LDS missions, and with her continuing faith has made peace with the whole experience. At the age of eighty, she says she still does not believe in suing for libel or slander, but she feels her family was disgraced and cheated by the woman she trusted with her son's story. She says that now, after many years have passed, she feels good about her lost son and that her other son, Scott, has come back to her. "I know for a fact that Alden is okay." In some miraculous way, she's seen and felt his presence. "He has even been in my bedroom, running around the bed . . . patting us on the cheek and saying he was sorry and that he didn't mean to hurt us."[18]

Shocked by the book that was published, the Barrett family at the time chose not to ask for a retraction or to sue the writer for the amazing fabrications in her book. The book portrayed Alden as a sixteen-year-old who was hopelessly drawn into a world of witchcraft and evil, who participated in violent satanic rituals, crazed sex, and outrageous acts of supernatural black magic. The elderly Sparks, who lives in Provo today, admits that she changed some of the facts by filling in details from some of the interviews she had with Alden's friends. She wrote a disclaimer to hide the identity of the family, but the details in the book, embellished and downright scary, make you wonder how this lady psychologist could have come up with such garbage. Her book includes stories of satanic rituals and chanting, Ouija board games, mutilating animals, drinking blood, levitating coins and other objects, rigging a high school election with the help of a voodoo doll, foretelling the future with crystal balls, having out-of-body experiences, participating in sadistic sex orgies, a wedding at the cemetery between Jay and his girlfriend wherein they cut each other's tongues and drink each other's blood, and a pact made between the six teens and the devil. In making this pact, they fill a bathtub with blood and one by one are baptized in it, their heads anointed with urine from a bull, drinking a nasty potion and droning and chanting.

From the book *Jay's Journal*: "I felt my spirit drifting out of my . . . earthly tabernacle . . . I wanted to scream, tried to scream but no audible sound came out. However my body was speaking! Saying things I would not have said . . . Our father which art in hell, hallowed be thy name. . . ."

In this pact, if even one of them breached his contract with the devil, they would all forfeit their lives through an injury to their right temples. Two of Jay's friends died in car accidents when they decided to confess to their LDS bishop. Ben Dieterle wrote the following in an article in the *Salt Lake City Weekly*: "The fatal blow for both of them strikes through their right temples. Jay, who becomes possessed with a demon named 'Raul,' shoots himself through the right temple. Moral of the story? Obey your parents' counsel, stay close to Heavenly Father, stay away from drugs, and forsake all ungodliness."[19]

In real life, the curse of *Jay's Journal* took a few more lives—if not literally, then figuratively. Alden Barrett took his own life, and soon after, two of his friends died in car accidents. Alden's only brother, infuriated by this fictitious story about his brother, went off on his own quest. He painstakingly compared the journal in Sparks's book page by page with that of his brother's actual journal and ended up publishing his own rebuttal book entitled *A Place in the Sun: The Truth Behind Jay's Journal*. Only 21 of the 212 entries in Alden's journal were in Sparks's book. "The rest came from Alden's letters, interviews of his friends, altered entries, and the author's imagination," says Alden's brother. Alden had been under house arrest once for drug use, had played around with the Ouija board a few times with friends (only one time is mentioned in an interview), and had briefly studied Hinduism. Otherwise, all of Alden's real letters and transcripts of interviews with friends revealed nothing about any sort of satanic or witchcraft involvement.

Alden's brother suggests that perhaps the author thought of Hinduism, Ouija boards, and a little pot as being satanic. One can guess that Scott Barrett's estrangement from his own faith involved his disappointment with some of its followers and leaders, rather than the faith itself. Most telling is the fact that *Jay's Journal* is still being sold by Amazon.com and at one time was offered by the LDS Church's bookstore chain, Deseret Book. And while *Jay's Journal* is still experiencing good sales, Barrett's book, *A Place in the Sun*, was never picked up by Deseret Book because of a few profanities.[20]

Interestingly, in the one seance mentioned in this interview, the group of six friends "asked the Ouija board three times if we would have long or short lives. All three times, it indicated that we would not live long," said Kim Lewis. "I almost died myself. I had carbon monoxide poisoning." Three of the six friends did die young. At least two of the friends were women, and now five of the six friends are dead. Kim Lewis is the only one still alive. Mike Wade and John Lundgren died in car accidents. Renee Richards drowned herself in a sink, and Jono Mason died on a motorcycle. The seventh friend, Alden's former girlfriend, lives on the east coast with her husband and family.[21]

Is it curse or coincidence that brought about the demise of these high school friends? Did a book that was filled with fantasies somehow cause other events to take place that might not have otherwise happened? Can a predicted outcome change the future? Perhaps it is Sparks's insistence that what she wrote was a true story. In one way or another, all seven friends suffered deeply as a result of her book. Prying, religious judgment, and sensationalism were the basis of this legend and its rumored curse. The book came out without the Barretts even being allowed to read it first, while in the meantime, the whole town was reading it and talking about it. Shortly after the book's release, Alden's tombstone portrait was defaced, and then the entire tombstone was stolen. When returned, it was positioned backward on its pedestal. Other pranks followed, the worst being Alden's mother finding a dead rat in her mailbox.

In August 1985, the Provo *Daily Herald* came out with a series of articles entitled "Satanism in Zion." Once again, *Jay's Journal* was presented as fact, and Alden Barrett was linked to the story. Two photographs appeared, one of Alden's tombstone and another of a ring with a pentagram that had never belonged to Alden. Alden's portrait, not yet defaced, was described as having eyes that pierced and were unblinking. "If the clay photograph had actually blinked, then the *Herald* really would have had a ghost story." Alden's family sent a letter to the paper asking for a retraction of this specific article in the series.[22]

Jay and Alden have now become urban legends in Utah, even though almost no one knows about Alden. Everyone knows about *Jay's Journal*, the ghost stories, the curse on the teens, and the rumored occult happenings there. Everyone knows that the folklore and the legend have merged. Everyone knows that these children died sooner or later, and in many cases it was sooner. People believe that things still go on in the Pleasant Grove Cemetery that are of both supernatural and hidden origin. Police do say that once the original book was published in 1979, there was an increase in occult-like activities in the cemetery. And some believe that this conservative community is still teeming with adolescent occultists and perhaps hidden underground movements that the dark force has infiltrated. Most know better, however, and life goes on in Pleasant Grove.

I would take this one step further and say that sometimes fiction can affect reality. Planting a seed in someone's mind, even if the thought was never there in the first place, can sometimes change the future. Because of this, I would never ask a Ouija board questions and never write a fiction book and claim that it was fact. I always allow individuality as much as I am aware of it in my students, and I never put dates on things to somehow assist those things into coming into fruition. I would never talk about nor predict evil—only good. I would never use evil to scare people into being whatever I thought was "good." It is a question of the cart before the horse. Which came first? Was it the curse or the prediction of it? Does everything happen simultaneously in linear time? Do ghost impressions come before or after the ghosts? Do curses come before or after their events? Did *Jay's Journal* cause a different outcome, or was everything just meant to be?

Whatever the cause, lives were lost, flames were snuffed out too soon, and a small-town cemetery has a legend, ghost, demon, and curse all tied to a family's tragedies and the unique history of Utah. The following poem appears on the front of Alden Barrett's tombstone.

Portrait of a Child

Whose eyes are these? As free as you please
A close up of a child playing, searching?
Whose thoughts were those? Me, first;
"I'm thirsty mama!" Poor mama.
The child, well protected from the watery days.
The summer haze of his life, yet to be realized
In his eyes he sees tomorrow's skies.
Who will question innocence?
The child was innocent,
Not knowing how well his life was spent,
Might find himself only too soon, bent.
If he had known the changes, the wrong decisions
Made in youthful haste, might the small smile,
Visible in his eyes, have been displaced?
Even erased?

—Alden Niel Barrett

Pleasant Grove High School and Kiwanis Park

The little town of Pleasant Grove has many ghostly tales. Perhaps they are related to the legends created by one little book that was probably mostly a fabrication, along with the amazing coincidence of so many teen friends dying. The author still insists that the parents were in denial about what their son was really doing. Still, several other tales exist, although the high school stories make perfect sense after studying the previous story.

Pleasant Grove High School students claim, "In the theater/auditorium under the stage is a door that is kept locked with six heavy-duty padlocks. Every morning the padlocks would be blown off the door and the door would be wide open. Everyone was given strict instructions to let the janitor know if the locks were removed. Every morning, the janitor was told the locks were gone and he would replace the locks."[23] I'm surprised that there are not more stories from this particular high school, considering such an intriguing history in the town.

Kiwanis Park in Pleasant Grove has a monument that memorializes a small skirmish between Indians and pioneers, and the usual haunted activity is reported. An interesting report states that the monument has an arch with trees and a spiral walking path. It is said that in walking this pathway you will hear the screams of the massacre and smell horrible odors.

The Grove Theater, formerly the Alhambra Theatre, has been made into a dinner theater. Being sure that things are securely locked, people in the building for rehearsals have heard strange noises and someone walking around upstairs. One time some members of the stage crew were painting the stage at about one o'clock in the morning, and they heard strange noises and voices. When they went to the front of the theater, they could see figures moving around. They yelled at the figures but got no response. They checked the lobby where they heard the voices, but nobody was there, and the doors were still locked. They also checked the upstairs. I was told by several people that it was one of the first buildings constructed on Main Street in the town of Pleasant Grove, and it has always been a theater of one kind or another.

Provo Haunts

Spirits, Myths, and Legends

The Utes massacred at Table Point and in Rock Canyon were never buried. They were left to the wild animals and the whims of nature. Is it any wonder that both of these places are haunted by the dead?

Old Bishop was a leader to his people and a friend to the white man. His spirit walks the shore of the Provo River in winter. Bill Hickman, notorious outlaw and lawman, told his tall tales about both of these events.

In Provo Canyon, the stories about Bridal Veil Falls are both old and new, according to the decade from which they came. Hermits, witches, healers, and old miners are said to have inhabited this canyon, and their stories might have been lost except for the tales told here.

Brigham Young University has its share of haunted buildings. Musical instruments play by themselves in the music department, and rumor has it that one of the museums is experiencing so much phenomena that a man was summoned to bless the place.

An old pioneer graveyard is buried under a building, which is, of course, "haunted." The old Utah County jail has spirited criminals, and the Hotel Roberts, which was razed in 2004, had an atmosphere all its own. Even Geneva Steel, once the largest employer in the valley, was silent, still, and definitely haunted until it was abandoned in 2005.

Provo was settled in 1849, but Utah Valley was the main home for the Ute

Indians long before the white man came. For hunting and fishing purposes, they lived in villages close to Utah Lake. It was a good location to defend themselves from their enemies. The explorers, Escalante and Dominguez, also came to the Valley in 1776 and promised settlements that failed to materialize due to other needs in the Spanish empire. Shortly after their arrival, the Spanish mined in the area and used Indians as slaves, the Navajo being a little less likely to rebel than the Utes. Fur traders and trappers frequently came to the area, and Provo is named after one of them—Etienne Provost. Because of the Ute Indian troubles and the wild ways of the early trappers and settlers there, a popular saying in the early days was "Provo or hell!"

When the President sent U.S. troops to quell the so-called Mormon insurrection, it was Provo that offered shelter to thousands of Mormons, including the Prophet Brigham Young.

Provo's early years were marked with consultations on the part of Brigham Young with mountain men such as Jim Bridger and Moses "Black" Harris. While there was a freshwater lake and rich soil for farming, Young was advised that this had been Ute territory for decades and that they were known to be great warriors who fiercely defended their lands. To avoid conflicts with the Indians, Brigham at first decided it would be safest to settle in the Salt Lake Valley. Ironically, the first settlers arrived at Utah Lake on April Fools' Day 1849. Thirty families founded Fort Utah. Before this, mountain men and trappers traded with the Utes and lived life like any other western community dwellers.

These Mormons were independent settlers who, rather than following the advice of their prophet, told Brigham they were going to settle by the lake and chose their own church leaders rather than allowing him to choose for them.

"After putting down roots, they seemed more intent on converting to the Ute's way of life than converting the Indians to theirs as their Salt Lake City brethren had done. The settlers also indulged in smoking, gambling, and racing horses with the Timpanogots Utes . . . Provo's pioneers tended to be violent, unruly, and less educated than their more genteel counterparts to the north." They were "ramshackle, dirty, and unkept," while at the same time, brave, cooperative, and nearly always having good intentions toward the Indians.[24]

In 1849 an incident occurred prior to the major conflict between the Utes and Mormons in the Provo Valley. The incident came to be known as the Battle of Provo River. This incident contributed to the later battle and has become one of the best ghost stories in the Provo area.

Three men set out toward Utah Lake to hunt for deer. These three men were confronted by a leader of the Ute tribe, Old Bishop.

Old Bishop was named after a real Mormon Bishop because he had many of the same mannerisms and gestures as the Mormon leader did and always tried to keep peace between his people and the settlers.

Old Bishop, according to the Ute version, was out patrolling the Ute lands and caught these men violating the treaty that had been made between the Utes and the settlers. According to the three men's version, one of the men recognized a stolen shirt that old Bishop was wearing and demanded it back. When the three men attempted to physically take the shirt off Old Bishop, he raised his bow and arrow to defend himself. At that, one of the men raised his rifle and shot him in the head.

Fearing reprisals from the Utes, the three men attempted to hide their crime by gutting Old Bishop's body like a deer and disemboweling him. They filled the old man's abdominal cavity with rocks so that the corpse would sink into deep water. The Utes immediately started searching for Old Bishop when he did not return to the village. Old Bishop's body did not sink into deep water and was caught in a cottonwood tree when the Utes found him.[25]

These three men, and virtually all the other settlers, were saved from Indian attack because of something that was happening at the same time. Hundreds of immigrants were camped in Utah Valley on their way to the goldfields of California. Providential for the settlers in two ways, these 49ers did a lot of trading of goods and protected the settlers from Indian attack by their sheer numbers.

The death of Old Bishop was forgotten, but only for a short while before more skirmishes between the Utes and the settlers brought about a final great conflict. According to Ute tribal lore, every year on the anniversary of his murder, which was in August 1850, Old Bishop's spirit appears along the bank of the Provo River. He roams the area, reinacting his death and disembowelment over and over again. His spirit rises from the river and takes the heavy stones from his abdomen one by one. As he removes each stone, he then tosses them into the river one by one. When all the stones have been removed from his body cavity, he slowly disappears into the river, only to reappear again and repeat this scene over and over. Many Utes say that they have seen his spirit but that no whites ever will. They say, however, that the time will come when Old Bishop's spirit will be seen by many. Even so, some people claim to have seen his apparition as a wispy white mist rising from the river and at places along the Provo River throughout the year.

Other apparitions, who were never able to tell their story, were the Ute people who were massacred or died from their wounds or exposure to the elements in the canyons by Fort Utah in February 1850. Settlers in the Provo Valley, while receiving militia help from Brigham Young, were chastised by their prophet for causing their own difficulties. Had they not been shooting, gambling, or running horses with the Indians, there would not have been any quarrels to pick, said Young. Young was also losing some of these settlers to the gold mines of California when they joined the 49ers who were headed there. He was upset with the entire situation, but he knew he would have to take a stand and force the Lake Utes into submission. They were robbing and plundering cattle and horses, and militia and settlers had been wounded or killed in the various skirmishes. However, they were Lamanites, and in Mormon doctrine, the Indians were brothers of the Mormons and were supposed to be taught to coexist peacefully with the Saints. It was a difficult situation for everyone, and although the course chosen, which was typical of the entire far west conquering, brought about an end to the conflicts, close to a hundred Utes died as a result.

The militia was sent to Utah Valley to descend on the Ute village, but they were surprised by the good defenses of the villagers. The Battle of Provo River lasted for two long days, and when it was over, the militia relentlessly pursued the Utes. They were chased south from Fort Utah, around the Lake to Table Mountain, and then cornered in a place called Table Point, where fourteen to thirty Utes were slaughtered by the militia.

Back at Fort Utah, another group of Utes were cornered in a place called Rock Canyon, where many of these Utes died from their wounds, fatigue, and exposure to the elements as they were trying to get away from their pursuers.[26] Old Elk died in this canyon from fatigue and exposure, along with several other warriors and women and children. He was considered the main resistance to having settlers on his land. He was heard to say that no whites would ever live in the Valley with his people.

When Bill Hickman, a notorious member of the militia, found out that Old Elk was dead, he went looking for the dead chief in Rock Canyon. Jim Bridger told him that he would pay $100 for the head of Old Elk, which Hickman took seriously. He cut the Chief's head off and took it back to Fort Utah.[27]

Since Hickman is known throughout history for his colorful memoirs, most of which are debatable, people questioned that he actually did this particular deed. Historians have found some confirmation of this in the words and interviews of people who lived in the Fort at the time. For example, Jane Park, a young inhabitant of the Fort, was interviewed several years later by a newspaper reporter and said, "Among others killed was Old Elk, the fighting chief, whose head was brought to camp (at Fort Utah) and hung pendant by its long hair from the walls of the roof of one of the houses. I well remember how horrible was the sight."[28]

None of the Utes in Rock Canyon or at Table Point were ever buried. Their spirits were never laid to rest, and their bones were left to the elements. These spirits could reside today in the canyons above Provo and in the Table Mountains to the southwest of the city.

Modern stories are told about a favorite place for rock climbers, which is located at the mouth of Rock Canyon. People who go there probably have little knowledge of what happened so long ago—or perhaps they do. Rock Canyon has been used for years as a favorite place for rock climbers. The huge rocks are enticing, and rumors are that more than a dozen climbers have fallen to their deaths there. While several accidents have happened involving rock climbers, "many deaths" may be an exaggeration. There may have been a few such deaths that started the rumors. To a believer in spirits of the dead haunting a canyon, a curse on the place is likely.

Rumors also exist that one or more murders have taken place in the Rock Canyon area over the years. I suppose the validity of this supposition can be checked out in local police records.

Another frequent rumor is that satanic rituals have been performed there by secret cultists whose names always remain anonymous. People have heard all kinds of unusual noises in the canyon and have reported feeling a presence following them as they either climb the rocks or attempt to leave the area.

It is interesting that many of the rock climbers do not know their own history and the likelihood of descendent connections to those who massacred the Utes as they ran from their pursuers in the canyon years ago. Trapped there and probably still angry, these guardian spirits would be unfriendly, especially to whites, and most certainly to anyone whose ancestors might have participated in the conflict.

The actual ghost sightings involve a man dressed in 1970s or 1980s clothing. He stands on one of the rock peaks and glides down the mountain at a faster-than-normal pace. These are more modern sightings, and several people claim to have seen this apparition. Most suppose that this man is someone who either fell to his death while rock climbing, or, more likely, due to the way he is dressed, was murdered in the canyon, his body never found. Perhaps some of the people who knew about the early history of Provo City started the rumors about Rock Canyon because of the strange phenomena they experienced there. Or perhaps stories of encountering Indian spirits have been told ever since the initial conflict, and in modern times the subjects of the stories have become rock climbers and murder victims. Or perhaps, as I believe, the spirits of the canyon are carrying out their revenge. Interestingly, Old Elk's pretty and intelligent wife accidentally slipped to her death as she was running from the militia near a place that was named after her, Squaw Peak.

In the ensuing years, Provo became a paradise of orchards and farmland, with the nickname of "Garden City" because of its types of orchards. Brigham Young Academy was founded in 1875 and eventually became the college that is now known as Brigham Young University (BYU). The academy building was recently renovated by donated and bonded funds,[29] and the new city library is attached to it. The old women's gymnasium across the street is another haunted place in town.

Mormon youth from around the world go to BYU to get an education from one of the world's largest church-owned universities. The University eventually became so overcrowded that other BYU branches were developed to accommodate the huge influx of converts from all over the world. Provo's label of "Happy Valley" has changed with the times, and the city has become much more cosmopolitan and accepting of differences because of the influx of converts from all over the world.

Early on, mills of all kinds, and eventually a huge woolen mill, were located in the area. Mining made a few men rich, and it was during World War II that a large steel mill was built. Geneva Steel was built on the east side of Utah Lake between the lake and the city of Provo. For years, Geneva Steel, while providing jobs for the townspeople, was the butt of jokes about the pollution in the valley. It closed permanently in November 2001, and its demolition began on June 30, 2005, and was completed in June 2007.[30]

Famous Mormon officials and politicians came from Provo, as did Jack Dempsey, the world heavyweight prizefighter. He spent his early adult years with Salt Lake City as his home base.

In 2008, the population of Utah County was estimated at 530,837. To the north of Provo is the city of Orem, which is rapidly becoming part of Provo. Together, the cities form one big mega city, with 85 to 90 percent of the population being Mormon, as compared to an average of 70 percent in the rest of the state. This area has one of the highest birthrates—three times higher than the national average.

Provo is famous for its university, and faithful Mormons like living there. The modern-day city has a few ghost stories, but in the old days there were several, and the old-timers still love to tell them.

Provo Canyon Tales

Bridal Veil Falls

Bridal Veil Falls, according to Indian legend, was created when an Indian princess jumped off the cliff because she thought her lover had forsaken her. Her lover cried so hard that the falls were formed from his tears. Because of the Indian maiden's death there, the spot has also been cursed.

I took the gondola ride twice, once as a little girl and once as an adult, apparently just a year or two before the accident occurred that stopped the gondola rides all together. When I recently went back there with my husband to take a ride up the canyon for nostalgia's sake, the place was deserted.

When I was a child, my family and several other families shared a cabin near the Falls, and we continued to go to the cabin for several years in the summer. Bridal Veil Falls is practically across the road from it. Now a large highway has surrounded the little summer homes and has made the area into a little island. I wonder how long these cabins will survive.

Bridal Veil Falls has always been a favorite of mine, and the spectacular drop is a wonder to behold, even without the gondola ride. We went down into the parking lot and found that the roof of the little building there had completely caved in and was abandoned. It looked as if a landslide had crushed it, and sure enough, when I asked someone about it, they told me that a snow slide had destroyed it. As I understand, no one was there at the time. I do remember when one of the gondolas got stuck and the passengers had to be rescued. The place is now closed and probably always will be because of the many dangers. Several citizens of Provo visit the area, especially on weekends, and climb the steep trails to the top. A few articles have appeared in the newspaper recently about the upkeep of the place. The cliff from which these spectacular falls descend is 1,228 feet high. If you have not been there, you will not understand the amazing danger of it, the steepness and majesty of Bridal Veil Falls. The curse upon the place seems to have been proven true, since it was once a popular tourist spot.

Lost Bride

A typical urban myth that probably comes from the name of the place is still heard in various versions all around the United States. Apparently people see a young woman dressed in a long white gown, hitching a ride up or down the canyon. People pick her up, and, of course, she disappears once the driver gets to his destination, either in the canyon or at the bottom, since she can be picked up going either direction.

In the original story, supposedly coming from the 1930s, when the driver looked around for the woman, the only thing left on the passenger's seat was her bridal veil, and that is when the driver realized that the young woman was wearing a wedding gown and holding her veil in her hands.

Another version has the veil floating in the stream at the bottom of the falls, where the girl landed after accidentally falling to her death. And a final version says that the young woman leapt to her death after being rejected by her fiancé. All of these stories prove an interesting metamorphosis of the original Indian legend, a tale that was probably made up by promoters years ago to get people to ride the gondola at the falls.

M. C., the Witch of Provo Canyon

In the second tale about Provo Canyon, M. C., an old woman, lived in a shack there. No dates or names are given. Kids would come up the canyon, sneak onto her property, and try to vandalize her place. Sometimes they would actually see her and taunt her with phrases like, "Burn, witch, burn" or "Witch's heart! Witch's heart!"

The woman finally got a big watchdog for protection. Someone killed her dog and she was heartbroken. Later, some of the kids that continuously teased her admitted to killing it. They were afraid she would put a curse on them, so one night they circled her shack, chanting and taunting her. She chased them off into the woods. The kids thought she had not returned to her shack, but she had returned. The kids sneaked back, set the cabin on fire, and then ran off again, not knowing that she had fallen asleep inside. When the old woman woke up, the entire shack was on fire. She tried to get out but could not. According to the tale, if you go up Provo Canyon today, you will hear her screaming or whistling in the spot where her cabin was located. The only thing that will save you is if you never whistle when the wind is high, and don't stop running until you get out of the area.

This story might be no more than an explanation for the wind that sometimes howls down the canyon, or for the other ancient spirits there, since the wind used to have much more significance to people than it does today. In the early days, wind was a signal that the spirits of the dead were near, and whistling at them brought them even faster. Ghosts were believed to use the wind as a way to activate their voices.

Since we have no idea where M. C.'s cabin was located, or just when the incident took place, we have to assume that it is a folktale explaining strange occurrences in the canyon. Such tales are often based on a little fact. For example, an old woman hermit might have lived up the canyon, and maybe kids did go up there to taunt her. Perhaps they did set fire to her cabin, but I doubt that she was in it at the time. Or perhaps the cabin was there but the old woman was not. We will never know the truth of this tale, so I will leave it to your imagination!

The Lost Gold Mine

There are also tales of lost gold mines, hermits, and ghostly things that happened to them. The most famous story is about the blind man's mine in Provo Canyon. The miner worked his tunnel until a mining accident blinded him. He then learned to work in his mine without his sight. He never found much gold, so people believe, although there are those who say finding his mine would make you a rich person.

Roy, or James L. Newman, was born in 1893 in Holladay, Utah. In 1929 Roy was out setting charges with his brother near the old Maxfield Mine in Big Cottonwood Canyon when the blasting cap exploded in his face. Roy was bleeding from an artery in his hand, and his face and sight were already gone. His brother helped him stagger into town for help.

Even after Roy was blind he was still considered a master engineer when it came to having perfect drainage and haulage engineering grades in his tunnels. The tunnels were so straight that you could "stand at the face of the tunnel and see the light of the portal."[31]

Roy said he was able to drive such perfect tunnels because he still retained light vision at the bottom of his left eye. "Through this small window, I get a faint sensation of light," he said. Thus, when he checked the tunnel bore for straightness, he set up a lighted carbide lamp in the middle of the track about three hundred feet from the face. "I then move up within fifteen feet of the face and stand up a pick with handle erect in the center of the track. These two objects thus mark the center of the tunnel."[32] He would then back up to the face, sight down the tunnel, and move his body to the left or right until the pick handle obscured the light. Without sight he performed all other mining tasks by developing his own unique methods.

Roy never found his gold. He died in 1974 at the age of eighty. Some say his lost gold mine was located in Big Cottonwood Canyon, while others say it was in Provo Canyon. Were there two separate mines, or did Roy only have one mine in an unknown location?

Brass Plates

For a long time in this spirit-filled valley, faithful Mormons sought to prove the truth of their church's scriptures about the ancient history of the Americas. In Mormon scripture, long before the Ute occupation of the valley, an ancient people known as the Lamanites roamed the area. They eventually killed off all the Nephites, who were their brethren.

Lehi, his wife Sariah, and their sons Laman, Lemuel, Sam, Nephi, Jacob, and Joseph crossed the ocean from the holy land. His sons became bitter enemies. The descendants of Laman and Lemuel became the Lamanites, and the descendants of Nephi, Sam, Jacob, and Joseph became the Nephites.

Archaeologists call these people from eight hundred years ago the Fremonts, and those living from seven thousand to nine thousand years ago, they call the Desert Culture. Archaeologists continue to dig in some of the ancient Indian mounds that carpet the area, thus explaining how differently from the rest of the world the archaeologists from BYU would view their history.

Frank Pray claimed he found a sealed tunnel at the foot of Mt. Timpanogos, which is halfway between Alpine and Provo. He said he found an ancient stone box in a cave containing brass plates with ancient Indian writings on them. Pray also claimed that the plates were photographed and examined and then went into the LDS Church archives, never to be seen again. He never went back to the cave, because when he and his companion discovered it, a hot wind blew at them from its entrance and they heard a voice say, "Leave at once!" They grabbed the box and ran from the cave, never to return.

Pray left Provo Canyon and moved to Alpine to finish his mining career there, because his visions had led him to believe that the canyon between Alpine and Provo was the right place to find both physical and spiritual treasures for his church. He spent the next thirty-eight years, 1900 to 1938, digging at an undisclosed site. He claims to have been blocked again from finding anything, since gravel continued to fill in his holes even as he dug them. He disregarded the two male angels who came to him and explained to him why he was not being allowed to dig his mine.

BYU Stories and the Museum of Peoples and Cultures

"The red brick Tudor building at the corner of First East Seventh North, lost in trees next to the Elms Apartments, has been there since 1938. The Museum of Peoples and Cultures, now full of artifacts, was once a Church Language Training Mission, according to the *History of Brigham Young University*. Before that, it was a bustling dormitory full of girls. It was originally a dormitory named Allen Hall that housed seventy-five men. It was named after the son-in-law and daughter of Jesse Knight, who funded the building. 'It wasn't set up to be a girls dorm at all,' said Jean Burnett, resident of Allen Hall in 1950. 'It didn't have any frills, but it was nice enough and comfortable.' While comfortable, life in Allen Hall was also structured. 'The doors were locked at 9:00 PM, and everyone was usually in bed by 10:00 PM.' " Meals were served at a certain time, and you didn't eat if you weren't there at that time. There was a weekend curfew, and the residents hung out at a hamburger stand across the street. Old Allen Hall was converted into a woman's dorm and later used for a museum.[33]

The museum director says that she still has a bathtub in her office and that showers are in the lab where she and her students store artifacts. The cultures museum occupies space at the Museum of Art on campus. While old Allen Hall is successfully being used at present, there has been talk of renovating it. The museum is still packed with artifacts and traveling exhibits, and there are a lot of stairs to climb in order to see everything.

The museum was established in 1946 at BYU but was moved into Allen Hall sometime in the late 1950s. The students produce their own exhibits and provide programs for visitors and the community. They learn necessary skills and knowledge along their way to becoming archaeologists in their respective fields.

Students who have worked at the museum in the past say that if there is any place on campus that is haunted, this is it. For years ancient Indian mummies were housed there until the Utah repatriation law went into effect in 1992. This law directed that all the tribes may claim their ancestors and bury them wherever they choose, but the state would prefer that they store them in the state repository, which was dedicated a few years back and is located under the mountain between the Pioneer Heritage Park and Hogle Zoo in Salt Lake City. Before repatriation the museum had so much trouble with ghostly activity that the staff supposedly allowed a Medicine Man from a local tribe to come and bless the place in hopes of quieting the spirits. It apparently worked, because the activity in the building stopped entirely after the holy man performed his rituals and chants. It has been my experience that "clearings" rarely work, and the spirits manage to return sooner or later.

With it having been a boys' and a girls' dorm for a few years, where something could have happened to contribute to ghostly activities, old Allen Hall has the ingredients for supernatural occurrences. The Language Training Center for Mormon missionaries could have some ghostly tales, although I found none. With the combination of the old building, the Indian artifacts, and captured spirits, probably anything could have happened in the past—or even today. The students talk among themselves about creepy lockups at night, basement sounds, and footsteps and things not where they are supposed to be.

The usual indications of a haunting are present, such as dimming lights and snatches of words or phrases heard when no one else is around. The Medicine Man probably quieted the spirits, but I doubt he got rid of them for good.

I am surprised that nothing has ever been reported about the old Maeser Science building, which was built on top of an old pioneer graveyard that was known as the Temple Hill Cemetery. When they were getting ready to construct this building, they offered families the chance to move their relatives and ancestors, which many of them did, but some of the bodies were unclaimed and are still buried there.

Strange activity is reported in the music section of the BYU library. People who were alone heard voices and conversations in the music reading room. The temperatures in the room can suddenly drop or rise for no reason. The music library also has a harp room, where a chair known as the "ghost chair" can appear and disappear at will. According to the students, this extra chair will appear, and no one can account for it being there. I wonder why librarians would waste their time counting chairs! In the music recording archives, the vast collection of old records can really spook the students with a feeling of being watched or even touched on the back of their neck when no one else is there. The old archive sections of libraries are notorious for hauntings. Is it residue energy or the old images and objects that draw the spirits?

Old Utah County Jail

From the looks of it, the old Utah County Jail, which was shut down a few years ago, was probably built in the 1940s or 1950s. For a long time, the county was renting out the facility next door to a youth recovery program and kept the police dog kennels in the old jail. It is still next to a police substation, and a brand new elementary school, which houses the students and faculty of the old Maeser School, was built next to it.

I toured the jail with my friends when we heard that ghost hunters had recently visited there, and I'm glad we did. Like most old jails, the haunted activity is pretty legendary: EVP recordings, orbs, shadows moving across film, voiced words and phrases, rattling jail doors, banging doors, lights going on and off at night, dogs barking, and more. This must have been hard on the K-Niners housed there, who are more sensitive to this kind of thing than humans are. Ghost hunters say that the old Utah County Jail is one of the most haunted places in the valley.

Hotel Roberts

Provo's old Hotel Roberts was built in 1882 and was one of the few buildings left from the early days of the city. Unfortunately, it was demolished in November 2004. At one point in history, Brigham Young noticed the hotel when he was staying in a home north of it and bought it.

Esther C. Pulsipher originally had the hotel built and called it the Occidental Hotel. The first structure was made of adobe and had two and one-half stories and a hipped roof. In 1890 a new wing with a partial third story was added, with a kitchen on the main floor. The new wing was connected to the original building through the dining room. In 1908 a third story was added in the rear, and in 1926, the hotel was totally remodeled to look like a mission style hotel.

A lot of famous people stayed at this hotel over the years. "Such celebrities as President William Howard Taft, Helen Keller, Keller's teacher Annie Sullivan, and Jack Dempsey have stayed in the Hotel Roberts. Dempsey worked for the tile company that laid the tile in the lobby."[34]

Jack Dempsey was born in Colorado and was a Mormon in his earlier years. He was raised in Salt Lake City and lived in Provo as a young man. He later made Salt Lake City his home and met his first wife on Regent Street in a brothel where she sang for the customers. Dempsey continued to have ties to Provo and Salt Lake, even when he moved on, first living in Hollywood and then in New

York City, where he ran a restaurant near Madison Square Garden.[35]

Hotel Roberts was a hotel or an apartment complex for years, but in 1995, a couple bought it and made plans to renovate it to its former glory days. The couple hoped to mix the modern with the historic in their renovations, since the old building was the only historic hotel in the valley. They made the décor old-fashioned but also brought the modern amenities to make it attractive for those staying there. The hotel had only one bathroom at the end of the hall on each floor. It once had a dining room and a restaurant, but these rooms were eventually lost. The place was run down and basically became a homeless shelter. The crime in the area was bad, and while the renovations were ongoing and people were hoping to see the downtown area restored, the Hotel Roberts continued to have a poor reputation. The Smiths worked hard to change the hotel's bad image and save the old building, but they didn't succeed, and the hotel was razed.

In 1999 police officers were still having problems at the hotel. A man climbed to the roof and threatened to jump. A typical college crowd gathered, and some of them were placing bets and urging the homeless black man to jump. It was not a typical crowd for Happy Valley, where people are usually more compassionate.

The police talked with the homeless man for a long time, and just as they had decided to close off the street, he came down without jumping. After two and one-half hours of discussions, the promise of an A&W root beer, and a lot of coaxing, the man stepped back from the edge of the roof and fell into the arms of the officers, crying and sobbing. Three weeks before, the same man had stood on the roof of the *Daily Herald* distribution center in American Fork and threatened to jump. He had lived at the Hotel Roberts for almost two years, kept to himself, and said that he was from North Carolina. There was no information as to whether he was an alcoholic or had mental problems. The hotel manager spotted him crying on the roof and called 911. He was taken to the hospital, and no more news stories appeared in the newspapers about him.

Other Possible Haunts in the Provo Area

I wrote in depth about Maeser Elementary and the old Brigham Young Academy in my first book, *Specters in Doorways: History and Hauntings of Utah*, where you can find their complete histories and hauntings. The McCurdy Doll Museum's story is forthcoming in hopes that a permanent home will be found before the entire collection is returned to the owners' families.

Provo has a few other haunted tales to tell. I was intuitively drawn to the superintendent's residence for the Utah State Hospital and the William Ray house. No true stories about them exist, but several made up ones do. Provo is not devoid of ghost stories, but it is not a city with a lot of obvious tragedies or mysteries to explore, except for in its earliest days. Not much has been said about the superintendent's residence, except that workers built the home during the New Deal days under the WPA in 1934. It is located down from where the old state hospital once stood.

The once magnificent and ornate state mental hospital building was torn down, probably not so much from the lack of soundness of the edifice, but to eliminate reminders of the horrors it must have housed back in the days when mental hospitals were much like chambers of horror. The huge old building stood against the beautiful mountain scenery on a high hill at the end of a long walk. It looked like something out of a Hollywood Gothic horror film. A picture of this building says it all! It was one of the most magnificently designed buildings in the entire state, and yet its purpose reminds you of *The Picture of Dorian Gray*—the outside remained beautiful while the inside grew more and more grotesque.

The William S. Ray house was constructed in 1898 and is an ornate and unusual structure built in the Romanesque Revival style. Ray was a banker, broker, and financier who for years ran the Ray Investment Company in Provo. He was the founder and first president of the State Bank of Provo and also served as mayor of Provo from 1910 to 1911. He was not a Mormon, yet he prospered in the town. His house, while on the historic register, is not located in the historic district of downtown where preservationists can keep an eye on it, and it suffers for it. It is run down and was obviously remodeled at some time as individual apartments. It is not in a good area and is in need of repairs and renovations. It is sad that its location has caused it to be forgotten, since a photograph of it shows how gorgeous the old mansion once was. It is now rented out for various functions, the most popular being a Halloween haunted house. The event producers advertised it with a story about a Frenchman who brought his young bride to the house, where she died under mysterious and tragic circumstances. Supposedly the Frenchman did away with himself in the house because he missed his young bride so much. This story was probably made up to make the house more interesting since I have not been able to find any substantiating evidence for it, even though it is romantic. On the other hand, my intuition tells me that some sort of tragedy did happen there, but we may never know what it was unless someone researches it.

As I walked through the house, which was open and empty at the time, I could see the different apartments and the layers of paint that hid the original natural wood staircase and window casements. Some of the stained glass windows were still there. Various additions on the back of the house made it so that you could not accurately judge which sections were part of the original mansion. The atmosphere was thick with activity, and I felt that more than one spirit was in the house. With so many occupants over the years, it was hard to discern from which eras these apparitions came. Ghost hunters would love the place if they could get permission to go there at night. It is definitely ripe for EVP recordings and ghost photography. I had the impression of a young woman who was sad and didn't want to live. I also had the impression of a young man, an older woman, and at least one dog. I felt that all of these spirits were from later eras except for the young woman who belonged to the original house. My feeling was that she was a daughter who either died in the house or outlived everyone and lived alone in it for a while. Whatever the scenario, she was an unhappy person who never got her life's wishes fulfilled and lived without "life" inside her until her death.

It has always struck me as strange that when we walked in the front door, after looking all over for someone to let us in or even talk with us, the house seemed to be expecting us, as though it had been waiting for our arrival and wanted us to stay a while and speak with it—which we did. No one ever came in, and we never found anyone around the place. It was odd to have this sort of opportunity, and I believe this young woman felt she owned the place and had waited for us, even as we were driving toward it. She welcomed us in, perhaps even unlocked the door for us. Whatever her story, she feels neglected and abandoned and hopes that her city will hear her cry and return this mansion to its former glory days.

Geneva Steel

When Geneva Steel was abandoned and guarded by just a few security people, ghost stories immediately started to emerge. With such a huge plant on the shores of Utah Lake and so much history associated with the number one employer in Provo valley, it was no surprise that they did. Lights would go on and off all over the plant in the middle of the night. Strange shadows and vehicles that should not have been there were reported. I wonder if ghost enthusiasts ever tried to get on the grounds, which would have been hard since it was well guarded.

Geneva Steel was located in the town of Vineyard, which is halfway between Pleasant Grove to the north and Orem to the south. I put this story in the Provo tales, because Geneva Steel has long been associated with Orem and Provo, and along with Brigham Young University, pretty much defined the area.

Geneva Steel Works was part of the United States Steel Corporation and was at one time the second largest employer in the state after the Kennecott Copper Corporation. It employed over five thousand people and processed ore, scrap metal, steel plates, sheets and coils, structural shapes, pipe, coal chemicals, and nitrogen products. After separation in the blast furnaces, these materials were processed in the rolling and structural mills to produce a wide range of products. The steel plant was constructed by the U.S. government between 1942 and 1944 as part of the industrial demands during World War II.[36]

It cost two hundred million to build and was sold to the United States Steel Corporation after the war.[37] From the end of the war until the plant was shut down, the people in the area considered Geneva Steel a mixed blessing. While it provided jobs and boosted the economy, it also caused all sorts of emission problems, and local farmers were constantly in lawsuits against the steel company since their crops and livestock suffered.

The company spent millions of dollars on emission controls, but the air continued to be so contaminated that on some mornings a bright golden haze would appear over the entire valley, darkening many days that should have been sunny. The drivers on the freeway had a hard time seeing the road in front of them as the stink blew over the valley in waves. Exposure to these emissions will probably cause myriad health problems for many years to come, not only for the plant workers, but also for the people in the surrounding towns.

The Environmental Protection Agency required even more emission controls in the 1970s that were so costly that the plant threatened to close, but it stayed open until the middle 1990s, when the plant shut down for good. Demolition began on June 30, 2005 and was completed in June 2007.

When the steel plant was abandoned, groups of people received permission to go into the plant. They were probably skeptical at first, but when they emerged, they also had unusual experiences to report. Apparently the locker rooms were the biggest source of ghostly activity in the buildings. People heard footsteps, and the showers turned on and off by themselves. Feelings of being watched or followed were strong, because accidents and deaths occurred throughout the years of operation.

Most of what is reported is residual haunting and impressions left in the buildings. One person reported seeing an apparition in the locker room. He tried to find the man he saw at the far end of the room, but the man simply vanished.

Notes

1. Jason Matthew Smith, "The Event," *True Ghost Stories: Ten Haunted Locations*, Oct. 28, 1999, no. 7.
2. Larry R. Gerlach, "Ku Klux Klan," *Utah History Encyclopedia* (Salt Lake City: University of Utah, updated Mar. 2010), http://www.media.utah.edu/UHE, accessed March 2008; Larry R. Gerlach, *Blazing Crosses in Zion: The Ku Klux Klan in Utah* (Logan: Utah State University Press, 1982); Wyn Craig Wade, *The Fiery Cross: The Ku Klux Klan in America* (Oxford, England: Oxford University Press, 1998).
3. Melvin L. Bashore and Scott Crump, *Riverton: The Story of a Utah County Town* (Riverton, Utah: Riverton Historical Society, 1994), 135.
4. Roxie Rich, "LDS Healers," *A History of Sandy City*, 2nd ed. (Riverton, Utah: Ensign Publishers, 2004).
5. D. Michael Quinn, "Blessed Objects of the Prophet," *Early Mormonism and the Magical World View* (Salt Lake City: Signature Books, 1987).
6. Rich, *A History of Sandy City*, 374.
7. Ibid.
8. http://hauntedhouses.com/haunts/states/ut/, accessed Jan. 6, 2010.
9. Ibid.
10. Ashley Boughton, "Fire Guts Vacant Magna Grade School," *The Salt Lake Tribune*, June 23, 2004, B.
11. Melvin L. Bashore and Scott Crump, *Riverton: The Story of a Utah Country Town* (Riverton, Utah: Riverton Historical Society, 1994), 135.
12. Ibid., 117.
13. *History of Annie Crane*, comp. Lyn Miller (Annie's oldest daughter), with help from members of the family and others, nd.

14. http://en.wikipedia.org/wiki/donner_party, accessed Jan. 6, 2010.

15. Julynn Ann Tanaka, *Hilda A. Erickson, Last Surviving Utah Pioneer* (Tooele, Utah: The Settlement Canyon Chapter of the Sons of Utah Pioneers, 1997), 53.

16. Caroline Monson, "Grantsville Lady's Painstaking Restoration: The Victorian Lady Comes to Life," *The Salt Lake Tribune*, Mar. 24, 1995, 2.

17. Ben Dieterle, "Teen Death Diary: Jay's Journal is the bizarre diary of a Utah Mormon teen caught in a web of satanism, sex, and suicide. But is it true?" *Salt Lake City Weekly*, June 3, 2004, 20–24.

18. Ibid., 21.

19. Ibid., 20–21.

20. http://www.motleyvision.org/2004/news-jays-journal-and-deseret-book/, accessed Jan. 5, 2010.

21. Dieterle, "Teen Death Diary," *Salt Lake City Weekly*, 23.

22. Ibid., 24.

23. "Haunted Utah," Utah Ghost Hunters Organization, http://www.utahghost.org/mainfiles/haunted_utah.html, accessed Jan. 6, 2010.

24. Robert Carter, "Founding Fort Utah," *Salt Lake Tribune*, Mar. 8, 2004, as quoted in the Provo City Corporation Newsletter, Jan. 2003.

25. "The Murder of Old Bishop," Blackhawk Productions, http://www.blackhawkproducts.com/fortutah.htm#The_Murder_of_Old_Bishop, accessed Jan. 5, 2010.

26. Ibid.

27. Ibid.

28. Carter, "Founding Fort Utah."

29. Brigham Young Academy and Brigham Young University High School, http://www.byhigh.org/history/garvinhistory/garvinhistory.html, accessed Jan. 6, 2010.

30. UtahRails.net, utahrails.net/industries/geneva-steel.php, accessed Jan. 5, 2010.

31. Christopher Smart, "Face in the Rock Keeps Its Secrets," *The Salt Lake Tribune*, May 16, 2003, B and B4.

32. Ibid.

33. Julene Thompson, "Life in the Dorms 50 Years Ago Was More Structured," *Daily Universe*, May 27, 2002.

34. Ed Quinlan, "Historic Provo Hotel to be renovated," *Daily Universe*, April 17, 1997.

35. Ibid.

36. "Geneva Steel," http://utahrails.net/industries/geneva-steel.php.

37. Roger Roper, "Geneva Steel Plant," in Utah History Encyclopedia, ed. Allen Kent Powell (Salt Lake City: University of Utah Press, 1994), 216.

BOOK THREE

SOUTHERN UTAH COUNTY TO GRAND COUNTY

Little Miner Boy: Young boys worked with their fathers in the coal mines in Carbon County. This photograph is thought to have been taken circa 1900 at the Castle Gate, Utah, mining camp. (Courtesy of Western Mining and Railroad Museum, Helper, Utah, all rights reserved.)

SPRINGVILLE TO MOAB

Springville

Springville Museum of Art

My great-great-grandmother's portrait hangs in the Springville Museum of Art in one of the rooms featuring famous Utah artists. Categorized by decade, it is famous because it is the first known portrait painted in Utah of a woman. It was painted by a famous local artist, George Ottinger, who came across the plains with his sister and widowed mother in the same wagon as my widowed great-great-grandmother, Eliza Thompson McAllister, and her daughter, Mary Ann. My great-grandfather, who was Eliza's son, William James Frazier McAllister, walked alongside this wagon from Florence, Nebraska, to Fort Laramie, Wyoming, when he was sixteen years old. He and George were around the same age and became friends when Will took over the cattle herd because George didn't know how to do it. George married Mary Ann one month later, but they were only married one year, because Mary Ann died four weeks after the birth of their son. During this time, George Ottinger painted a portrait of his mother-in-law, Eliza. The families arrived in the Salt Lake Valley sometime in 1863 and lived together in Immigration Square (where the old city-county building stands today), and later they each bought a home across the street. Eliza lived in one of the homes with the family of her son Richard Wesley, a Methodist Episcopal minister turned Mormon, until she died in 1872. There are no pictures of her except for this portrait that, I am glad to see, hangs in a beautiful spot in one of the gallery rooms. If ghosts can speak, I am sure I had a conversation with her when I visited the gallery, since most portraits not only carry a piece of the artist's soul with them, but also a piece of the soul of the sitter.

The beautiful Springville art gallery was the brainchild of Cyrus Edwin Dallin, who became an internationally known sculpture and educator. He was born in 1861 in a Springville log cabin and attended a one-room school house there. He developed an early interest in art and Indian life. At eighteen, he moved to Boston and studied under the gifted sculptor Truman H. Bartlett. He also studied in Paris at the Julianne Academy and the Ecole des Beaux-Arts. Eventually, he became an instructor at the Massachusetts School of Art and lived with his family in Arlington Heights, Massachusetts. In his lifetime, Dallin sculpted many Western themes, including Buffalo Bill and other characters in his Wild West Company. He was also an archery champion.

When Dallin married in 1891, he moved back to Utah for a few years and created both the Brigham Young monument on Salt Lake City's Main Street and the large golden Angel Moroni on the Salt Lake City Temple. Later, he returned to Philadelphia and taught at the Drexel Institute. Dallin, in gifting one of his famous statues to his hometown of Springville in 1903, initiated not only an interest in art at the local high school, but also eventually the establishment of the Springville Museum of Art.

The original title of the gallery was the Springville High School Art Gallery. The name was later changed to the Springville Museum of Art. The museum has continued to house a broad spectrum of works representing Utah artists and international art collections, along with an unusual permanent collection of Soviet socialist realist art.

When Dr. Swanson from Springville visited the USSR in the 1990s, he got the museum interested in displaying a continuous collection of Russian art. The Springville Museum of Art was the first American art museum to display and collect Russian art pieces that are mainly from the 1950s through the 1970s. Other collectors also began contributing to the gallery's Russian artworks. Dr. Swanson wrote two major books on Soviet impressionism.

For years, a second, smaller collection of Russian realist art has been housed on the first floor of the McCune mansion in Salt Lake City. Upon viewing them, you can see why ghost stories were started about this Russian art collection. Many of the paintings are life-sized portraits of groups of people or two or three people joined together by a crisis or misery that was going on at the time of the painting's inception. The figures are at the front of the pictures, and you can easily imagine them stepping out of the paintings with their high emotions intact. Nurses caring for wounded soldiers, parents caring for a sick child, school children, and Russian ballet students seem to walk from the portraits toward the viewer. Even groups of soldiers or laborers stare out in despair at gallery visitors who are assaulted by their high emotions and haunted stares.

The McCune story, directly related to these Russian paintings, involves an electrician repairing faulty wiring in the three chandeliers that hang in a row from the middle of the ceiling in the smaller west main floor ballroom. It happened when the mansion was being renovated a few years ago. On the east wall is a large

Russian painting of a ballet school for little girls. One life-size little girl, with blonde pigtails, stands in the foreground in her ballet outfit. On the west wall is a sectioned mirror. The McCune mansion is famous for mirror ghosts, since there are many mirrors there, especially in the huge third-floor ballroom, where people claim to have seen long-dead dancers from time to time, dancing from one mirror to the next. The electrician was on a ladder and looked down just in time to see the little ballerina float down from her portrait, walk across the middle of the floor, leap into the mirror on the other side of the room, and disappear into it. The electrician was so startled and frightened by this event that he immediately left the mansion—and his job there—never to return. He told the other workers about it before he left, and had them witness the tiny wet foot prints going across the middle section of the newly polished floor.

It would therefore be no surprise to me that with the introduction of the Russian paintings to the Springville Museum of Art, a few ghost stories will eventually emerge involving these haunted and eerie paintings.

Art collections are notorious for stories about paintings. Gallery attendants report having to move particular paintings to a new location, or even to a storage vault because of someone complaining that the subject's eyes follow them around the room. And since Russians are known for being passionate and intuitive, paintings of people in times of great stress and tragedy would carry these intense emotions. I certainly have my own experiences with these paintings every time I go to either art gallery. It seems their eyes follow you, their hands reach out to you, their emotions touch you intensely, and their intuitive natures connect with your own. Beyond this, they often appear to step out of the painting onto the floor in front of you, or you feel as if you are being pulled into the painting. Either way, to an intuitive, ghosts would seem inevitable.

For years people have said that the museum is haunted, even though those who work there say there are no ghosts. Perhaps it is the deceased artists visiting their works, or maybe some of the visitors are ghosts who have come to see their self-portraits or the landscapes of their births. Maybe they just want to see the artistic works of their own ancestors or descendents. If ghosts stay in places that remind them of their past, then why wouldn't paintings also be visited?

Visitors and former employees alike report having on occasion seen a woman in a long gown and hat, or a young boy wandering through the museum. The woman and the boy are dressed in clothes from different time periods. Shadows move about in the hallways or across door frames between the galleries. People have seen the shadows out of the corner of their eyes. Having visited this museum on several occasions, I tend to agree with the people who make these claims. An eerie atmosphere definitely exists in the building, and for some reason, it is an active site for ghosts. The basement has a heavy, dark atmosphere that is helped along by the unusual lighting. Oddly enough, the present employees never report anything unusual.

My favorite painting at the museum is the portrait of a young woman in a long black dress and a broad-brimmed black hat. She was painted by an artist from Utah who eventually painted the portraits of a few Hollywood celebrities from the silent era and the talkies of the 1930s and 1940s. Legend has it that it is a portrait of young Margaret Hamilton, twenty years before her role as the wicked witch of the west in *The Wizard of Oz*. If this story is true, then the artist might have done some prophetic foreshadowing of his own, because the outfit in the painting matches the witch costume she wore in the movie. Or, like many stories, perhaps the film came before the painting was noticed, and the likeness became a futuristic vision after the fact.

Grant Elementary School and the Reynolds Mansion

Springville has other tales, one of them concerning the old Grant Elementary School. A band teacher apparently died in a car accident on his way to school one morning. Shortly after his death, people heard piano music played by invisible hands in the combination cafeteria and auditorium.

The other story involves a one hundred-year-old tree that the city was going to remove as part of a new housing development. The first house was built and the residents moved in. With no explanation, they began experiencing a constant noise. Other phenomena occurred in the brand-new home, such as clocks and pictures flying off the walls, cupboards opening and closing by themselves, and glasses moving across the counter. The basement had such an awful feeling that the owners didn't like going down there, and their dogs refused to go. When it was decided that the old tree would stay, a lot of the phenomena stopped. One theory is that perhaps there is an old pioneer or Indian grave near it, or it may be that the tree itself doesn't want to go.

The old Reynolds mansion, which is presently the Cowan photograph and framing Gallery, is also purported to be haunted by the last Reynolds family resident, Valite Knudsen Reynolds. Valite's husband, John T. Reynolds Jr., located two houses in town for possible purchase. One had two turrets, and the other had one. He asked his wife which one she wanted, and Valite immediately said that one turret was fine with her. The Reynolds extended family owned properties in Springville, so Valite and John Reynolds moved from Provo to Springville. They married in 1918 and had eight children. Vilate lost two of them—a girl, Elizabeth, who was eighteen months old, and a boy who was only fourteen weeks old.

After her husband's death, Vilate lived alone in her home until her own death from respiratory illness in 1983. The Reynolds mansion became an art gallery and then law offices, and it is now a photo gallery and framing shop again.[1,2] Neighbors report seeing the woman apparition staring out of an upstairs window on occasion, and lights being on when they shouldn't be.

The current owner, while not a strong believer in such things, has a label over the basement door that reads, "Ghost Underground." Old Mrs. Reynolds, as she is known, was a next-door neighbor to one of the Daughters of the Utah Pioneers member's grandmother. The DUP member recalls stories her grandmother told her about Mrs. Reynolds. She portrayed her as a good and loving mother and friend, who probably didn't want to leave the home she so loved. The present owner only had a few ghostly experiences to relate, such as leaving lights on by mistake and finding them turned off, and turning lights off before leaving only to find them on the next morning. He also reports shadows walking across doorways where he is working, or the front door being opened, the sensor going off, and noises downstairs on the main floor. When he goes to check, no one is there, and there isn't enough time for someone to leave without being seen.

The strongest energies I felt in the home were in Valite's bedroom on the main floor and in the upstairs bedroom. The energies were not strong enough for me to be convinced of a ghostly presence. The possibility exists that Mrs. Reynolds wasn't there at the time and I simply missed her!

Springville Cemetery—A Sexton's Musing

Chad Daybell has written several fiction and nonfiction books, but one particular volume, *One Foot in the Grave*, is about the years he worked as sexton for the Springville Evergreen Cemetery.[3] He never mentions where it is, but people in town kept telling me that his book included ghost stories I should add to what I already have about the cemetery.

Most of his book is about weird and strange happenings that living people pull in cemeteries and the almost comic side of the business of dying in America. He has plenty of odd, peculiar, and downright funny stories to tell, but he also includes a few ghost tales and some faith-promoting stories as well. His "ghosts" are composed of a few urban myths that we hear about all across the country, and some are tied to the cemetery in Springville. All are brief sketches from Utah.

Springville's cemetery is one of those odd ones with a paved county road dividing it in half. To the east are newer graves, and on the west side of the road are pioneer graves, as well as more recent ones. The cemetery is well taken care of but does not have any of the old fancy statues and pedestals that people love to photograph, so most of the cemetery is covered in flat or low gravestones that are easier to mow with a tractor mower.

Chad Daybell says that on foggy, frigid days, the ghosts get bored and come out to play tricks on those who work there. Among other things, they have been known to move his pen to different positions on his desk when he left for a few minutes, or flip pages in his day planner.

He tells one urban myth story whose details are varied according to the area it comes from. Neighbors driving by see a middle-aged woman walking on the road by the cemetery. She looks sad and has a baby in her arms. She isn't wearing a winter coat, even though it's cold and snowing. The couple stops and offers her a ride. The woman gets in the back seat with the baby in her arms, and neither the driver nor his passenger turn to look at her until they arrive at the cemetery gate,

141

where she says she's going to visit a loved one. The driver and passenger turn to find the backseat empty.

Thinking she has taken shelter under a tree, the couple gets out of the car and searches for her. When they look around, they discover that their own tracks and those of their vehicle are the only ones in the snow.

"This ghostly apparition has been seen on at least three separate occasions by cemetery visitors, each time in the middle of a snowstorm. I hope to see her myself one of these days."[4]

Daybell also mentions some of his own experiences. He never liked to dig a new grave around Halloween, especially on All Hallows Eve or the day after. It was rare that he had to, but he always felt weird about doing it. The police heavily patrol the area during this time to prevent vandalism in the cemetery.

Daybell jokes about wanting to dress up as a ghost, go for a ride on his backhoe, and wave at people who pass by, but his parks superintendent boss tells him this would be in bad taste.

Daybell also admits that he really believes in ghosts because of his own experiences in the cemetery. For example, he was always seeing a dark shape that seemed to be watching him from behind a particular tree. The dark shape darted back and forth from behind the tree as Daybell passed it.

One day he was digging a grave plot when the backhoe turned up some human bones and part of a blue blanket. He and his assistant soon realized that they had stumbled across an ancient Indian grave, and they hurriedly reburied the bones and blanket and never said anything to anyone. Worried about disturbing something sacred, they dug a new grave plot nearby and left the Native grave undisturbed.

His local ghost stories are good ones, and the best one involves a town vagrant who liked to steal things. He died and was buried not far from the sexton's office. Almost immediately after his burial, odd things began to happen around the building. The women's restroom window would be slightly open each morning, even though Daybell shut and locked it the night before. A rusted walkway gate he could not close no matter how hard he tried was suddenly closed four days after this man's burial. Then one morning the combination lock on their equipment compound was found open. He double checked it each evening, but by morning it was wide open again, and this continued every once in a while for the next week or so.

Daybell decided to do some research, so he came back late in the evening to check the lock. Not only was the lock open again the next morning, but the gate was also pushed open a few more inches so he would notice it.

"The biggest surprise came moments later when I checked the shed by my office. I lock it with a large lock that requires a key, but not only was the shed unlocked, but the lock itself was now hooked on a peg two feet above the door![5]

Daybell's best comments are about the balance of good and evil impressions within the cemetery. He would pass the graves of exceptionally "good" people that he knew personally and would get a warm feeling. On the other hand, he tried to stay as far away as possible from three particular graves of people he knew who were not so good. In one case, a man had shot and killed his wife and then killed himself. The two families were bitter toward each other, but due to financial reasons, the couple was buried side-by-side. While he felt that the woman had moved on, he knew that the man had not, because every time Daybell got near his grave, he felt him making attempts to draw him closer or at least was watching him as he passed by. This feeling made Daybell uncomfortable, and he believed that the man was still trying to tell his side of the story to anyone who would listen.

He also felt someone watching him whenever he passed the second grave. Other people would mention that they either did not like to be in this section of the cemetery, or they felt as if someone was watching them. People who did not know anything about this particular grave reported that an unseen force played with their hair or blew on the back of their neck.

In the third case, a well-known "haunted" grave in the cemetery was always avoided by visitors and cemetery personnel. One day, the sexton was required to dig a plot next to the haunted grave. He was alone and was using a metal probing rod to locate the grave so he could dig a new grave next to it. The probing rod hit the haunted vault, and a jolt of electricity went through his body. He immediately dropped the rod and just stood there, wondering what had happened.

He tried again, and this time, as he probed for the grave, he was shoved quite forcefully in the chest by invisible hands. Almost falling down, he turned and ran for his office, feeling as if someone—or something—was chasing him. Whatever it was, he says, he knew it was not of this earth.

As soon as he reached his office and one of his employees walked up to him, the entire feeling vanished. It was his opinion that whatever followed him was not from this grave, but rather something that had been drawn to this spot where the "haunted" grave was located. The next day he moved the new grave as far away from the spot as he could, not wanting the woman to be buried where she would have to deal with this evil entity after her death.

The practical, everyday occurrences in this graveyard are wonderful examples of the phenomena experienced by those saying good-bye to a loved one or visiting them from time to time. We have all had them; we just rarely discuss them. Chad Daybell's little book is refreshing and a good read for those interested in the business of preparing and housing the dead.

Santaquin

Buzzy Lamb was a real person who lived in Santaquin and ran a trucking line in the area. I don't know the time frame for his story, but my intuition tells me that the event occurred in the early 1950s when trucking stories were popular. He and the ghost lights or UFO lights that follow him or appear near him is

Santaquin's most famous, decades old ghost story. Santaquin is also the home of a haunted family restaurant where poltergeist activity takes place.

Santaquin was settled in 1851 by pioneers who were also sent to settle Payson, which is only six miles north of Santaquin. At the time, the settlement was named Summit City. Local Indian Chief Guffich developed a friendship with the leader of the pioneers, Benjamin F. Johnson, and this helped the pioneers settle peacefully in both towns.

The early settlers left the area because of the Walker War but returned in 1856 when the Summit City Fort was built around their settlement. A short while later, the local chief warned Mr. Johnson of a planned raid by the young braves that included his own son, Santaquin. Chief Guffich told the young braves when they arrived at the empty fort that the Great Spirit had warned the whites of the attack. No more incidents took place between the Indians and whites in either settlement.

When the settlers wanted to name the town Guffich in honor of their friendship with the chief, Guffich asked if they would name it Santaquin, after his son, instead.

Santaquin had a school by 1856 and a church by 1896. The town had a flour mill, sawmills, a molasses mill, and a furniture shop. The railroad came to town in 1875, and ore was discovered in the nearby Tintic area, which attracted the miners.

When the Geneva Steel plant was built in the 1940s, fruit farmers relocated to Santaquin from the Provo area. Santaquin is predominately LDS, and the majority of people are of Scandinavian descent. According to the July 2008 census, more than 8,400 people live there now.

Buzzy Lamb was a trucker in Santaquin and drove his rig between the small towns in the area. A terrible accident occurred in the canyon. Buzzy's huge truck overturned and he was decapitated. High school kids sometimes went to the Santaquin Creek looking for Buzzy and were taken by surprise when he appeared. He supposedly roams the area searching for his head. You may not see him as you walk along the creek, because few people have, but you will hear his footsteps behind you on the trail. Buzzy has recently been seen by those brave enough to search for him. Sometimes he is searching for his head, and sometimes he has it in his hands.

A recent haunting in Santaquin took place at the Family Tree Restaurant. According to the story, a little boy drowned in the canal that ran through the back of the property behind the restaurant. After the building was remodeled and turned into a restaurant, several patrons reported seeing and hearing unusual things on a regular basis. The doorbell rang when no one was pressing the button, and it would sometimes stick straight out in the air. Pots and pans suddenly slammed into walls, startling the employees. But the most interesting part of this modern-day haunting is that a few people on occasion have seen a lady dressed in blue walking into the back rooms when no one is supposed to be in that area. Those who have seen her consistently agree on her appearance. This means at least two full-fledged apparitions have been sighted on the premises. The little boy is responsible for the poltergeist activity, such as moving things around and touching patrons, while the woman can merely be seen.

Payson

James Pace settled Payson in 1851. It was originally known as Peteetneet Creek when the first settlers came in 1850, but in 1851 it was renamed after James Pace, who was one of the original settlers.

Spring Lake Villa, a third settlement, is located south of Payson and southwest of Santaquin. Ute Indians shot and killed the guard outside Payson Fort, and the incident started the Walker War. Skirmishes continued until May 1854. A treaty with Chief Wakara was signed that month, but two years later other conflicts erupted, which became known as the Black Hawk War. The Black Hawk War lasted two years before the settlers in Payson could return and develop a farming community. Payson today has more religious diversity than other small towns in Utah, mainly because the Presbyterians established a mission school there in 1877. The school ran until 1910 and was such a good school that Mormon children also attended it. The Methodists, Baptists, and Jehovah's Witnesses eventually established churches in Payson.

Payson Cemetery is of great interest to ghost hunters in Utah. Several groups have visited there and say that it is an actively haunted cemetery. They have several EVP recordings and ghost lights or orb pictures that were captured there. A study of the people buried there would help identify the possible ghosts.

Another interesting place in Payson is the Peteetneet Academy, which was opened in January 1902. It was architecturally and academically one of the most outstanding schools in the country at the time, and its beautiful location, high on a hill in the middle of town, is still a sight to see. The town is proud of its restoration of the building and grounds and has turned the old academy building into a town museum. It is one of the best examples of historical buildings in the state, along with the Beaver County Courthouse Museum in Beaver, Utah.

The academy was named for Chief Peteetneet, who befriended the white settlers and lived in the settlement for a while. It cost $22,000 to build, and its ornate architecture was unusual for a small town. One educator said that in its day the academy was the most outstanding school in the country. It served students from first to eighth grade. One of its teachers, Irene Colvon, was returning from a European holiday when she met her fate as one of the passengers on the Titanic.

The school for a long time was the oldest continuously operating school in Utah, and when it finally shut down, the town rallied together to save the building. It is now a wonderful town museum and art gallery, with beautiful grounds and fountains on a hill overlooking Payson.

When I visited the museum, I felt that the building itself was full of ghosts, which were coming from the various collections held within the building, especially a huge roomful of all kinds of inventions and early technologies collected by one man, a longtime citizen of Payson. Among other things, the room contained old-time radios, telephones, toasters, telegraphs, and lights. It was also full of the collector's personality, and he would visit from time to time to check on his collections.

The art gallery and other exhibits are also of interest. The interior is absolutely incredible, and more than one haunting is probably occurring there all the time, whether the museum people are aware of it or not. As for me, one time in that particular collection room was enough. Spirits from other eras are in that room, and their residue energy hangs around the objects there, which made my experience overwhelming.

Payson also has some great early ghost stories. One involves an event that happened in 1858, when a man, his wife, and her two sons from a previous marriage arrived in the settlement. They were poor, and the townspeople tried to help them as best they could. They showed them a good place to build their dugout, provided poles for the construction, and gave them provisions. The man and woman were constantly quarreling, and the man finally left the woman and her boys.

> Sometime in May the woman or boys laid plans to steal some of the settlers' horses. They would drive them to the mountains and sell them to the soldiers in the army camp west of Lehi. Three others were involved in the plot, and then one of the group revealed the plan to his older brother and others, and the corrals were then more closely watched.
>
> On the appointed night the raiders came to get the horses, but the guards closed in on them. Three escaped, but the sons of the woman sought shelter with her in the dugout. The guards and the owners of the horses surrounded the home and called for the eldest to come out and deliver himself to them. This he would not do, but at length came out and began shooting in the direction from which the voices came.
>
> The night was extremely dark and none of the shots took effect. The man then tried to escape by running toward the east, but he was overtaken at the corner of the Pond Town Field and killed. On returning to town, the mob shot the old woman and tore the dugout down around her. A few days later the younger son was reported missing and was never seen or heard from again.
>
> More than 80 years later workmen discovered skeletons of three human beings and a dog while digging a trench for the city sewer system. The find was located on Second North between Fifth and Sixth West Streets. This would have been outside the fort, some distance from the west wall. Under the date of March 16, 1939, the Payson Chronicle stated that an effort was being made to discover if they were bones of Indians or were early white settlers.[6]

Most old-timers felt that they knew exactly who the skeletons were. They were also certain that this area of town was haunted by the ghosts of these victims of early day mob violence. The bones were never identified, but some people in town who remember the story believe that the old woman and her sons were buried in this makeshift grave. There are some who believe that their ghosts still haunt the area, so the homes or businesses on or near this address would have the ghosts of a man, woman, and dog hanging around. Perhaps the younger son was found and murdered, and his ghost is also lurking about.

The mayor of Payson, in his 1935 autobiography, told the following story that involves a dead man, his ghost, and the gold coins he left behind.

When I was a lad of 17, back in 1894, I was herding sheep for Bill and Jesse Miles on Loafer Mountain. There were several herds of sheep in Payson Canyon, and we used to visit with each other in the daytime.

One day Jesse and I rode to George William's Camp near the Payson reservoirs. Herders were a man by the name of Fred Winward, who had gone to the canyons to see if his tubercular condition might be improved, and Frank Coombs. It so happened to be the Fourth of July, and Frank had gone to town for the celebration, leaving Winward there alone.

When Jesse and I reached the Camp, we found Winward dead as a mackerel and terribly flyblown. We cleaned him up the best we could and Jesse lit out for town to get help in taking the body home. That left me there alone with the corpse and I didn't relish the idea that there was nothing else to do.

That year the road was all washed out, and it was impossible to get a vehicle of any kind up where we were without going around through Spanish Fork Canyon and coming down from the Thistle Valley side of the Mountain. Consequently, it was nearly morning before Jesse, Frank Ballard, and Dave Mitchell got to us (the corpse and me) with a white top buggy. I was sure glad to see them, for it was kinda spooky sitting up all night with a dead man and a howling dog.

I had amused myself most of the afternoon by carving names upon the aspen trees. I had carved Winward's name, date of birth and death on a big tree that stood just in front of the camp. Forty years later I went back and found the tree with the carving still legible. Joe Barnett was with us and knew exactly where the tree was. The tree has since been removed in making a road to the Recreation Center above the Box Reservoir. Other trees still have my name carved on them.

Well, there was an old cabin near where Winward had camped, so we tore up the door and made a large box, and we just picked up the body, bedding and all, and put it in the box and loaded it into the white top buggy. We left for town just after it started getting daylight.

A few days before Winward died he told Jesse Miles and me that he had saved a few hundred dollars and was going to use it to file on a piece of land known as the Clark Springs where Genola is now located.

We thought no more about it until some two years after his death. George Todd, who had worked with Winward in George William's harness shop, got a letter from Winward's folks in England. They asked if he knew the people who were with Winward the last two days of his life. They said Winward told them in the letter that he had saved his money and yet they could not trace it down.

Mr. Todd wrote them that the folks who were with Sam last were above suspicion. That was the last we ever heard of Fred Winward or his folks. [It is probable that Fred was related to Pete Winward for whom the Pete Winward Reservoir is named.]

About twenty-five years later, workmen were tearing up the foundation of the Williams building where Fred Winward had worked in the harness shop when they found an old can. Inside they found a cache of $600 in $20 gold pieces.

The building which adjoins my property [80 South Main Street] had burned down years before. Workmen were now cleaning up the remains to make space for the Knowles Building.

No one ever claimed it, but I felt the money and the can belonged to Fred Winward. However, it was "Finders Keepers," and the men who found it were allowed to keep it.[7]

Some people who still remember this story believe that Winward's ghost has haunted the area for years. Since the early 1940s, people believed that additional gold coins were hidden on his property. Naturally, people were said to have secretly looked for the coins but never found anything. The ghost sightings of Winward disappeared with time.

Other interesting unsolved murder cases in Payson add to the mystique of the area. Stanley Douglas, a longtime resident of Payson, recalled the following events when he was being interviewed by a local historian. Douglas was eighty-three years old at the time.

One winter day in 1920, I was standing in front of father's store with Ammon Nebeker Sr. It was snowing. Two boys, Red Peery (George A. II) and Ralph McBeth came along with a strange story. Said they were rabbit hunting in the Meadows east of where Max Depew built his house. Right near the Union Pacific tracks they came upon a dead man who had hung himself in the willows. Max Wilde and Keith Vance, who'd been hunting with them, said they heard he had been in the pool hall the night before, wearing a long black coat.

I and Ammon started out in my new model T. Ford. We could drive only to the fence, then got out to walk down to the meadow. The going was rough, so Ammon turned back. I went on and found a young man with dark hair, dead, with a necktie as a noose; he sat on a stump with a necktie around the willow too limber to have held his weight.

The death was advertised and his folks came from the Midwest to claim the body. They took him home for burial. But on Christmas Day they received a phone call from their son, indicating that he was alive. Who they buried is unknown. The body had likely been placed in the meadow after a murder, possibly by hitchhikers on the railroad.

About 1940, a suicide actually did take place, when the body of the man was found hanging from a tree at Nebeker's Grove near the D&RG railroad tracks. People thought he'd been traveling by freight train, stopped here, and ended his own life.

In another case, two young boys were murdered. The year was about 1904, when I was about ten or twelve years of age. These boys had immigrated from the old country after inheriting quite a large sum of money. They had been here long enough to learn the language fairly well, when their bodies were found under the ice at Utah Lake. A hole had been cut and the bodies pushed under. A man was tried for the murder, then released.

A murder took place in our neighborhood when my mother was a young girl. An Indian was shot by a white man, and knew the Indian had witnessed him kill another white man. The Indian did not die immediately and seemed to be recovering. Food was carried to the Indian daily by my mother, Emma Jane, and her sister Mary Dixon. The shack where he lived was located either east or south of my mother's family home, 340 West 4th North. One morning when they arrived with a basket of food, they found the Indian dead. He had been shot again. People surmised who the killer was, believing that the Indian was shot the second time to keep him from recovering and telling the name of the killer.[8]

After hearing all these other stories about the early days in the town of Payson, one could surmise that the Payson Cemetery would have a lot of interesting energies for ghost hunters. Besides these tales, there are probably a few other tamer tales of pioneers, miners, and settlers that might be uncovered with more research about the older part of the Payson Cemetery. The Cemetery is already famous for having a lot of artistic headstones and is well known among state historians for its beautiful stone masonry and artistic sculptures. Any town would "shine" with a lot of interesting stories if someone would "dig" to find the town's interesting historical tales. Many towns are now having "living history" walks through there cemeteries, with locals dressed as the cemetery residents while telling their stories. Perhaps Payson has already begun such an event in their town.

Madoline C. Dixon deserves great praise for her excellent research on the town of Payson, and for writing one of the most interesting small-town books I've ever read.

Payson Canyon and Santaquin Creek

For several years people have reported unusual sightings and hauntings in Payson Canyon and Santaquin Creek. The canyon has some old abandoned mines, and both canyons were a stopping place for early Indian tribes, supporting the claims that ancient Indian burial sites are all over in the mountainsides. People claim to have seen such burial sites and have experienced their own private hauntings after stumbling across them.

The canyons are also famous for unusual noises, cold spots in the middle of hot summer days, and, most famously, strange, floating lights. However, it is the area around Santaquin's Canyon and Creek that made the national news recently and has appeared on the Internet sites where UFO researchers post. Lights seen at night have been reported there over the years. These occurrences have some UFO researchers attributing them to alien visits, but others say it is the ancient ones buried in the canyon who do not want to be disturbed. Perhaps these lights in earlier days were behind the Buzzy Lamb story that was so popular in the 1950s. Apparently, even the pioneers sighted these strange lights and sounds up the canyon. The ghostly trucker might simply have become UFO lights and sounds later on.

Locals in Payson not only have excellent stories with ghosts attached, but they also have stories connected to two giant floods in 1907 that came down the creek bed and buried the entire town under several feet of water. With ancient Indian burial sites, hundreds of abandoned mine sites, a history of devastating floods, and strange lights hovering over the towns of Payson and Santaquin at night, is it any wonder why so many stories of ghosts and apparitions, as well as UFO sightings, have developed over the years as a means to explain them?

My grandmother's people came from Santaquin back in the days when these stories may or may not have been told. My father's mother was a Cushing, and she believed in "spirits." She even had a few horse whisperers in her family, who worked intuitive miracles with their horses. Not knowing this grandmother well, I always thought she paid little attention to the netherworld. My cousins, who knew her and the family stories, recently set me straight. They said that Grandmother Madsen had several intuitive experiences regarding her own children and even predicted a few future events.

Benjamin

Benjamin is a little town about halfway between and a little to the west of Spanish Fork and Payson. It is close to the southern end of Utah Lake.

Benjamin has an old pump house that isn't used anymore. At one time it regulated the irrigation flow of water to the different farms in the area. Those living nearby have called the local authorities on several occasions, because they believed that they saw trespassers in the old pump house.

The neighbors claim they can hear people talking, music playing, and sometimes even see lights coming from inside. Since the electricity to the place has been turned off for decades, any lights coming from inside would have to be flashlights, lanterns, and candles. When authorities investigate, they don't find evidence of any of these things, nor do they find evidence of car tracks or anything else that would suggest that anyone has been there. People who drive past the pump house at night say that they can see light from an unknown source coming through the cracks at the edges of the boarded-up windows. They have heard voices and music when no one was there.

The story about the pump house relates to an incident that happened to two men working in the pump house one evening. One of the men got accidentally pulled into the machine. The other man tried to save him, and in doing so, he got one of his arms caught in the pump. The first man was dragged all the way into the machine and died. The other man died shortly after because of the loss of blood.

It would probably be impossible to find out if this story was true, unless someone in Benjamin had lived there long enough that he or she would remember the event. It does make a good story and provides an explanation for all the strange happenings there. This could simply be a teenage story, or there could really be some phenomena occurring there, either connected or not connected to the event. Either way, further investigation might be warranted by one of the ghost hunter groups in the northern part of the state.

Another place in Benjamin purported to be haunted is the old Arrowhead Swimming Resort. The resort was built in 1923 and had a large dance hall next to the pool. A drowning occurred there before 1950, which is supposedly the reason for the haunting. A little boy died, and visitors to the resort reported seeing his outlined shape moving through the rooms. Over the years, other stories were added to this one, including sightings of a "ghost cat" who is supposedly buried behind the main building. Voices and conversations are heard at night and some claim that the two downstairs bedrooms seem to be the center of the ghost sightings. Even an old woman has been seen, adding a warm presence to the building. Guests claimed that all these things made them uneasy there.

A call to the family who owned the resort from 1950 until it was closed down in 1975 confirmed that they had never had any ghostly happenings at all. The old swimming pool building has been torn down, and the woman I talked to said that her son has converted the remaining building into a home. She did say that the pool was fueled not by a hot springs, but by an old well, and wells are often the center of such activity. However, the owner was adamant about never having had any ghosts about the place.[9]

Spanish Fork

Spanish Fork got its name from the Spanish explorers Dominguez and Escalante, who explored the Utah Valley along with what became the Spanish Fork River in September 1776. In 1850 Enoch Reece settled with his family along the river and soon had neighbors, including John Holt, John H. Reed, and William Pace. In 1854 they built a fort where Spanish Fork is located today and called it Fort Saint Luke. Nineteen families from the nearby settlement of Palmyra lived in this fort whenever they needed protection from the Indians.

In 1855 the city of Spanish Fork was established, and the four hundred plus people of Palmyra moved to Spanish Fork. Over four hundred other families from northern settlements, afraid of Johnston's Army, also fled to Spanish Fork, and many of them ended up staying there after the army left. Archibald Gardner built one of his flour mills there in 1859, and a foundry that turned out iron and brass castings was also built in 1884.

Agriculture and livestock have always been important in Spanish Fork, and a packing company for the local farmers' peas, beans, and tomatoes operated there in 1925. At one time Spanish Fork had the largest livestock show east of the Mississippi River. Held every May, it was the oldest show of its kind and included popular activities such as stock judging, horse pulling contests, parades, rodeo, sales and a horse show.

A Presbyterian Church was established in 1882, and its school functioned for all the children in town until the state public school system began. An Icelandic Lutheran Church was also established early on and served its congregation for years.[10]

In July 2008, Spanish Fork had a population of a little over 31,538, as compared to 5,000 in 1950.[11]

Spanish Fork has at least two haunted places. The first haunting relates to the Spanish Fork City Cemetery and is an old story that has been told for years. A beautiful grave marker in the cemetery, referred to as the "Weeping Widow" or "Weeping Willow," is of a woman sitting on her knees and leaning against a gravestone. One arm is extended to the top of the stone, with her hand clutching a small bouquet of real or artificial flowers, and the other is drawn up to her face, her hand covering her face. Her long ringlets drape around her. The woman in the grave died in 1929.

The legend of the weeping woman probably began because of the old water markings on the gravestone. An infant grave is nearby, which makes me think that she may have lost a child. She is said to cry real tears and call out for her baby in the night. People have reported hearing her cry when passing the cemetery in the dark, or have actually seen tears stream down her face. The woman was only thirty-three, and headstones of the couple lie side-by-side. On the monument the inscription reads, "Warm summer sun shine kindly here, Gentle breeze blow softly here. Mother earth above lie light, lie light, Good night Sweetheart, good night."

The other story of a haunting is relatively new and involves the Spanish Fork High School. The auditorium where the students put on their plays has been nicknamed the Little Theater. Shortly after the little theater was completed, the custodian went up onto the catwalk to install the light bulbs for spotlighting, and while he was working on them, he slipped and fell. He was alone at the time and apparently died shortly after falling. Various superstitions have developed among the students over the years. For example, you should never go to the theater alone but should be in a group of five or more students. If you go into the theater alone, the spirit of the old custodian will make the curtains rise and fall, start playing the sound effects for theater productions, and cause the stage lights to flicker on and off.

Parowan

Eerie solstice lights and ancient markings in the narrow notch of a canyon, as well as the Indian name Evil Waters from a curse put on the town, makes the town of Parowan intriguing.

The "Quilt Walker" pioneer story is an interesting tale, and in Helper's historic mining district, the old Albert Hotel is full of apparitions and spirits who are not always quietly "helpful."

Fairview has an old 1940s haunted motel, an old school house turned museum, and a hundred-year-old pioneer home up Fairview Canyon where an apparition sighted there was supposedly one of Ted Bundy's victims.

The Thistle mudslide disaster produced two eras of ghost stories, one in the lake where the town is buried, and one after the lake was drained.

Parowan was Southern Utah's first settlement and county seat. It is the gateway to Brian Head Ski Resort and Cedar Breaks National Monument. Fremont and Anasazi Indians inhabited the area as early as 750 and up to 1250, and Parowan Gap boasts plenty of evidence that it was a major Native American thoroughfare.

The Spanish Trail also passed through this area. Parley P. Pratt explored there, and with the discovery of rich iron ore deposits, settlement of the area began in 1851.

The first settlers traveled in the bitter cold winter weather to establish a settlement by what they called Center Creek. In 1861 the town built a rock church with timber and yellow sandstone. The building served many functions, such as a church, a school, a town council hall, a social hall, and a tourist stop. In 1939 the Daughters of the Utah Pioneers helped restore the meeting house, and it is now Parowan's town museum.

Parowan was called the "Mother of the Southwest" because of all those who traveled through the town on their way west. The early pioneers planted crops, as well as mining coal and iron deposits. They built mills and tanneries and several factories and established dairy farms and sheep ranches.

In the early 1900s, mining became the main employer in the town, but by the 1980s, the mining industry had declined and the town pulled together to come up with other ways of making a living. Along with dairies and ranches, tourism is now one of the most important businesses there. The town has a memorial park, several restored historical sites, and even a community theater. Parowan is noted for the quality of its cemetery's gravestone etching and art, which is thought to be the best in Utah.

One of the legends about Parowan concerns the Indians who lived there long before the white man came. The area where Parowan was built was supposedly cursed for all eternity. A story is told that when ancient Lake Bonneville covered the entire area, an Indian maiden drowned in its waters. The site of her drowning is where Parowan is today. Parowan is an Indian word meaning "Evil Waters."

The town has prospered nicely, so the story of the curse does not seem to have come to fruition, or perhaps the Indian maiden likes what they have done with the town and has forgiven them.

Parowan Gap is another interesting mystical place outside of Parowan. The town had a Summer Solstice Observation a few years back to celebrate the ancient Fremonts who lived a thousand years ago. They left behind thousands and thousands of petroglyphs in this narrow canyon notch, while using shadow markers for a calendar and to leave messages. It is believed that this natural mountain passage tells the story of how these people lived and what their beliefs were. On June 20, 2005, almost three hundred people came to watch the sun set perfectly into this narrow passage in the mountains. The ancient people used their observations of the day and night skies to guide them as to when they should plant their crops and when to conceive their babies.

In a recent study, archaeologists found fifty areas of significance that included not only hunting and habitat sites, but also evidence that these people used the Mesoamerica calendar as it was used in ancient Mexico. The ancient Fremont Indians knew the night sky a lot better than we do, because their survival depended on it. People who study these sites believe that the high rock piles found there were where the ancient people climbed to observe the solar and night sky cycles.

In an article dated June 20, 2005, Mark Havnew of the *Salt Lake Tribune* wrote that, "John Fullmer . . . said the name of his ancestor, David Fullmer, is on a plaque at the gap commemorating the first white settlers to discover the petroglyphs in 1850."[12]

The *Salt Lake Tribune* also reported that Nal Morris, an archaeoastronomist, believed that he was observing a nineteen-year cycle when the sun set in the gap that evening. The sun rose from the notch at precisely 9:44 PM, in line with a petroglyph panel explaining this lunar event.

"In addition, the planets Mercury, Venus, and Saturn will also line up Tuesday night in the gap." None of this will so precisely be seen for another nineteen years. Our fascination with the mysteries of the past just might someday solve some of the mysteries of the future.[13]

Another interesting story from the Panguitch-Parowan area is that of the Quilt Walkers. This is a beautiful example of the faith and fortitude that saved the Mormon people many times.

One winter, early in the settlement of both towns, one of the communities was starving. They had no wheat, and they needed to get to the other town forty miles away to bring back food for the settlers.

A group of men volunteered to make the journey through the deep snow. Hungry themselves, they set out with wagons, oxen, horses, and warm quilts made by the women of the settlement. It was not long until the wagons, oxen, and horses became mired in the snow. The men were stuck, unable to go on in the waist-deep snow.

One of the parties got the idea to spread out a quilt on the snow and see if he could walk across it without sinking. He tried, and it worked. The other men tried it and discovered that no matter how heavy they were, not one of them sunk if they walked across the snow on a quilt. So for the rest of the forty miles, which was most of the distance, each man carried a quilt under his arm. They laid the quilts one in front of the other like a game of leapfrog or ants crossing a river, walking over each one to form a bridge of quilts on the snow.

In the July 24th 2003 Pioneer Days of '47 Parade, which is a much bigger event than July 4th in Utah, the Panguitch-Parowan float depicted this famous local event. Seven young men dressed as pioneers laid their quilts end to end and walked the entire parade route in front of the float in a record 110-degree heat on the black pavement.

Helper

Early in 1880, Teancum Pratt and his two wives, Annie and Sarah, settled Helper. In 1887 the railroad brought more settlers there. A lot of people mined coal, but it was Teancum who did most of it.

Helper's main economics was as a freight terminal for the railroad. The town got its name from the helper engines that carried freight over Soldier Summit, a steep grade that required more than one engine to make it over the summit. In 1892 Helper became the junction point for two major railroad companies to Ogden and Grand Junction, Colorado. Helper was a railroad town first and a mining town second, and did not experience the mining boomtown effect like so many other towns in the area. The town had a diverse population since immigrants came to mine and to work on the railroads.

By the 1900s, Chinese, Italians, and Austrians had poured into the area as laborers and merchants, which were the two main occupations at the time in Helper. The coal miners' strike of 1903 and 1904 at Castle Gate forced people to change their occupation, and a lot of them came to Helper to try either business or farming. Greeks, Chinese, and Japanese men were brought in to break the Castle Gate strike, and coal mining became the chief occupation since coal was shipped out in several directions from Helper. Helper was nestled among the mining camps and became a refuge for both union organizers and strikers from Castle Gate.

The town survived the Great Depression well, and by World War II, coal production had increased dramatically. Coal production still continued strong into the 1960s, but since then, the industry has had its highs and lows. Helper continues to thrive with an amazing ethnic diversity not found in many small Utah towns.

The legends from Helper are fairly obvious. Ancient Indian spirits might be roaming around everywhere, and people who traveled the Old Spanish Trail also haunt the area. The railroad men and miners killed in the area have haunts of their own, and several ethnic stories tell about these hauntings. The campfire tales are numerous and are not tied to any certain area of town but are related to many sites. The layers of history in this town are numerous, which means that the stories of hauntings could be endless.

Helper has a grand museum called the Western Mining and Railroad Museum. It is housed in the old Helper Hotel building that was built in 1913–14. Each room on each floor boasts a different theme: the Italian room, the blacksmith's shop in the basement, several model train rooms, the coal mine disaster room, an old camp house, a simulated coal mine, part of the old city jail cells, a complete company store, a schoolroom, medical offices, World War I and II rooms, a communications room, and an old beauty shop. Two lots filled with old coal mining equipment are located outside. The museum's brochure invites visitors to take a stroll along Helper's historic Main Street to visit the "phantom" galleries and businesses there.

A call to the old Albert Hotel did not confirm any stories of phantoms. While no one in town mentioned any ghosts there, I got my own ghostly impressions of the museum and wrote them down. Active areas were the blacksmith's shop in the basement where the old transported jail cells are, and all of the second floor. The area around the old 1929 Wurlitzer piano, apparently used in the Castle Gate Amusement Hall at one time, seemed haunted.

The third floor was populated by three different male apparitions, one of whom died in the hotel—more likely of old age—and the other two were suicides. Fourteen men had something to do with the old back entrance that no longer exists. Perhaps they did construction work on the place or used this entrance instead of the front one.

The two medical rooms had heavy and oppressive atmospheres. It was difficult to breathe there, as well as in the television-radio room next door. I saw two children's spirits and their mother. She seemed to be the wife of the man who had managed the hotel and might have managed it after he died.

Most interesting was the extreme pressure on my chest and the feeling of being unable to get enough air when I walked into the medical rooms and the room full of miner's breathing equipment. The pressure would disappear when I stepped out of these rooms, and when I stepped back in, it would build in my chest again. I could also hear some sort of strange breathing apparatus that I have never heard before.

The heaviest ghostly activity was in the two rooms dedicated to those who fought in the two World Wars. Every inch of a narrow hallway leading to this room is covered with neat, even rows of 5 by 7 black frames of young men's photos. I am assuming that some of them lived and some of them died, but there were no indications as to who died in the war and who did not. Even my husband felt this eeriness, as if the spirits of some of these men returned here from time to time to pay a visit to this tiny hall of remembrance. Having served in a later war himself, my husband said it felt as if voices whispered to him in that hallway, telling him or asking him things. I felt as though the voices were asking me to stay a while and listen to their stories and requests for loved ones.

The old Albert Hotel, later to be called the Helper Hotel, was in business until 1941. In 1942 the Denver and Rio Grande Railroad Company bought the building for accommodations for their train crews. In 1981 a local woman spearheaded the drive to save the building since the railroad company no longer wanted it. Plans were made to convert it into a museum. Twenty-seven different nationalities are represented in the museum, with collections from the turbulent union organizing days.

The museum only had two floors completed when it opened. It now houses over 3,000 objects, with the same number of photos catalogued there. If you are a lover of history and want to see historical displays in an old historical building with nothing slick or new about it, you will be wowed by this one. It was quite a journey for an intuitive person. The unseen folks there have a lot to say, whether those who lived there at one time or another, or those who have memorabilia on display there. For a quarter you can purchase five postcard reproductions of the photograph portrait hanging at the top of the stairs in one of the hallways. It is of a five- or six-year-old boy dressed in dirty miner's clothes, a helmet and light on his head, his seemingly oversized mining tools in his hand, and a huge tobacco pipe in his mouth. He looks directly at the camera like an old man, and his brows are furrowed with worry. It is a haunting portrait of the times.

I wrote this section on Helper several years before the museum decided to have Halloween ghost tours and began documenting their ghostly experiences in the hotel. I was surprised to learn that many of my intuitive thoughts were true when I heard a radio interview in 2007 after having visited the museum in the mid-nineties. It only goes to show you that ghosts are not aware of time. The Western Mining and Railroad Museum has jumped on the bandwagon of the new century with ghost tours, documented employee and visitor experiences with the paranormal, and even a ghost hunter society that visited the place in September 2007 before Halloween and caught orbs and dramatic EVPs. It seems that historically there was at least one murder in the hotel and three suicides, all on the third floor. Two of the men who committed suicide were Chinese, museum employee Sue Ann Martell says. She also says that the most haunted places in the museum are the jail cell areas, the mining room (where the Wurlitzer is), and the doctor's two rooms. It was an understatement when she said that spirits were attached to their stuff, and this is why the World War II photos are so overpowering.

Two personal experiences were given on the radio show, and I am sure they would tell you more if you went to Helper to visit the museum. It is, after all, the best mining and railroad museum in our entire state because of the size of its collection and the space it has for growth. They have identified at least three separate ghostly presences that people have encountered consistently enough to reveal the ghosts' habits and patterns.

Sue Ann Martell says that she had an experience that another woman employee also had a few days later. She was the last one in the building and had just turned out the lights, which makes it really dark until you get to the front desk. She heard a male voice, and thinking she had locked a visitor inside, she quickly turned on the lights to apologize to him. Imagine her surprise when no one was there! When she turned the lights back off, the male voice was right next to her and whispered directly into her ear. She quickly vacated the premises, but not without realizing that he was speaking either Chinese or Japanese. The other woman employee confirmed this story a few days later when she had the same experience. The women feel that one of the Chinese men who had committed suicide in the building was trying to communicate with them.

Another employee went into the men's bathroom, and while he was there, he heard the bathroom door slam behind him. When he went to investigate, he discovered that he was locked in the bathroom from the outside. No matter what he did, he could not get out. He struggled with the door for what seemed to be an eternity, and when he was just about ready to call for help, the door suddenly opened with no effort at all. Both employees mentioned that when they had their haunted lantern tours in the museum in 2006, two people ran out of the building in terror. It was the late night tour, and whatever happened to the two tour members was never discussed. The tours are so popular now that they've had to limit them to thirty people per group, and you must call ahead to get a ticket. Martell says that this is no childish spook alley but real ghosts instead. In my experience, ghosts are usually suffering in one way or another because of the life they did or did not lead, so games and ridicule by live people will bring out the worst in those who have something to overcome or are just playing around with the living. Now under new management, the Helper Museum and the town of Helper is fast becoming a small-town artist's haven for many.

Thistle

The Thistle Mud Slide Ghosts

The town of Thistle was a farming and ranching community in 1883, and with the advent of the railroad in 1890, it became a railroad town with 228 residents. It was the junction of the Sevier Railway and the D&RGW railroad. As a junction on a major line on the railroad, Thistle had an eight-stall roundhouse built to store water tanks, a coal tipple, and a machine shop. At that time Thistle had a post office, barber shop, schools, pool hall, saloon, depot, water system, beanery, and stores. Helper engines were needed to make the tough climb to Soldier's Summit, but when locomotive diesel engines were developed, helper engines were no longer needed, and Thistle began to lose its citizens. But even after this, Thistle was an important junction for the railroad.

A hundred years later in 1983, several families still lived in the area, and a service station and an abandoned school house were left standing in the town. There was an unusual wet cycle from 1982 to 1986, and in April and May 1983, there was a late and sudden snow melt. Several large landslides took place in the northern part of the state. The heavy season of rainfall and a severe winter caused the mountain just west of Thistle to begin sliding down. Stream beds and deposits in the canyon just above Thistle rose about one foot an hour, and the earth piled up against the buttress of Billie's Canyon and dammed the river. The huge mud slide that ensued was a mile and a half long and a thousand feet wide, and it completely flooded the town. Eventually there was a dam formed from this slide, which was a hundred and seventy feet wide.

Railroad experts decided to form the landslide into a dam and construct an overflow spillway tunnel to keep the river from forming an even larger lake. Many workers and lots of heavy equipment worked furiously to direct the flow of the mud slide in such a way that three newly drilled tunnels would drain the water. The Army corps of engineers set up a pumping system to help pump the water out of the newly formed lake. Trains were able to safely pass around the lake through the other two tunnels, while the third tunnel was used to drain the water from the lake. Thistle lay at the bottom of the lake for a while as the new lake was slowly drained to avoid flooding Spanish Fork.

The town of Thistle was no more. The railroad never reopened the tracks through the area once the lake was drained. Thistle was declared a disaster area, the first one declared in Utah. It was the most costly landslide in the history of the United States. Trucking companies had to lay off workers. There was a rerouting surcharge for each ton of coal, which pretty much stopped its shipment. Coal mines in the area had to lay off miners. There were shutdowns and canceled contracts. Some miners suddenly had to drive for two hours or more to get to their new jobs. Due to this one landslide, coal production dropped 30 percent in 1983. Even the uranium producers and oil companies lost money. Tourism dropped. Because the local highway route was blocked, all of the local companies that had to find another way to transport their goods lost money. Total cost of the Thistle landslide was estimated to be about 48 million dollars.

The only thing left when I drove through the area a few years back was the old turn-of-the-century school house whose interior was completely destroyed. Evidence of the flooding can still be seen around the area, and no one lives there now. As I rounded the corner from a long, slow descent into the valley, the school house suddenly came into view. It was standing all alone with its back to the road, a sea of mud still surrounding it. I was not aware when I drove through the valley that any of this had happened, and someone had to tell me about it later. Because of the lack of foliage and all the dirt piled up, I thought it was an old mining area. I got out and explored the old school house. It was beautiful and unique and was constructed of brown sandstone. I do not know why, but I had a strange feeling of desertion long before the school was abandoned. Today the school house is almost entirely gone. Transients have used what remains of it for shelter, and the company on whose property it sits seems to have ignored its existence. When I first saw it, the entire school was there—roof and all. I remember the date chiseled over the stone entrance as being in the 1890s. I regret not taking any photos.

Local stories are mostly about what was found in the lake after the flood and before it was drained. According to what I was told, it took almost two years to drain it.

Both reasonable and exaggerated stories abounded while the lake was still there. One story was that a forgotten baby in a closet was found by an amateur diver, obviously a story that is completely untrue. Unbeknownst to company and state officials, divers did go down to look for salvage. They sometimes found poignant items, like a doll or other kinds of personal keepsakes. It's probable that they found and kept valuable items that they never told anyone about.

Stories were also told about the man-made lake. The most famous is about a group of amateur divers who went down together to explore on their own. One of the divers got separated from the others, and as he swam along in the murky water trying to find his companions, he suddenly felt something grabbing at his ankles. He felt as if something was trying to hold him down there for good. When he finally did get free, he found his companions and led them back to the spot where he'd been caught. All of the divers' ankles were grabbed, and they really had to struggle to get away. Each of them told the same story and confirmed that no one was unaccounted for when they were struggling to get to the surface.

Urban or rural myths are told about the lake where the town of Thistle was completely submerged under water. It is supposedly a haunted and scary place after dark.

A story is told of a forgotten old woman who drowned in her home, hidden away where no one could find her. Perhaps since she lived alone no one remembered to look for her. On the other hand, you would think that a family member here or there might have missed her.

An old hermit that no one knew was living in the valley is supposed to have been smothered in the mud slide even before the lake was created. His apparition is supposed to walk the valley at night.

The hermit, the baby, the old woman, and those who grabbed at divers' ankles during this time were thought to be ghosts haunting the lake. These ghosts and apparitions, according to some, still haunt the area even though the lake is long gone.

Some people talk of what they saw while on the lake—strange things that they could not explain, such as ghosts, eerie lights, and midnight boaters. Hunters and campers have reported seeing spirits on the shores of a lake that is no more. Fishermen in the streams nearby report seeing something walk toward them in the shape of a man, but it disappears when they get closer. Stories suggest that people died there, taken by surprise as the mountain disintegrated before them, somehow forgotten as the slide made their grave in the muddy water. Yet records confirm that everyone got out safely.

Last, people passing through the area at night sometimes report seeing lights in the distance when they know nothing is there. It's as if the light of the full moon is still reflecting off the lake's surface, even though the moon is not full and the lake is no longer there.

Fairview

Fairview is the largest town in Sanpete Valley. Twenty Mormon families left Mt. Pleasant and constructed a village by the San Pitch River and Cottonwood Creek in 1859. By 1864, the town of Northbend had changed its name to Fairview, because it commanded an excellent view of wheat fields all the way to Manti.

During the Black Hawk War, for better protection, Fairview was abandoned for Mt. Pleasant, but by 1866 a fort was built with thick, ten-foot-high rock walls.

Fairview continued to grow, though it lost most of the diversity it had in the early years. Early on, Fairview and Mt. Pleasant were in a rivalry to be the hub of the valley. The Mormon Church's United Order was established in 1874, but poor crops and economics led to its demise in 1875. Agriculture and livestock have been the mainstays of Fairview, though some sawmills were also established there at one time. The railroad arrived in the 1890s. In present-day Fairview, industries include dairies, roller mills, coal mining, and fur ranches.

Like Spring City, Fairview still has many historic buildings. Several churches and homes exist from the early days, as well as a two-story rock school and brick town hall, built before the 1920s. The Fairview Roller Mills is another monument, one of the first agrarian buildings in the state. Fairview has done a lot to preserve its historical sites. The school house is now a large museum, and next to it is a more modern art museum. When I visited Fairview, I spent time in the town, enjoyed a walk to the cemetery, and rode all around the area. Friends also told me more personal stories about the area. It was the Fairview School, though, that caught my attention. While there are no town legends about the school, I got several impressions of my own in it.

It seems the little school housed about twelve classrooms, and the thick walls kept it cool inside. The museum that it currently houses is excellent. Created by a local artist, it features theme rooms, such as tool and farm equipment, ancestors and antiques, and a great collection of miniature scale houses, carriages, and wagons. There is also an outdoor farming equipment display. The art museum next door, along with other ever-changing local art exhibits, has a history of the town in photos that patrons can view.

When I was there, I had an experience I often have in such places. A person at the museum, whose heart and soul has gone into renovating and preserving it, talked a mile a minute about the museum's interesting facts and features. Town museums often become town senior citizen centers, with seniors who have garnered these riches bandying all the old town stories. This is especially wonderful for a first visit. While visiting the second time, however, an intuitive wants peace and quiet in order to "listen" to the building as it talks to her in the silence. An old building will display its recollections visually and with many feelings. It will also often speak in snatches of phrases and words from different times and eras, or sometimes even from the present. Stories of individuals will be told, as well as groups of people who speak to you in unison. Visions will be painted on a rich canvas in one's own mind, and the intuitive must have all her senses readied without interruptions.

The second time, I went with a friend, who understood my need for silence. She kept the curator busy until another couple came in, and he left us in peace by going with them to another part of the building. While my friend looked at the pioneer women's theme room upstairs, I sat in the ancestor room to rest my feet. In my mind's eye a woman came up to me—a teacher like myself—and told me her story. She told me of all the years she had taught in the building, and how I was sitting where her desk had been. She also talked about the students who had passed through her doors. She mentioned three special high school students she taught at one time or another. All three of them were killed in accidents—car or wagon—I don't know. She had chosen to stay in this room, mourning their loss, expecting them to return at any moment.

I did some research to find out if any of this was true, but I failed to find anything. In former days I would have dismissed this vision as a flight of fantasy. Now I know better and file such incidents away in my head, waiting until the day that they are proven true—if that day ever comes. Quite often they are. People call me, or I run across something in a magazine or newspaper somewhere, and the incident is confirmed, but hardly ever in the way I had pictured it. More of these visions are never confirmed, so they just sit there as experiences I can never prove, that seem so real at the time in my mind.

Also in Fairview is an old motel called the Skyline Motel. The manager I talked to at the time said that the ghost of the former manager seems to be haunting the place. The motel has been there for about thirty-five years, and the present owner has owned it for six. Before him, a woman named Bobbi Tucker owned it.

The present managers had a psychic visit the place, who told them that the motel was haunted by a little girl, as well as by Bobbi. But long before the psychic visited, everyone knew that the place was haunted. Lights dim or go on and off on their own in front of people. The present manager was staying in the room that was once Bobbi's. One day, as she was lying in the bed, it started shaking for no discernible reason. Nothing else was shaking in the room, just the bed. Guests have awakened to find an older woman standing over them, who then promptly disappears. Once the manager's husband got up to go to the bathroom in the middle of the night, looked back down the hall toward their bedroom, and saw an older woman standing in the hall. When he walked toward her, she vanished.

It is mainly the electricity that this ghost affects. Besides lights flickering or going out, sometimes the stereo will suddenly not work, or the coffee pot mysteriously starts up on its own. There is a mirror in the living room where people have reported more than once seeing a figure cross in front of it. One time the manager was lying on her bed because she was in so much pain from a bad hip. She suddenly realized that someone was massaging her hip to make her feel better, but, of course, no one was there. One summer she and another person were in one of the rooms. She was making the bed and the other person was cleaning the bathroom, when all of a sudden, all the old, heavy wooden hangers attached to the rod by the bathroom began swinging back and forth, hitting each other violently. On another occasion, the manager's mother was sound asleep in her room when she woke up to hear a woman humming. She got up and looked around. As soon as she did, the humming stopped. She got back into bed and the humming started again. Finally, the mother decided to let the woman hum. She sounded happy, almost as if she were humming while she was rocking in a rocking chair. The manager feels that every night when she and her husband go to bed, Bobbi leaves the room and doesn't return until morning.

Guests have told the manager that they have seen the little girl and the old lady haunting the motel, but no one has ever died there. This seems to be the sort of haunting in which two people are attached to a place because they are most familiar with it.

People who work at the motel talk to Bobbi all the time. Employees also feel that whenever anything upsetting happens around the place, Bobbi appears as a comforting ghost.

The manager had a troll doll collection, and for almost two years one of her favorite dolls disappeared. During that time, she found out from Bobbi's daughter, who lives near the motel, that Bobbi also loved troll dolls. After two years, the doll reappeared on her pillow in Bobbi's former bedroom.

One time a brother-in-law was visiting, and he saw a little girl walk past the other people in the room. He thought it was his daughter, until he glanced up and figured out that he didn't know who the little girl was. When he asked everyone if they had seen the little girl, they said yes, but because they had assumed it was his daughter, they hadn't paid attention to what she looked like. They realized that nobody knew who she was. No children were living in the area, and they couldn't find the little girl anywhere.

People in Fairview agree that the motel is haunted, but what confirmed the belief that the main ghost is Bobbi Tucker was when Bobbi's son took his own life. The cuckoo clock that still hangs in the motel, which belonged to Bobbi, stopped ticking at two o'clock, the exact time that the people in the motel received the news that Bobbi's son was dead. When everyone was visiting after the funeral, the manager decided to start the clock up again. As she set the clock, everyone in the room felt a cold breeze come through, and an invisible figure brushed past two people near the kitchen door and then went out the back door. Everyone present believes that it was either Bobbi's son leaving, or Bobbi herself grieving for her lost son. Everyone who works at the motel has experienced ghostly phenomena and expects more strange things will happen in the future.

A hundred-year-old house, which is still heated with woodstoves, is located up Fairview Canyon. It was built by a family named Green and was originally in the middle of a large apple orchard. Railcars used to come through, the apples were loaded into them, and the cars were joined to a train to distribute the apples to the different buyers. The old home has partially burned down at least five times, and every time it has, the LDS Church, who now owns the property, rebuilt it, finally using white cinder block to keep it from burning down again. After the Greens left the home, a series of families tried to live in it, but no one lasted long.

Finally, another family, who also happened to be named Green, moved into the home about six years ago. The Green family reports that things have disappeared and then reappeared in odd places. They experience the usual phenomena of lights going out or dimming and movement and footsteps upstairs where one big room was built when the LDS Church used it as a meeting hall. They have also heard banging and tapping sounds coming from that same room.

The family also reports being sound asleep and then waking to soft, old-time music playing when they do not have a radio, CD player, or anything else that would produce it. Sometimes the family hears a baby crying when there are no babies around. When grandchildren come to visit, they are often found sitting in closets, playing with invisible playmates, or talking to them in the room. These grandchildren normally don't do this—except at Grandma's house.

A ghost has been sighted around the Green house and seems to be an American Indian woman with long dark hair. The grandchildren talk to her, and the apparition's favorite place to wander is in the backyard, where she has been seen the most. The house is near a large creek bed in a small canyon, where it is possible that nomadic Indians might have frequently stayed in their travels. Or perhaps one of the owners of the home had an Indian wife.

Another theory—a total rumor—is known around Fairview. It seems that one of Ted Bundy's victims was killed in this vicinity, and this ghost may be one of his victims that was never found. People believe that her body lies waiting to be found in the field next to the Greens' old orchard house. The Greens have wondered if this is the woman they are seeing, since Bundy's victims often had long dark hair. If this is true, then perhaps she is trying to get someone to locate her. If it is not true, then perhaps the woman is an apparition from a time much earlier, who simply loved her house or the land that it is on and returns from time to time to check on things. It seems that if it were a murder victim, more signs to help find her would be heard or seen. It is an isolated area, and not too many people would know how to go about finding this girl.

Manti and Spring City

The Indians weren't the only threat the early settlers had to face. In their book *The Gold of the Carre-Shinob*, Kerry and Lisa Boren mention another enemy the pioneers had to face when settling Manti.

There was a compelling reason why Isaac Morley chose Temple Hill as the site of the new city. Chief Walker had pointed out the hill as being sacred to the Utes. His ancestors, he explained, the "Old Ones," once had an altar on the hill's crest where human sacrifices were performed. Morley inquired whether there were any remains of the stone altar still visible, but the chief said there was not. There were caverns beneath the hill, however, he said. Morley's curiosity was instantly piqued and he asked Walker to show him the caverns, but the chief balked: "Heap bad place," he said fearfully. "You no go there—never come out!"

"Why is it dangerous?" asked Morley. "Are there evil spirits there?"

"Worse," said Walker. "You will see when the warm weather comes." [Rattlesnakes!][14]

Manti and Spring City are only a few miles apart. I was entranced by the area when I visited these towns. I especially enjoyed my visit to the local graveyard, where rows and rows of spectacular old tombstones tell stories of their own.

The saddest stories were of the women whose children were stillborn, or those who lost their babies due to what is now known as sudden infant death syndrome. Other children died as toddlers, from fevers or other unnamed maladies. Polygamous wives, along with many of their children, sometimes surrounded a patriarch's grave marker. Many of the names we no longer hear, which made the experience entrancing but deeply saddening for an intuitive person.

The people I stayed with in Manti gave me the grand tour. It was like a fantasyland of history, warmth, and community. I also realized that as a non-Mormon I was vastly outnumbered. Still, I was impressed by the Mormon values and faith, and how all of this had created a sense of timelessness. I was impressed by the pride that many of them had in their ancestors, the pioneers, who came across the plains with little and suffered greatly in so doing. It seemed as if the earlier eras had a real sense of place in each town I visited. But I also felt that my individuality was out of place. While it was a wonderful visit and full of great comfort and love, I also realized that I could never belong there. The people welcomed me with open arms, and I will always have fond memories of my visits there. I can't say enough about how friendly, open, and charitable they were.

I was also pleasantly surprised that two interesting stories of the Manti–Spring City area were included in this grand history. One is a sad religious myth that has been told many times through the years, and the other is a dark tale of some families who built a small fort there.

Brigham Young asked several families to settle the area near a creek. This creek was named Canal Creek during the time it was used as a campsite for both Indians and scouts. James Allred and forty families settled Springtown in 1852. By 1853, the settlers had built a fort, and the settlement was known as "Little Denmark." During the Walker War, the settlers of Fort Hambleton, later known as Mount Pleasant, left their fort behind and moved into Springtown.

Eventually the families from both settlements had to abandon the Springtown fort and flee to Manti. The Indians burned the fort and took all their belongings.

In 1854 James Allred formed another group of settlers, mostly composed of newly converted Danish immigrants, and tried again to settle the area.

In 1866, during the Black Hawk War, they had to temporarily abandon the area due to more Indian hostilities.

In 1867 the settlers returned and built sawmills in the mouth of the canyon. Indian hostilities had subsided, and the town began to flourish, growing in population from 850 in 1880 to 1,230 in 1900.

The town was resettled for a third time and christened Spring City. From 1867 on, the town grew, with new canals, schools, and churches. The early buildings were of log or sod. Most of the Danish residents were sheep men, cattlemen, or farmers. The official name for the town was adopted in 1870, and Orson Hyde, who was an apostle of the LDS Church, lived there.

In 1890 the Rio Grande Western Railroad was built through town, and the town's population boomed to 1,250. By 1895, however, the town had lost two-thirds of its population and was down to approximately 400 people.[15] Spring City's population in July 2008 was 1,044, more than two hundred less than it was in the early 1890s.[16]

The Utah Heritage Foundation and the Historic American Buildings Survey Foundation have made sure that Spring City will never be forgotten, since Spring City is one of the most interesting and beautiful pioneer towns in Utah. It has remained, at least up to this writing, almost totally unaffected by the march of progress, and many of the old original stone pioneer houses and nineteenth century mansions remain. Many of Spring City's buildings are listed on the State Historic Register, and I am sure a lot of them have their own hauntings. Ghosts and apparitions of times past are everywhere, since the entire town is filled with old mansions, log houses, and commercial buildings.

Like Spring City, Manti had a lot of Mormon Danish converts who settled there in 1853. People also came from England and other Scandinavian countries, as well as from the Ohio Valley in the United States. It is much like Spring City in that it is the home of several historic buildings, the most famous being the Manti Temple, located on Temple Hill. The second Mormon temple to be built in Utah, it has one of the most interesting architectures and histories of the Mormon temples.

Construction on the temple began in 1877, and according to Cynthia Larsen Bennett, "Brigham Young described a vision in which he had seen the Prophet Moroni (who lived in the Book of Mormon times) dedicating the spot for the building of a temple. It was built with volunteer labor from beautiful buff-colored oolite sandstone quarried on the construction site. Funds were raised by members. All eggs laid on Sunday were set aside and sold as 'temple eggs'; the chickens were said to be very busy on Sundays. Men came from every town in the county to work on the temple, some walking miles every week. The road between Ephraim and Manti became well trodden in those days from the Ephraim men's feet going back and forth between home and the temple (some say it was smoother than it is now)."[17]

The temple was dedicated in 1888, a few months before Brigham Young's death, and cost a million dollars. The architect was William H. Folsom.

The word *Manti* is taken from the Book of Mormon. There were 224 settlers in Manti in 1849, and they lived peacefully with the Ute Chief Sanpitch's encampment. The first year, many of the settlers lived in dug-outs on what is now known as Temple Hill. They survived terrible blizzards, and at the risk of their own lives, the men brought in supplies by sled.

Throughout the summer the hill might as well have been known as Rattlesnake Hill, since the settlers did battle with them all summer long. Surprisingly, no one is recorded as having been bitten.

During the Walker War, three separate forts were constructed in Manti: Little Stone Fort, Log Fort, and Big Fort. Manti was one of the first five towns to ask to be incorporated in the state of Deseret.

With its unusual and striking architecture, the Manti Temple has always been the dominant man-made structure in central Utah. It suddenly comes into view as you round the curve and enter the valley. It's like a beautiful European castle on a misty and distant hill.

In modern times, the town of Manti has hosted "The Mormon Miracle Pageant," which is performed in July on the hill behind the temple. Thousands of people throughout the world come to see this pageant every year, which brings the town tourist revenue. It is also one of the most popular temples for weddings in the LDS faith. Couples come from all over the world to be married there and have their picture taken in front of it.

Inside the temple is a gorgeous, hand-carved wooden spiral staircase that winds up several stories. Not being a Mormon myself, I cannot enter the building, but I can look at it from the outside. People who go to the temple say that the inside is as magnificent as the outside. No elevators were in the building for a long time, so people in wheelchairs had to be carried up the stairs.

Rumors were told of finding a sealed-off room in the side of the mountain when they did renovations on the temple a few years ago. Stories ranged from the room being entirely empty and perhaps never needed, to finding it filled with hidden records, and even golden plates. The best stories come from the more distant past, when locals spoke of all kinds of things that existed, or had been found to exist, under the temple or inside Temple Hill. Even the sword of Laban is rumored by some to be buried or hidden in a secret room in the temple for safekeeping. (Laban was a wicked man who was beheaded with his own sword by the prophet Nephi in the Book of Mormon.)

The hill itself is spectacular. In the middle of a relatively flat valley, it seems to rise out of nowhere. One rumor is that it originally was an ancient Indian mound and that the temple was built over it. Part of the rumor is that people have had visions of Indians walking about within the temple walls, visitors from a long ago past, long before white settlers were in the valley.

Later tales describe a labyrinth of tunnels built under the temple and deep into the hill, which house sacred records.

Speculation even exists that there are temples of gold in the hill and that the Mormons built their temple over them to both hide and protect them from outside scrutiny.

Many Mormons say that they have a much deeper spiritual experience in this temple than in any other LDS temple they have attended.

Diaries and Mormon writings about personal experiences are kept near this temple. Some examples of ancestral stories include when Isaac Morley and others were discussing a temple site in the area with Brigham Young in 1850. One of the settlers, "Betsy Bradley and her three-year-old son Hyrum saw a white horse ridden by a personage dressed all in white appear on the hill northeast of the new settlement of Manti, and then watched in amazement as horse and rider disappeared."[18] The settlers speculated on whether they had seen the angel Moroni or God, but either way they considered it a divine dedication of Temple Hill.

In 1888 another man had a vision as he was traveling to the Manti Temple. He saw a multitude of spirits, among them his deceased father, who told him that they were his ancestors who needed to be baptized for the dead. This is a practice where Mormons research their dead ancestors and give them an opportunity to become members of the faith (if their ancestors so choose) by performing their temple ordinances for them by proxy. This explains the importance of genealogy work and why the LDS people are internationally known for their excellent resources in this field.[19]

Another tale taken from an 1890 *Young Women's Journal* article is a great example of the dozens of angel and Nephite stories told by the early settlers. The first janitor of the Manti Temple, Peter Alstrom, was cleaning when a terrible windstorm struck. As he was rushing around to close all the windows, he suddenly saw a man in a dark suit wandering through an area that was locked and off-limits to visitors. Anxious to get the windows closed, the janitor went about his business closing the windows, thinking that the man was a visitor who had somehow gotten in. After all the windows were closed, Alstrom tried to find the man but couldn't. When he tried the door to that particular area, it was still locked.

A few nights later, shortly after the dedication of the building, a fierce rainstorm hit Manti. The janitor had just settled in for the evening when he remembered that a window in one of the rooms was still open a little. He went to the room to close the window, and when he opened the door, he saw a "personage clothed in white robes, a brilliant light surrounding him and filling the whole room."[20] Frightened and overwhelmed, the caretaker ran upstairs and began to pray. The next day he was assured by the president of the temple that angels were often in the temple but not everyone was allowed to see them.[21]

Being the second oldest Mormon temple in the state, this building rises spectacularly above everything else on Temple Hill. No matter what is hidden beneath it, or goes on within its walls, this structure continues to fascinate and empower the people who visit it. Since it is a religious edifice, whatever happens inside would be attributed to angels or prophets and never to apparitions and ghosts. The age of the building and its placement on sacred—and possibly consecrated and energized land—makes this particular temple special above all the others in the state. In the nineteenth and early twentieth centuries, people believed in magic much more than they do today. This particular place has carried its ancient Indian and pioneer spirits, its ghosts, and its angels and prophets into the twenty-first century with ease.

Spring City also has its share of beautiful old buildings. Louisa Bennion writes beautifully about growing up there:

> We watched the old Spook house on the corner burn down. It was an adobe house, melted down to the lathe in many spots, and full of the evidence of sheep having been its only recent inhabitants. The people who had inherited the property lived far away, and were worried the house would fall down on kids sneaking into it (I had, and found some old playing cards before I got spooked and ran home), so they let the fire department do a practice burn on it. My mother stood in the road and cried. To her it was a lovely, soulful old house, and it could have been saved. . . . Our neighbor, renowned artist Ella Peacock, captured the image of the burned-out shell of the "Spook House" the day after it was practiced on by the local fire department. She shook her fist at them in frustration on the day it was burned.[22]

Bennion states that her parents moved there in 1977 around the time she was born. As a little girl she heard about the ice cream parlor, candy store, and theater that had already met their demise before her time. By then it had been declared a historic district, and those with money were coming into town to renovate and preserve some of the buildings and homes in the area. Those who lived in Spring City were a bit upset about being told what to do with their own properties. It wasn't easy to tear down Grandma's old home and build a new one on the inherited property.

The May home tour in Spring City has become a tradition for outsiders to attend. Before the 1970s, Spring City was rapidly becoming an official ghost town. Once known as Allred's Settlement, it would never die completely. It returned again and again, with several names and nicknames before Spring City became the final one.

Both Manti and Spring City are full of ornate mansions, stone pioneer houses, and a few original log houses. Manti has nineteenth century homes, churches, and public and commercial buildings that are on the National Historic register. It requires driving down the side streets to see all of the beautiful homes. The most famous is the Patten rock house, constructed in 1854 by John Patten, which is now the Spring City museum. Due to the layers of history there, it is one of the most spectacular homes. The Beck home, the Monson home, the Masonic lodge, the old school house, and the bishop's storehouse are all on the historic register. An easterner would be amazed to find such detailed architecture in a small western town like Spring City. Structures like these would normally be found further east.

Spring City has a premier ghost story, one of the best I've heard, but establishing the truth of this story is another matter!

The story relates to the Johnson mansion and has existed ever since the mansion was built—or soon after, since I was able to find several versions of the story from throughout the last hundred years.

The Jacob Johnson home was built in 1875, and in later years became known by some of the local people as the "pink castle." Judge Johnson lived in the home until 1892, and a large Victorian section was added in 1892. Johnson had a law office in Spring City, and he had an office and library to the north of his house. He later became a judge for the Seventh Judicial District of Utah and used a part of his mansion for the courthouse. He was a circuit judge for courts in Manti, Moab, Monticello, Price, and Castle Dale. This makes the stories even more intriguing, because he certainly must have made a few enemies in covering such a wide area of the state, no matter how fair and just he might have been. Using part of his house as a courtroom would certainly attract a few disgruntled spirits to his house. I have visited such places where a home was also used as a courthouse, and without a doubt, such houses have a lot to say or show you from the past.

In doing research for other stories, I ran across a bit of information on Judge Johnson's character. It seems he was well known throughout the region for rigidly following the rules, both in his private life and in the courtroom. He stuck to the letter of the law and often imposed the stiffest sentences he could. If you went before Judge Johnson, you knew you would end up with the maximum sentence for whatever crime you had committed. He had a reputation that indicated he would have created enemies, as well as rumors about him, both in his personal life and as a courtroom judge.

The *Utah History Encyclopedia* states that in 1854, shortly after his father died, Johnson immigrated with his mother from Aalborg, Denmark. He first lived in Ogden, Utah, then in Sacramento, California, and later in Carson City, Nevada. He eventually moved to the White Pine Mining District and studied law.

In 1872 he moved to Spring City to practice law and to farm the land. He was a United States District Attorney from 1880 to 1881 and United States Commissioner for Utah from 1881 to 1883. He was a probate judge for Sanpete County from 1883 to 1890, prosecuting attorney for the county from 1892 to 1894, and a judge for the Seventh Judicial District from 1896 to 1905. He was a Republican and a Mason when he was elected to the United States House of Representatives and served there from 1913 to 1915. He did not get re-elected by his party for another term. He returned to Salt Lake City to practice law and died in 1925. He is buried in the Salt Lake City Cemetery, and his funeral was held in the Salt Lake Masonic Temple.[23]

"He had married Margaret Anderson in October 1873, and the couple were the parents of two sons. After her death on 15 December 1885, Johnson married Matilda Justesen of Spring City, by whom he fathered two sons and four daughters."[24]

It only adds to the mystery and legend of the house that Judge Johnson spent a lot of money and time to build the expensive and quickly constructed addition to his home and then moved out of it right away. The version told in several older accounts says that a man (keeping the judge's identity safe) who owned a house in Spring City killed his wife and buried her under the porch. His wife just disappeared one day, and people were told that she ran off. This was not that unusual in those days, when an unhappy wife had no other alternative but to run away.

No one knew that the wife from the Johnson house was dead, but her ghost supposedly haunted the husband to the point that he was driven out of the house and left town for good. Her ghost has been haunting the house ever since, and anyone who has tried to live there has also been haunted by her.

These tales were from the turn of the century. A 1920s version states that the house stood empty at that time and simply lists it as one in existence in Spring City.

As I read the nebulous accounts, I realized from the descriptions that the story might be about Jacob Johnson's house. People tried not to pinpoint him, but he was the only famous judge who lived there.

The 1920s version also states that over the years attempts were made to explore the basement crawl space, but to no avail. No evidence was ever found of a body buried under the porch, but the story remained and was added upon by different storytellers. It is described in written folklore accounts, told by word of mouth, and even told on radio stations at Halloween time. None of them identify the house, for obvious reasons.

The modern version of this story is a much better one. Early on, especially when the wind was high, a woman weeping loudly could be heard coming from the house late at night, so that even the neighbors heard things they could not explain.

One hundred and twenty years later, a young couple, unaware of the house's history, dug up the foundation to put in a new plumbing system. They supposedly found bones that were later identified (not by any officials) as human. The owners had the bones privately analyzed, and they were discovered to be the bones of a young woman. The couple did not go any further than this and never called the authorities for fear of losing their new home. The bones soon disappeared, and the plumbing was put in and covered over. The whole affair was quietly forgotten.

The couple soon told a few trusted friends that odd things were happening in the house. Lights went on and off or dimmed when the couple had not touched the switches, and the water turned on by itself when no one was there. Cupboard doors swung wide open, especially if someone was telling a ghost story around Halloween, and, of course, doors opened, shut, or locked on their own.

What really got to the couple was hearing children's voices upstairs when their own children were definitely not in the house. Or the sounds of a woman crying down in the narrow cellar or crawl space near the old porch's location.

It would be interesting to find out what Judge Johnson's first wife died of. Did she die of a broken heart as well as of some mysterious ailment? Did the rumors start because he so quickly married again and had more children?

The fact that Judge Johnson was a Gentile in a small Mormon town, especially a Gentile who could convict you harshly if you committed a crime, was probably enough to start several rumors. Masons were known to practice secret rituals, and Mormons and Masons were certainly at odds at the time. Any number of reasons existed to be suspicious of this judge. Isn't it fascinating that we will never know the truth to any of these rumors and ghost stories, even though the children's voices are still heard and the woman still cries in the cellar, and will do so as long as the house stands?

Richfield, Glenwood, Sigurd, and Fillmore

Black Hawk was a Ute Chieftain who fought his own private war against the whites. He left behind ghosts and spirits in the skirmishes of the Black Hawk War. The battles and massacres near Richfield, Sigurd, and Glenwood left their own hauntings on the land. Wherever a battle took place, the spirits who didn't survive are sure to be haunting the area.

Art Accord, the famous silent movie star, was from Glenwood. He was young when he died in a terrible and mysterious way in Mexico.

Fillmore was the original territorial capital, with a haunted county jail of its own, as well as another famous chief, Wakara. Wakara's claim to fame is having one of the most unusual burial sites in the mountains near Fillmore. This, if you can find it, is not a place to visit at night, or even in the daytime, since it is haunted with the spirits who suffered and died there in honor of their chieftain.

Richfield

Richfield was once considered the the hub of Central Utah. In 1863 George W. Bean took an exploring party into the area, where they found a big spring near today's Richfield.

In January 1864, a party of ten men, led by Albert Lewis, arrived in the area to establish a settlement. By that winter, several families had been called by the Mormon Church to settle there, and through necessity, they lived in dugouts for more than a year. The first two white women in the area were Ann Swindle and Charlotte Doxford.

The town went through several names before becoming Richfield. It was first called Big Springs, then Warm Springs, and even Omni after a prophet in the Book of Mormon.

By 1865, about one hundred families lived in Richfield. A school was immediately built, and the settlers started construction on a fort, with each man being asked to build a section of the wall as payment for his land.

After Black Hawk stole ninety head of stock near Salina and two settlers were killed while working in the canyon, many of the families moved to Richfield, along with the families from Glenwood.

The Black Hawk War had been brewing for years, but the official date given for its beginning is April 1865. Some Ute Indians and settlers met in Manti to settle a dispute over some cattle that had been killed by starving Indians. The meeting ended in violence when a Mormon pulled a young chieftain off his horse, thus insulting the entire band.

The Ute Chieftain Black Hawk took his band on a rampage and killed five Mormons, stealing hundreds of cattle as more and more Indians flocked to his side for food and protection. By the end of the first year, Black Hawk and his followers had stolen over two thousand head of cattle and killed more than twenty-five whites, which succeeded in uniting several tribes, including the Navajos and Paiutes.

The war went on for two years before Black Hawk decided to make peace with the Mormons. His followers fell away, but Indian troubles of one kind or another continued until 1872, when two hundred federal troops arrived in the valley.[25]

In 1871 Richfield was resettled by 150 families. The town continued to grow, becoming a commercial and cultural center for most of the Central Utah area.[26]

Later in the history of Richfield, Ralph Ramsey, a locally famous sculptor who carved the Eagle Gate in Salt Lake City, built the Ramsey House. It is now a museum that houses furniture and memorabilia. The museum has over two hundred local oral histories stored in its library.

Glenwood and Sigurd

Glenwood was the site of a bloody incident during the Black Hawk War. Originally called Prattsville, Glenwood was founded in 1863 when twenty-five families spent their first winter inside rock-walled cellars with roofs only a foot above the ground. They also spent their first years there in constant fear of an Indian attack.

In *Roadside History of Utah*, Cynthia Larsen Bennett wrote, "One mother gave birth to her baby in the back of a wagon while she and her family were fleeing an Indian attack. Merrit Stanley, the town blacksmith, was shot several times by Indians when he went outside to fill his coal bucket."[27]

Bennett continues, "On the morning of March 21, 1867, news came that a fresh shipment of goods had arrived at the Glenwood co-op. Jense Peterson and his wife left their eighteen-month-old daughter with a neighbor in Richfield, and, along with another neighbor, fourteen-year-old Mary Smith, started to Glenwood ... When the family reached Black Ridge, east of the Sevier River, they saw Indians in the river bottoms stealing cattle. The Petersons attempted to flee on foot but they were overtaken and killed. The Indians scalped them all and stripped and mutilated the women's bodies. White boys hiding in the river bottoms had witnessed much of the episode and ran for help. Within a month the entire county was evacuated."[28]

These massacres usually took place when two or three people were traveling together unarmed and unsuspecting. In an earlier incident in June 1858, Indians massacred Jens Jergensen and his wife, along with Christian E. Kjerulf and Jens Terkelsen, who were traveling unarmed on their way to Sanpete Valley. This became known as the Salt Creek Massacre. Many of these massacre sites go unmarked, unless the local citizenry decides to erect a small monument or they come to the attention of the Utah Daughters of the Pioneers, who have done a great job of marking most of these sites in Utah. The Salt Creek Massacre does have a large rock monument by the side of the road. The smaller monument in Glenwood is a little harder to find.

In 1874 Erastus Snow established the United Order in the Glenwood and Siguard area. (The United Order was a Mormon attempt at utopian living.) This system continued to flourish for the next five years. All property was given to the bishop, and people received credits for their labor, which they could turn in to the bishop's storehouse for goods or services. Two gristmills, a sawmill, a shingle mill, a cording mill, a tannery, and a sugarcane factory were established. A telegraph was installed, and business and individual dwellings were built during this time. Eventually the Zion Cooperative Mercantile Institute, which was built in 1878, was where all town members would cash in their credits in exchange for money to purchase items. The United Order system in Utah failed, broken by outside influences and internal friction among the members. The ZCMI store continued to operate until 1930 and is still standing on Main Street in Glenwood. The Joseph Wall Gristmill, built of black lava rock and brick in 1874, was still standing in the 1980s and was on the National Historic Register.

Because of its heat and humidity, Sigurd was originally called Neversweat, but due to the colorful sandstone cliffs surrounding it, the name was soon changed to Vermillion. As the population grew, the Mormon community or ward was divided into two wards. The south ward became Sigurd, and the north became Vermillion. Eventually the entire town was called Sigurd, but there are still those who call the north end Vermillion. Today Sigurd, with a population of approximately 432 people,[29] is located twelve miles south of Salina and depends on agriculture and a local paper mill and gypsum plant to keep its economy going.

Two Indian battles took place at this site before Sigurd was settled. The Cedar Ridge battle occurred when settlers were fleeing to Monroe from their settlements in Sevier County. They were ambushed by a small group of Indians. One man was killed, one was severely injured, and the rest managed to escape. The other incident involved two men, Charles and George Wilson. They tried to cross the Sevier River at Rocky Ford. Charles was immediately killed when the Indians attacked them, but George managed to escape by digging a hole for his whole body in the riverbank, completely burying himself in the mud and using a reed for a vent hole to the surface. He stayed like that all night and was able to escape in the morning.[30]

People around Sigurd and Glenwood, Utah, which are directly east of Richfield on the other side of the Sevier River, say that there is an old road in Glenwood that leads out to a place called Hepler's Pond. The story is from the late 1800s and has been added upon over the years. In this tale, an old log cabin belonging to a man called Hepler sits next to the pond. As the story goes, Hepler lost his temper one night and went completely out of his head. He murdered his entire family and threw all their bodies in the pond. Hepler was never brought up on charges of any kind and continued to live by himself in the cabin. His family simply disappeared. The road to the pond has added to the mystique of the place, because it winds and curves and has a lot of sharp turns that force you to drive slowly so you can witness things that might otherwise go unnoticed. No one knows how long the old log cabin has been there.

One unexplained phenomenon along the road is that your car's headlights will sometimes go on and off repeatedly as you pass the log cabin and pond. Also, a lot of people claim to have been run off the road, with no explanation as to why it happened. Other times people do have an explanation. They say they saw something in the rearview mirror—a shadowy figure holding a lantern and standing in the middle of the road behind them. The figure sways back and forth as it slowly walks down the road.

An old tree that looked like a hand sticking out of the water used to be in the pond, and when the moon hit it just right, people would say that one of the drowned family members was trying to get their attention. A few years ago someone shot the end of the tree off, but it didn't stop the tales. People also see lights in the cabin in the middle of the night.

Those brave souls who ventured into the cabin say they could hear footsteps at the other end of the house. Legend has it that old Hepler, whose spirit still walks his property, is a interactive ghost. People have been pushed, shoved, and touched on the back of their necks, which made the hair on their arms stand up. It is said that the spirits of both the murdered family and old Hepler continue to haunt the area. Perhaps someone who lives in the Glenwood and Sigurd area knows more history about the cabin and the pond and can set us straight about these ghostly spirits.

Glenwood has one more claim to fame that comes from back in the days when it was still called Prattsville. The silent movie star, Art Acord, was born there. He went from a runaway ranch hand at age twelve to a rodeo circus star, stuntman, and eventually a cowboy star in Hollywood where he made over a hundred movies. He was the best horseman among all the stuntmen at the time, and his good looks got him into the movies. He married three times, began drinking and fighting, and eventually ended up in Mexico where he still had a huge fan following.

Art died in 1931 from cyanide poisoning and complications related to hepatitis.

His death was listed as being self-inflicted, but some say he was murdered. Since he met such a tragic, untimely, and mysterious death in Mexico, perhaps his spirit comes back to visit his hometown from time to time.[31]

Fillmore

Fillmore was settled in 1852 with thirty houses and a log school house for the thirty families who were led there by Anson Call to settle. The first territorial capital, Fillmore was named after President Millard Fillmore because he appointed Brigham Young Utah's first territorial governor.

The first session of the Utah legislature convened in December 1855 in the monumental Fillmore statehouse. The fifth and sixth sessions were held there, but the rest were moved to Salt Lake City, because Fillmore was too far away from the hub of the state and did not have adequate accommodations. Fillmore was centrally located, but Southern Utah was not developing as fast as the northern part of the state. With at least three or even four giant wings planned, the statehouse was never completed, because the federal government reneged on its deal to fund the project. Today it is a museum for the town.

Rumors abound about ghosts in the statehouse, and any reported stories center around one room that was a temporary county jail. Visitors say that the room has a strange feeling and report being touched on the shoulder or arm. Some have even come away with a photo or two of streaks of light or orbs.

The famous Gunnison Massacre happened in Millard County, not too far from Fillmore. Eight men were killed by the Indians, and the survivors made their way to Fillmore and reported the tragedy. Captain John W. Gunnison was taken to Fillmore for burial, and William Potter, a Mormon guide, was buried at his home in Manti. Six other men rest in a common grave near the site. The men were warned about the Indians by Gunnison's friend, Bishop Anson V. Call, but since Gunnison was friends with Kanosh and Moshoquop, he wasn't worried. Two Indians saw the group's military uniforms and army equipment and reported their whereabouts to their chief, but they did not get close enough to see that it was Gunnison. The first shot was fired at the rising of the sun, and minutes later, eight men were dead, killed by the Indians' guns and arrows.[32]

Chief Walkara died in the vicinity of Meadow Creek in 1855 and was buried in the mountains near Fillmore. The burial was in a secret location (now known to be Dry Canyon, the first canyon north of Corn Creek) that is believed to have been robbed by whites in 1909. Rumors circulated that his wives were also killed and buried with him. A little boy was fastened alive to the pedestal beside Walkara's body and was left there to die, buried alive.[33] People passing could hear the boy calling to them, but they were afraid to do anything. The barbaric burial also involved the killing of several horses so that the great chief could have his possessions with him in the afterlife. Material goods were buried with him. The grave was later robbed of everything in it, including the bodies. Supposedly, a Charles Kelly located and visited the site soon after it was robbed and found it to be empty. Certainly a spirited place for those aware of ghosts, the gravesite would be a place best left to its own!

Had the old statehouse been completed, it would have been massive. Only one of its four wings was completed. Each wing was supposed to represent and serve the four directions of the vast Utah Territory. The Daughters of the Utah Pioneers worked diligently to save the old building when it was deteriorating and abandoned in the 1920s. They obtained state funds for renovations and operated the place until 1957, when the State Parks and Recreation Commission took over. Dances, meetings, schoolrooms, and jail rooms all occupied this building at one time or another. The usual things are claimed to be ghostly activity in the old statehouse, including footsteps, knocking on walls, misplaced items that turn up somewhere unexpected, and an occasional voice calling out an employee's name when no one but the employee is there. If permission were given, it would be an interesting place to investigate.[34]

Notes

1. *Springcreek Camp DUP Histories* (Springville, Utah: Daughters of the Pioneers, 1943–48), 27–33
2. Marie Jensen Whiting and Jerri Sorensen Fackrell, *Early Springville Homes*, 2 vols., 1979.
3. Chad Daybell, *One Foot in the Grave: The Strange but True Adventures of a Cemetery Sexton* (Springville, Utah: Bonneville Books, 2001).
4. Ibid., 2.
5. Ibid., 95.
6. Madoline C. Dixon, *Peteetneet Town: A History of Payson, Utah* (Provo Utah: Press Publishing, 1974) 202.
7. Ibid., 203–4.
8. Ibid., 204.
9. Personal interview on February 2, 2010, with June Bartholemew who owned the resort with her husband from 1950 to 1975. Her son Jim Bartholemew now lives on the property.
10. *Utah History Encyclopedia*, edited by Allen Kent Powell (Salt Lake City: University of Utah Press, 1994), 523.
11. City-Data.com, http://www.city-data.com/city/Spanish-Fork-Utah.html, accessed January 8, 2010.
12. Mark Havnew "Parowan Gap Displays Yearly Spectacle," *The Salt Lake Tribune*, June 20, 2005, B4.
13. Ibid.
14. Kerry Ross Boren and Lisa Lee Boren, "Isaac Morley—One of God's Footsteps," *The Gold of the Carre-Shinob* (Springville, Utah: Cedar Fort, Inc., 1998), 29.

15. Allen Roberts, "Spring City," *Utah History Encyclopedia*, 525–26.
16. City-Data.com, http://www.city-data.com/city/spring-city-utah.html, accessed on Jan. 11, 2010.
17. Cynthia Larsen Bennett, *Roadside History of Utah* (Missoula, Montana: Mountain Press Publishing Company, 1999), 199.
18. Shirley Bahlmann, *Unseen Odds* (Springville, Utah: Bonneville Books, 2004), 55–56.
19. Ibid.
20. *The Young Woman's Journal*, edited by Susan Young Gates (Salt Lake City: Young Ladies' Mutual Improvement Associations of Zion, 1889), April 1890, 1:213.
21. Bahlmann, *Unseen Odds*, 84–88.
22. Louisa Bennion, "My Own Private Ghost Town," *Utah Preservation*, 9 vol. series, 5:72–76.
23. *Utah History Encyclopedia*, http://www.media.utah.edu/UHE/, accessed on Jan. 12, 2010.
24. Ibid.
25. John A. Petersen, "Black Hawk War," *Utah History Encyclopedia*, 43–44.
26. Judy Busk, "Richfield," *Utah History Encyclopedia*, 466–67.
27. Bennett, *Roadside History of Utah*, 206.
28. Ibid.
29. City-Data.com, http://www.city-data.com/city/Sigurd-Utah.html, accessed Jan. 14, 2010.
30. *Utah History Encyclopedia*, http://www.media.utah.edu/UHE/, accessed on Jan. 12, 2010.
31. Answers.com, http://www.answers.com/topic/art-acord, accessed on Jan. 13, 2010.
32. Utah State Research Center, http://history.utah.gov/, accessed Jan. 14, 2010.
33. Ibid.
34. Ibid.

BOOK FOUR

IRON COUNTY TO
KANE COUNTY

Cedar City to the Grand Canyon

Cedar City

Cedar City (Coal Creek) Apparitions

Not only is Cedar City famous for its replica of an ancient Shakespearean theatre, but it is also paranormally famous. Multiple haunted mansions and buildings are located there, along with a Union Pacific Junction Depot, an old retirement home, and a former pizza place, all hopping with paranormal activity.

On the Southern Utah University campus is the famous historical story about "Old Sorrel," a horse whose likeness lives on in a statue. The Old Main Bell Tower also hosts some ghosts, one of which is the subject of the most famous ghost story in the southern part of the state. Versions exist from several decades of students, and the stories have become more embellished with each generation. The spirits of Old Main reflect the changing times. Haunting music can still be heard today from the long ago vanished stringed instruments that were once stored on the third floor. The crows caw as they stop to rest in the bell tower, whose knell was once a warning to early settlers that death was approaching.

Settled in November 1851, the place known as "Little Muddy," and later Coal Creek, became Fort Cedar. The initial settlement consisted of a group of thirty-five English, Welch, and Scotch miners, who planned to establish an ironworks twenty miles north of Parowan. These miners were part of Brigham Young's Mormon militia, and they traveled to the area in two groups: a foot soldier company and a cavalry company. They settled on the north bank of Coal Creek, built small houses within the fort that they were constructing, and named the placed Fort Cedar because of the cedar or juniper trees in the area. They used the boxes from their wagons, turned upside down, for shelter while building their cabins. Once the cabins were built, the men brought their families—over one hundred people—from Parowan.

The Iron Mission had begun. As more and more ironworkers arrived, the little fort could not support them all, and so another site was selected on the south bank of the stream where the settlers could also better protect themselves from Indian attacks. The Walker War forced them to abandon the original fort, and in just two days they moved to the new site. The new fort was a half-mile square, with a high wall around it.

Two years later, in 1855, with the help of Brigham Young, they selected the third site, which was on the floodplain of the valley. This site was closer to the ironworks blast furnace and the site where the present city resides. Fort Cedar covered sixty-three acres and contained 120 lots. The walls of the fort were nine feet tall. An interesting note is that Butch Cassidy, born in Beaver, often used this area as a hideaway. In 1923 the railroad arrived in town and brought even more iron with it.

Cedar City sits in the middle of the Dixie National Forest and has a total of six state or national parks around it, as well as the Brian Head Ski Resort. It is referred to as the Gateway to the Parks because it is situated close to Zion National Park, Bryce Canyon, and Cedar Breaks National Park, to name a few. Not only is it the home of the Utah Shakespeare Festival and Southern Utah University, but it is also the home of the annual Utah Summer Games.

State Normal School, a branch of the University of Utah, was established in Cedar City in 1897, but not before the town established a school in the old LDS ward hall on private land. Two months after the school opened, the state school system was established. The State Attorney General told the people of Cedar City that the school would have to be shut down because it was not on land deeded by the state. They were told to build a new state school by September on state-deeded land. By this time it was winter, and in order to get building materials, a party of four men were sent on an expedition to the lumber mills in the canyons. They pushed through shoulder-high snowdrifts and would have been lost if it wasn't for a sorrel horse that was determined to push on. The old sorrel steadily walked in front of the party, resting on his haunches like a dog when he tired, and then pushing on. He led them to the mills and back again. Thus, the legend of the Old Sorrel was born. In time the school was built, and the old sorrel was honored by a statue on the grounds of the university.

Old Brickhouse and Dragon King Restaurant

Betty's Café closed, and the old Brick House stood empty and deserted for a while. At present the Dragon King restaurant occupies the building. Stories of ghostly activity in the café have been reported on several Internet sites over the years, and for decades people have felt a ghostly presence there. It is an active entity that pinches, places its hands on people's backs and shoulders, and roughly pushes and shoves patrons. Besides the usual door openings and closings, lights turning on often by themselves, and objects being moved about, the ghost even appears late at night, sometimes as a full apparition dressed in blue jeans and a plaid shirt. I was unable to find any history about the original home. I can only surmise that behind the restaurant's locked doors a ghostly presence still awaits its chance to frighten the new owners—who aren't talking!

Adrianna's Restaurant and the Garden House Restaurant

Once the home of the mayor of Cedar City, this building has been rumored to have active ghosts. The present owners feel otherwise, though, and the old home has been operating as a restaurant for the past few years.

James Smith was a sheep farmer who built his house before World War II. He became a millionaire, and his house is one of the biggest in town.

The Smith family had ten children, and their last child was a baby girl who died at birth. Some locals believe that this child is haunting the old home.

Smith was a millionaire, but he drove around town in an old truck and usually wore old work clothes. Once he drove all the way to Salt Lake City to deposit some money in his bank. When he got there, he was arrested, because the police did not believe the money was his. Smith liked to show off his wealth in front of people by rolling up ten-dollar bills and smoking them like cigarettes.

Another interesting story about the Smith family concerns his wife, Mary. A Peeping Tom was in their neighborhood, and Mary was worried about her nine children, so she conceived a plan to catch the Peeping Tom. The next time she spotted him around their house, she climbed up onto the roof and drenched him with a pot of hot water.

Smith descendants lived in the home until the early 1970s, and it wasn't until 1989 that the Rolands purchased the home and turned it into a restaurant. Rumors of ghosts started during the time the home was empty.

In the entryway of the restaurant is an old rolltop desk that Jim Smith had built into the wall. This is where his study was located. The old desk even has writing carved into the wood by his daughter, Belle, who was learning to write cursive at the time.

The owners do not notice any strange or odd happenings, but some of the employees do. Mr. Roland did have one experience while locking up alone at two o'clock in the morning. The soda machine clicked on by itself as he passed it and then turned off as he went out the door.

A psychic visited the restaurant and told the owners that she'd seen a little girl laughing and running around. The employees were surprised at this, because the restaurant rarely has child diners. The psychic was immediately drawn to the attic and said that she sensed a strong spirit dwelling there. Now, no one, if they are alone, will go up to the attic to turn off the lights. Either the lights stay on all night or the ghost occasionally turns them off for the employees.

The ghosts are supposedly the little girl who died there and old Mr. Smith. Both apparitions are becoming well known in Cedar City today as the stories become more colorful and creative with time.

Leigh Mansion

The Leigh family has been prominent in Cedar City for several generations. Henry Leigh is considered one of the founding fathers of the city. He not only contributed financially to the town and the building of its university, but he also put in many man-hours to make things happen. He was a Mormon bishop, the mayor of the city in 1893–94, superintendent of schools, and a College of Southern Utah board of director. One fun story told about his superintendent days relates to him visiting each of the schools as part of his job. The principals would hear his buggy coming and add a lot of fuel to the fire to warm up the school so that the superintendent would think the school was always that warm. Inevitably, Henry would come in, sit down, become sleepy, and doze off right in the middle of his observation.

It is not known which Leighs originally lived in the home, but it eventually became student apartments. A young couple with small children finally bought it and spent a lot of time renovating and restoring it, but they no longer live there. The current owners could only tell me that Mrs. Leigh (probably the wife of a son of Henry Leigh) was raised in Toquerville. This family of Leighs owned Leigh's Carpet and Furniture in Cedar City, and Mrs. Leigh's husband built the house for her. When her husband died, Mrs. Leigh moved back to Toquerville but missed the large home so much that she moved back to it and had a small side home built next door for her youngest child, Ravenna. Ravenna lived in the smaller home and took care of her mother. When the mother died, her daughter Ravenna Leigh lived in the smaller home alone.

Apparently some of Ravenna's sisters died in the mansion. One of her sisters, who had recently been married, contracted meningitis and came home to be nursed. She passed away a short time later. Another sister died in the home when she was young.

It is said that Ravenna worked as a World War II pilot carrying supplies back and forth across the United States. Ravenna did have some children but must have outlived her husband by several years. She was the last person in her immediate family to live on the Leigh property. She lived in the smaller home until she could no longer take care of herself. During this time, the mansion was made into a girl's dormitory for the college and then later divided up into apartments.

While the Leigh family knows nothing about ghosts or apparitions in the mansion, everyone who has had any contact with the place feels that it is haunted, especially the young family who restored it. It is one of just a few eclectic Victorian homes in Cedar City. The sandy red brick house had the first black roof ever in Cedar City. The home has parlors on the left side, and the kitchen is in the back where coal stove heating is still evident. The home has a front porch, and on the left side of the house is a high turret with a balcony over the front porch. It is one of the most charming homes in Cedar City. Unfortunately, others like it have been torn down. The couple put in central heating, new plumbing, and totally restored the house before they moved out of town. It was during the renovations that family members noticed that the house was haunted.

The first thing the mother noticed was that when she yelled at her children to stop making so much noise, she would hear a loud bang as though some heavy piece of furniture had fallen over. She noticed that it happened every time she yelled at or called her children. When they would go to investigate, they couldn't find anything turned over. One day she was in the parlor and had all her children lined up on the couch. From this vantage point she could see the stairway. She was giving her children a lecture about behaving when they heard a big bang upstairs and at the same time all the lights around them flickered on and off. The upstairs noise made all the children look toward the stairs. When the mother saw her children's ashen faces, she turned to see what they were staring at. A young girl was coming down the stairs, and one of the children cried, "She doesn't have any legs!" This frightened everyone, especially when the girl disappeared at the bottom of the stairs.

In the front window was a welcome lamp that was only turned on if someone was late getting home. The mother noticed on several occasions that the welcome lamp was on when she hadn't turned it on. Her husband didn't believe her and was getting frustrated with having to constantly turn it off. One night her husband said to her, "Why do you keep that light on all the time? It's a waste of electricity!" He turned the light off, and as he did so, it promptly came on again, right while he was watching it. From that day forward the light came on by itself every night, and they had to turn it off every morning.

The mother also discovered that the ghost couldn't stand it if she didn't finish the vacuuming. If the mother stopped vacuuming and went to do something else for a minute, the vacuum would come back on by itself. One day her husband came home for lunch while his wife was vacuuming. She went in the kitchen to talk to him, and the vacuum came on. Her husband checked it and couldn't find anything wrong. He turned it off and went back to the kitchen, but as soon as he left the room, the vacuum turned on again. It even came on one time when the wife had pulled the plug.

The more upset family members got with each other in the home, or the more irritating the talk between two family members became, the more poltergeist activity there was. The basement light in a storage room would turn on by itself, and the more her husband complained about it, the more the light would go right back on after he had left. Once while doing her oldest daughter's hair in the downstairs bathroom and laundry room, her daughter pointed to an area in the room where the mother could see nothing and said, "Mommy, I want my hair like hers." When questioned, the little girl repeated, "Like hers, Mommy, like that little girl's over there. I want a big blue bow like hers!"

The family had purchased an old piano that was manufactured in the 1850s. One day the mother left the house, and the children were alone for a few minutes. When she returned, her children, even the oldest one, were hiding in bedrooms under their covers. When she asked what had happened, they said, "The ghost plays the piano." The children were twelve, ten, and six years old at the time. The mother later heard the piano playing from time to time. It was never a tune, just scales, over and over again. The family had a St. Bernard dog whose hair would go straight up, and he would attack something in the living room. After a couple of episodes of this, the dog refused to go into that room.

On another occasion, visiting relatives were staying in the home. At least five of the children were under four years of age, and youngsters were sleeping in sleeping bags all over the house. Most of them were in the upstairs back part of the house in an area that at one time was a private apartment. One bedroom had a bunk bed where a seventeen-year-old was sleeping on the top bunk. In the middle of the night, he saw a young woman leaning over the child in the lower bunk. She was in a long white dress, and he thought she was a real person. He said, "Excuse me, can I help you?" The woman ignored him and turned and went out the door. He got out of bed and went looking for her. He watched as she went from room to room, checking on all the babies and kids, until she came out at the end of the hall and disappeared before his eyes. He looked everywhere but couldn't find her. The next morning he asked everyone who the young woman was. His aunt told him that no such lady had ever been in the house. This young man was not one to make things up and was a total skeptic when it came to ghosts and spirits. As the family talked about it, they decided that this lady ghost was a guardian angel who was especially protective of children.

A friend who came to visit put her baby in an upstairs turret bedroom. The young mother closed the door while she chatted with her friend. As soon as she got back downstairs, the door to the bedroom opened by itself. This routine happened seven times in a row, until finally the visitor gave up and brought her baby back downstairs. From this experience, the owners learned that the ghost would not allow a baby to be left alone in the house at any time. She was apparently a warm and loving spirit, who besides loving her home, felt highly protective of young children. It is the couple's theory that she lived in the home and lost an infant there. Perhaps she lost more than one and doesn't want anyone else to go through what she did. For some reason, the spirit never liked the husband. It might have been because he was constantly complaining about the poltergeist activity and found it unpleasant to deal with. Or perhaps he reminded her of someone else who treated her badly when she lived in the home. It seems clear that this apparition liked harmony, peace, and quiet in her environment, and she especially wanted little babies and young children to be safe.

The best story concerns one of the couple's young daughters, who was constantly sick with ear and throat infections. She was ill at home when the mother got a call from her children's school, telling her that her son was also sick and needed to be picked up right away. It was truly a dilemma, since she could not find anyone to watch her little girl while she went to get her little boy. The school was five minutes away, and after calling everyone she knew, the mother decided to take a chance and leave her five-year-old daughter alone while she drove to the school to pick up her son. Her kindergartener was sleeping in an upstairs bedroom, so the mother figured she would stay asleep while she was gone. She hurried to the school, picked up her son, and drove back. As she and her son came in the front door, they both saw a pair of little legs running along the hallway from the bottom level stairwell. They heard giggling and watched as the legs ran the full length of the house and into a bedroom on the far side, slamming the door. The mother, thinking her daughter had awakened, ran to the far bedroom and opened the door, but no one was there. She ran back down the hall to the other end where she had left her daughter and found her sleeping peacefully right where she had left her.

The couple always felt that one or two little girls and also the young woman, who seemed to watch over them and all the children who visited the home, haunted the house. Once, their grandmother from Salt Lake City had been to a Hopi ceremony in the Four Corners area, and at one o'clock in the morning, instead of driving all the way home, she stopped and crept into her daughter's house through the back door. She didn't want to wake anyone in the house and figured she could surprise her daughter in the morning. Knowing the back door was never locked and the light was on to welcome her, she went in and put her sleeping bag on the couch. She crawled into the sleeping bag and attempted to go to sleep. As soon as she was in her sleeping bag, something pounded up through the bottom of the couch as hard as it could on her back. She got up and checked under the couch, as well as under the cushions, but nothing was there. She waited a few minutes and then got back into her sleeping bag. The same thing happened again and again. Finally, she sat up and talked to the ghost in her mind. She explained why she was there, why she had crept in the back door, and that she was part of the family and it was okay for her to be there. After having this conversation with the ghost of the house, she was finally able to go to sleep without any thumping on her back.

Old Main Bell Tower

In order to understand the evolution of the Bell Tower Ghost in Old Main, you need to be aware of a few interesting events in the history of the college that might explain the colorful stories told by the students today.

A special committee was appointed when the school was originally being planned, which included a woman named Rebecca Little. This is possibly where the name Little came from in the later story of the Bell Tower Ghost, or Rebecca Little might have had an ancestor involved in this story.

Lillian Higbee MacFarlane was a renowned pianist in the early days of the school. She gave a remarkable recital that included music by Beethoven, Chopin, and Mozart that for years was considered legendary by the music department, as well as the college and the entire town. It might be Lillian who has been confused with the later girl who plays the piano at night in Old Main. For years after the school was first built, the library and music department were located on the third floor of Old Main.

Above the third floor of Old Main is a small bell tower that for years did not have a bell. The Home Economics Club was organized in the 1920s by prominent local women to give financial assistance to special contributions for the high school. One of these contributions was a large cast iron bell that the high school's flat roof could not accommodate. The women offered the bell to the Branch Agricultural College, to be placed in the cupola on top of the main building, which at the time was called the Library Building. One major problem existed—the bell weighed eighteen hundred pounds, and the small tower would have difficulty housing it.

Using the department hoist and some steel cable, an inventive teacher and some of his students managed to fit the bell into the small tower. They fashioned a way for it to be rung by extending the bell rope from the operating crank to a loop below the ceiling. Every morning at 8:00 the bell rang to remind students and townspeople of the hour, and it also rang for special events, both in town and at the college. Some of the mystery surrounding the tower involves the bell ringing even after it was no longer in the tower. The college has replaced the old bell with a mechanized system, but there are some in town and at the school who believe the bell is still in the old tower. The great fire in December 1948 signaled the demise of the bell when the roof of Old Main was destroyed and the bell crashed through all the floors and landed in the basement.

The lore of the fire on December 12, 1948, has also contributed to the rumors and stories about the bell tower and Old Main's apparitions and ghosts. On a wintry Sunday morning, a newspaper boy spotted smoke coming out of a ventilator on top of the building. The first to arrive were the manager of the college farm and the school custodian. The custodian cut the power to the building, but flames were already visible on the roof. Students rushed to the scene and formed a human chain up the fire escape and passed precious books and artifacts back down the stairs in an orderly fashion. As the third floor was consumed, students grabbed armfuls of books and threw them out the windows. The students left the building only moments before the roof collapsed, and no one was hurt in the fire. The bell could be heard clanging from floor to floor, almost as if it were crying as it fell to the ground below. When the fire was finally out, only the roof and the third floor were damaged. One professor, Mary Bastow, lost her entire collection of materials, books, and paintings. Twenty percent of the library's collection survived, and while space was found for classes, it was difficult to find space for the books, so books and artifacts were stuffed into closets and stairwells all over campus until a new place for the library could be located. According to student tour guides, there are still two small rooms on the third floor near the bell tower, but no one knows what they were used for.

In his book, *Popular Beliefs and Superstitions from Utah*, Cannon states,

"People going past the old Branch Agriculture College Auditorium at midnight have heard weird strains of 'Deep Purple' coming from a piano somewhere in the darkness. The performer is said to be a young woman, an accomplished pianist, who suddenly died of a heart attack after completing a rendition of 'Deep Purple' at a recital in the auditorium."[1]

One librarian at the school said that an elderly Cedar City native gave this account of the haunting of the Old Main building. The woman, Afton Topham, claimed that this incident had taken place seventy years ago.

> A young lady by the name of Little was practicing playing the piano in the Old Main Building for the junior prom. Apparently there was a piano in the upper room. The piece she was going to play for the dance was something like "Deep Purple." The day before the prom, Miss Little died of a ruptured appendix and never did play for the prom. Since then, people have heard her playing this tune on the piano in the bell tower of Old Main. When people pass by late at night, they can hear this music coming from the building.[2]

Most people agree on the song being "Deep Purple," and that for years after the tragedy it was never chosen for the junior prom. It was considered bad luck. It was the song that people heard echoing from the bell tower around midnight.

Over the years, students at the college have added amazing stories to this original tale. Their creative additions can be traced to parts of the school's history and Old Main itself.

One of the stories began with the laying of the foundation for Old Main's construction in 1897. According to the student stories over the years, "A laborer was guiding a large slab of sandstone into place when letters began to appear as if written by the finger of a supernatural being. As the finger traced the letters, the workmen read them aloud, 'Virginia.' When the workmen said this, the stone began to bleed human blood where the inscription had been."[3]

The article claimed that the inscription can be seen in the special collections section of the college library, but the librarians say they have never seen any such thing in their library or anywhere else.

The stories of bloodstains on the brick in front of Old Main have persisted. An example of this is the story the student tour guides used to tell to visitors on campus. The guides had been asked by the administration to stop telling the story, because they say the story isn't true. A little old couple supposedly lived up in the rooms by the bell tower. The man was a custodian for the school. The couple had a fight and the man got angry with his wife. He ended up murdering her near the bell tower and dragged her down the stairs to the front of Old Main. Her blood dyed the bricks in that spot red.[4]

Until the fire of 1948, the haunting of Old Main consisted of hearing piano or flute music coming from the bell tower at midnight as young couples strolled by. They were treated to the mystical strains of a beautiful waltz. Also over the years, unearthly lights glowing from the third story windows were reported, as well as shadows moving around in the belfry. No birds but crows would perch atop Old Main.

In the old days, people believed that crows knew where a spirit had passed, and that black birds always visited farmhouses on the anniversary of an occupant's death. For example, as a child, my husband's father stood with his grandmother and other family members on a small farm in Indiana while she told him of his great-grandmother's passing on that very day a year before.

"It was just around this time," she said, and then asked everyone to have a seat on the front steps. From the timber about a mile or so from the house, a clutch of crows rose out of the trees and flew straight toward his grandmother's yard. They landed in all the trees around the house and barnyard and cawed and cackled for five or six minutes. Then they flew off to the west. His aunt Cora piped out, "Same thing they did last year!"

The Old Main fire on December 12, 1948, which happened at 7:30 AM on a Sunday morning, started a whole new set of rumors about the old building. The prominent rumor was that a Dr. Jerode Spear, supposedly a famous parapsychologist from the University of Utah, was hired that same year to investigate the hauntings at Old Main. His diaries about this investigation were returned to Southern Utah University by his grandson, who was a student at SUU in the late 1980s. It is hard to believe that there were any parapsychologists at the U of U in 1948, but it is possible to believe that a psychic might have passed through town at the time and made a comment or two about the spirits.

Regardless of who supposedly researched the hauntings, the fire inspired two stories, one being that when the bell crashed to the basement, it took an employee of the college with it, smashing him into the basement floor. Obviously, no skeleton was found. The second tale is that a malevolent force inhabited the bell tower as the result of a violent incident that took place there.

After the fire, stories of murders on the third floor were handed down through the years. People were supposedly axed, strangled, gutted, chopped up into pieces, and then disappeared into the old coal furnace sitting in the center room of the third floor. Other stories state that the remains were carried down to the basement and thrown into the furnace. The mysterious Dr. Spear started a rumor that Old Main's bell tower was a dimension door to other worlds, or at least to the netherworld. Some people believe that spirits from other dimensions come through this door to visit or do evil. Dr. Spear claimed that such an event caused the fire. Probably none of this is true, but Dr. Spear supposedly recommended that Old Main be torn down to rid the town of an entrance to the netherworld.

The premiere murder story about Old Main was probably fabricated. The story concerns a young sixteen-year-old girl who was supposedly murdered near the site of Old Main in 1886. Perhaps the murder has some truth to it, but the rest of the story is rather hard to believe. Two years before Old Main was built, a young woman named Virginia Loomis was murdered east of Cedar City in the red hills. Her throat was slashed, and her blood-soaked body was left lying over a large red sandstone boulder. The stones used in the construction of Old Main in 1898 were out of the same red sandstone boulder quarry in which Virginia was killed. Supposedly, the only suspect was her boyfriend, but he was released due to lack of evidence and left town.

Years later, the boyfriend returned to Cedar City just two weeks prior to the fire in 1948. At the unbelievable age of seventy-eight (if he was sixteen at the time of the murder), he took a job tending the furnace in Old Main. This boyfriend was supposedly the man who was crushed to death when the bell fell into the basement during the fire. Even more bizarre, in Dr. Spear's version, the murdered girl's apparition appeared in the flames, laughing as her murderer received his retribution. It is rumored that in the dead of night you can hear Virginia's voice echoing through the bell tower, along with other voices from the spirit world.

Virginia is probably a made-up name. The real young lady was a senior in high school in the late 1930s when she died of appendicitis. By the year 1939, this local high school student was making a name for herself as an accomplished pianist. She was especially known for her rendition of "Deep Purple." A local doctor performed the surgery to remove her appendix, and soon after, she developed peritonitis and died of septicemia. Not long after, people began reporting lights flashing on and off, crows on the roof, and the strains of piano music coming from Old Main. One young woman, who attended the school at this time and had her own experience with the phantom piano player, required the same operation, which was performed by the same doctor soon after her classmate's surgery. While she thought nothing of it, her parents were afraid to let the same doctor perform the operation.

Winona Cowen relates her experience:

> There were three students in the Old "A" building one night for some reason, and all of a sudden they heard music coming from somewhere upstairs. They went upstairs to find out where it was coming from. When they got to the auditorium, they could tell the music was coming from the piano at the front of the hall. Even though it was dark at the time, they could see that no one was sitting at the piano. That's when they realized something was strange. They got a little closer to make sure nobody was really at the piano. When they discovered there wasn't, they practically fell over each other trying to get out of there.[5]

After a few more experiences like this, she and her classmates decided to quit sliding down the large tin rain gutters outside the old administration building, probably because they suspected that someone was playing the music to scare them away from the building.

While other students who went to school during the 1930s and 1940s didn't believe the ghost story, variations of this story became well known around campus. People wondered why any spirit would choose to play the same song over and over again, but the lyrics in the song suggest that nothing is really final, and just because the physical body isn't there, it doesn't mean that a spirit can't linger.

The words to the song "Deep Purple" are haunting and beautiful: "When the Deep Purple falls over sleepy garden walls, and the stars begin to flicker in the sky, Thru the mist of a memory you wander back to me, breathing my name with a sigh."[6]

Those who did not believe the ghost stories at the time explained the whole thing away by stating that there used to be a lot of instruments stored in the music room on the third floor. The building was drafty, and the wind would blow down through the instruments, causing different sounds to reverberate through the huge, old auditorium. The sounds would get louder and louder and begin to echo, but this does not explain the playing of a tune.[7]

Even in those days, students came up with wild stories based on this tale. Bessie Dover remembered the story she heard from friends who went to the old agricultural college in the 1940s. "I had always heard that it was a ghost of a former ballet dancer, and she had died from an infection she got in a blister from dancing a lot," she says. "I heard that the ghost was dancing up in the auditorium to that old poplar song 'Deep Purple.'"[8]

While the stories of today surpass the old ones in their colorfulness and blood and gore, the thing that has been constant for decades has been the reluctance of students to pass by Old Main late at night, or especially to enter the building and stay on the third floor alone. I am sure school officials discourage this practice as well. The transformation of this spirit from a gifted, forlorn, and mournful artist, whose life was cut short, to a malevolent force out to spill blood on the stones from which the structure was built, is something each generation of students has contributed even more to.

Other Haunts in Cedar City

Two other suggested haunts in Cedar City are an old abandoned retirement center and a former Godfather's Pizza also known as the Depot Junction. The retirement center has eerie lights coming from it when people drive by it. One room is lighted half red and half green. Besides shapes and strange movements around the building, people have reported seeing an old lady staring out of one of the windows.

The pizza place has changed hands and names several times, but no matter what its current name might be, it still has ghostly activity and has had for years. It was the Union Pacific Railroad Depot at one time, so it has a history. One rumor is that an employee supposedly died in the boiler room. This is according to a psychic who visited the place, but no one seems to know how, why, or when he died, which makes the story a bit suspicious—unless, of course, it was a railroad worker from a distant time. All sorts of strange phenomena have supposedly occurred in the building. Besides people hearing moaning and clanking noises coming from downstairs, objects seem to move around by themselves, and the electrical equipment in the place is affected quite often. The TV and various lights in the building will go on and off by themselves. Pizza bags have flown out of their holders, and the piano will play the same notes over and over again all by itself. People have heard a little girl crying in the front part of the pizza place.[9]

Blanding

An old Mormon ghost tale from the Blanding area dates back to 1908. A stranger approached me after one of my speaking engagements and said he'd heard I was collecting ghost stories. He offered me a story, which I gladly accepted. The man may have been connected to the family in the story somehow, but I've not seen him since to ask him. All I have are his two typewritten pages that I will quote exactly as he gave them to me. Not only is it a marvelous story that shouldn't be lost, but it is also typical of old-time Mormon resurrection stories or visions that were reported in early pioneer times. Intuited and interpreted in a different fashion than it would be today, it is a great ghost story with a spiritual tinge!

Blanding was first named Grayson, a maiden name of one of the town's founder's wives. In 1914 the town changed its name when a wealthy easterner named Bicknell offered to donate a thousand books to the town if the citizens would change its name. Thurber, a nearby town, vied with Grayson for the books, and when both towns got the books, they split the prize. Thurber became Bicknell, and Grayson became Bicknell's wife's maiden name, Blanding.

Many new settlers arrived from 1912 to 1916. Among them were several of the families who fled to Mexico during the polygamy purge. They returned to Southern Utah because it was an area in which they might still be left alone. The town's population rose to 1,100, and the refugee families returning from Mexico were called Pachecoites.

Zeke Johnson was the son of Joel Hills Johnson, which I question, since Joe Hill is a pretty famous name in Utah. Johnson is a common name in the early settling of Blanding, and someone did take an awful lot of extra time to include all the bracketed corrections in this interesting story. I tend to believe that the story was told from an intuitive experience that this old man had years before. Of course, like any ghost story, it is up to the reader whether he believes it. What I find poignant, however, is that had these bones been found today, none of the mystical, spiritual magic of the late 1800s and early 1900s would have followed them. Recently, three teenage boys accidentally dug up some Fremont Indian bones in their backyard, and they were quoted as saying that maybe their "find" would get them a little more interested in history.

Zeke Johnson's 1908 Witness of a Resurrection

[The following narrative is reproduced as I received it—except that I have corrected spelling and grammatical errors as indicated in the brackets.

It appears to be a transcript of a talk. Note that San Juan County is in eastern Utah.][10]

Experiences of Zeke Johnson, now eighty-five—1954.

I have been requested to relate an experience I had in 1908 or 1909 in San Juan County. I was just making a home in Blanding and the whole county there was covered with trees and sagebrush. I was working hard to clear the ground to plant a few acres of corn. We had five acres cleared and we started to plant the corn. My little boy Roy, seven or eight years old, was there to help me plant the corn. I'd plow around the piece and then he'd plant the furrow with the corn. Then I'd cover it and plow again. While I was plowing on that piece of ground, I discovered there were some ancient houses there, that is, the remnants of them.

As I was plowing around I noticed that my plow had turned out the skeleton of a small child—the skull and the backbone. Most of the bones, of course, were decayed and gone. Part of the skeleton was there, so I stopped immediately as my plow had passed it a little. I turned and looked back against the bar of the plow between the handles. As I was looking at that little skeleton that I had plowed out, and wondering, all of a sudden to my surprise, I saw the bones begin to wiggle. They began to change position and to take on a different color. Within a minute there lay a beautiful little skeleton. It was a perfect little skeleton.

Then I saw the inner parts of the natural body coming in—the entrails, etc. I saw the flesh coming on and I saw the skin come on the body after the inner parts of the body were complete. A beautiful head of hair adorned the top of the head. In about a half a minute after the hair was on the head, it had a beautiful crystal decoration in the hair. It was combed beautifully and parted on one side. In about half a minute after the hair was on the head, the child raised up on her feet. She was lying a little on her left side with her back toward me. Because of this I wasn't able to discern the sex of the child, but as she raised up, a beautiful robe came down over her left shoulder and I saw it must be a girl.

She looked at me and I looked at her, and for a quarter of a minute we just looked at each other smiling. Then in my ambition to get hold of her, I said, "oh, you beautiful child," and I reached out as if I would embrace her and she disappeared.

That was all I saw, and I stood there and wondered and I thought for a few minutes. My little boy was wondering why I was there because he was down at the other end of the row, anxious to come and plant the corn. Now, I couldn't tell that story to anyone because it was so mysterious to me and such. Why should I have such a miraculous experience? I couldn't feature a human being in such a condition as to accidentally plow that little body out and see it come alive. A body of a child about five to seven years old, I'd say.

I couldn't tell that story to anyone until finally one day I met a dear friend of mine, Stake Patriarch William H. Redd of Blanding. Stake patriarchs are men who do what is known as patriarchal blessings for members of the LDS Church. The blessings are a blueprint for each member's life in terms of their spiritual and earthly gifts and experiences. They are to be kept sacred by the people who receive them. He stopped me on the street and said, "Zeke, you have had an experience on this mesa you won't tell. I want you to tell it to me." Well, I told it to him. Then he had me tell it to other friends and since then I have told it in four temples in the United States and many meeting houses and socials, fast meeting, and at conference times.

I wondered, and it worried me for years as to why . . . was I, just a common uneducated man, allowed to see such a marvelous manifestation of God's power. One day as I was walking alone with my hoe on my shoulder going to hoe some corn, something said, "Stop under the shade of that tree for a few minutes and rest." This just came to me and I thought I would, so I stopped there and the following was given to me.

It was an answer to my prayer. I prayed incessantly for an answer as to why I was privileged to see that resurrection. I was told why. When the child was buried there, it was either in time of war with the different tribes or it was wintertime when the ground was frozen and they had no tools to dig deep graves. If it was during time of war they couldn't possibly take time to dig a deep grave. They just planted that little body as deep as they could under the circumstances. When it was done the sorrowing mother knew that it was such a shallow grave, that in her sorrow she cried out to the little group that was present, "That little shallow grave, the first beast that comes along will smell her body and will dig her up and scatter her to the four winds. Her bones will be scattered all over the flats." There just happened to be a man present (a Nephite or a Jaredite, I don't know which because they had both been in this country). The man said, "Sister, calm your sorrows. Whenever that little body is disturbed or uncovered, the Lord will call her up and she will live." Since that time, I have taken great comfort, great cheer and consolation and satisfaction, with praise in my heart and soul, until I haven't the words to express it, that it was I that uncovered that little body.

Thank you for listening to me. I just can't tell this without crying.

Zeke Johnson, son of Joel Hills Johnson

The Nephites and Jaredites were the names of two groups of people in the Book of Mormon, who crossed the ocean and settled in America. The LDS Church believes that the Lamanites are the ancestors of our present-day Native Americans.

It would be normal and natural for an early Mormon settler to interpret what he had seen in the manner that Zeke did. I have had experiences such as this and would probably interpret them similarly. I would attempt to understand the person in the vision and their time frame and belief system. Perhaps the little girl appeared to Zeke Johnson to comfort him. Perhaps it was a time in Zeke's life when he needed such comforting, and the apparition appeared to him for a reason. I know we interpret such events by our own life experiences, and they don't have to be esoteric.

I was on a radio talk show answering questions when a man called and asked me about the old Union Fort where a shopping center now stands. A fight to preserve the history of the Fort had erupted with the locals, and compromises were made to placate the angry descendants when the developers wanted to build the center. When I told him that I had plenty of ghost stories about the area and was still investigating them, he told me a story that made me leap back in my chair in the studio. Rumors of pioneer graves abounded but had not been proven. He had worked for the company helping to clear the land and dig the foundations. One day they dug up two gravestones with the names and dates of children on them. They were ordered to keep their mouths shut, and the gravestones were removed to a company building, never to be seen again, because the developers didn't want any more trouble that would delay their work.

But the man on the line had worried about this incident for years. Just like Zeke Johnson, he wanted a resolution to what he had been a part of. He said that he had two little girls of his own and was often bothered by the memory of being the one to find the gravestones. He was pleased that someone was listening to him, especially after he tried and failed to get others to investigate the incident. He was sure that the little girls' bones were down there, buried under a Walmart forever.

When I put the puzzle pieces together, it did make sense. Even though there is an old Union Fort cemetery just two miles away, there was a three-year gap between the time the fort was founded and the first person was buried in one of the first pioneer cemeteries in the valley. During that time there were two diphtheria epidemics, and several people died, especially small children and elderly people. Plenty of ghost stories come from the buildings where the fort once stood. This man hadn't seen a child resurrect, but in his thoughts he had been bothered by a similar apparition in a more modern time.

Recapture Creek

Along with the rediscovery of the sacredness of this land, stories also exist of lost gold along Recapture Creek, which is located between Bluff and Blanding.

The stories originate from when the Spaniards came through this country centuries ago. Supposedly a pack train of gold got lost in the desert, and all those escorting the gold died there. Rumor says the gold can still be found today.

After finding the gold, the Spaniards closed down the mine, set their Indian slaves free, and were headed home. The freed Indian slaves suddenly attacked the Spaniards, and everyone was killed. The Spaniards, their burros, and all of the gold were buried right where they fell, which was supposedly somewhere between Bluff and Blanding, along Recapture Creek.

The gold bars are thought to be valued between $500,000 and $1,000,000 on today's market. Men who have claimed to have found even one of these gold bars have not lived long. Stories abound about the curse put on this gold by the Native Americans who killed their captors and buried their gold. Anyone who finds the gold, whether white or Native American, will die a short time after finding it.

The stories told about this gold start with John C. Fremont, who claimed to have found the skeletal remains of some burros in the period between 1842 and 1844. The local Indians told the first settlers in the area about an old Spanish mine in the Abajo Mountains near Bluff. Oral traditions in the tribe were that the Spaniards carried gold south along a trail near Recapture Creek and that the pack train was attacked and the Spaniards were buried where they fell. Over the years, some of the descendants of the enslaved Indians claimed to know where the gold was, but no white man was clever enough to trick them into telling.

An old Snake Indian woman, who used to trade at the trading post, supposedly brought in her little gold nuggets in small buckskin bags, claiming to have gotten them from potholes at the base of the Abajo Mountains.

A young lawyer from the east, who claimed to have found gold in the potholes, came into town, showed it around, and was never seen again. He either died because of the curse, was robbed and murdered, or took the little he found and left town.

Mysteries and stories about the lost gold run rampant in the area. Was the gold originally found from the lost pack train, the lost Spanish mine, or perhaps a more recent lost mine, such as that of the local prospector John Howard? Was John Howard's lost mine the rediscovered Spanish mine, or merely the gold remnants of the pack train? Or is this the famous lost Josephine Mine said to be in one of three places in Utah—the Henry Mountains northwest of the Abajo Mountains in the Uintahs, or in the La Sals near Moab, Utah?

The pack train, the mines, and all the other stories continue to revolve around Blanding and Bluff more than any other site in Utah. All I can say is that when I drove into Bluff for the first time, I had no idea just how interesting this little town could be under its dry and dusty surface. Each year Bluff has a special event called the Fandango, which is a gathering of writers and storytellers who speak in six different languages and represent several beliefs and cultures.

One last story about Recapture Creek is worth noting here. In 1905 a cowboy named Andy Laney stopped to water his horse along the creek bed. He supposedly found a small gold bar about eight inches long with a cross on it. He immediately sold the gold bar for $1,800 and headed for a tavern called the Blue Goose in Monticello, Utah. He picked up a partner named Blaine and returned to the site to look for more gold. They apparently found more bars of gold and headed for Dolores, Colorado. Blaine was killed in a card game dispute when he was accused of cheating, and Laney spent all the remaining money and then went back to being a cowboy. He was killed a short time later by outlaws near Navajo Mountain. Their deaths continued the rumored curse on the gold.

In 1964 two artifact hunters found more gold along the creek but disappeared without a trace. In 1979 a couple camping along the creek supposedly found a gold bar, but no one knows who they were or what happened to them.

In 1994 a group researching a book on the Old Spanish Trail claimed to have found a small cache of the gold bars stamped 1761. As far as I know, no one ever saw these gold bars other than the people who supposedly found them.

The legend of the gold bars—supposedly lost somewhere between Bluff and Blanding—and the curse they are rumored to possess continues on.[11]

Monticello

The old Monticello Flour Mill, built in 1933, has a haunted reputation. The old mill produced flour for the community until the mid-1960s and has been restored and converted into an inn. It is now a bed and breakfast with seven guest rooms in the main building and three in the granary next door. A gift shop, a main sitting room with a huge fireplace, a second-floor TV area, and a third-floor library are available for the guests' convenience. The inn has a screened-in porch and a hot tub, free breakfast, and fine dining as well. On top of all this, the Grist Mill Inn seems to house several ghosts, so many that the Utah Ghost Hunter Society held their annual October investigation there in 2003. Their reports on the inn's hauntings are quite intriguing.[12]

Monticello rests at the foot of Blue Mountain and was ideal for settlers because of the springs located east and west of town. Before 1880, an exploration party was sent from Bluff to look for another Mormon town site. At the time, the region was being used by the Carlisle Kansas and New Mexico Cattle and Land Company for grazing their cattle. Four men started to plant crops and laid out the town site and surveyed for an irrigation ditch. In July 1887, the first settlers moved into the area after an eight-year-long fight with the cowboys from the cattle company.

Typical of the fights between the cattlemen and the settlers in the old West, the skirmishes involved warning shots, heated disputes, and legal wranglings over water rights. The local Ute tribe added to the tensions as the town was being established. It was eventually decided that the Mormons had the legal rights to the water, and by the spring of 1888, the construction of the town was underway, with wheat, oats, and potatoes being planted. Monticello was first called North

Montezuma, and later, Hammond. Eventually the town took the name Monticello in honor of Thomas Jefferson's estate.[13]

The farmers in the area arrived in the 1930s during the Great Depression, and many families still live on the original homestead of their parents and grandparents.

One famous historical story was written into a song called the "Blue Mountain Song," and people in Monticello love to tell it.

> In 1880 Monticello was a typical rough-and-tumble Western town. Stories abound, and one of the best is of a cowboy who rode his horse into Mons Store, grabbed the end of a bolt of calico, dallied it around the horn on his saddle, and rode out on a run, unwrapping the bolt as he sped up the street.[14]

There are chuck wagon and guest ranches and working cattle ranches in the area. There is also a large Hispanic community. Monticello houses a small Mormon temple and is really quite a beautiful town with fences and green lawns.

It's reported that during its operation, the mill produced nearly all the flour sold to the Navajo nation. The main reason the mill shut down was that the federal government decided to purchase flour companies based in Salt Lake City and gave the Navajo Indians all the flour they needed free of charge.

Several accidents and one recorded death occurred at the mill during its operation. When a group of Cub Scouts was touring the mill, one of the scouts climbed on the grain elevator and was accidentally crushed to death.

During the renovation process to turn the gristmill into an inn, it was decided to bring in equipment from other mills to give the inn its atmosphere, because a lot of the original mill equipment had fallen into disrepair. One theory is that additional "haunts" arrived with the equipment from other flour mills around the country.

Because the ghost hunter's group was conducting an EVP recording class at their October convention, they managed to capture some unusual voice phenomena while they were there. They made a list of encounters that employees and guests have had in the different rooms in the inn. In the Breakfast Room, an old man in coveralls was seen walking between the flour mills' bagging machine and the back door. In the front lobby near the elevator, a young boy was seen playing ball and running up and down the steps while stopping occasionally to peek at people from around the stairway. In the kitchen area, the same young boy was sensed whenever someone was baking, especially chocolate chip cookies. In the Walton Room, footsteps are sometimes heard on the stairway near the front door, and noises come from the elevator. In the Corbin Room, the presence of a large dark man wearing work clothes and work boots has been felt. He is not a friendly spirit, and people do not feel comfortable in this room when his presence is there.

In the Family Room, an old man has occasionally been seen, but he is more often heard walking from the Nielsen Room to the top of the stairway and back. And in the Nielsen Room, an old man was seen sitting on the bed, watching TV. A female spirit has also been seen walking around the room.

In the library, several people have sensed the presence of a female and have speculated that she might be a scout leader. In the Palmer Room, evidence is sometimes found of someone sitting on the bed, or while a guest is in the room, an indentation on the bed can appear. Finally, in the Keller Room, another female spirit is often felt and occasionally seen as well.

The Utah Ghost Hunter Society was able to obtain several voice recordings and photographs of orbs. An exceptionally clear voice kept saying the name Nathan. Other repeated phrases included, "I'm going to put it over here," "Do you?" and various yes and no answers in response to questions that people were asking. Photos sent in by other people after they heard about the investigation at the inn included orbs, rope-like lights, and even the outline of a torso in one of the inn's windows.[15] In 2009 the Utah Researchers of Paranormal Activity did an investigation at the mill, which is now up for sale.

St. George

I had not been to St. George since I was a little girl, and it was a shock when I saw the small town gone and in its place a sprawl of fast food places, expensive hotels, and huge mansions on the bluffs surrounding the city. I had to go into the heart of town to find its historical section, because it had been swallowed up by the beautiful scenery, expensive homes, businesses, and tourist hot spots. While city planners had not expected such growth, and there are not enough streets to support all the traffic nor enough homes being built to house all the people, they are happy that many of their young people are now staying, because plenty of jobs and opportunities are available there. From a historical point of view, I was somewhat disappointed by what I saw, even though the city has taken great pains to preserve its historical places and haunts. The ghosts probably have to hide out more now, forgotten beneath the suburban sprawl.

Reading about St. George in Mr. Roylance's book, which was written in 1982, you can see what was coming since he talks of the city having been "yanked rudely into the hectic current of mainstream America, and in the process, their characteristic local color is being overwhelmed by the contemporary culture of the region and the nation. . . . to a marked degree they have become—or are becoming—miniature models of Las Vegas, Los Angeles, or even Salt Lake City. At the same time it must be acknowledged that deliberate effort has been made to keep some development as architecturally attractive and environmentally compatible as possible."[16] Now million-dollar homes are built on the Dixie Sugar Loaf vermilion bluffs overlooking the town, on a bluff once described by pioneers as being as bald as the prophet Elisha.

In 1852 settlers first came to the future site of St. George. The Mormon settlers established an Indian mission in 1854, just two miles north of where St. George is today, at a place called Santa Clara. St. George was not officially settled until 1861, when Brigham Young sent settlers to the area after establishing experimental farms there in 1857 and 1858.

Before the Mormons arrived, the Dominguez-Escalante Party had passed through the area, along with trappers and government survey parties. This was the legendary Jedediah Smith's trapping area. Even before the Spanish and the trappers arrived, native tribes, including the Virgin River Anasazi, roamed the area. Native American rock-art sites have been found there.

The desert land was unforgiving and harsh for the first settlers, and they suffered greatly because of their inability to understand or cope with the land's rhythms and cycles.

More than 200 wagons and about 309 families settled in the valley. They were called to the Cotton Mission, as Brigham Young referred it, in Utah's Dixie. Settlers had come from the South, and with the Civil War going on, cotton was thought to be a realistic and profitable enterprise. One of the pioneers noted that he believed they were close to hell, because it was surely the hottest place he had ever been. On the other hand, when the first settlers arrived, they had to endure a rain of biblical proportions, with forty days and forty nights of flooding.

Mr. Roylance also noted in his book that "Erastus Snow was the Apostle designated to build up Dixie, and if life was hard for him and the other men, it was heartbreaking for some of the women. David Cannon's young wife, living in a willow lean-to in place of the luxury she had known, told her husband that if he could find just one flower fit to pin on a lady's dress, she would try and be satisfied. In the spring he presented her with a bouquet of orchid-colored sego lilies, and she thought them as beautiful a flower as she had ever seen."[17]

St. George was named after George A. Smith, just one of those selected to settle in the area. He was dubbed "St. George," because he discovered several medicinal properties of the potato peel, which were used to treat the first settlers who became ill. These tough pioneers endured more hardship than any others in the state because of the weather and climate there, so they named their town St. George in honor of the miracles George Smith provided with his potato peels.

Unfortunately, a few miracles did not prevent the hardships from forcing them to desert the mission, which many did. In 1863 St. George became the county seat of Washington county. Building was begun on the St. George LDS temple in 1875, and the temple was dedicated in 1877. Several other important buildings were also constructed, such as the courthouse in 1870 and the social hall and opera house in 1875. Silk was being produced in the area as early as 1874, along with other products such as molasses, dried fruits, and wine. The Dixie Academy Building was dedicated in 1911 and was operated by the LDS Church until 1933, when it became a two-year state college. In the 1960s, a new college campus was opened in the southeast corner of the city, and this new Dixie College has approximately twenty-five hundred students enrolled today.

St. George offers several buildings in the Heritage Square section of town, where ghosts do linger. The LDS temple and tabernacle in the square are probably still housing spirits of angels and churchmen. Another building in the area is the old Washington County Courthouse, built between 1867 and 1870, with a pioneer museum next door. In a one- to two-block radius are several inns and Brigham Young's Winter House, which is now maintained by the LDS Church. With advance notices, you can arrange a tour of it during the summer months. Otherwise, it is used for private Latter-day Saint functions.

While little is advertised about the spirits in St. George, there are lots of other hauntings in the old town section of the city, and the pioneer legends concerning them are enticing. One such legend tells of a small mountain pass near St. George, where it was said that the voices of ancient Indian children could be heard laughing and playing as they hurled rocks down onto the pioneer workers.

The Devil's Saddle

To get their children home before nightfall, pioneer mothers created one of the most famous local haunt legends in St. George. Devil's Saddle is located on the west end of the airport road. Looking at the west end of Black Ridge, you'll notice a clearly defined mountain pass where the Devil's Saddle formation is located. Pioneer mothers supposedly told their children that they needed to come home before the devil swooped down through the saddle and carried their souls away to hell.

Another local haunt is a dark cavern located on Red Hill just north of St. George. When the town was first settled, it was believed that American Indians used this area as a burial wall for their children, and townspeople were warned against going near the place, because the cries of these children could be heard still echoing from the wall.

When construction began on the LDS temple, the route to the rock quarry went past the cavern on Red Hill. Rock slides occurred when the workers quarried for the temple, probably as a result of the increased traffic. People believed that the spirits of the buried Indian children hovered over the area and pushed these rocks into the narrow chasm. When public access was determined too dangerous, religious leaders supposedly gathered there and offered prayers on behalf of the wandering spirits. As part of the ceremony, an etching of a lamb was chiseled into the narrow passage. This etching can still be seen in the Red Rock Canyon along the old quarry road near the present-day Elks Lodge above the Dixie Red Hill's golf course. Rumors of the Gadianton robbers also marked the area, since their ghosts were believed to push rocks down onto people from the narrow chasms. Freighters told stories of these evil men who lived in Book of Mormon times, whose spirits were thought to have brought harm to the Mormon people in the early days of the LDS Church. Passes around St. George were also said to be part of their stomping grounds.[18]

The Winter House

The Brigham Young Winter House was Young's winter residence, and social and religious events were held there for the community from 1870 until Brigham's death in 1877. From 1959 to 1975, the house was maintained as a Utah state historical monument. The LDS Church has maintained the residence since 1975 and offers tours that are conducted by missionaries. One interesting fact about the home involves Brigham Young's superstitions. He supposedly believed that the earth's energy forces traveled in an east to west direction, and therefore, when he visited the home, he slept with his head toward the east and his feet pointed toward the west. Stories of ghosts in the house are kept private and are seldom told to outsiders. I am sure there are some apparitions because of the stories told by owners of other old residences within two blocks of the Winter House.

St. George Opera House

The old opera house, which I talk about in more detail in one of my other books, was once an old winery built in 1864, and with later additions, became a social hall. Eventually it was the opera house, followed by a sugar beet factory. It was abandoned for a while and then was renovated in 1995 to once again shine as a performing arts center known as the St. George Opera House.

Old Dixie Hotel

In the earlier days of St. George, the old Dixie Hotel, now no longer standing, had quite a few reports of ghosts. One of the rooms in the hotel had a reputation of being especially haunted. Apparently, the bed in the room would rattle, jump around, and bang into the wall in the middle of the night. A visitor to the hotel finally solved the mystery of the haunted room. He looked all around and checked every nook and cranny, until he discovered that the "signboard of the inn was fastened to the outer wall by a nut and screw, which came through to the back of the bed, and when the wind swung the signboard to and fro, the movement was transferred to the bed, causing it to shake violently."[19]

Other Possible Haunts around St. George

Several historic private homes, a school, the old *County News* building, and a club hall are also located in St. George. A historic walking tour complete with photos is offered on the internet: http:/Aivww.infowest.com/utah/colorcountry/historywalking.html.

The Woodward Elementary School was completed in 1898 and still stands today with its bell tower intact. Of special interest is the fact that the County

News Building was originally a saloon in Silver Reef in the 1880s and was moved to St. George, where it has housed a town newspaper ever since. It is my experience that when buildings with a violent past are moved to a new location, they continue to have ghostly activity within them. And there certainly was plenty of violence in the mining town of Silver Reef with over 2,000 citizens, 275 mining claims and 37 mine companies in operation during its peak in the mid-1880s.

Located northeast of St. George, Silver Reef was one of the larger mining boomtowns in the 1870s. When Silver Reef went bankrupt, the town dance hall was used as a jail for twenty-five union leaders. Some of the buildings were sold for taxes or torn down, while others were dismantled and transported to other towns for building materials. A few were transported as they were, but those that were made of stone had to be moved piece by piece.

One man who dismantled his newly purchased saloon discovered over $10,000 in gold hidden in a secret wall panel, which started a rush on building ownership in the defunct town of Silver Reef. A few more post-hole treasures and small caches of gold were found in buildings, but the biggest rumored gold cache belonging to casino owner Henry Clark was never found.

Several killings occurred in Silver Reef, and one of note was that of Henry Clark, who took the location of his gold to his grave with him. Clark made a fortune as a Mississippi river boat gambler and killed several men in Silver Reef who accused him of cheating. One night he broke the bank roulette, was once again accused of cheating, and reached for his gun. The saloon owner beat him to the draw. Henry reputedly cached several fortunes at Silver Reef and never told a soul where he had hidden them. Encircled by a little wrought iron fence, his grave can still be seen in one of the cemeteries outside the ruins of Silver Reef.[20]

Silver Reef has an old pioneer park with a pioneer dwelling in it. The dwelling is located between two huge overhanging rocks and has a downright eerie feeling inside. The ancients who lived there before the pioneers probably also inhabit this spot from time to time.

A restored 1927 movie theater is in town, along with the Quicksand and Cactus Bed and Breakfast that was originally the home of famous author and historian Juanita Brooks.[21] Brooks was the first to write bravely about the Mountain Meadows Massacre. Several books have been written since this, but her book was the first. *Mountain Meadows Witness*, written by an LDS woman, Anna Jean Backus, is my favorite because she poignantly wrote about her own ancestors.

Hardy House

The Hardy House is located on a major thoroughfare and is no longer a restaurant you can visit. The home is now divided into offices. I talked to a lot of people in order to get information on the ghost that is rumored to be haunting the place. Back when the house was a restaurant, people were in tune with the spirits in the building, and this home is listed on the Utah ghost websites.

Augustus Hardy, who was the town sheriff, built the Hardy House in 1871. It was remodeled after an incident in which a vigilante group broke into the sheriff's house in the middle of the night, took his jail keys, removed a prisoner they were afraid might escape justice, and hanged him. A stray bullet from this incident was lodged in one of the doors of the house, but it may have been lost in the recent remodeling.

The little stone jailhouse was built around 1880 by Sheriff Hardy. It is a one-room, black lava rock building near his home and still retains bars in the windows. It is in the Hardy house that people claim to have seen the ghost of sheriff Augustus Hardy, who people say was quite a character of the times.

Penny Farthing Inn

One old home, built by George Whitehead and located only a block away from Brigham Young's Winter Home, was turned into a bed and breakfast inn. The owners of the Old Penny Farthing Inn talked freely about the two ghosts who playfully inhabit their inn. When the owners first moved in, their dog kept acting as if he saw something. He would bark and growl and sometimes stand on his haunches if anyone headed toward the basement.

A lady staying at the inn told the owners outright that they had ghosts, but they didn't have to worry because the ghosts were good and would never bother them in a negative way. Their guest had apparently lived in a subdivision in California where she experienced poltergeist phenomena similar to the famous Black Hope Cemetery story that the movie *Poltergeist* was based on. After relating her story, the woman told the inn owners that if anyone should know the difference between a positive atmosphere and a negative one, she should!

The new owners began to notice a few unusual things during their renovations. Doors opened and closed for them. One night the wife heard footsteps coming up the stairs and woke her husband to find out if he had closed the downstairs door. He was sure he'd closed it, but he went down to check it. Just as he got to it, the door slammed shut in front of him.

One day the wife was wallpapering alone in the house and heard someone calling her name. She thought her husband had returned home, but when she checked, the front door was locked and there were no footprints from the rain outside. She heard two different voices calling her husband's name and heard laughter right behind where she was wallpapering. She realized that the voices were little children and told them to stop, just like she did with her own children years before, and they stopped!

When guests began to arrive at the inn, they reported some interesting things in addition to doors opening and closing before the doorknobs were touched.

Some of the guests heard voices and laughter when no one else was around. It was children they could hear—singing, laughing, and talking. The guests also heard toilets flushing during the night when no one was in the bathrooms. Things moved around and were rearranged during the night. The owners would often be watching television, hear the doorbell ring, jump up to answer it, and find no one there. This "spirited" game went on for a long time, until one of the owners told the ghosts to knock it off, and they did. Guests sometimes suddenly feel a warm tingling in their room. On occasion, when the couple is alone in the house and it has been raining, they find little wet footprints on the stairs.

One interesting incident involved an old jacket. For several years the owners left some keys in a pocket of a jacket. One day they needed the keys, so they went to get them. The jacket hung on a hook in the hallway. They checked the pockets, but the keys were gone. Even though the owners were sure the keys were in the jacket, they searched the entire house anyway. After two days of searching, the husband went back to check the pocket where the keys were originally placed and found them there as if they had never been missing. Another time, after they had searched all day for them, lost car keys were found under the wife's pillow on the bed. She said no one had put them there, so it had to be one of the spirits.

In the 1880s, the brother of Erastus Whitehead, Mayor George Whitehead, built the home that eventually became the Old Penny Farthing Inn. E.G. "Ras" Whitehead and sons ran a large mercantile downtown and were always interested in any newfangled stuff they could find and order. If they could find it somewhere, they would order anything that anyone wanted.

The George Whiteheads lost one of their seven children—a little girl. People think she died as a child of a fever in the old house.

Ice was kept in the basement, and the family made ice cream and packed it in hay and newspaper and kept in the basement. Sometimes the aroma, either of the ice or the ice cream, is still noticeable down there.

The Whiteheads' store downtown eventually became a pharmacy and then a fabric store. The Whiteheads continued to live in the house after Mr. Whitehead passed away at thirty-four years of age, leaving his widow and seven children. Not long after his death, the little girl died in the home.

Several families lived in the home afterward, but it was a family living there during World War II that they remember the most. It is believed that they also lost one of their little girls. No one remembers their name or how the little girl died, but they do remember that the father of the girl became so despondent over her death that he eventually became an alcoholic. Townspeople say he would go up to the attic and stay there for hours, grieving the loss of his little girl. Rumors say the girl died of leukemia, but no one knows for sure. The current owner's son-in-law had a dream about the two little girls, and when he saw pictures of former residents of the home, he was sure he recognized one of the girls. He also felt that one child was a baby, while the spirit from World War II was a little girl.

The owners of the inn said they enjoyed having the two little girls around, except for when the girls play tricks on them that impede the progress and upkeep of the house. The owners said that when necessary, they talk to the girls just as if they were two real little girls. "It's like talking to my own grandchildren," the wife says.

While the atmosphere throughout the house is light and full of laughter, the attic does have a certain sadness to it, with the possibility that the ghost of either old "Ras" or the father from the World War II era inhabits it from time to time.

The owners named the inn after a nineteenth-century bicycle that had a large front wheel and small rear wheel. The proportions of the two bicycle wheels are reminiscent of old British coins: the larger "penny" coin, or front wheel, and the smaller "farthing," or rear wheel.

The inn has a large collection of antiques and Americana, and some stern portraits of Brigham Young and Joseph Smith glare down from the walls. The main floor has a country breakfast room. One of the guest rooms, the Sego Lily Room, has an iron-frame bed transported from Salt Lake City by Mormon settlers. The other theme rooms are entitled the Morning Dove Room, Honeymoon Suite, Sir Winston Room, and Betsy Ross Room. Since the inn is so close to the Winter House, I asked the innkeeper about ghosts at Young's winter home. She assumed there were a few, but being Mormon herself, she said that if there were any, no one would talk about them.

Seven Wives Inn

The Seven Wives Inn is of interest, because the same Edwin G. Woolley, who did so much to promote the Grand Canyon, built his home next to his friend Benjamin F. Johnson. These two homes, along with the George Whitehead residence, have been combined to make what is now the Seven Wives Inn. Woolley built the larger house in 1873 and hid polygamists in his attic using a built-in secret door. Woolley's house was the largest and most magnificent in town. Johnson lived in the smaller home and had seven wives, and some of his descendents run the inn.

Next door to these homes is George Whitehead's house, which was built in 1883. His home was called the President's House, because the Whiteheads and others who owned the home were hosts to some of the early presidents of the LDS Church. Apparently George's wife was an excellent cook.

The seven bedrooms in the Johnson portion of the inn have been named for each of his wives: Melissa, Sarah, Harriet, MaryAnn, Lucinda, Julia, and Jane. Because of hosting the presidents of the LDS Church, the bedrooms in the Whitehead home are named after the presidents' wives: Eliza, Caroline, Rachel, and Mary.

Rumors of ghosts come from the guests and the employees and not from the owner. It seems that because of being so near to Brigham Young's winter home, the spirits must keep quiet. They may not be that active, but they are certainly there.

A visit to the St. George historic district is well worth the trip, especially with the added bonus of the spirits of two little girls who welcome guests happily at the Old Penny Farthing Inn, and its owners who are just as cheerful as any "grandparents" could be. The historic district of St. George has other colorful places to visit, including the previously mentioned Washington County Courthouse and the totally renovated St. George Opera House, with performances running through much of the year. I'm hoping you will take the time on your visit to this fast-growing city to check out its ghostly dwellings as well.

Washington City

Washington Cotton Mill

Washington City, which is located ten miles west of St. George and not far from Zion Canyon, has two intriguing ghost stories. I told one of these stories concerning the old Washington Cotton Factory in more detail in my first book.

The cotton factory building was constructed in 1865 and is now the Star Nursery. It was part of Brigham Young's plans to introduce cotton and silk production into Utah's Dixie. Mormon converts from the southern states relocated to Utah to oversee industries with which they were familiar.

Life in Utah's Dixie turned out to be extremely difficult, with epidemics, a constant lack of water, and, ironically, constant flooding. Neither industry did well for Young's Cotton Mission. The cotton factory helped the Mission endure as long as it did, and somehow the factory endured as well.

The three-story stone structure granary and cotton factory is thought to be haunted. By 1910, after a series of owners, all the machinery was sold and the factory sat idle. For about a thirty-year period, sometime between 1910 and the present, the Rio Virgen Manufacturing Company ran the factory through a series of crises involving more flooding, fires, and several financial disasters. Finally, the building was again idle and was used as a storage facility until about ten years ago. At that time, Norma Cannizzarro, visiting from out-of-state, fell in love with the place and turned it into a nursery.

People working at the nursery hear a young woman crying at night, which is still a mystery to them. They haven't given the female ghost a name, but her presence is always there. While no one has seen an actual apparition, employees have heard her beautiful voice humming and singing in the empty building, either at closing time, or when they first open up in the morning. Entire groups have heard the singing, and when they ask each other if someone has been singing, no one has. Voices have also been heard in the empty building, and water faucets turn on and off by themselves.

Rumor has it that there was a big fire at the mill several years ago, and one or two people died in it. One person who works at the nursery said that late one evening, when she was alone and locking up, she heard a voice talking and then humming, and finally a huge moaning sound that frightened her so badly that she ran out of the building and didn't finish locking up. Perhaps the woman who haunts the old factory is simply a reminder of the difficulties the Cotton Mission in Southern Utah endured. The settlers lost much of what they worked so hard for. Many young ones did not survive. They were near starvation and could not fight off the outbreaks of malaria, typhoid fever, and dysentery.

John D. Lee Mansion

The John D. Lee mansion in Washington City was the biggest and finest mansion Lee ever built. In her book *American Massacre*, Sally Denton stated that it was built "using lumber from Parowan, native mica for the windows, and millstones hauled from the local mountains by a full-time crew of ten men."[22] Lee had a good income from a molasses mill and a cotton farm in nearby Toquerville. According to Denton, "His wives and children were the best dressed in the county."[23]

Twenty years later, Lee was executed for his crimes at the Mountain Meadows Massacre. Some of his riches supposedly came from the booty that was taken from the bodies of the Arkansans that were left for the wolves at the massacre site. While estimates say that over fifty Mormons were involved in this massacre, it was John D. Lee alone who was executed for the crime. He was able to enjoy several good years in between, with many wives, children, and grandchildren. He achieved a lot of important progress for his community and enjoyed a lot of wealth and prestige, but after the massacre, the locals were hostile toward him and "turned their cattle into his grain fields and diverted his irrigation ditches."[24] Lee went about the county telling anyone who would listen how the Indians had massacred the immigrant train.

Due to the rumors of being haunted, the Lee mansion was torn down in the late 1890s. The original tale is rather gruesome, and while it's probably not true, it's easy to see where it came from since John D. Lee certainly committed similar crimes at Mountain Meadows. This horrific tale was "later recounted by one of his wives that she had seen him slit the throat of a child survivor of the massacre who had spoken out of turn. The young victim had commented on Lee's wife Emma wearing the silk dress and gold jewelry of the girl's mother."[25] According to local legend, "figs ripen black over the grave" of the murdered child who is supposedly buried in Lee's orchard. It is a known fact that Lee took at least two or three of the surviving children to live in his home. It is the private opinion of many people that some of the leaders of this massacre took surviving children as a form of atonement for their sins.[26]

All but seven of Lee's nineteen-plus wives abandoned him as public opinion grew more and more against him, and only three stood by him at the end. It has been suggested that one of the wives who abandoned Lee made up the story of the murdered child in order to disassociate herself from him, but perhaps not. Stories of Lee's brutality abounded, but the more accepted rumor was that the stolen child had simply died in the Lee home from complications of the injuries she received at the massacre site.[27]

During the years that the Lee mansion was abandoned, rumors of a little girl's ghost living in the deserted mansion surfaced, and people claimed to see her wandering the grounds. The mansion was sold to the Presbyterian Church, who added a bell tower. Because the minister rode a circuit and was only there one day a week, teenage boys would sneak into the church and ring the bell in the middle of the night, making everyone think that the ghost was doing it. The town council decided to have the church torn down in the 1890s to rid themselves of both the tales and the mischief of any ghosts or real young people who continued to hoax this haunt for their own amusement. Nevertheless, the ghost child truly had been seen wandering around in the church and the outside gardens.

Conflicting rumors abound as to where the child was buried—in a small family plot on the grounds, or just somewhere near the house. Some rumors even claim she was buried under the house. A few versions say the child was a boy, and others say it was a girl. I doubt that such an apparition, if there were one, would have left when the house was torn down. Ghosts of this magnitude and tragedy stay with the land forever. And whether the child died from her wounds or at the hands of John D. Lee at his own dinner table really doesn't make a difference to the spirit. If the child was real and her death was documented, she would continue to walk the grounds where she was buried, if only for justice's sake.

Kane County

The Kaibab National Forest, where my granduncles and grandfather went cowboying and ranching when they were young, housed mystical places for my mother in her childhood. Born in Glendale and raised in Kanab, my mother was an unknowing and powerful intuitive who probably never understood this magical tie to the spirits of the land there, thinking it merely the protective environment of a small Mormon town. I have often wondered what she saw and felt while growing up in such a haunted place. And to say these areas are haunted is an understatement. This is a gorgeous country, full of plateaus and colorful cliffs with names such as Grey, White, Pink, Table, and Vermillion Cliffs. This part of Kane County also has some original lake names: Duck, Cave, Hidden, Three Lakes, and the largest one, Navajo Lake. Tales are told of canyons full of Anasazi and Aztec relics, of the Basketmakers and later Indian spirits, the residue energy of Spanish miners and their slaves, mountain men and explorers, cowboy rustlers and outlaws, pioneers and settlers, all contributing to the legends and lore of the area. Zane Grey wrote about the area and lived there for a while, as did the infamous John D. Lee, executed much later for his part in the Mountain Meadows Massacre.

Kane County, especially the area around Kanab and Glendale, was my mother's home country. Her relations and ancestors were from both Glendale and Kanab. Some of the Kane County towns continued to flourish, while others became ghost towns, crumbling into dust. Upper Kanab became Alton and Berryville. Pocketville became Glendale, named for the town of Glendale in Scotland. Orderville, because of its past history, remained Orderville. Winsor became Mt. Carmel, and Pahreah or Paria was integrated into an old movie set near Johnson Canyon where another old movie set stands. The towns of Fredonia, named for "Free Women," and Pipe Springs, whose fort still stands, were the Mormon Arizona towns just across the border. Paria, White House, Skutumpah, Adairville, and Moccasin Springs, which was named from finding an Indian moccasin between two rivers, disappeared all together, along with several other smaller settlements whose ruins are still listed on present-day maps. Kanab and all the small towns around it are gateways to the Coral Pink Sand Dunes, Zion and Bryce Canyon National Parks, Glen Canyon National Recreation Area, and the north rim of the Grand Canyon.

According to Indian lore, Navajo Lake, Hidden Lake, and at least a dozen other lakes are haunted. It seems that in the moonlight the guardian spirits arise from the mists to protect a sacred land. Even the Paria River is said to be haunted by a mythical creature. I was told that in the Paiute language *paria* means "muddy waters," or beast of the muddy waters. Modern-day reports of Bigfoot sightings in this area may explain what this mythical animal was so long ago. People who traveled the Paria River claimed to see not only this creature, but also the "hoodoos," a legendary people punished by Coyote and given this name. (Coyote tales are a famous series of Native American stories told about "Coyote," who was always tricking the people.[28])

The "hoodoos" haunt the entire region, although their look-alikes are the rock formations they are named after in Bryce and Zion Canyons. Three Lakes, it is claimed, is the site of an ancient Aztec treasure and underwater cave. Johnson, Stout, Cave, Cottonwood, Kanab, and Angel Canyons are full of ancient Anasazi and Fremont culture artifacts that people believe are guarded by ancient spirits of the canyons. The first explorers, fur traders, and trappers may have left a ghost or two in these canyons, and echoes of the first settlers and early pioneers may also remain. Later, when Kanab became "Utah's Little Hollywood," more apparitions were added.

In 1923 the novelist Emerson Hough photographed my mother at five years of age. He was visiting the area for the filming of his novel, the 1925 Academy Award winning western, *The Covered Wagon*, which was directed by former Ogdenite James Cruze. It was the biggest movie ever made for Hollywood at the time. Kanab Creek was lined with cameras for one of the scenes where the pioneer wagons crossed the river, but this scene was never used in the film. Mr. Hough sent my mother's parents an autographed photo postcard of the pretty little girl dressed in her Sunday best. He wrote something to the effect that she ought to be in the movies. Had her family stayed in Kanab after her childhood years, I wonder if she would have been in a western or two as an extra. This world was a fairyland to my mother. Even in her old age she spoke and wrote of Kanab and Glendale with tears in her eyes and great fondness.

Glendale

The first settlers of Berryville went through some harsh times and left behind the spirits and imprints of their passing. One story reveals the characters of some of the Native Americans and pioneer settlers. Their ghosts still echo down through the decades.

John and William Berry were from Kannaraville and went searching for good grazing land for their cattle. They ended up founding Berryville (Glendale). The land looked so promising for settlement that by the spring of 1864, all four Berry brothers moved there to establish a settlement. Robert and Joseph came, along with their wives, sisters Isabella and Dena Hales. Robert married Isabella and William married Dena. They named their settlement Berry Valley and built their log cabins in a square facing each other like a small fort. Joseph and Ann Hopkins, my great-great-grandparents, were among the new settlers to Berryville.

About a hundred Indians lived in the area, mostly Paiutes and Moquis, although the Navajo regularly came across the border from Colorado to hunt and fish. All of the local Indians seemed friendly to the settlers. It was the Navajo who were incensed that their hunting grounds, which they had hunted and fished in for decades, were being settled by whites.

Almost immediately several skirmishes and conflicts arose. More than once raids and massacres forced the settlers to flee from the smaller settlements to the larger town forts for protection. Brigham Young's solution to this problem was to send more settlers to increase the population and therefore give them more protection. He also provided his militia to escort the settlers whenever they had to flee from an Indian attack.

Most of the settlers made occasional trips to Salt Lake City. On one such visit, the Berrys stopped at their former home in Kannaraville, where Isabella's two-year-old child took sick. Robert and Joseph Berry stayed behind with Isabella and her child, while the rest of the party went on to Berryville. When Robert and Isabella's child died, the three of them resumed their journey home while mourning the loss of the child.

Between Short Creek and the Cain Beds, the three Berrys were attacked by the Cedar Band Indians and massacred. Wood haulers found their bodies. Joseph and Isabella were in the wagon, and Robert's body, which was showered with arrows, was leaning against the wagon. It was later heard that the same Indians reported that Robert had fought bravely and well.

Shortly after this atrocity, my great-great-grandmother Ann Spendlove Hopkins and her friend Mrs. Cornwell and her five children were placed in a wagon while their husbands stood guard outside as they prepared to be escorted by the militia to the local fort.

According to my great-great-grandmother's history, the Hopkins and Cornwell families had a frightening experience of their own: "To their great relief, an Indian came to the wagon, raised the cover, gave an Indian grunt, and went away. The

Indian was dressed in clothes taken from the Berrys. He had on the white shirt so that the endowment marks were on the back."[29]

The Indian who looked in Ann's wagon was the leader of the band who had carried out the massacre. His nickname was Coal Creek John, and he was wearing a shirt that belonged to one of the murdered brothers.

Her history continues, "At the sight of this, William Berry, another brother, was determined to have revenge by killing the chief. He was restrained by other settlers by being locked up until his anger had subsided to the point where he could realize that retaliation would only cause more bloodshed and make a difficult situation more difficult."[30] The Berry brothers were buried in the Grafton Cemetery.

This is the town that the movie *Butch Cassidy and the Sundance Kid* made famous as a backdrop for its filming.[31]

Joseph Hopkins was Glendale's blacksmith, and his blacksmith shop can be seen at the Smithsonian Institute today, since it was donated to the institute after his death. Boyd and Margaret Stewart are other ancestors of mine who lived and died in Glendale, Utah.

No dates are given, but the best pioneer story from Glendale is from the author of the 1970 version of *The History of Kane County*.

> One of the finest stories depicting the character of the local Indians comes from Glendale. James Blazzard and his wife Mary Catherine Jolly Blazzard had the tragic experience of having their little three-year-old Mary Ann, who was playing in the doorway, disappear. Tracks of Indian ponies were found leading out of the river; it was thought that the Indians had stolen her.
>
> The hunt continued far and wide for traces of the child, to no avail, and even though scouts were sent out from Salt Lake City, the search was futile.
>
> More than a year passed. One evening a dark face was pressed against the Blazzard's window, and then an unexpected tapping at the door: One-two, one, one-two.
>
> "That is Old Choog's knock." Mr. Blazzard said. "The one he used when he was sick."
>
> Jim crawled toward the door and slid the bolt, expecting Choog to come in, but instead, the Indian thrust a small girl with tousled hair and ragged clothes through the door.
>
> "Me bring you Indian papoose," he said and disappeared into the darkness. Jim hunted around outside, but Choog was gone.
>
> "We'll have to keep her overnight," he said.
>
> In combing her hair with coal oil in case of lice, a long dark mole, Mary Ann's birthmark, was discovered on her neck. Jim held the lamp close to her face. Her eyes were blue. When they undressed her they found that her armpits were white. Her skin had been stained with wild berries and her hair dyed black with walnut bark.
>
> News of Mary Ann's restoration spread rapidly up and down Long Valley. The settlers crowded around to see her and to discuss the circumstances of

her return. They were all agreed that Choog himself had not stolen her, but that he had rescued her for her parents, because they had taken care of him when he was sick.[32]

When we visited the Glendale Cemetery years ago, it was before the town took it over and planted more lawn, cleared away bushes, and turned the pioneer graveyard into a beautiful place. At that time, neither my mother nor I had any awareness of our intuitive gifts, and the cemetery seemed more real because it was overgrown and a bit abandoned. We walked all over together but could not find any of our ancestors' graves. We finally located them under some large, overgrown bushes in the back of the cemetery and had to dig through the foliage to read their names on their very old markers. Had I known then what I know now, I would have had a much deeper understanding of their trials and tribulations, as well as the mystical lands from which my mother came. I will always be curious about which ancestors carried the so-called "gift" and how they handled it.

Fredonia and the Roll Away Saloon

The early histories of Fredonia and Pipe Spring, which are just across the border in Arizona, are closely tied to Kanab's history. I mention these towns because of the Roll Away Saloon legend that is told in different versions and argued about even today.

Fredonia was settled mainly because of water problems in Kanab. Kanab Canyon's waters began to dry up due to a prolonged drought. By 1882, the drought ceased and a cloudburst caused a large flood, which contaminated all the wells the settlers had dug. Kanab citizens built a dam to keep the water close to town. After the drought, they discovered that the dam had more water than Kanab needed. They decided it could be used in the little valley beyond Kanab, which became Fredonia. The first house was built there in 1885.

Located eight miles south of Kanab, Fredonia became a convenient place to send plural wives whenever the United States marshals made raids. By slipping across the border, these women were safe from arrest. Apostle Erastus Snow suggested the name Fredonia, which means "Free Women."

The Roll Away Saloon story is taken from Rowland W. Rider's book *The Roll Away Saloon: Cowboy Tales of the Arizona Strip.*[33] It is a tale about a real saloon located right on the Utah–Arizona border, four miles from Fredonia and four miles from Kanab. It sat on a little hill called Halfway Hill, where riders could be seen coming from a long way off in either direction. The saloon was built on a series of logs that could easily be rolled with a few crowbars. The men of both Fredonia and Kanab took advantage of this saloon to the consternation of both the "free women" of Fredonia and the women of Kanab. Both groups were upset about their men spending their hard-earned money in a saloon.

One day the women in Kanab met at a quilting bee, got to talking, and got all fired up about the saloon. They decided to get on their horses, ride down to the saloon, and burn it to the ground—which they tried to do. The owner of the saloon saw them coming, called the men out, provided crowbars, and they rolled the saloon across the Arizona border so that the women couldn't do anything since the saloon was now subject to Arizona's laws and not Utah's.

The women of Fredonia heard what the Kanab women did, and a few days later planned their ride more carefully, keeping it secret. They rode up to the saloon, but the saloon keeper had a lookout, and once again the men came out and rolled the saloon into Utah. The women of Fredonia could do nothing because now the saloon was subject to Utah's laws. Apparently this happened a lot when the local law came around.

Rider tells a lot of cowboy tales in his book, including one about meeting President Roosevelt and putting on an impromptu rodeo for him, and one about camping out with Zane Grey, who they always had to wait for because he couldn't do any kind of cowboying well. He says that Grey went to live at Lee's Ferry but traveled about the area stealing stories from cowboys—especially him. He tells of a man who owned a buffalo herd near Pipe Spring. He saved his own life one day by getting down on all fours and pretending to be a buffalo so that the big bull in front of him wouldn't charge.

Rider tells only one ghost story about camping by himself one night and having an old prospector walk out of the mist from nowhere with seven bags of gold on his burro. The man showed him the gold and then walked off into the mist, never to be seen again. But these are cowboy stories, and my granduncles and grandfather were also good at telling them!

Pipe Spring

Pipe Spring is full of spirits, including the ghosts of early Native Americans, a few famous white explorers, and settlers who had to defend themselves against attacks.

Whites first discovered Pipe Spring when a party led by Jacob Hamblin camped there in 1858. Later, Brigham Young, John Wesley Powell, and Jacob Hamblin met there to turn the land into a fort and ranch for the Mormon Church.

In his book *The Roll Away Saloon*, Rowland W. Rider told his granddaughter the following:

A legend exists of a humorous event that prompted the naming of the spring. William "Gunlock Bill" Hamblin, a noted marksman, was tricked into trying to shoot through a silk handkerchief that was hung in a tree, but the bullet just pushed the silk aside without marking it. Vexed by this, Gunlock bet he could shoot the bottom out of one of the men's (Dudley Leavitt) smoking pipes without touching the rim. When he succeeded, the place was called "Pipe Spring" in honor of the event.[34]

The Navajo Indians began their raids along this Arizona Strip. The first two white fatalities happened near Pipe Spring when two Mormon men were killed trying to retrieve their stolen stock from the Navajo men trying to find meat for their families. Pipe Spring became an important location for the Mormon militia, who were not stationed there but kept a storehouse and shelter there as they fought the Navajo in the area.

Only one battle took place in the Pipe Valley, when the militia engaged about forty Navajo, and some of them were killed. The rest escaped back across the Colorado border. Anson Perry Winsor built a stone ranch house complex there, and this "fort" was completed in 1872. It was named after him as the Winsor Castle Pipe Spring Fort and eventually became the Winsor Castle Stock Growing Company owned by the Mormon Church.

John Wesley Powell stayed in Kanab but got most of his supplies from Pipe Spring when he and his men surveyed the Grand Canyon. Eventually, the Winsor Castle Cattle Company was deeded over to the federal government (due to the Edmonds-Tucker Act of 1878[35]) and then later went under private ownership. In 1923, with the grazing lands finally given out in the area, Stephen Mather of the National Park Service convinced President Warren G. Harding to make Pipe Spring a national monument to preserve the unique fort and its lands. This old fort and all of its outbuildings can be seen today with little change, just as it was in the 1870s. Pipe Spring is considered a haunted location, although little has been done in terms of EVP recordings or videotaping.

Kanab's History

My mother was born on a ranch where her father was working. She was soon taken to Kanab, where her mother and father moved in temporarily with her great-grandmother who ran the old Cole Hotel (Hick's Place) in Kanab.

Kanab was settled three different times, in 1864–65, 1868, and finally 1870. Jacob Hamblin negotiated treaties with the Navajo, Paiutes, and Moquis after years of conflict.

The name Kanab means "Willow Basket," like the baskets the Indian women carried their infants in on their backs. Another story is told that the name "The Place of Willows" came from the willows along the riverbank in Kanab that Paiute women would use to make their *khans* (papoose baskets).

A land already spiritual was blessed once more in April 1870 when the prophet Brigham Young visited the area with gifts of cattle, sheep, and horses for his people. Farming was difficult in the dry, waterless area. Before irrigation ditches could be built, the people planted a group farm in 120 acres south of town so that their crops would have a better chance of surviving.

In 1881 the first gristmill was built in Kanab Canyon, three miles north of town. Two more mills were built in the 1890s, and a final, larger mill was built in 1915. A flood washed the first mill away. The second one in Hog Canyon was hit with a series of difficulties and had to close down. The third, located near the town cemetery, burned down before it was completed.

The Deseret Telegraph came to town in 1871. Fort Kanab had no dance halls, saloons, or any other accoutrements of the wilder side of most frontier western towns. Brigham Young sent Levi Stewart to lead the community in Kanab as the LDS bishop, mayor, and founder of the settlement. He was a polygamist and had several wives like most Mormon leaders did at the time.

Tragedy struck part of his family on December 14, 1870. One of his wives, Margery, and three of her children perished in a fire inside the fort. As the fire spread, the roof of the cabin caved in, barring their exit from the wooden home. Two grown sons of other wives rushed in with Margery to save her children, and they were also killed. All in all, six people perished in the fire: Margery, Levi, Charles, Urban, Heber, and Edward. Another son managed to save one of the children but was badly burned. To commemorate and honor the fallen pioneers, the entire community built a stone school house on the same ground. The school was completed in 1873, and eighty students and a teacher filled the little one-room school house the first year. I would imagine that the first children attending the school probably had the remarkable experience of having an occasional spirit child sitting among them.

By the turn-of-the-century, Fort Kanab was no more, and the town of Kanab had a growing population. By the time my mother was born in 1917, Kanab was the gateway to many Southern Utah scenic wonders, and tourists rich enough to travel overseas to see these marvels were arriving from all over the world. My mother recalled when the king and queen of Sweden visited Kanab and how disappointed she was. She expected a handsome king and a beautiful queen, but both turned out to be plain. My mother's heart sank, but she soon noticed the queen's beautiful smile and realized that she was kind, compassionate, and loving.

Other famous foreign dignitaries and homegrown celebrities stopped in Kanab on their way to visit the canyons. The movie people came to town more frequently after 1922. They added another layer of hauntings to Kanab from the early days of the silent films. Stunt doubles were rare in those early days, and actors and actresses often performed their own stunts. The first early stuntmen and their horses were often injured, sometimes severely, while performing daring stunts.

One man with a promising career in Hollywood died instantly on the set of the film *Nevada* that starred Gary Cooper. Leon Ward graduated from stunt double to small parts in the cowboy movies. Local doctor M. J. McFarlane, who treated the Hollywood stars involved in the filming, stated, "During the shooting of a milling battle on horseback for *Nevada* on June 3, 1927, the fighting became the epitome of realism: Leon Ward of Parowan was shot through the heart and killed."[36] This Utah born actor suddenly disappeared from my research, until I ran across this quote in Dr. Mac's book.

Buffalo Bill Cody came to restock his animals and see the wild country, Zane Grey stayed at the old Cole Hotel when writing *Riders of the Purple Sage*, Theodore

Roosevelt came through, and John Wesley Powell stayed in town often, as did others before the movie era in Kanab. The old Paria movie set near Johnson Canyon and the Parry Lodge in Kanab, where many of them stayed, have their own haunting tales to tell. Several Hollywood celebrities and movie stars fell in love with the area once they made a film there. According to Jackie Rife (Kanab's famous and only stuntwoman), the nicest big-name western stars were Joel McCrea, Clark Gable, John Wayne, Audie Murphy, and Ronald Reagan. Some of them returned for vacations or to go hunting and fishing. Among these were Wallace Berry, Harry Carey Sr., Clark Gable, and later, John Wayne and his entourage.

One funny and yet tragic story that Jackie Rife told me was that right after Clark Gable's wife, Carol Lombard, was killed in an airplane crash, he took another hunting trip to North Fork. Jackie's father took him hunting, and he shot his first mountain lion. They took it back to camp, and when Gable was really drunk, they told him it was tradition for a hunter on his first kill to eat some of the animal. They cut off a piece and Gable ate it. The next morning when he woke up with a hangover, he asked them if they had eaten dinner the night before, because he couldn't remember. They said, "We ate dinner, but you had a piece of your mountain lion." Rather than wounding him more, it probably lightened things up a bit and got Gable to laugh a little.[37]

The infamous John D. Lee lived in Paria Canyon with his wife Emma before establishing Lee's Ferry. He left another wife, Caroline, in Kanab when she was expecting her eleventh child.

Along with this is the legend of the John D. Lee mines, possibly two mines and a third cache of gold kept secret and hidden between Kanab and Lee's Ferry on the Colorado border. Lee apparently had a secret silver mine near or in the Grand Canyon, and a gold mine near where he eventually settled in Paria Canyon when he was hiding out from the federal investigators. He had eighteen wives and their families to support, and no one knows where his gold cache was hidden. One adopted boy often went with him into the canyons near Lonely Dell to a place called Soap Creek Canyon. Lee knew these mysterious canyons better than anyone and could always lose anyone trying to follow him. The secret locations of these mines went with Lee to his grave.

After Lee was executed for his part in the Mountain Meadows Massacre, his wife Emma found a cache of ore under their bed worth $7000. Emma married a man named Frank French, and they spent years trying to locate these mines and the gold cache but never found anything. Rumors still persist that Paria Canyon might have been the location of his other secret mine.[38]

One poignant story about John D. Lee is that when he tried to settle Fort Harmony near Kannaraville in 1852, it had to be abandoned because of the Walker War. (Fort Harmony was the first settlement in the area and was located four miles southeast of the present New Harmony.) Two years later, Lee came back and built a new fort and was living in it at the time of the Mountain Meadows Massacre. He acted as the town assessor, probate judge, clerk, and collector. He lived there until

1862 when, as he called it, "Harmony number two" was destroyed by a twenty-eight-day rainstorm. Two of his children were killed when the walls of his home gave way. Lee stayed in his wet clothes for eight days straight fighting to keep his home and the settlement.

After the rain and flooding were over, the entire settlement buried family members and moved one last time to the head of Ash Creek to found the tiny New Harmony that exists today. Lee and his family certainly paid many times over for that fateful day in the Meadows. He was executed some twenty years after the incident as the sole scapegoat for the fifty or so Mormon participants.[39]

Haunted Canyons and Lakes

Four layers of hauntings are in the Kanab–Glendale area of Kane County—the Indian myths and legends, the Spanish explorers and gold mines, the pioneer and settler stories, and the famous and infamous who passed through the area during the peak years of "Utah's Little Hollywood."

Lakes said to be haunted are Navajo Lake, Cave Lakes, and Three Lakes. The haunted canyons are Stout Canyon, Cave Canyon, Johnson Canyon, Cottonwood Canyon, Paria Canyon, and Kanab (Angel) Canyon. Haunted places in Kanab, besides the massacre sites during the Indian conflicts, are the Cole Hotel, the Heritage House, the Parry Lodge where all the movie stars stayed when they were in town, and the old Paria movie set and ghost town ruins.

Navajo Lake is supposedly haunted by ancient lake spirits, but only in Indian lore since no whites have ever seen any mists rising out of the lake. Three Lakes is supposed to house an underwater cave that the ancient Aztecs dug hundreds of years ago. The present owner had so much trouble with treasure hunters that he now prosecutes trespassers.

The Aztecs supposedly dug a cave 750 to 900 feet into the rock in order to store their valuables in this man-made water trap. In the past, the owner has allowed several sets of divers to try to reach the end of the tunnel. No diver was successful, and most returned covered in soot, saying they would never go down there again. The soot came from large bonfires built by the ancient Aztecs to heat up the rock, causing it to crack and fall apart. The tunnel seems to be shaped like a menorah, with several branches leading to small chambers, each with separate treasures of their own.

Before using divers, the owner tried to drain the lake but soon discovered that it was fed by several underwater springs, so this option was impossible. He was also informed that the lake is a protected environment for the amber snail, and the local rangers told him that he could never drain the lake.

In the meantime, he hired divers, none of whom were successful. Equipment was constantly failing, and these were skilled professional divers who knew what they were doing. They had not been believers in guardian spirits who attempted to keep them from going down the main tunnel, but all the divers refused to go down a second time. They described seeing ghosts or spirits that attempted to choke them. They also claimed to have encountered supernatural forces, which many of them did not believe in before exploring Navajo Lake.

Eventually one diver did make it to the end of the main tunnel, only to discover that it was closed off with solid rock. They tried a different tactic by drilling holes from the top of the cliff down through the rock, and this was when they discovered that there were several branches leading off the main tunnel. They decided to drill a hole big enough so someone could enter the tunnels from there. When they hit seventy-five feet, the drill stopped and would not go any further. They used a heavier bit, but the drill still stopped at that exact depth. So they drilled smaller shafts and eventually punched into one of the rooms at the end of a branch tunnel. They discovered that all of the smaller rooms had been closed off, and that was why the divers had not noticed the other tunnels.

More strange things happened after the drilling. The next driller they hired died, and his wife passed away soon after, both of them dying of natural causes. The owner of the land decided to stop trying to access the chambers at the end of the tunnels. He felt he had exhausted all the possibilities, and the place seemed to be protected by supernatural forces that were beginning to frighten him and his family. The owner eventually died, and his family stopped all exploration of the lake and its underwater Aztec cave.

Before the family stopped their exploration, they located five large stone altars on the cliff by the lake. The altars overlook the valley floor. An unusual symbol was found carved in a rock above the canyon floor. It looks like a giant arrow, spear, or paintbrush, with a large circle around its middle. The arrow is pointing to a nearby natural spring. Another symbol is located about one hundred feet from the lake ponds and looks like a yoke.

There are theories about what these symbols represent, although archaeologists will tell you they could mean just about anything. Religious scholars say the yoke represents subservience to another, or work being done to please God or "the gods." Others say the yoke predates even the Aztecs, and others say the ancient Indians put the yoke above the graves of loved ones so that their journey to the underworld would be a good one. The symbols could have been carved at any time, or may even be present-day hoaxes. Still, the fact that so many people were affected negatively by trying to discover the underwater caves' secrets does suggest it has either a man-made water trap to choke divers, or guardian spirits who will not allow the place to be explored any further. Speculation is that the caves could be tombs, which would explain the yoke symbol as well as the guardian spirits.

Kanab (Angel) Canyon, long before the Best Friends Animal Sanctuary was located there, had few visitors, but those who did go into the canyon felt that the spirits of the Basketmakers were still dwelling there. Now that the sanctuary is in the canyon, people can feel its energy. It just so happens that two employees of the animal sanctuary are also members of the American Ghost Hunters Society and are especially interested in EVP recordings. They decided to explore the canyon on their off hours, where a variety of unwanted and exotic animals that cannot find a home anywhere else are now housed. The sanctuary is one of only a few large complexes in the United States where animals can live out their lives without fear or retribution for their natures, wounds, or handicaps. It houses horses, cats, dogs, exotic pets, and wildlife. These ghost busters took recorders and cameras with them and came back with orbs and sounds. But most interesting were the consistent pictures of a single, very large orb of energy in a particular spot in the canyon. Their electronic meters also indicated a strong presence of electromagnetic energy in this same area. I wonder if this could be the guardian spirit of the canyon, one who watches over the animals as well.

The ghost hunters also believe that the animals in the shelter sense the presences in the canyon and in the buildings on the property. One incident they like to relate concerns them going to the main house each evening, to the same room, where they watched a cat playing with an invisible friend. They decided to take photos, and after developing the photos, the women discovered a vortex of light energy where the cat was looking and playing with his invisible friend. The sequence of pictures revealed that as the cat played, the energy vortex grew bigger and bigger. In each photo, the cat backed a little further off from the vortex. The vortex finally got so big that the cat would jump back and run away into another room.

The ghost investigators, Jodi Chavez and Michele Page, also talked about how pet and person often continue to have a bond for a while after the pet is gone. People often report seeing or feeling the presence of their pet for a while after they have died.

"Some people keep seeing them," says Michele. "Or they feel like they've just jumped up on the bed. Just accept that this is happening. It can be quite comforting."[40] Spirits of this canyon must be enjoying the Best Friends Sanctuary and all the animals that they have brought to the canyon.

When I talked to Michele Page on the phone, I learned that she has over twenty years of experience with her own ghost hunting group in Nevada. She has been quoted in several magazine articles and in several documentaries on the History, Discovery, and Travel Channels. She was amazed at what she was videotaping, recording, and sensing, not only in Angel Canyon, but also in Peekaboo Canyon right behind the animal sanctuary. She said that the untouched petroglyphs interested her because kids today have computers, but children then had to write their messages in stone. "People had to write on the rocks to tell their stories," she commented.

When Michele and her husband were building a new home on their property in Kanab, the workmen digging the foundation found an ancient Indian burial site. She told her husband previously that she kept seeing an Indian man walking around in their old house (on that same property) from doorway to doorway, especially at night. When they began building the new house, they found a lone Indian grave, and work was halted while the authorities figured out what to do. After the house was completed, they continued to see the Indian spirit, which often startled Michele and even her cat. He would sit on the edge of the bed while she and her husband were sleeping and wake them up just in time for them to turn on the light and see the indentation on the bed. Michele says that the Kanab area is a haunted place, both from ancient times and from pioneer times.

Stout Canyon is twenty miles from Kanab, and campers claim it is haunted. What the campers and hikers see besides Indians spirits are mountain men trappers. The area had lots of good game, so it was trapped a lot in the early days. The tall trapper, who appears wearing a deerskin shirt and pants and a Scottish-looking military hat, is carrying an old muzzleloader. He mostly appears in the woods near a campfire. Once a flashlight is turned on the apparition, he will disappear. Since several people have seen the same ghost, perhaps it's a real man of flesh and blood, such as a hermit who lives in the woods nearby and likes to appear at campfires. On the other hand, he could be the spirit of a man who died there a long time ago.

Cave Lakes Canyon, Kanab Canyon, Cottonwood Canyon, and Johnson Canyon all carried amazing artifacts from the Anasazi period, as well as the later Fremont period. Indian legend claims that guardian spirits, who guard not only treasures but also the ancient dead, inhabit all of these canyons. Johnson Canyon was the scene of a treasure-hunting scam in the late 1920s and early 1930s, when a man came into the area claiming that gold had been discovered in the canyon, and a small boom started as more and more people arrived there. It was over almost as soon as it started, when people discovered the scam and moved on. Imprints of these often desperate gold diggers probably remain.

Paria Movie Set

Later, Johnson Canyon was the site of a western town movie set, with the original remains of Paria just a couple of miles away. The old Paria only had a building or two and the little cemetery left, but the new Paria had false front buildings and a never-ending succession of movie props that were built for a particular movie and then destroyed. The Joel Johnson Ranch was also the site of a lot of films, as were other sites around the area. Cave Lakes, Duck Creek, and Navajo Lake were also places where films were made. The original town of Pahreah (Paria) was situated thirty-five miles north of Lee's Ferry and forty-two miles northeast of Kanab. Some of the old cowboys called the place Par-ree. The Paiute translation is interpreted by whites as "muddy water," but the Paiute story is that one of their hunters cornered an elk, which forced the elk to jump into the river, thus the name "elk water." Peter Shultz and others staked claims there in 1865 but had to leave in March 1866 when the first whites were killed along the Arizona strip.

Paria was resettled in 1870 by a party of Mormon missionaries who got some of the starving local Paiutes to work for them by giving them half of the food they needed to survive. The other half of the Indians' diets were berries, roots, and seeds. Constant flooding became a real problem, and even though the settlers of Pahreah built a U.S. Post Office, it was abandoned in 1915.

By the 1930s, Pahreah was a ghost town. The movie companies had come to Kanab, and after discovering the remains of the old ghost town Paria, they built a movie set of their own a couple of miles away from it. Today the western movie set is open to tourists and offers daily gunfights. The set includes the open-air dance pavilion, which was originally used for my favorite movie from Kanab, *Westward the Women*.

Robert Taylor, the star of the film, was just as grumpy in real life as he was in the movie, but he had a good reason. During the filming he was in the midst of a divorce from Barbara Stanwyck. Later, the same set was used for *Pony Express*, which starred Charlton Heston and a Utah-connected actress Rhonda Fleming. *Westward the Women* is my favorite movie, because at least 150 women extras and one Utah stuntwoman, Jackie Rife, from Kanab, came from all over the area to be in the movie. The extras came from Kanab, Orderville, Mt. Carmel, Alton, and Fredonia, Arizona, to participate in the filming. They got hot and dirty and were exhausted by the end of filming. People said afterward that they had gained a new respect for, and an understanding of, what their own ancestors had gone through to come west. People do not know that a young Frank Capra, my favorite film director, wrote the screenplay. To a believer in ghosts, I find it interesting that descendants of some of the women, who really made such a journey, carried out their story in some deeply moving scenes of loss, death, and forgiveness. One can just imagine these women in the desert scenes with their own ancestor walking behind them.

The Paria movie set burned down soon after a big community drive to build it up and repair it following an area flood. To date, what is left of these buildings is under discussion, and some people in the community are working on a plan to rebuild. It was never proven that the fire was caused by arson, but people believe that's what it was. The surviving sets were moved to Movietown, another western tourist town, and recently ghost hunters investigated all of these buildings, catching actual ghost photos.

Moqui Cave

Garth Chamberlain purchased Moqui Cave in 1951, and everyone thought he was crazy for doing it. He couldn't get a bank loan for the project, but he and his wife went ahead with it anyway. They cleaned up the cave and used 286 bags of cement (which they mixed in a small fruit sprayer) to coat the walls. They painted the cement with white paint and brought in 150 tuck loads of dirt to level the uneven floors. Each load had to be taken inside in a wheelbarrow. They built a stage and an orchestra pit and opened their cave to dances and socials. A bar was even installed in the south wing.

After years of Friday and Saturday dances, they closed it down and decided to open a museum instead. They gathered Anasazi artifacts and minerals, and even built small replicas of Anasazi cliff dwellings to display. They ran the museum for several years.

Today the cave is a museum of paleontology, geology, and western history. A gift shop displays carvings and sculptures by Garth Chamberlain, and Lex Chamberlain and his wife run the place.

Thousands of tourists drop by each year on their way to the canyons on old Highway 89. Lex's great-grandfather was part of the Orderville communal experience. Lex's father raised a few eyebrows, Lex says, because his father was sort of an "outgoing rebel with a gift for colorful, earthy language." His son smiles as he acknowledges that his father was, "let's say, less active in the (LDS) Church when he decided to buy the cave. Dad bought the cave for the purpose of opening it up as one of the first dance halls and taverns in this good ol' part of Southern Utah," Lex says, chuckling. Unlike his father, Lex is an active Mormon. The bar was handcrafted with inlaid stones and specimens that Garth had collected from around the world.

The crowds became rowdier and rowdier, and after twelve years the Chamberlains decided to change the atmosphere by creating the museum. When Lex's father died, the family wanted to sell the cave, but in the end, Lex and his wife, Lee Anne, argued themselves into taking over the business. They call it a hidden treasure of local history, and so do a few others.

The following is from an article in *The Salt Lake Tribune*, written by Bob Mims: "Chamberlain picks up a long, carved wood panel crafted by his father. It is a family portrait; generations lovingly etched for posterity from a reunion held years ago. 'Out of all the things here, I am proudest of this,' Chamberlain says. 'It's my family.'" Apparitions hang around such places that they loved so dearly, especially when it all remains in the family.[41]

Moquis were little people that came from Hopi legends. They were an even smaller race than the Hopi, standing about three feet tall. They caused all kinds of mischief for the Hopi and other tribes that believed in them. They especially liked to raid the granaries of the Indians, and even some of the granaries of the early settlers. The Moqui supposedly lived in the river bottoms or in caves in their own specially designed houses. They became such a nuisance that local tribes, Hopi or not, waged war against them and drove them out of their communities. In one version, the last of the Moquis were rounded up and chased off the Kaiparowits Plateau (Five Mile Mountain) near Escalante. In another version, the Moqui simply vanished after their defeat in battle, never to be seen again. For years, a lot of cowboys claimed to have gunned down the last of the survivors. Moqui Cave was supposed to have been one of their hiding places long before anyone lived there.

Kanab's Spirits

The old Cole Hotel, located in the town of Kanab, is where Sy Hicks, the last of his family to live in one of the largest homes in town, grew stranger as he got older. He was known for scaring kids by jumping out of the bushes around his house and telling them that his dead wife was upstairs in the bedroom. Sy never married and let the home get so run down that it was known as the town's "spook" house for years. Sy eventually took to living in the old chicken coop out back and did not live in the house at all—probably because it scared him! After Sy died, the house stood empty and was threatened with demolition until a couple from California came along, bought the place, and spent years on its painstaking renovations. It is now a beautiful bed and breakfast not far from the Heritage House.

The Heritage House was restored by townspeople and is used as the town museum and a showpiece for Kanab. I talked to the tour guide last time I was there, and she said that while there were no definite sightings of ghosts in the house, it certainly had all the signs of one, from creaking ceilings and dimming lights to doors discovered open when they had been left shut the day before. She also said that once in a while she felt as if she were not alone in the house, as though someone was following her around to make sure that the house was well taken care of. Her own ancestors lived in the house, and she thought that perhaps it was her connection to them that made her not only feel at home, but also feel like she was being watched.

By the 1930s and 1940s, Johnson Canyon had become a complete fort built for the movie *Buffalo Bill*, and the new Paria had become a complete movie set for many films. Echoes of film crews and famous movie stars can be heard in this canyon.

In town, the Parry Lodge, looking like a miniature white southern mansion or a 1940s country cottage, has really capitalized on its famous past. The suites are even named after the stars who stayed in them. Even though the peak years for films being made in Kanab are over, the lodge is still a favorite place for tourists to stay. Some people enjoy staying in a room where their favorite Hollywood star from the classic era also stayed, including stars such as Charlton Heston, Glen Ford, John Wayne, Barbara Stanwyck, and Ava Gardner. The yearly Western Legends Festival has grown bigger each year, and the town is flooded not only with tourists, but also with the old westerns' great stars, directors, stuntmen, and stuntwomen. Cowboy poets, chuckwagon dinners, old westerns films, and much more is offered during the four-day event, which will probably soon be a week-long event. The old barn behind the Parry Lodge is now The Old Barn Theatre, which was originally owned by Gid Findlay, another original pioneer of Kanab.

While not boasting of any celebrity spirits, Parry Lodge does claim to have one apparition—the ghost of Whit Parry, the original owner and renovator of the lodge. One of the original waitresses, who worked there for a long time, was often quoted as saying that Whit told her he would come back to haunt the lodge because he loved it so much. Apparently Whit was a bit of a jokester who liked to play practical jokes on the waitresses. Mostly though, he was a perfectionist. His waitresses had to be in perfectly starched uniforms, and leftovers were unacceptable. So the ghost stories really do fit a person who wanted everything just so. Some say that he still expects perfection. That is why some people are thoroughly convinced that the only ghost at Parry Lodge is Whit's.

The Parry Lodge was once Justin M. "Jet" Johnson's home. It was one of the original pioneer homes in town. Jet Johnson came to Kanab as a sheep man and ran his large herds during the 1890s. There were several Johnson brothers who were among the first men to carry the mail to Kanab. This was no small feat! Nephi, Joel, and Jet Johnson and a few others braved a route from Toquerville to Pipe Spring, to Kanab, to Johnson, and to Paria on horseback. The carrier traveled a small trail through two canyons and two ranches. He had to dismount and carry the mail on his back down a 1,000-foot cliff where he met the carrier from the other end of the route and exchanged mail sacks. The carrier then climbed back up the cliff in the dark and camped for the night in a small cave on a ledge. Eventually, Joe Hamblin devised an easier method. The mail was attached to a windlass that was raised and lowered down the cliff in Zion Canyon.

In 1891 Jet, Nephi, Joel, and Sixtus E. Johnson decided to go into the mercantile business. Joel quit his partnership with another man and agreed to go into business with his brothers. They bought a store from an ancestor of mine, James R. Stewart, and went into business as the Johnson Brothers Store. It prospered for a few years but then went under in 1894. Some other men bought the Johnson Brothers Store, and when one of the new owners stated that it might be a white elephant for them also, they renamed it The Elephant and painted a big white elephant on the front of the building.

In 1909 the Kanab Equitable was organized. A group of men and one woman bought the Wonderland Store building to open up another mercantile business. Jet Johnson was one of the men in the organization, and my great-great-grandmother was the only woman, Eleanor J. McAllister. In 1914 Jet Johnson and Gid Findlay, who owned the barn behind the Parry Lodge, were involved in organizing a private water company, because Kanab was always looking for new water sources.

The development of the film industry in Kanab was due to the combined efforts of brothers Whit (Whitney), Gron (Gronway) and Chaunce (Chauncey) Parry. The Parrys started out by conducting tours through Bryce and Zion Canyons. Once *Deadwood Coach*, with Tom Mix, arrived in 1922, it was the Parry brothers who sold the idea of filming movies around Kanab. By the 1930s the movie industry had come full force to Utah. In the 1920s, Chaunce filmed the area by plane and on horseback, and with his album in hand, he went to Hollywood to visit all the major studios. Gron managed the transportation, props, and even the extras for the movie companies as they arrived, but it was Whit who created the Parry Lodge and provided housing for everyone, including making arrangements with other motels in the area to accommodate extra guests. Whit and Chaunce bought the place in 1930, but it was Whit who did the renovations and built the new cabins on the north lot.

All of the brothers got to meet and mingle with the Hollywood greats, especially the western stars. But according to some employees, it was Whit's ghost who decided to stay to keep an eye on things. Whit served an LDS mission in France and brought back some chandeliers that still hang in the lodge today.

In the old days, whenever anyone walked across the second floor, the chandeliers would swing back and forth. Now, sometimes when employees are working late at night and no one can possibly be on the second floor, they don't hear footsteps, but the chandeliers will sway back and forth as if someone were walking through the second floor rooms. For years employees would leave their paperwork on their desks only to come back the next day and find all the papers gone. They would have to search all over upstairs and would eventually find the papers stacked neatly in an odd place.

Employees also sometimes found the water turned on full force in the women's bathroom when no one was around. They turned it off only to came back later and find it on again. Employees expect that some startling and specific incidents will happen again in the future.

In one incident, which happened in the wintertime, two women were alone in the building painting. Suddenly, three fruit glasses on the other side of the room flew off a table, hurtled across the room, and shattered at their feet. Another time, a woman was walking alone past the dishwashing area in the kitchen when the spray hose squirted her in the back, and there was definitely no one else there. One of the employees was filling the juice pitcher while all the glasses on the table were turned upside down around her. She looked down to see all of the glasses being turned over by invisible hands. The people at Parry Lodge say that as long as the lodge is there, Whit will probably hang around to make sure things are done right.

In 1957, almost as a requiem after the peak period of movie making in Kanab, and after the late 1920s to 1950s celebrity visitors to the lodge, a "B" movie entitled *The Girl in Black Stockings* was filmed in its entirety at the Parry Lodge. The stars of this low-budget film noir murder mystery seemed as if they were paying homage to the history of this star-studded retreat, because many of them went on to greater stardom in Hollywood: Lex Barker, Anne Bancroft, Mamie Van Doren, and even Dan Blocker of *Bonanza* fame. Marysvale's hometown beauty and movie star, Marie Windsor, also starred in this production, and all of them probably stayed in the lodge where the movie was filmed, as if they were on a brief vacation out west. Since Marie Windsor, Dan Blocker, and Anne Bancroft are all gone, as well as others who stayed there, more haunting tales might yet surface about the place.

My mother spoke of her hometown and its beautiful surroundings with great love and respect. She probably saw a few spirits when she was growing up but didn't recognize them. I do know that she wrote of a special upstairs room in the old "Hicks" place (Cole Hotel), which was the north bedroom. She had adventures there putting on plays with friends, going to see her little brother there after he was born, and even taking her turn to take ice to her grandfather who eventually died in that room. She said that all of life's pageantry was presented to her there when she was a child, her great-grandfather and great-grandmother having been the stars in many of the town's plays. She went out with her grandfather to visit his bee farm and cavorted in the forests by Jacob Lake. Her family made homemade ice cream, and with the help of her little red wagon she would bring ice from the icehouse. She saw royalty and movie stars and enjoyed her favorite activity—eating freshly made clabber with her father in the pantry of their house. The ghosts of Kanab and Kane County are especially real to me, because they came alive in my mother's words and eyes whenever she mentioned her favorite place, her childhood home.

Jacob Lake Inn

My sister worked at Jacob Lake six days a week and had no car. It was rare to get a ride into town, so she spent her time off on the Bowman's ranch down off the Kaibab, where she met "Shorty," who taught her to ride and wanted to teach her to shoot.

Shorty rolled his own cigarettes, was bowlegged, and never took his cowboy hat off. He was the epitome of a true cowboy. My sister only wanted to learn to ride, so Shorty taught her on several visits. The funny part is that she never rode a horse again.

My sister wore gingham blouses and a circle skirt and worked as a waitress. She enjoyed meeting people from around the world. She also went with others to the North Rim of the Grand Canyon and really enjoyed it. She found it fascinating that the Kaibab Plateau was a little forest-covered mountain in the middle of the desert. She was always looking for the Kaibab squirrel, which she was told is not found anywhere else in the world. The whole experience was enjoyable, but she only worked at the inn for one summer and then moved on.

Jacob Hamblin had to travel around the Kaibab Plateau to get to the lake ponds, until the local Paiutes showed him a way to go across the top of the Kaibab, which reduced his travel time by two days. The biggest pond, Jacob Lake, was named after Hamblin. It is small, but it is a permanent source of water, which is a rarity on the Kaibab Plateau because of the porous Kaibab limestone. Melting snow seeps through the gravelly soil to emerge as springs several hundred feet below the rim of the plateau.[42] Hamblin tried to deepen the lake but was unsuccessful due to the springs that created the lake in the first place. He named some of the other ponds, such as Crane Lake, for a crane someone once saw there; and Crocodile Lake, because someone said the tall grasses and reeds surrounding it made it a good place for crocodiles to hide.

In 1962, when my sister worked at the Jacob Lake Inn, our family piled in the car, dropped her off at the inn, and went to see the Grand Canyon. At the end of the summer, we traveled down, picked her up, and went to see the Grand Canyon again.

The Jacob Lake Inn is a six-generation family owned business. It is thirty-five miles south of the Utah border on the Kaibab Plateau and is owned by the Rich family. It is part frontier outpost, part highway rest stop, gas station, general store, gift shop, and café. The Rich family drives from Salt Lake City to Jacob Lake, making the six-hour drive look like a short commute to work.

Half a million tourists come to the North Rim of the Grand Canyon, and traces still remain of the celebrities who stayed at the inn, such as Clark Gable, John Wayne, Wild Bill Elliot, President Ford, Priscilla Presley, the Rat Pack and Frank Sinatra, the Prince of Siam and his sons, and singer John Denver, who bought a fishing license there just a few months before his death.

Effie Dean Bowman Rich was born in 1923, the same year the inn was built. She says it was a wonderful place to raise children. Her seven children worked at the inn as soon as they were old enough, and every one of them enjoyed it. Each child runs a part of the inn, and the family hires college kids to work there in the summers, as my sister did. Effie's twenty-nine grandchildren and nine (so far) great-grandchildren have worked at the inn.

The Bowman's pioneer ancestors date back to the 1860s. They used to hunt and fish by the North Rim of the Grand Canyon and were among the first whites to see the area. Frank Woolley was a Utah militiaman who mapped the area three years before John Wesley Powell, but he was killed by Indians in 1869. His brother, Edwin D. Woolley, carried on his mapping work after his death. Edwin was instrumental in getting celebrities to visit long before the movie industry was persuaded to invade the area.

Edwin Woolley took Zane Grey, Buffalo Bill Cody, and President Theodore Roosevelt to see the Grand Canyon and the Kaibab Plateau. He persuaded Cody to come with a party of English noblemen, hoping to gain their interest in the wild game hunting they so loved. He later brought Theodore Roosevelt and his hunting party across the Colorado River in a little wire cage tram system that he built himself with wire cable strung across a narrow gorge.

Brandon Griggs of the *Salt Lake Tribune* said, "Woolley blazed the first trail from the North Rim to the canyon floor, strung a cable across the Colorado River, and rigged a tram that carried passengers and their horses over the water. Woolley also brought in Union Pacific railroad executives to try and convince them that the North Rim needed a railroad to the rim just like the South Rim eventually had. Two years later he made the first automobile trip to the North Rim—a journey of eight days from Salt Lake City."[43]

He stashed gas cans ahead of time on his way up to Salt Lake City so he could just stop and fill one of the first automobiles in Salt Lake City as they went along. He got caught in the sandy soil in Kanab and used tarps covered with sage and tree limbs to drive across the sand, tarp by tarp.

Totally in love with the Kaibab, Woolley's granddaughter and her World War I veteran husband opened a store by Jacob Lake. Nina, Edwin Woolley's granddaughter, and her husband, Harold Bowman, sold gasoline from a drum and added onto their store so that travelers had a place to eat or sleep. It was the Depression, so Nina made her own soap and found auction furniture, while Harold strolled down the road to greet stranded motorists and help them out. Harold had planned it this way. Automobiles in those days had to stop at the bottom of hills and then get a running start to make it to the top, so building a store in the right spot was crucial. A store at the bottom of the hill was enticing to weary travelers before they charged up the next hill and had to keep going. When the road was changed, it no longer went by their store, so Harold made a road that branched off the new road and went directly to their store. Nina died in 1959, and Harold was killed two years later when his plane struck a mountain near Bryce Canyon. Nina and Harold Bowman's daughter, Effie Dean Bowman, inherited Jacob's Lodge.

Jacob Lake Inn is operated under a thirty-five-year lease from the forest service and is one of only three lodges on the North Rim on federal land. All who live in the area pick up their mail and hunting licenses there and consider it a community center. The inn cannot close down during the winter months even though the family loses money, because the federal lease requires them to stay open. "We have to have a menu that can be made by a disinterested nineteen-year-old. . . . With some of these boys, the only thing they have made before coming here was toast."[44]

In 1946 Effie Dean Bowman was proposed to at the inn, and she and her husband, John Rich, a Utah geologist, began splitting their time between the inn and Salt Lake City. Effie's brother piloted a small plane back and forth bringing guests to the inn.

The forty-five seasonal employees live there and come from Utah and colleges from surrounding states. They sleep in dormitories and meet for evaluations, gripe sessions, and group hikes. Teamwork and community spirit are encouraged, and the Riches have lost few employees over the years. Not many have gotten out of the place without learning something. A few years ago, Jacob Lake Inn had a reunion and invited all the college kids who worked at the lodge to come and chat with each other. A lot of "kids" showed up, revealing that their experience there had been an important one.

The forest service has asked the Riches to expand their property, so they are in the process of building a twenty-four-unit motel besides the little log cabins they now have, and they are enlarging the dining room. It is unlikely that the ghosts in this inn will move to their new lodgings. They will probably choose to remain in the original areas of the inn and the small log cabins behind it.

Eighty-two-year-old Effie Dean Rich spoke fondly of her years running the inn. She loved her horseback rides out into the Kaibab, where sinkholes dot the landscape. She remembers being entranced by the Prince of Siam and his sons. She says that President Ford and his wife were charming and really impressed her. She is proud of her ancestor Edwin Woolley, who came from Kanab. Her grandfather, Franklin B. Woolley, was one of the first to map the area. She says her first job as a girl was to empty the chamber pots each morning from the row of little log cabins, because few guests wanted to go out in the middle of the night to find the outhouses.

Hundreds of high school and college students, including those from the Navajo nation, have been changed by their experience at Jacob Lake, but Effie would modestly say that she and her husband didn't really do anything.

Grand Canyon

No story about Kane County would be complete without the ghosts of the Grand Canyon, since the North Rim is only about sixty miles south of Kanab in Arizona. Only 10 percent of Grand Canyon tourists go to the canyon from this direction. According to Hopi legend, the Grand Canyon is where the Hopi Indians emerged from another dimension, coming out of the Third World and into the Fourth World. The Canyon is a spiritual gateway to the Fifth World. The Hopi are considered the most spiritual and psychic of all the North American tribes, and their ancestors occupied areas around the South Rim of the canyon. The ruins there, such as the Tusayan; the falls there, such as the Havasupai Falls; and the kivas, such as the Ceremonial Kiva, are all considered sacred sites to the Hopi.[45]

The original Indian legend says that the Hopis' ancestors lived in an underworld in the Grand Canyon. The Hisat'sinom of the Homolovi (Anasazi) are considered to be these ancestors. The underworld people broke into two groups: the good people, who were the One Hearts, and the bad people, known as the Two Hearts. These two groups could not get along with each other, so they were counseled that one of them must leave and go to the surface. Machetto, their chief, caused a tree to grow so high that it pierced the roof of the underworld. The people of one heart climbed out and stayed on the surface to grow grains and corn, and the people of two hearts stayed in the underworld. The one hearts sent a messenger to the Temple of the Sun and asked for a blessing for their people, but the messenger never returned. The Hopi believe that one day their messenger will return, and when he does, all their lands and ancient cliff dwellings will be returned to them. Because of this, for centuries the Hopi have honored a tradition that the old men of the tribe go outside at sundown, gaze toward the sun, and look for the messenger.[46]

People of the Hopi nation continue to make pilgrimages to the ancient dwellings in and around the Grand Canyon. They are sacred sites to the Hopi and should not be disturbed. Guardian spirits are angered if they are, and according to the Hopi, you are taking chances if you bring any of the relics home. Three places within the Grand Canyon are not only sacred, but also eerie and frightening for white people. One is the Watchtower Kiva, which has petroglyph symbols on its walls. Another is the Tusayan Ruins, which houses a collection of ancient Anasazi dwellings. The third is Havisupal Falls at the base of the canyon. All three are said to be haunted by ancient spirits of the canyon.

The Grand Canyon is an exceptionally deep, steep-walled canyon that is 277 miles long, 15 to 18 miles wide, and 4 to 6 thousand feet deep. It contains buttes, mesas, gorges, valleys, and cliffs that together with the plateaus make it one of the most spectacular of all America's national parks, with 1,218,375 acres of wilderness around the canyon itself. The flow of the Colorado River cut and sculpted the canyon, and water from the North Rim has formed tributary valleys. The canyon is relatively recent, having been sculpted from the river's eroding flow during the last 6 million years. Nine rock layers can be seen, which show the layers and fossils of the canyon's history.

Tom Wharton of the *Salt Lake Tribune* noted, "Rock at the top of the Grand Canyon, Kaibab limestone, is 270 million years old. Rocks at the bottom, gneiss and schist, date back as far as 1.8 billion years."[47]

The Grand Canyon was declared a national monument in 1908 and a national park in 1919. It was designated a World Heritage Site in 1979. In 2004, 4.3 million people visited the Canyon, and these visitors come not only from around the United States, but also—and most especially—from foreign countries. You must reserve a room at least one to two years in advance to stay in the park, and the burro rides to the bottom take up to four years advanced booking, unless you are lucky enough to get a cancellation.

It is interesting to note that "the Park is home to more than 1,500 plant, 355 bird, 89 mammalian, 47 reptile, 9 amphibian and 17 fish species." It contains three of the four desert types in North America and five of the seven life zones in North America, which are the Lower Sonoran, Upper Sonoran, Transition, Canadian, and Hudsonian.[48]

Indian myths abounded in the early days of the canyon. When John Wesley Powell surveyed it, a man named James White supposedly haunted it, and he has been haunting American historians ever since.

In her book *Hell or High Water*, Eilean Adams wrote, "White was a Colorado prospector, who, almost two years before Powell's journey, washed up on a makeshift raft at Callville, Nevada. His claim to have entered the Colorado River [from] the San Juan River with another man (soon drowned) as they fled from the Indians was widely disseminated and believed for a time, but Powell and his successors on the river discounted it."[49]

Adams, who is White's granddaughter, wrote her book about him and in the process became a great history detective. She is out to prove that her grandfather did discover the Grand Canyon first.[50]

Adams presents a convincing case in her well-written and thoroughly researched *Hell or High Water*. If true, James White also made the first recorded river run in the history of the canyon. White has been a legend among river runners and rafters in the area for decades. They not only talk about believing his story, but some of them also say they saw his ghost on the river when they were rafting. He is said to be reenacting his harrowing ride at points along the Colorado.

Some of the Indian ghost dances, influenced by a Paiute religious leader named Wovoka, who was also known as Jack Wilson to the whites, took place in 1889 at the nearby Grand Canyon West Ranch. The Southern Paiutes copied Wovoka's lead from the Northern Paiutes in Grass Springs.[51]

Wovoka was a prophet of peace who taught the Native Americans that they must live righteously and perform religious dances if they wanted to regain their lands from the white man. He believed that through clean living, an honest life, and cross-cultural cooperation, the Indian people would eventually live in a prosperous society, free from sickness, pain, and death. Unfortunately, his interpretation of the dance varied with each tribe, and some of them believed the dance would cause hurricanes and storms, as well as wake up their forefathers, who would rise out of the ground and drive the white man out of the Indian lands for good. The ghost dances were held for several months, with representatives from the Navajos, Havasupais, Moquis, Utes, and other Native American tribes. The dances were to bring on a pestilence that would wipe out all the whites so that Indians could return to their lands.[52] This belief played a major role in the tragic Wounded Knee Massacre on December 29, 1890.[53]

A 1909 edition of the *Arizona Gazette* states that explorers in the Grand Canyon found evidence of ancient people migrating from the Orient. The article claimed that tablets of hieroglyphics were found inside a cavern, along with copper weapons, Egyptian deity statues, and even mummies. It also claimed that the Smithsonian Institute had financed the expedition. These caverns were never found again, and the Smithsonian Institute denies any knowledge of such an expedition. Some people believe that this was an elaborate newspaper hoax, while others say that a front-page article from such a prestigious institution, which was highly detailed and went on for several pages, lends the story credibility. In 1909 *The Phoenix Gazette* ran the story, which maintained that mysterious tunnels were found in the Grand Canyon that housed oriental statues holding lotus blossoms in the palms of their hands.

Just a few hundred yards from the Bright Angel Trail on the south rim of the canyon sits the old EL Tovar Lodge. Built in 1905, it is one example of the original haunted lodges on both the North and South Rim of the Grand Canyon. The most expensive log cabin in America at the time, the lodge was designed by architect Mary Jane Colter, who completed the interior with Indian artifacts and mounted animal heads on the walls, which made it look like a grand hunting lodge or a European Villa. She designed other buildings at the site, but some of them have since been demolished. The Bright Angel Lodge, Hopi House, Desert View Watch Tower, Lookout Studio, and Hermit's Rest still exist today. Colter designed other southwestern hotels and railroad stations, but she is remembered primarily for creating the image of the Grand Canyon with her imaginative and natural designs.

The El Tovar was named for Don Pedro de Tovar, who was an explorer with Coronado in 1540. Tovar was the first European to learn of the existence of the Grand Canyon. The lodge is a huge, one-hundred room, Swiss chalet influenced resort hotel. It originally did not have private baths in the rooms, but guests could reserve one for an additional fee. It featured a fifteenth-century dinning room and several art galleries that sold works from famous landscape artists who came to paint the canyon. A solarium, music room, club room, amusement room, and roof garden were available for the guests. The El Tovar had electricity (a real feat in such a remote area), a greenhouse with fresh fruits and vegetables, and a dairy for fresh dairy products. Fresh water was offered daily and was hauled in by train from Del Rio 120 miles away. The original building cost $250,000 to build. The dairy has since become the Kachina Lodge, and the greenhouse is now gone.

The El Tovar just underwent a $1,000,000 renovation, and visitors need to book a room one to two years in advance. The rates in 2004 were $124 to $201 a night, with luxury suites going for $286 a night. The renovations apparently brought out additional ghostly activities, because the lodge's owners have their own parapsychologist who visits once a week to tell the ghosts' stories in the lobby of the hotel. The parapsychologist says she has identified at least fourteen ghosts and presents a free program entitled "Guests That Checked In, But Never Checked Out." The most famous resident apparition is Mary Jane Elizabeth Colter, but the ghosts of other famous people may be there also since George Bernard Shaw, Guglielmo Marconi, President Taft, President Theodore Roosevelt, and a French marshal have all visited there.

Colter, the official architect of the Grand Canyon, designed Bright Angel Lodge, Hermit's Rest, Hopi House, the Lookout Studio, Watchtower, and the Phantom Ranch at the bottom of the canyon.

Colter was born in 1869. Her father died young, leaving Mary Jane, her mother, and an older sister behind. Mary Jane decided she would have to earn a living for the family and convinced her mother to pay for her to attend the California School of Design in San Francisco. Colter then taught mechanical drawing at a high school in St. Paul, Minnesota. The Fred Harvey Company operated all the concessions at the Grand Canyon and hired young women (the famous "Harvey Girls") from all over the country to run them. After successfully designing a New Mexico hotel, Colter was hired by the Harvey Company from 1902 to 1948 to design the Harvey House gift shops, newsstands, restaurants, and hotels along the Atchison, Topeka, and Santa Fe Railway.

In 1899 Fred Harvey realized the big market for Indian baskets, rugs, pottery, and silver jewelry, and Colter was originally hired as a decorator for these new Indian shops in the hotels. When the Santa Fe Railway extended their line to the South Rim of the Grand Canyon, the Harvey Company contracted to build a hotel there, and Colter was to design the Indian store across from the new hotel. She was soon designing other buildings at the Canyon from the ground up.

Her Native American motifs are easily recognizable and were the foundation for others who followed in her footsteps. Colter was a mystic in her own right. When she designed a building, she believed she had to be inspired by something supernatural, or influenced by a good story with mystical elements. Examples are the hermit story for her Hermit's Rest, or Phantom Ranch, which was supposedly named for its supernatural echoes and nearby Phantom Creek. She insisted that each of her buildings have an imaginary story to it, as well as "contain all the character and ghosts that might accompany such a past."[54] So it is easy to see why many of the ghost stories concerning her buildings revolve around Mary Jane Colter, who would surely return to her beloved Grand Canyon if she could.

Colter's buildings have since been demolished, most going quietly and without protest. The Hotel Alvarado in Albuquerque, razed in 1943, caused a huge outburst of public protest long before preservation had become important to people. Colter died in 1958 at the age of eighty-eight, so she lived to see some of her buildings come down.

Today, most of the South Rim buildings are on the damaged or threatened natural historic landmarks registry, and some of her hotels have been renovated. The Los Angeles Union Station still stands as well. Colter's first love was the South Rim of the Grand Canyon, and according to the resident parapsychologist, she is often seen in the buildings she considered home.[55]

The town of Williams, Arizona, is practically the same distance south of the Grand Canyon as Kanab is to the north. While Kanab residents are less likely to talk about their resident ghosts, they have just as many as Williams does. The Red Garter Bed and Bakery in Williams is a good example of capitalizing on ghost stories. With one hundred years or more of traumatic history, the place boasts of at least one resident ghost.

The Red Garter is a two-story, Victorian-style building that was constructed as a saloon with a bordello upstairs. The ghost there is called Eva. Eight upstairs rooms were occupied by one madam and seven soiled doves. The rooms have been remodeled into four guest rooms and a shared bath. The place was originally called William's Saloon Row and operated up until the mid-1940s. A steep flight of stairs led to the women's rooms, and for years these stairs were nicknamed the Cowboy's Endurance Test.

August Tetzlaff was a German tailor who decided to invest in building and owning this establishment. With the silver and copper boom going on, as well as the building of the Grand Canyon railroads, there were plenty of miners and railroad workers to frequent his place, especially on weekends. In fact, the street in front of this old saloon is called Railroad Avenue, where the girls used to call down to the street from their rooms above. Tourists who took the Santa Fe and Grand Canyon Railways often stopped at William's Saloon Row as well. Longino Mora was the operator of the saloon. He was a scout for the U.S. Cavalry in the Indian wars, had five different wives, twenty-five children, and lived to be ninety years old. Even though Arizona outlawed prostitution in 1907, like other illegal businesses, Tetzlaff kept both his saloon and prostitution businesses open.

A murder was committed on the stairs of the saloon that touched off a citywide crack down on prostitution. This infamous murder and the advent of World War II, which took all the men away, led to the closure of the saloon and bordello. The building housed several reputable businesses after this until 1979, when John Holst bought the place and leased it out. In 1994 he decided to renovate the place and make it into a bed and breakfast inn, and his first guests began to report the typical phenomena of a haunting. There were phantom footsteps up and down the stairs, a strong presence was felt in the rooms, and some people had dreams of a woman with long dark hair in a floor-length gown walking the halls. Sometimes a guest would suddenly hear a loud clunking sound for which no one to date has found an explanation.

Right behind The Red Garter were two large rear rooms that comprised William's Chinatown. In these rooms the Chinese railroad workers or "celestials" operated a restaurant, chophouse, and opium den and used them as apartments for the workers. The local sheriff was often called to these rooms because of some disturbance or the report of a murder. The bodies, if there were any, and most people believe there were a few, mysteriously disappeared every time. In her book *Haunted Arizona*, Ellen Robson noted that "There are even tales of the town garbage collector, Heine, being lowered into the cesspool below the outhouses to look for bodies, only to come up empty handed."[56]

The man murdered on the stairs in the 1940s and the Chinese man murdered during an earlier era contribute to the ghostly log at the bed and bakery, but the young woman who slams doors and makes other noises gets more attention. Wearing a white nightgown and holding something in front of her that no one can see clearly enough to identify, this Hispanic woman walks the halls and rooms of the old building and seems to have something to say to people with what she carries. Interestingly, a picture of the Mora family hangs in the building. A dark-haired young woman, who fits the description of the ghost that some people have claimed to see, is in the picture. Those who have seen the girl's apparition say she has long dark hair, smiles happily, and can't be seen in mirrors. The picture of the Mora family has a mirror in the background, and most of the family members are reflected in it. On close examination, this particular girl doesn't seem to be reflected in the mirror as everyone else is. While all the family members are standing in front of the bar, she is standing behind it. She is the only one smiling. Is she one of Mora's wives or daughters? Or was she around as an apparition even before this? Perhaps someday a ghost investigation will reveal the truth of the matter.[57]

By the 1920s, Emory and Ellsworth Kolb, the foremost photographers of the Grand Canyon at the time, took tourists down into the canyon on burros to see the canyon floor. In 1928 a young newlywed couple, Glen and Bessie Hyde, approached the Grand Canyon guides and asked them to take their picture. Glen Hyde was a farmer from Twin Falls, Idaho, whose hobby was river running. He built his own twenty-foot scow, and the Hydes had already gone down the first

160 miles of the Colorado, hiking out at the Phantom Ranch that Mary Colter had always said had "supernatural echoes." They met famous boatman Emory Cole there, who encouraged them to wear life jackets. Being an experienced river runner, Glen Hyde told Cole that Idaho boatmen didn't wear life jackets. What makes the story so intriguing—besides the Hydes' disappearance—are the facts that they were honeymooners, Bessie Hyde would have been the first woman on the Colorado, and she was a hauntingly beautiful, petite tomboy.

The Hydes wanted their photo taken by the rim of the canyon, and the Kolbs obliged. They said they would be back to get the picture after rafting a little further down the river in the canyon. The Kolbs talked to them on November 16, and by early December, the Kolbs had not heard from the Hydes. They contacted Hyde's father, and along with him, they initiated a search of the canyon. A small plane pilot spotted the Hydes' homemade raft caught in some rocks in the river. The rescue party hiked down and found nothing out of place in the boat. Nothing was taken, and everything was packed neatly. The only thing missing were the Hydes.

The Hydes' disappearance has become one of the great unsolved mysteries of the twentieth century, probably because of the location and the fact that Bessie would have been the first woman to navigate the rapids on the Colorado in the Grand Canyon. They both vanished without a trace. Several books have been written about this incident, as well as articles that appeared in national magazines at the time of their disappearance. River runners and rafters on the river have told stories for years of this young honeymoon couple's spirits haunting the Colorado River in the canyon. Hikers and campers have also told about having seen or felt their presence around the river.

In 1971 a new mystery about their disappearance was added to the story when a gray-haired old woman, who was on one of the rafting tours, claimed to be Bessie Hyde. She told a campfire story of her disappearance and said she murdered her husband, left his body to the river, and hiked out of the canyon to start a new life back east. She claimed that Glen Hyde was beating her and it was her only way out of the situation.

In 1976 a skeleton with a bullet in its skull was found on the South Rim of the Grand Canyon. The size and age of the skeleton seemed to fit the time of Glen Hyde's disappearance, as well as his physical description. Around the same time period, an old man came forward, claiming to be Glen Hyde.

In 1992 a famous Grand Canyon boatwoman, Georgie White Clark, died. Her given name was Bessie DeRoss, and she was raised in Denver, Colorado. Few people had been inside her Las Vegas home, and when her friends went through it to close it up, they supposedly found among her personal effects the wedding certificate of Glen and Bessie Hyde, along with a small pistol. On the wedding certificate were the names Bessie Haley and Glen R. Hyde.

These unsolved mysteries were the inspiration for two books from 2002 about the Hydes. The first was entitled *Sunk Without a Sound: The Tragic Colorado River*

Honeymoon of Glen and Bessie Hyde,[58] by Brad Dimrock, a twenty-eight-year veteran river guide of the Colorado River. The second, *Grand Ambition,*[59] is a novel by Lisa Michaels. It is part fiction and part fact and is interwoven with Reith Hyde's account of his son's disappearance. Michaels says she became intrigued when she first saw a photo of the Hydes. She noticed their bomber jackets, wool fedoras, fur collars, and Bessie's short haircut, all representative of the 1920s adventurers and explorers. She wanted to write her historical novel because of its "riveting suspense." A half hour spot about the Hydes was aired on *Unsolved Mysteries,* and other versions of their story were presented on documentaries about the Grand Canyon.

Another rumor is that Georgie fell for Emery Cole, the Colorado River guide and famous boatman of the time. She did not want to continue on the river run and refused to go with her husband. Her husband became angry and forced her to continue down the river with him. Bessie stabbed him in the back or shot him in the head with a pistol, depending on which version of the story is being told. She pushed him overboard and walked out of the canyon, leaving both her new husband and her new love interest behind.

If ghosts of retribution exist—and I believe they do—perhaps coming back to the scene of the crime was not a good idea. On the other hand, the man and woman who claimed to be Bessie and Glen certainly got some notoriety by telling their stories, whether they were true or not. Georgie's story was told by what she left behind, which is certainly a ghost story of its own.

In Troy Taylor's article "Haunted Arizona: the Ghosts of the Grand Canyon," Taylor tells a ghost story about "the wandering woman."[60] She is seen on the North Rim searching for her husband and son who were killed in a hiking accident there. The family came to stay in the old lodge on the North Rim in the 1920s, and after hearing the news of her family's deaths, the woman grew despondent and committed suicide. The lodge burned down in 1926 but was soon rebuilt. Visitors and staff have seen her on the North Kaibab Trail. She wears a flowered white robe and has a scarf on her head. She once appeared in the doorway of a forest ranger's sleeping quarters, which really startled the awakened ranger. Ellen Robson and Dianne Halicki talk about this ghost in their book *Haunted Highway: The Spirits of Route 66.* They say that the "wandering woman" wears a shawl on her head.[61]

Besides those in the old lodges, other ghosts are just now being discovered and reported. Phantom children move the swings and merry-go-round in the park's old playground. The playground was torn down years ago, but voices and laughter—and even fighting—can still be heard in the same area. In their book, *Haunted Highway,* Robson and Halicki report that workers watched as a little ghost girl pushed the merry-go-round around several times and then promptly disappeared before their eyes.[62]

The lodges and buildings of both the North Rim and the South Rim of the Grand Canyon are haunted. Along with Mary Jane Colter's spirit at the El Tovar Hotel, Fred Harvey often appears on the third floor during the holidays and invites people to the annual Christmas party. In the middle of the parking lot is a marked grave of one of the Harvey Girls who worked for the Fred Harvey Company. Apparently someone who knew her wanted her to be buried on hotel property. A black-caped apparition has been seen there more than once. It walks up the path leading to the front steps of the El Tovar, passes the Harvey Girls' grave, and disappears as it rounds the back side of the Hopi House.

The Colter's Hermit's Rest structure was designed in honor of the most famous hermit ghost of the Grand Canyon, who lived in the early days of canyon exploration. His name was Louis Boucher, and he lived at the head of a canyon near the South Rim. Because of him, the canyon was eventually named Hermit's Canyon. In the 1890s, Boucher earned his living guiding tourists in and out of the canyon, and after he died, stories of his ghost haunting the area began to spread.

When Mary Jane Colter designed her buildings for the Grand Canyon, her plan for Hermit's Rest was to have a partially open resting place for weary travelers passing through the canyon. She specifically designed it so that tourists could imagine they were resting in the old hermit's home. Hermit's Rest is shaped like a cave entrance and is made out of large square stones. A big fireplace, benches, and chairs fill the structure. It is reasonable to assume that Boucher's spirit might choose from time to time to visit a place that honors him.

Another famous ghost was seen at Maricopa Point. This ghost is of a man who fell over the edge of the canyon in the 1930s while installing railings. He was a worker for the Civilian Conservation Corps (CCC) and slipped and fell to his death. People report seeing a black misty figure near the railings at sunset. They also report hearing a loud shoveling or scraping sound.

While some owners of the inns and resorts say nothing about their ghosts, others capitalize on them, and visitors have plenty of their own experiences to share. The canyon keeps its secrets of lost spirits, and the ancient spirits who guard the ruins keep their secrets as well.

The surrounding towns have haunted places too. I often think of my mother in her wide-brimmed, turned-up hat, Buster Brown haircut, and baggy coveralls that children wore in the 1920s, camping with her family at Jacob Lake and taking the short drive to the North Rim for the day.

The last time I was there, a crow landed on the edge of the canyon at sunset and cawed at me. It was as though I could hear music on the wind, and all my memories of my mother and her tales of Kanab and the Kaibab came drifting back to me. I knew at that moment why I was a Westerner, why I longed to be out of the city, and why the intuitive journey is such a rich one, regardless of those people who do not understand my gift. I was partially in my mother's shoes, and it felt comfortable to be there.

Notes

1. Cannon, *Poplar Beliefs and Superstitions*, 335.
2. This version, told by Afton Topham, was retold by Janet Seegmiller, special collections librarian at the Gerald R. Sherratt Library on the Southern Utah University campus in Cedar City, Utah, February 2, 2010.
3. Tom Braun, "The Haunting of Old Main," Southern Utah University *Thunderbird*, Oct. 31, 1991, 5; and Chris Taylor, "Dr. Spear Exposes Haunted Old Main," *Southern Utah University Journal*, Oct. 31, 1994, 3–4.
4. Ibid.
5. Dean O'Driscoll, "The Ghost Story of SUSC," Southern Utah University *Thunderbird*, May 26, 1983, 14–15.
6. Peter DeRose and Mitchell Parish, "Deep Purple" (Nashville, Tennesee: EMI Music Publishing, the Songwriter's Guild of America, 1933/1938).
7. O'Driscoll, "The Ghost Story of SUSC," *Thunderbird*.
8. Ibid.
9. Utah Ghost Organization, www.utahghost.org, accessed Jan. 26, 2010.
10. Recorded in the *Johnson Family Bulletin*, September 1973.
11. George Thompson, *Some Dreams Die Hard* (Salt Lake City: Dream Garden Press, 1982), 83–84.
12. "Utah: The Grist Mill Inn Story," *Encyclopedia of Haunted Places*. Compiled and edited by Jeff Bellanger (New York: Castle Books, 2008), 184–85.
13. Robert S. McPherson, "Monticello," *Utah History Encyclopedia* (Salt Lake City: University of Utah Press, 1994), 372–73.
14. Harold George and Fay Muhlestein Lunceford, *Monticello Journal: A History of Monticello until 1937* (Utah: self-published, 1988). In Tom Perry Special Collections at the Harold B. Lee Library, Brigham Young University.
15. Utah Ghost Hunter's Society, www.ghostwave.com, accessed Jan. 26, 2010.
16. Roylance, *Utah, a Guide to the State*, 648.
17. Ibid.
18. Ibid., 79.
19. Bart Anderson, "Restless Spirits and Other Things That Go Bump in the Night," *St. George Magazine*, Sept.–Oct. 2002, 78–80.
20. Thompson, *Some Dreams Die Hard*, 26–27.
21. Read Sally Denton's *American Massacre: The Tragedy at Mountain Meadows, September 1857* (New York: Knopf, 2003), or Will Bagley's *Blood of the Prophets: Brigham Young and the Massacre at Mountain Meadows* (Norman, Oklahoma: University of Oklahoma Press, 2004) to learn more about this infamous event in Utah's history.
22. Denton, *American Massacre*, 209.
23. Ibid.
24. Ibid.
25. Ibid.
26. Ibid.
27. Ibid.
28. For an example, see William Bright's *A Coyote Reader* (Berkeley and Los Angeles:

University of California, 1993), which is a definitive collection of Coyote's various adventures.

29. Quote taken from author's family history documents.

30. Ibid.

31. Adonis Findlay Robinson, "A History of Kane County" (Kane County Daughters of Utah Pioneers, 1970), 422.

32. Ibid., 442–43.

33. Rowland W. Rider, as told to his granddaughter Deirdre Murray Paulsen in his book *The Roll Away Saloon: Cowboy Tales of the Arizona Strip* (Logan, Utah: Utah State University Press, 1985); "Roll Away Saloon," 3–4; "Seven Bags of Gold," 37–46; "Enter Zane Grey," 56–59; "Scaring President Roosevelt," 71–73; and "Buffalo Jones Out Buffalos the Buffalo," 100–101.

34. Ibid., 490.

35. Edmunds-Tucker Act, see http://en.wikipedia.org/wiki/Edmunds-Tucker_Act, accessed Jan. 26, 2010.

36. L. W. Macfarlane, *Dr. Mac: The Man, His Land, and His People* (Cedar City, Utah: Southern Utah State College Press, 1985), 294.

37. Author's personal interview with Jackie Rife, Kanab's famous and only stuntwoman. Information used by permission, February 5, 2010.

38. Thompson, *Some Dreams Die Hard*, 51–52.

39. Roylance, *Utah, a Guide to the State*, 642.

40. Ghost investigators Michelle Hardison and Jodi Chavez, "Tomato the Cat's Special Investigative Report: The Ghostbuster," *Best Friends Magazine*, Mar./Apr. 2003, 38–39.

41. Bob Mims, "Legacy in the rock," *The Salt Lake Tribune*, Dec. 7, E-1 and E-8.

42. Wikipedia.com, "Jacob Lake, Arizona," accessed Jan. 26, 2010.

43. Brandon Griggs, "Heart of the Rim," *The Salt Lake Tribune*, Sept. 2, 2003, sec. B.

44. Ibid.

45. Dennis William Hauck, "Grand Canyon," *Haunted Places* (New York: Penguin Books, 1996), 16.

46. Four Corners Clamor, www.ausbcomp.com/redman/clamor7.htm, accessed Jan. 22, 2010.

47. Tom Wharton, "Grand Canyon on the Go" *The Salt Lake Tribune*, May 22, 2005, B.

48. Ibid.

49. Eilean Adams, *Hell or High Water: James White's Disputed Passage through Grand Canyon*, 1867 (Logan, Utah: Utah State University Press, 2001), 2–4.

50. Ibid.

51. Wikipedia.com, "Wovoka," http://en.wikipedia.org/wiki/Wovoka, accessed Jan. 21, 2010.

52. Ibid., "Ghost Dances," http://en.wikipedia.org/wiki/Ghost_Dance, accessed Jan. 21, 2010.

53. Ibid., "Wounded Knee Massacre," http://en.wikipedia.org/wiki/Wounded_Knee_Massacre, accessed Jan. 21, 2010.

54. See Arnold Berke, *Mary Colter: Architect of the Southwest* (New York, Princeton Architectural Press, 2002) or Virginia L. Grattan, *Mary Colter: Builder upon the Red Earth* (Flagstaff: Northland Press, 1980).

55. Ibid.
56. Ellen Robson, "The Red Garter Bed & Bakery," *Haunted Arizona* (Phoenix: Golden West Publishers, 2003), 114–16.
57. Ibid.
58. Brad Dimrock, *Sunk Without a Sound: The Tragic Colorado River Honeymoon of Glen and Bessie Hyde* (Flagstaff: Fretwater Press 2001).
59. Lisa Michaels, *Grand Ambition: A Novel* (New York City: W. W. Norton & Company, 2001).
60. Troy Taylor, "Haunted Arizona: The Ghosts of the Grand Canyon," www.prairie.com, accessed 2001.
61. Ellen Robson and Dianne Halicki, *Haunted Highway: The Spirits of Route 66* (Phoenix, Arizona: Golden West Publishers, 2003), 147.
62. Ibid.

About the Author

After thirty-five years of teaching special education and gifted and talented children, Linda Dunning has retired to her "real" life, following a spiritual path, authoring books, and doing intuitive counseling. The eight-part Utah Tales series will continue to come out after this third book, *Restless Spirits*, is published. Having enjoyed a lifetime of writing, attending writer's workshops, publishing poetry, and receiving various writing awards for short stories, nonfiction, and autobiography books, she is now looking forward to finishing this twenty-year ghost project series and journeying off to some other new and exciting adventures as a writer.

Before working on this series, Linda wrote *Soyala*, a historical romance trilogy about Southern Colorado and centered on Hopi beliefs, mystical animals, and women healers in the early nineteenth century. *Soyala* was followed by *The Rainbow Bridge*, a sci-fi fantasy romance, and a collection of nonfiction short stories entitled *The Suede-Like Petals of a Giant Crimson Glory*. *A Year for the Dayroom Child* is about teaching the severely multihandicapped. Next was *Shadow Wife*, a nonfiction book about Vietnam combat veterans and their wives, and *Light on a Sensitive Surface*, a mother-daughter memoir about the life of intuitives and the death of a mother who never quite owned her "second-sight" abilities. Since all these books won awards but were too artsy to publish, the ghost and night creatures won out!

Linda is often asked what the most important thing is that a writer can do, and she always answers, "Just keep writing." She adds that you either love writing or you leave it, and in her case, she never suffered from it. She has always enjoyed the amazing journey it brought her throughout all her teaching years. Like any passion, writing is one part joy and two parts hard work. The history and lore of her native state continues to intrigue and enthrall her.